Highlander The Cursed Lord

By

Donna Fletcher

Highlander The Cursed Lord

Cover art
Kim Killion Group

Visit Donna's Website
www.donnafletcher.com
http://www.facebook.com/donna.fletcher.author

Chapter 1

Bliss had forced herself to stop crying not long after she had left Clan Loudon. Tears would do her no good. She had to stay strong if she were to survive, and she would survive. She had to. She had to keep her sisters, Elysia and Annis, safe and see them wed to good men who would treat them well.

She prayed that Elysia had paid heed to her advice and gained the courage to ask Saber, a farmer of good strength and character, to marry her. He would keep her well protected. It made it easier that Elysia and Saber favored each other. That alone would be a good start to the marriage.

"It won't be long now until we arrive."

Bliss turned to Lawler, riding beside her. He had been kind to her the two days they had spent traveling. She had thought him of advanced years when first meeting him, his white hair a good indication of it and the few wrinkles attesting to it as well. But the sharpness of his blue eyes and the strength he'd displayed the last two days made her think he was of less years than she had first thought.

"You worry for your sisters, but there is no need. You struck a good bargain, and they will wed who they choose because of you," Lawler said. "You are a wise and brave woman."

"Some would argue otherwise since few if any would agree to wed the cursed lord," Bliss said, recalling the bargain she had put forth to Lawler.

She would not only wed Lord Rannick, the worst cursed lord out of the three lords whose families had had a powerful curse cast upon them around twenty years ago, but she

3

would need to get with child. It had been the only plausible solution to prevent a forced marriage of her sister Annis to Lord Brogan, the condemned lord. He was the one who death did not touch. She also had wanted to make certain Elysia would be able to wed a man of her choosing and not take a chance that she'd be forced to wed a man who would treat her badly, since she was such a sweet, kind soul. As long as Bliss could keep her sisters from harm, that was all that had mattered to her.

When Lawler failed to comment on her remark, she said, "Tell me Lord Rannick is not a bad man."

Lawler's body stiffened and his shoulders squared. "I will not lie to you. Lies will do you no good in this situation. Lord Rannick was once an honorable man. He made the most of his first marriage to Lady Cecilia that his father had arranged for him. He treated her well and when she got with child he was pleased and looked forward to the birth of their first bairn. He was devastated when they both died in childbirth. He did not wish to wed again, fearing the woman's fate, but his father ignored his wishes and wed him to Phedra. They were married barely a few months when a riding accident claimed her life. He refused to wed after that and once again his father ignored his wishes. It was after a vicious fight with his father that Lord Rannick went to meet his new wife, three days after they'd been wed through proxy, and tell her that he would not consummate or commit to the marriage. He did not have a chance to say a word. She collapsed upon seeing him and he caught her in his arms, and there was where she died."

"How horrible for him and those women," Bliss said.

She was a healer and well understood that death struck unexpectedly in childbirth, accidents happened, but a young woman dying for no apparent or understandable reason made her wonder the cause of her sudden death.

"More horrible than you can imagine. Lord Rannick

departed the clan not long after his wife was laid to rest. He traveled to foreign shores in search of a way to end the dreadful curse and in so doing—he lost his soul. His father sent men to bring him home and it took most all of them to capture him and forcibly restrain him to accomplish the task."

"Lord Lochlann was shocked when he laid eyes on his son. His skin had deepened from the heat of the sun in some of the heathen lands he had traveled, and a scar on his cheek marred his once fine features. No one knows how he got it, he never speaks of it. Many believed he sought death, no longer wanting to live with the curse, but the curse refused him a reprieve. He's doomed, as are his heirs to suffer the curse." Lawler turned silent for a moment. "There is something I feel you should know, though I was ordered not to tell you. But I feel you have a right to know, to be prepared. Lord Rannick told his father that if he forced another wife on him," —Lawler hesitated— "he would kill her and save her the trouble of whatever miserable death would surely befall her."

Bliss stared at Lawler. What could one say to the news of one's own impending death? Only one thing came to mind. "Do you think he means it?"

"If you asked me that of the man he was before he left his homeland, I would say nay, I do not believe Lord Rannick would do such a heinous thing. But since his return," —Lawler shook his head— "I cannot say for sure what Lord Rannick would do. He is a man full of never-ending pain and mounting anger, and I do not know if he will ever be able to rid himself of both."

"I am grateful for your honesty," Bliss said even though his words had spiked her fear.

"There is more you should know."

Bliss waited, Lawler's silence an indication that he was hesitant to tell her.

5

Lawler took a heavy breath before he finally continued. "When the men Lord Lochlann sent to bring his son home found Rannick," —he stopped again and shook his head— "a hole was about to be made in his head… voluntarily."

Bliss shut her eyes a moment and shook her head.

"You do not seem as shocked as most do when they hear that," Lawler said.

"People do strange and horrible things to those they believe are possessed by evil. A hole in one's skull would be considered a good way to rid someone of evil, though it would do little to solve the problem. Lord Rannick must have been desperate that he would agree to such a procedure."

"From what I heard from those at Clan Loudon, you are a skillful healer and speaking with you, I see how true it is. I pray by some miracle that you can help restore Lord Rannick to the honorable man he once was or as close to it as possible."

Anxious over his remark, Bliss quickly asked, "Lord Lochlann will not expect a miracle from me, will he?"

"It will be a miracle if Lord Rannick allows you near him, let alone gets you with child."

"You believe I am doomed to fail, don't you?" Bliss asked, after hearing what Lawler had to say, it seemed the likely outcome.

"I have come to admire your courage, Lady Bliss. I would rather see you fail than die." With a nod, Lawler rode ahead.

Lady Bliss.

Lawler's formal acknowledgment made her marriage to Lord Rannick all the more real as well as her fate. Did death at her husband's hands await her? Or punishment by Lord Lochlann when she failed to fulfill the marriage agreement and get with child? Or would she succumb to the curse before anything else could touch her?

It would not be long before she found out.

***

The village was impressive, as was the towering keep that occupied a large space to the right side of the village in the distance. Defined pathways ran like tentacles through the village, cottages aligned neatly along them with gardens alongside each. The people of Clan MacClaren went about their chores with few smiles and not a bit of laughter. Their faces were solemn as if resigned to their fate—to the curse.

The keep loomed large over the village, intimidating anyone who looked its way. Two sentinels stood to the sides of two tall, wood doors and pulled them open when she and Lawler approached.

Bliss wished she had a chance to freshen herself before meeting Lord Lochlann, her garments dusty from the journey. At least her plain, pale-yellow shift and green wool tunic didn't appear worn, thanks to Elysia's skilled stitching hand. Her brown wool cloak wasn't as warm as it once had been. It had seen many years, having belonged to her mum, who died ten years ago when she was barely twelve.

She slipped her cloak off and draped it over her arm and moved her long braid off her back to rest over her shoulder on her chest. Her brown hair held only a slight curl to it but did well braided.

"Wait here a moment," Lawler said and disappeared.

Servants were busy with chores and cast curious glances her way, some even gathered to whisper. They quickly spread apart when Lawler returned with a man who she assumed was Lord Lochlann.

His was a formidable man, tall with wide shoulders, a broad chest, and a well-defined body for a man whose gray hair showed little sign of the dark color it once had been. He was also a man of good features, and no doubt the reason she

7

had heard tell that at one time Lord Rannick possessed even finer features than his father.

His gait was as intent as were his brown eyes as he fast approached Bliss, but she remained where she stood, determined to show no fear, though her stomach twisted in knots.

"You agreed to this marriage freely?" Lord Lochlann demanded, stopping in front of her.

Bliss was not a short woman, but she had to tilt her neck back to meet his eyes. "I did, my lord."

"Lawler says you are an excellent healer," Lochlann said, his eyes roaming over her.

Bliss did not like his blatant perusal, but she had little choice then to ignore it. "I do my best, my lord."

Lochlann spoke to Lawler but kept his focus on Bliss. "She's plain, no features that catch the eye, and thin, no shape to her at all." Lochlann shook his head. "How will you ever bear a bairn?"

"Thin, wide, large, small, I have found in the countless bairns I have delivered that size matters little," Bliss assured him.

"You are not young either," Lochlann said as if he accused her of a crime.

"Twenty and two years, my lord," Lawler said. "Still within the range to bear children."

"How can you be sure?" Lochlann questioned skeptically.

Lawler kept his frustration out of his voice. "Bliss agreed to wed Lord Rannick and get with child as soon as possible. No other has come near to agreeing to such a proposal."

"Why did she agree?" Lochlann asked again, skeptical.

"She struck a bargain," Lawler said and explained how she agreed to wed Lord Rannick in exchange so her one sister would not be forced to wed Lord Brogan and that both sisters would have the freedom to choose their own husbands.

Lord Lochlann rubbed his chin. "She knows how to bargain that might help her with Rannick. And she is protective of family. Will you be protective of your husband?"

"Is it not my duty to do so?" Bliss asked.

"Aye," Lochlann said, his tone commanding. "And you will do well to see to all your wifely duties no matter how difficult it might be."

"Who are you admonishing about wifely duties?" a woman round in size asked upon entering the Great Hall.

"This is none of your concern, wife," Lochlann snapped.

"It most definitely is if you are speaking to a woman about wifely concerns, husband," the woman shot back at him with the same sharp snap of her tongue.

"Helice, you will leave this to me," Lochlann demanded.

"What is it I am leaving to you?" Helice asked. Her dark hair barely held a gray strand to it and fell softly around her pretty, full face in gentle waves. When a glare was his response, Helice gasped and clutched her chest. "You did not go against our son's wishes again and marry him to someone, did you, husband?"

"I did," Lochlann admitted, his chest rising proudly as he purposely squared his shoulders.

"How could you do that, Lochlann?" Helice admonished. "Hasn't Rannick suffered enough? If he loses another wife, we will most certainly lose him, and I am not ready to bury my son."

"Bliss is a healer. She can help Rannick, and he has a duty to see that the Clan MacClaren lives on," Lochlann said.

"Rannick feels his duty is to see the curse end with

9

him," Helice argued.

Lochlann turned a glare on his wife that would wither most women. "That is not his decision to make."

Helice paid his scowl no heed. "He thinks of saving future MacClaren from suffering."

"We all suffer in our lives. The curse is nothing but nonsense, and I will not let it destroy our lives," Lochlann argued.

"It already has, husband," Helice said and turned to Bliss. "Have you been offered any food or drink, my dear?"

"Nay, my lady, but I am good," Bliss said, not wishing to add to the strife.

"Nonsense," Helice said and waved a servant over. "Food and drink."

"Bliss has no time for that. She is to be taken to Rannick immediately."

"Bliss, what a lovely name," Helice said and hooked her arm with Bliss's, and walked over to the table to sit.

"Helice!" Lochlann commanded with warning.

"Bliss will do better facing Rannick with food and drink in her," Helice said without a glance to her husband.

Lochlann walked to the table to face his wife and Bliss. "You struck a bargain. I expect you to do as you agreed or else I will see your two sisters wed to men of my choosing. Lawler will take you to Rannick as soon as you are done here. Do not take long." He marched off without a word to his wife.

Bliss turned to Lady Helice. "I am not hungry. I should take my leave now."

"At least have a calming brew before you go," Helice offered. "Besides, I wish to ask you something."

Bliss remained silent as servants placed food and drink on the table, one servant filling the tankard in front of Bliss with wine.

Tears pooled in Lady Helice's eyes as she spoke softly

after the servants walked away. "You are a healer. Please, I beg of you, Bliss… heal my son."

***

Bliss followed Lawler on foot through the woods, after leaving their horses tied to a tree branch, her stomach knotting with each step. It took only ten minutes, though it seemed like hours, to reach the dwelling she now spied through the trees. It was a pleasant looking dwelling, the lone window shutters open, letting in the brisk autumn air and what light there was from the overcast sky. Wood sat stacked in a pile on the side of the dwelling and a rough-hewn bench sat to the right of the door. A garden took up a sizeable area off to the side with an abundance of harvest yet to be picked.

Surely, a man who could maintain his dwelling so well could not have lost that much of his humanity.

Bliss clutched the bundle that held all she owned. This was her new home. This was where she was to live with her husband. This was where she would meet her fate one way or the other.

"You will explain who I am to Lord Rannick?" Bliss asked, stopping before taking a step out of the woods and into the clearing where the dwelling sat.

"Unfortunately, that's left to you," Lawler said. "If I remain, Lord Rannick will demand I take you with me."

"He could demand I leave," Bliss said, fear shivering her.

"True, but you won't leave. It is your duty to remain here, no matter what he says to you."

Bliss did not know what to say. Her legs trembled so badly that she feared she would not be able to take a single step.

"Go and be done with it, and may God be with you,"

Lawler said and turned and hurried away.

Bliss stared at his retreating back, her eyes not leaving him until he disappeared into the distance, not having glanced back once. She was alone. Completely alone. Alone with a possible madman.

She took a cautious step and was relieved her legs did not collapse beneath her. She forced herself to take more steps until she stood not far from the dwelling's door. She listened for any sound that someone was inside but heard none.

Thinking he could be asleep, she called out, "Good day. Is anyone there?"

She got no response. She stood where she was not knowing what to do. She dared not enter the dwelling, fearful of being trapped inside when Lord Rannick found her there. At least outside she could run if necessary.

She heard the footfalls then. They were heavy and determined and coming from behind the dwelling. They drew closer and closer, sounding as if they pounded in her ears, and she wondered over his size. He had to be large to have such a heavy gait and thick perhaps, which meant he'd have strength to him. She recalled Lawler telling her that it had taken many men to capture him and return him home. That meant he was beyond strong.

Bliss's stomach roiled and her legs grew weak once again and she braced herself as best as she could to meet her husband.

Chapter 2

Bliss clamped her lips shut to stop the gasp that rushed up in her. She had thought she'd been prepared to meet him, that his appearance would not shock her—she was wrong.

He was a sight, his skin-colored bronze, far different than the fair-skin of his countrymen. The scar she had been told about ran down his right cheek from just under his eye, disappearing into his mustache and short-cropped beard that were lighter in color than his brown hair, though they matched the golden strands that ran through his shoulder-length hair. The scar barely marred his fine features, unlike his scowl that gave a sinister look to his brown eyes dashed with green.

He was tall. Her head would probably reach no more than his shoulders that were wide, as was his chest. He was not broad with muscle but more defined with it from what she could see with his shirtsleeves rolled-up and his chest partially exposed, the ties at the neck of his shirt hanging open. The strip of plaid that usually ran over the chest hung at his side while another part of his plaid hugged his narrow waist tightly.

The one thing that troubled her the most was the axe he gripped in his hand and Lawler's words came back to warn her.

Lord Rannick told his father that if he forced another wife on him, he would kill her and save her the trouble of whatever heinous death would surely befall her.

"Begone from here," Rannick ordered with a sharp tongue, caught unaware by the thin, plain woman standing not far from his dwelling and staring at him in obvious fear.

13

Bliss gathered her courage. She gave a quick thought to keep the truth from him, let him think she had lost her way. But lies only birthed more lies and the deeper the lies, the more difficult for the truth to finally surface. Did she dare begin her marriage on lies? Or did she speak the truth and suffer death?

"I am parched. May I have a drink?' she asked and so the lie started, but what else was left to her?

"Nay, be on your way," he ordered again and pointed the axe for her to leave, then walked to stand in front of the dwelling, raising the axe to grip in both hands.

The weapon frightened her. However, the truth of him learning why she was there, frightened her even more. If a lie would save her, then she would let it spill from her lips and worry over the consequences later.

"Please, sir, I need a drink," she begged.

Rannick eyed her skeptically. He trusted few if none these days, his father insisting he wed and worried he would do something foolish and wed him against his will as he'd done twice before. However, this woman was of peasant stock with plain features and slim. She would not meet his father's standard for a wife for him. He would worry that she was too slim to bear children and while she carried herself well, it was not with the regal bearing of nobility.

A sudden thought struck him, and he raised his axe, a snarl turning his face angry. "If you have men with you who plan to rush me, I will see them dead."

"I give you my word, sir, I am alone," Bliss said, though almost turned to look with the way Rannick's eyes scanned the woods behind her.

"Why are you alone?" he demanded.

Bliss almost faltered, but a quick thought came to her. Dare she add more lies? Would it do her more harm than good, but what harm would come to her if she did not try? She prayed to the heavens to forgive her for the lies that

14

would fall from her lips.

"I have no one." At the moment that was true, she was on her own far-removed from her sisters. "I am all alone." She spotted the mistrust in his eyes. "And I trust few people, so I keep to myself as much as possible."

Rannick understood that, but nonetheless wanted her gone as quickly as possible. She might be plain, but there was something about the woman that stirred his long dead senses. Not that she aroused him, it was something else inside him she stirred... empathy? Impossible. He had compassion for no one. So why did he feel the need to see her quench her thirst?

The thought troubled him, and he was quick to say, "There is a stream beyond the cottage. You can quench your thirst there and be on your way."

"Could I not shelter here for the night?" she asked, worrying what excuse she could make to linger tomorrow.

"NAY! Have your drink at the stream and be gone," he ordered threateningly while shaking the axe at her.

Bliss hurried off, as fast as her trembling legs allowed, fearing his anger and the sight of the axe. She made a large berth around him and disappeared beyond the cottage, stumbling her way through the woods until she finally came upon the stream and dropped down on its bank. She hugged her sack against her chest, her heart beating wildly. How was she ever to accomplish her task when he frightened her so badly?

She shuddered. There was no way she could tell him that she was his wife. She feared at what that news might bring. She couldn't give up, her sisters' futures depended on her. But how did she make this work when he chased her away?

She scooped a handful of water up and realized she hadn't eaten all day. She was wise enough to know she needed her strength and rummaged through her sack to find

15

the meager food she had packed away in case she might need it. She also was well-versed in the plants in the area and, if necessary, she could forage for food that would sustain her.

A plan. She needed a plan, but how did she form one that dealt with a madman?

She moved to sit under a large pine tree. She leaned her head back against the trunk. All the fears and worries of the last few days had caught up with her. She was exhausted. She closed her eyes, not that she would sleep, but a brief rest would do her good.

A rumble of thunder had her eyes shooting open and she was shocked to see that dusk had claimed the land and night wasn't far behind. She would need a fire, the night turning cold of late.

She hurried to her feet and was about to step out from under the tree when the sky let loose with a downpour. She scurried back under, hoping to keep herself dry, but the rain didn't cooperate. It rained bucketsful and in no time she was soaking wet.

With no recourse left to her, she sat once again under the tree and prayed the storm would pass quickly. It was a prayer that went unanswered.

The night seemed endless, the rain and thunder relentless and the lightning frightening. Bliss gave thought to finding shelter elsewhere, but not knowing the area she concluded it was a foolish move. The rain kept the animals away, at least she hoped it would.

She huddled beneath the large pine branches and tried to think of anything but her dire situation. She cringed with every clap of thunder and shut her eyes tightly against every flash of lightning. If she were home, there would be no worry. She would be tucked safely away in the cottage with her sisters.

So much had changed in such a short time and her heart ached over being separated from her sisters. She always thought that Elysia would wed and have bairns and the family would grow. She worried over Annis. She wasn't particularly interested in marriage. She was far too interested in constructing dwellings to be bothered with a husband, especially one who would deny her a chance to do what she loved. At least they both were safe and were able to choose their own husbands and not be shackled to men who were complete strangers to them and would possibly harm them. Her sacrifice would not be in vain.

She jumped when a streak of lightning split the dark sky and she waited for the thunder and it came, rumbling the land with its enormous crack, and she shivered. She wiped the rain from her face, not that it did much good, the rain continuing to pour down on her. She would need to start a fire when the rain stopped. It was the only way she could dry her garments, but with how soaked they were, it would take forever for them to dry.

The night wore on and so did her strength and after a while, tears joined the rain that ran down her cheeks. She was alone and her heart ached at being separated from her sisters.

Bliss yelped when lightning struck, the bolt appearing as if it slashed through the tree. She heard the sound of a branch cracking somewhere overhead, and she fought to get to her feet, but her soaked garments were too cumbersome, slowing her down. She heard branches snap as the falling branch took other branches with it as it came tumbling down and all Bliss could do was squeeze her eyes shut and plant herself as tightly as she could against the trunk of the tree and pray that the branches missed her.

Another of her prayers went unanswered.

***

The crack of thunder woke Rannick, not that he had

17

been sleeping well. He could not get the woman he had sent on her way out of his thoughts. Had she made it to safety? Was she stuck somewhere in this storm without shelter? And why the bloody hell should he care?

He had isolated himself here for a reason, a damn good reason. He would not let his cursed life touch another. He had lost three wives, two of which he had not wanted. His first wife, Cecilia, had been an arranged marriage he had agreed to. He could not say he loved her, but he had cared for her, and he had been delighted when she had gotten with child.

Rannick threw the blanket off his naked body and swung his legs off the bed to sit at the edge. It had hit him hard when she and their bairn had died in childbirth, her screams that had lasted throughout the night still haunted his nightmares. He had promised himself he would never wed again.

His father had thought differently and wed him again, though this time without his permission, to Phedra, a woman who spoke her mind and did as she pleased and believed no curse could touch her. She died in a riding accident, though she was a skilled horsewoman. Shona, his third wife, a sweet soul from what he had been told since he had wanted nothing to do with her for her own good, died in his arms only three days after his father wed them by proxy. It had been the one and only time he had touched her.

"Never again. Never again," he whispered, staring into the flames of the small stone fireplace.

The image of the woman who had begged for water rushed into his mind. Why she haunted him, he could not say though he had gone far longer than usual without a woman. He had not touched a woman since his return home. He had coupled with many a woman while away, not one having meant anything to him. But then none had been a wife to him. He and his father had had a vicious argument after his

18

father forced his return home. His father had insisted he wed and produce an heir for the clan. He had refused and made it clear that that would never happen. He had threatened that any wife his father forced on him, he would see dead before the curse could claim her. He left the keep that day and sheltered here in the remote cottage. And here was where he planned to stay until the end of his life.

Unfortunately, the woman's arrival today had disrupted his plans. He could not keep her from his thoughts. He did not know what it was about her that kept her lingering on his mind. She was plain featured but not unpleasant to look upon and had little shape to her, being too thin. Her long brown hair had been secured tight in a braid and her eyes were brown in color and nothing to speak of, so why then did she continue to occupy in his thoughts?

It was that damn feeling he got when his eyes connected with hers. It had touched something inside him, stirred it, and left him feeling... he shook his head. What the bloody hell was it about her that tormented him?

It also tormented him that she was out there in an awful storm, probably soaked through and probably without shelter or without the chance of a fire to keep her warm.

"Not my concern," he barked at himself and slipped under the blanket.

He winced, a quick, sharp pain running through the scar on his cheek. He recalled the attack well. He'd been caught off guard and had fought with blood pouring down his face. He had briefly thought to surrender to the large man and see the curse upon his family die there and then, but his warrior instinct forbid it and he had fought to survive. A weakness he had found in the man, an injury that had not healed well, soon made it apparent that he could easily be defeated. His opponent had realized it as well and fled.

Light pierced the few small cracks in the door from the flash of lightning and the mighty thunder that followed felt

19

as if it shook the small dwelling.

"Damn," he mumbled and shook his head again.

There was no point in going out in the dark of night to find the woman. She could be anywhere. She probably moved on once she drank her fill at the stream, too afraid to remain near him. A wise decision on her part.

But what if she hadn't?

He hadn't realized he had been rubbing his shaft while lost in his thoughts until it hardened in his hand. He quickly released it. He had only satisfied himself that morning, and he didn't need to spill his seed in waste again. Though, he would not spill his seed in a woman even if she was willing. He and his two friends, Odran and Brogan, the other clan lords that had been cursed, had pledged to sire no bairns so that the curse would end with them, and that was a pledge he intended to keep.

Thunder continued to rumble, and rain continued to fall heavily, and sleep continued to elude Rannick. Not so thoughts of the woman. She remained busy in his mind. He finally got out of bed and hurried into his garments. It was a fool's errand, but he would get no rest if he did not go to see if she had remained by the stream.

He made sure to tuck a knife in the sheath at his waist and one in his boot, then he grabbed his cloak and swung it around his shoulders. He went to the door and swung it open.

He jolted, startled by the rain-drowned figure standing there.

"Help me," the woman begged and fell into his arms.

Chapter 3

Rannick held her in his arms, for a moment, not sure what to do. Her soaked garments threatened his own and he hurried her to the bench to sit and to rest her back against the table's edge. It was close enough to the fire to help dry her clothing. He rid himself of his own cloak before struggling to remove hers, heavy with rainwater.

He stepped back away from her as her eyes fluttered open and that was when he spotted the blood at her side.

"You need to stop the bleeding," she warned through painful breaths. She continued to struggle to talk. "A pouch—my side—healer."

He removed the pouch, dropping it on the table and crouching down beside her to take a look at the wound.

"Tree branch—clean before treating," she said, and her eyes rolled back in her head then closed.

He steadied her with his hand, preventing her from tipping to the side and tried to get a better look at the wound. If a tree branch had stabbed her, then she was right in warning to cleanse the wound. Splinters of wood could have embedded themselves inside her and if not removed, the wound would turn putrid, and she would die.

"Bloody hell," he mumbled. He had no choice. He had to strip off her garments so he could see the wound clearly and that was not going to be easy with how wet they were.

He would have preferred her to remain in a faint at least until he got her garments off, but she came to.

"I need to take your garments off," he said, his face planted close to hers as he slipped his arm around her waist to get her to her feet.

21

"Aye," she agreed and draped a weak arm over his shoulder.

A groan of pain rumbled in her throat as he launched her up off the bench.

Her tunic gave him little trouble, the shift beneath was a different matter.

"Please," she pleaded after a few unsuccessful attempts and lowered her head on his shoulder.

Her ragged breathing and the way her weight, little there was of it, rested against him told him she was exhausted. How far had she walked to return here? How long had she been bleeding?

"The wound cannot wait. It needs immediate attention. I am going to cut your garment off," he said, leaving her no choice. Surprisingly, she nodded.

He kept his knives sharpened, prepared for anything… anything but this. His blade sliced through the wet cloth more easily than he expected.

She shivered when all that was left on her were her boots and she moved closer against him. He needed to get her dry before he laid her on the bed, and keeping a firm hand around her, he eased her along with him as he reached for one of the cloths that he used to dry himself after a dunk in the stream.

He rubbed her shoulders with it and ran it down along her back as he turned her to the fire. He swiped the cloth over her backside quickly and couldn't help but think that though she was slim, her bottom rounded nicely. It was not a thought he needed to be having at the moment. He turned his attention to her chest, his eyes glancing at her small breasts as he gently ran the cloth over them. He stopped when his eyes fell on the wound.

It continued to bleed, though slowly, and not knowing how long it had been bleeding didn't help.

"The wound," she mumbled.

He lifted her in his arms and placed her on the bed, running the cloth over her flat stomach and slim legs, after taking off her boots and before pulling the blanket up to her waist.

"Still bleeding," he said, placing a cloth along her side to catch the blood.

"Splinters," she reminded.

"I will look," he said, "but with the wound still bleeding…"

"Sear it," she groaned.

He was glad she said what he was about to.

Rannick set to work, lighting a candle and holding it near the wound while he examined it.

"What do you see?" she asked.

"It looks clean enough," he said, hoping he was right, and no sliver of wood remained.

"Run water over the wound before you sear it."

He had seen wounds flushed out with various liquids in foreign countries. It didn't always make a difference, but who was he to say what made the difference. Besides, with the way her strength was waning, he feared it was already too late and was surprised at how much the thought troubled him.

"I will fetch the water," he said.

She raised her hand with effort, and he almost jumped back when it fell gently against his scarred cheek. She shocked him even more with what she said.

"I trust you."

He removed her hand from his cheek and leaned down close to her face. "Never make that mistake. Never trust me."

She shocked him again when she said, "I have no choice."

It was ironic that she turned to him for help since it was probably his fault that she had suffered the wound, but she

23

was not his wife, and he need not worry the curse would affect her.

Prove it. Save her. The challenge reverberated in his head like a tolling bell.

He needed no challenge. He did not want to see her die. He'd had enough women die around him. He set the blade of one of his larger knives in the fire to heat, then snatched a bucket up and stepped outside.

Thoughts ran randomly through his head. She would need to stay with him and heal. It could take weeks. Winter could set in by then. How could he send her away on her own to face the cold or possibly heavy snow? An easy solution. He would return her to his village. His mum would see her well-cared for.

My bed would be much warmer in winter with her in it.
And why did he even think such a foolish thought?
She is not your wife. She is safe. She is in need.
"Nay!" he whispered harshly.

He would send her to the village to heal as soon as possible.

He set the bucket on the table when he returned and went to the bed. Her eyes were closed and her face pale. She was thin, though there was a gentle curve to her waist and her breasts were small, though adequate enough to enjoy.

He shook his head and mumbled, "Too long without a woman."

Her eyes opened slowly, and she licked her lips before asking, "Your name?"

He thought not to give it to her, his name widely known due to the curse, and she was already suffering, she did not need to be frightened as well. But that might work well for him, for then she would want to get away from him as quickly as possible.

His chin went up slightly as he said, "Rannick."

"Rannick," she repeated on a whisper. "Thank you for

24

helping me."

The woman's reactions continued to shock him.

"Bliss," she said.

Bliss had eluded him, and he was not foolish to believe he would ever find it. How could she think this was bliss—could she mean? "Your name is Bliss?"

"Aye, Bliss," she repeated.

He smiled—barely—a surprise since he could not remember when last he smiled. It looked like he was wrong... he did finally find Bliss.

"This is not going to be pleasant," he warned.

"I know," she said and shut her eyes.

He could not imagine what her thoughts might be. Here she was naked and vulnerable in front of a strange man and yet she trusted him. And people thought him insane. Yet, the urge to help her, see her kept safe, overwhelmed and surprised him.

She winced when he dribbled water on the wound, but managed to say, "Look again for splinters."

Rannick was surprised to see a few had washed out with the blood. "We got some out."

A heavy sigh had her chest rising and falling with relief.

"I am going to give you a stick to hold on to—"

She hurried to interrupt him. "It would be better if you held me tight in case I flinch."

She shivered and he wasn't sure if it was from fear or from being cold. "We need this done. You need rest, and warmth."

"Aye," she agreed and reached out to him.

He settled her in the crook of his arm, leaving the wound exposed where he could easily sear it. Her hand latched onto his arm that held her and she buried her face against the side of his chest.

He did not wait. He reached to the corner of the hearth where he had placed the knife and grabbed the handle with

25

the wadded cloth he had left there. He did not hesitate; he pressed the scorching blade against the wound. She cried out against his chest, then her body went limp in his arm.

The odor of burning flesh permeated the room. He eased her out of his arm and arranged blankets over her, keeping the soft wool away from the seared wound so it would not irritate it. The only thing left was to pray and he had long ago lost any faith in that.

***

Rannick woke to soft groans. He had fallen asleep sitting braced against the end of the fireplace where he could keep an eye on Bliss. He looked at her now and saw how she shivered. He hurried to her and felt her head, thankful to find it cool. Since she had no fever, it was either dreams or discomfort that had left her restless enough to chase the blanket off her.

He placed it over her, but she did not stop shivering. He tried another blanket, but it did little good. He could not let her shivers continue, and he needed some solid sleep himself. He made a hasty, if unwise, decision and slipped off his boots and shirt and eased himself beneath the blankets to carefully take her in his arms.

His warmth drew her to him, and she turned and snuggled against him as if she could not get close enough, then finally as if she found the perfect niche, she settled quietly, her shivers fading away.

He shut his eyes, not so much to sleep, but to let himself have this moment with this woman in bed. It had been years since he had slept beside a woman, held her while she slept, felt the warmth of her naked body against his.

Strange that he should find with her what he so ached for… "Bliss."

***

Bliss woke with a wince and cuddled closer to the warmth that embraced her. She didn't want to leave it. It was far too comforting. She pressed her face against the heat, and an earthy scent, quite pleasant, filled her nostrils. She should open her eyes. She needed to start the day and see to those in need.

Her eyes flew open to see she was pressed against a hard chest, and everything came rushing back at her. She went to move and winced.

"Easy," Rannick said, his hand going to her shoulder and easing her onto her back, relieved to move her away since he woke aroused against her.

Bliss shut her eyes for a moment, partly against the pain that jabbed relentlessly at her and partly at trying to focus and recall all that had happened. Good Lord, she was in bed with her husband where she needed to be—he, however, had no knowledge of that. She felt him slip out of bed and a shiver of relief ran through her.

"You need to leave here," Rannick said with intentional roughness. "I will have you taken to my clan village where you can rest and heal."

Bliss had to think fast. She could not allow him to return her to the village. His father would claim she failed, and all would be lost. Her sisters would no longer be safe.

"I am not well enough to travel," she said, which was the truth, at least for a few days, but she needed more than a few days reprieve.

"I do not want you here," he said with a snarl, and he meant it. His foolish thoughts of last night were just that— foolish thoughts. Never would he know bliss, the feeling of joy, or Bliss the woman in front of him. And he certainly would not be the evil that destroyed Bliss.

She remembered him to be much kinder last night, but

27

then he had had little choice. Though, he could have just let her die and be done with it, but he hadn't. That had her believing he was not the evil man so many claimed him to be.

"I am sorry to impose on you," she said apologetically and winced as she shifted in bed.

"A day or two, no more," he snapped, seeing the truth of her words. She was not fit to travel yet. "Then you go to the village."

She silently thanked the heavens when a thought came to her. "I do not think it would be wise of me to go to the village."

"You will go. I command it," he ordered, jabbing a finger her way.

The way his face twisted with anger sparked fear in her, but she stayed strong as best she could. "I will do as you say, my lord, but I fear if you send me to the village, it will be known that I spent time here and—"

A string of oaths flew from his mouth before she could finish. Once his father found out, he would get what he wanted—a wife for his son. He would force another marriage on him.

His eyes narrowed in suspicion. "You know who I am yet last night you asked my name."

"To be sure it was you," she said quickly. "I made my way through your village yesterday and was warned about you." There was truth to her words since Lawler had warned her what to expect. She winced when she moved to turn.

"Stay as you are," he ordered sharply. "You need rest. You were warned away and yet you came here anyway?"

She spoke another truth. "I did not want to."

"Stumbled across me by accident?" he asked once again suspicious.

"Aye, I certainly did that," she said, thinking it had been stumble after stumble that left her no choice but to come here.

"Where have you come from and where do you go that brings you this way?"

She saw the suspicion in his brown eyes, the green specks sparking, though the scowl that had deepened his brow lines between them had eased.

"I lost what home I had and traveled in hope of finding a new one." Another truth, since she hoped that somehow all would go well, and she would at least find a modicum of peace here.

"A new home where?"

A partial truth was the best she could do. "Wherever I landed."

"It is not here," he snapped in warning.

She went to turn again, and the blanket slipped off her breasts.

"Cover yourself, woman!" he yelled.

Bliss quickly pulled the blanket up to her neck. How had she forgotten she was naked?

"You have no qualm of being naked around a man. Are you overly familiar with men? Is that what you search for a man to shelter with for the winter and see to your needs?"

His insult so infuriated her that her anger gave her the strength to push herself up in bed while keeping the blanket tight against her chest. However, her wound was quick to remind her that she was far from healed. The pain hit hard and fast.

She had just enough time before the faint devoured her to call and reach out. "Rannick."

Chapter 4

Oath after oath flew from Rannick's lips after reaching
Bliss in enough time to stop her from tumbling out of bed in
an effort to reach out to him. He wanted to berate her for
foolishly trusting him and berate himself for letting himself
care. It did no good to care about or for a woman. In the end,
the woman suffered for it, and he did as well, for the pain
could be unimaginable and the results for the woman...
deadly. Never again would he allow himself to care for a
woman.

He brushed the wisps of hair that had fallen free from
her disheveled braid off her face. They were soft to the
touch, plain brown in color, a deeper brown than he had first
thought, and held a slight curl. Her face was more oval than
round and creamy in color and free of any blemishes. Her
features were pleasant enough, though she did not possess
the beauty that captured a man's eye and held it. And yet for
some reason, her features captured his eyes and held them.

Her eyes drifted open, and his name fell softly from her
lips, "Rannick."

"I am here," he assured her, and as if it was
commonplace, he wrapped his hand around hers. A sting to
his heart had him catching a breath that almost erupted into a
strong gasp when she squeezed his hand.

"Trust," she whispered.

Was she reiterating her trust in him or telling him that
he could trust her?

"You will remain abed until I say otherwise, or I will tie
you to the bed," he ordered briskly.

Her eyes fought their way open, fear heavy in them, and

she paled. "You would not."

Guilt stabbed at him but then it was his constant companion, a companion of his own doing. He had given no thought to marrying his first wife, but he should have prevented his father from wedding him to the two women that followed. This woman was not his wife, but he would not suffer guilt over her death if he was able to prevent it.

"Try me," he warned. "You will do what is necessary for you to grow strong enough to take your leave. Or I will make certain that you do." He released her hand abruptly, a sudden pain stabbing his chest as he did. "And do not think to work your womanly wiles on me. I have no need or wont of a woman."

Bliss almost laughed. "Womanly wiles? I have no experience with such things."

"Say you, but heed my warning, for I am far from an honorable man." He went to a chest near the end of the bed and pulled something from it and tossed it at her. "Put this on and keep it on."

It was a shirt, a string tie at the neck, and far too large for her, but it mattered not, it would cover her and that was all that concerned her. She stifled a groan as best she could as she moved to sit up to get the shirt on her. The pain stole her strength with each move and that was not good. She needed all the strength she had to heal. And with the way she grew lightheaded when she struggled to sit up, she knew she had already used what strength she had left for the day.

Bliss did not want to ask, did not want to rely on him even if he was her husband. But wasn't it better she did? Wouldn't it be wiser to gain his trust and perhaps, at least, his friendship before she told him they were husband and wife?

With a tremble in her voice, she did not need to fake, she said, "I need help."

Rannick had seen that but had hoped she would

31

somehow manage on her own. More the fool he. He grumbled as he went to her and slipped his arm beneath her back to ease her up to sit.

Bliss grabbed his arm and shut her eyes when a slight dizziness struck her.

"Stay as you are. It will pass."

His voice was powerful and yet gentle, and she kept her grip on his arm, taut with muscle.

Rannick's eyes went to her hand, her slim fingers tried to grip like an iron cuff around his forearm but lacked the strength. He should dislodge her hand, not allow her to touch him, but he did not want to. The foolish thought had him disengage his arm and snatch up the shirt.

"One arm at a time and keep that blanket covering your chest until the shirt is on," he ordered sternly and readied it to slip over her head.

Bliss made no comment. What was there for her to say or do for that matter? She was where she was supposed to be—in her husband's bed. Now she only needed to heal enough to have the strength to see their marriage consummated. And pray that she got with child before he discovered her deceit, a deceit with which she was growing more uncomfortable.

She cried out as a stitch of pain caught in her side and her hand instinctively went to her wound, the blanket falling away from her breasts.

Rannick dropped down beside her on the bed. "Rest your head on me."

She did not argue, she rested her head on his chest, another part of him hard with muscle, and surprisingly she relished the strength and comfort it provided. His thumb brushed the side of her breast as he eased her arm into the sleeve. It was a faint brush and not unpleasant or on purpose. It was good to know since intimacy with him might not prove as daunting as she had feared.

He quickly slipped the shirt down to her waist, eased her on her back, then pulled the blanket up to her waist before he planted his hands on either side of her.

The strength of his hands pressed on the blanket pinned her to the bed. She could not move. He rested his face far too close to hers. So close, she could see that his scar and scowl did nothing to diminish his exceptionally fine features and the specks of green that dotted his brown eyes seemed to enlarge with his mounting anger and that sent a streak of fear racing through her.

"You tempt me, woman. Keep your distance from me and leave here soon," he warned with a snarl. "Or I will see that you stay the winter and poke you nightly, then send you on your way with the first sign of spring. You will find no home here. No man who cares. No love. Only endless pokes that mean nothing."

Rannick stood, turning away from her, annoyed with himself. Had it been seeing her naked or the trust she had placed in him that made him say such a foolish thing? And yet the thought to have her warm his bed for the winter would not leave him. It nagged at his mind and body. Bliss was not his wife. She would be in no danger if he did nothing but poke her. He could see her sent off in the spring with good coin and a place where she could settle safely.

INSANE!

Aye, it was insanity to even think it. Why then had he? It did not matter. It would never happen. He would make sure of it, starting now.

He turned to face her, his snarl returning. "Think hard on my words." He shoved his plaid aside, his hand grabbing hold of his rock-hard shaft. "For I will slip into you every night with no thought but to satisfy myself." He turned away and swerved back around just as fast. "You need to know I am evil—pure evil—and evil can easily destroy bliss."

He turned his back to her once again, grabbed his shirt,

and stormed out of the cottage.

Bliss stared at the closed door. His warning had sent a chilling shiver through her right down into her bones.

Leave as soon as you are well, she silently warned herself.

"I cannot," she whispered, she had to protect Elysia and Annis.

She should be grateful, for he unknowingly made her task easier and a bit more frightening. If she spent the winter with him, she would surely get with child, though some thought her past child-bearing years. A foolish thought since she had delivered bairns from women older than herself. Her only worry was that since her first monthly bleed had begun it did not always come when it should. That could make it difficult to tell if she was with child.

She shook her head. There was no need to worry about that until the time came. She had been offered a way to see this task accomplished without much difficulty. She could not let fear stand in her way. The image of his sizeable shaft flashed in her mind. She had learned that some shafts could be too large for some women. She hoped that would not prove a problem for her. Though, something else might.

I will slip into you every night with no thought but to satisfy myself.

A slight shudder ran through her. She had tended enough women to know not all of them enjoyed the marriage bed and for various reasons. Some simply disliked coupling, calling it disgusting, some felt their husbands selfish, some quite enjoyed it, and some felt their husband lacked skill. Some women laughed about it, others cried, and some were simply indifferent toward it, claiming it was part of the chore of being a wife.

Bliss wondered where she would fall among those women. Her hope was that sharing the marriage bed with Rannick would at least be tolerable. Tolerable was something she could manage. Though truth be told, she had envied the women who had spoken with not only delight about the marriage bed, but also with pride in their husbands' skills.

She yawned, finding herself tired, though she had slept well. Her body was letting her know she needed more sleep to heal, and she did not fight it. She let herself drift into a light sleep.

***

Rannick clinched his fists, wanting to pound something but wisely refrained from doing something he'd regret. A broken hand would serve no purpose. How had he allowed himself to even let the foolhardy thought slip past his lips?

A way to get rid of her.

That was it. He wanted her gone and what he had said to her would chase her away as soon as she was fit to leave. He wished that was today, but she was not nearly healed enough to leave. And it had annoyed him that she was right about what would be assumed if he delivered her to the keep for his mum to look after. His father would have them wed in no time.

Then Bliss would die.

Anger shot through him at the thought, but so did a tingle of fear. He would not want to see anything happen to her. She was an innocent woman caught in the evil that surrounded him, much like the insects that get caught in a spider's web. Once captured there is no escape only certain death, and like the spider, he was the evil that delivered that death.

He clinched his fists so tightly that his knuckles turned white. He would not let that happen to Bliss. She was an innocent in all this. He would make sure she was anxious to take her leave as soon as she was well enough to do so. Then he would return to live out his days alone until death saw fit to take him.

Rannick stepped away from the door after slipping on his shirt. The rain had stopped, though the gray skies warned of more. He made his way to the lean-to, a few short steps from the cottage, where he stored the firewood and gathered an armful. He would see to the fire then go hunt food for them. Rest and food would help build her strength and make for a quick healing and a quick departure.

He entered the cottage, relieved to see she slept. He added logs to the dwindling fire, hunching done to poke at the logs with a good-sized stick so the flames could lick at the new logs and set them ablaze.

"Does it still rain?"

He shut his eyes a moment against her soft, sleepy voice and the unexpected memory of how much he had enjoyed having her rest comfortably in his arms last night. He had known loneliness throughout the years, but never had he realized the pain of that loneliness until he had felt the deep pleasure of her warm naked body snug in his arms.

It tore at his heart, and his heart had felt nothing in years, and he intended to keep it that way. It was the only way he could survive and keep others safe from him.

"The rain has stopped, but the skies are gray," he said, without glancing her way as he stood. "I go hunt food for us. Sleep, heal, and be on your way." He gave her no chance to respond. He grabbed his bow and quiver, stocked well with arrows, and hurried out the door.

Once again Bliss stared at the closed door. This time, however, she was too tired to care. She closed her eyes and let sleep once again take hold.

Bliss woke, not sure if it had been minutes or hours that she had slept, but with one worried thought.

Fever.

She felt the uncomfortable warmth that preceded a fever

and needed to see to it before it worsened. There was a brew she could make that would help, but she was not foolish enough to think she had the strength to do that. A cool wet cloth would help for now, then when Rannick returned, she could explain to him how to fix the brew.

Her hand struggled with the blanket as she tried to toss it off her. She was weaker than she thought. Had the fever taken stronger hold than she had realized? She had to at least get a cool cloth to her head. She could not lie abed and let the fever worsen.

Her struggle to sit up was more of a battle and by the time she got herself to sit on the edge of the bed, she was exhausted. She spied the bucket of water barely two steps away and hoped Rannick had placed a fresh one there. It took a couple of tries before she finally got on her feet, though it was with an unsteady sway. With caution, she stepped forward and her sway worsened. She stumbled to the table, grabbing the edge.

"Foolish," she admonished herself as she would have done to someone in her condition for even attempting to get out of bed. Her side felt on fire, or was it the fever that caused the stinging heat? Her head was too fuzzy to be sure of anything.

She had to get back to bed or she would collapse where she was and lie there until Rannick returned. A few steps were all it would take to get to the bed. She could stumble to it and hopefully collapse on it.

A few calming breaths, a moment to regain her strength, and she turned to head back to the bed. The pain tore through her side and she had no time to react. She went down in a faint.

***

Rannick had the two rabbits cleaned, speared, and ready

37

for the hearth. A light rain had started on his way back to the cottage and with the skies darkening it was sure to grow worse. Once in the cottage, he intended to focus on cooking the meat and seeing to cleaning his weapons, anything that would keep him from engaging with Bliss.

He entered the cottage, keeping his eyes on the hearth and shrugged off his cloak before crouching down to adjust the spear on the spit he had fashioned in the hearth. The quiet suddenly struck him and his eyes shifted to the bed and seeing it empty, his eyes hurried around the room as he rushed to his feet, only to stop when he spotted Bliss on the floor by the side of the table.

Heat struck him as soon as he had her in his arms. She had a fever and that was not good. He got her to the bed and stripped the shirt off her and left the blanket off as well. In one of the foreign lands he had traveled, they treated fever differently. They kept the person cool and made sure the person drank frequently. It worked more than it had failed, and he hoped it would not fail Bliss.

He hurried to fill the bucket with fresh water and bathed her face with a cool cloth, then he bathed the rest of her body as well, his only thought ridding her of the fever. Even though she shivered, he would not cover her.

A shudder woke her, and she whispered, "Cold."

"Aye, and you will stay that way until the fever breaks," he ordered.

She struggled to get out, "Brew."

"Aye, I will fix one for you."

She sighed, shivered, and reached out her hand to him.

He took it and she wrapped her slim fingers around his. "Trust you."

The oaths that had been lingering on the tip of his tongue fell loose, though quietly so she did not hear. He did not want her to trust him. No one trusted him, not any longer, especially since his return. He had lost all of his humanity while he'd been on foreign soil, though he had hoped, and prayed—not that his prayers were answered—for death. Death would end the curse for his family, for there would be no heir for the curse to cling to.

"Keep hold of my hand, please," she pleaded.

Her hand barely had any strength to it and yet she kept hold of his. He spoke without thinking. "I will not let you go, Bliss. I will see you kept safe."

"Promise," she murmured.

"Aye, Bliss, you have my word." He scowled. How did he, a cursed and evil man, keep her safe?

Chapter 5

Rannick split the thick log in one swing of the axe. He had cut down a tree and split it into logs and was now splitting those logs into firewood all since early this morning. He had to do something to combat the frustration building in him in the last six days.

He had managed to get Bliss's fever down after spending the remainder of that day bathing her with cool, wet cloths and having her drink the brew he had made following her instructions. By evening the fever had left her. He had placed a light blanket over her, and she had slept peacefully. Not so he. He had barely slept sitting braced against the end of the hearth, his concern for her keeping him awake.

Another crack of wood rang through the brisk air.

He had two wives he had coupled with, and several willing women years afterwards, but never had he felt the intimacy he had felt while caring for Bliss. There was not a part of her naked body he had not touched with the wet cloth, or his fingers had grazed in the process and not once had she protested. She had laid there trusting him and had thanked him repeatedly for his help.

He swung the axe again and with such force, the log split, and the two pieces went flying.

Rannick snarled. If Bliss only knew what he had been thinking at times. He truly was evil, having thought, much too often, how he would like to do more than cool her body down with a cloth. He wanted to heat it to a feverish pitch until she begged...

"Rannick."

40

"What?" he snapped without turning, his lascivious thoughts having turned his shaft hard against his plaid, not something he wanted Bliss to see. "And what are you doing out of bed?"

"I am feeling better."

"Good, drink some more of the brew and get back in bed," he ordered.

"I drank much of the brew already and—"

"Drink more. Now let me be," he said with an angry snarl.

"I truly am sorry to bother you, but I need to…"

"Say no more," he ordered and smacked the axe into the top of a log. His anger had managed to shrink his shaft, so his arousal wasn't obvious—to his relief—and he turned to face her.

He did not think oaths would ever stop falling from his lips with Bliss around. She stood in the doorway wearing his shirt. that fell past her knees, and her boots, worn as they were. Her shiny brown hair hung loose, the sides tucked behind her ears and her cheeks glowed pink as they always did when she had to let him know she needed to see to her private needs.

The first few times she was too weak to walk, and he had carried her into the woods. She had refused to let him help her and had insisted he brace her against a tree and give her a moment of privacy. The last two days she had managed, with his help, to walk into the woods and he would wait patiently for her while she saw to her needs.

"I think I may be well enough to go on my own," she said and stepped toward him, a slight sway to her gait.

"Not yet," he said abruptly and took hold of her arm.

She did not bother to argue. She had learned he could be stubborn at times and those times she chose to let it be.

They entered the woods and after she almost stumbled twice, he swung her up into his arms. "I will not have you

41

suffer another injury and delay your departure."

Strangely enough she had gotten used to being in his arms and even stranger was that she found herself comfortable there. He held her firmly but with a gentleness that did not threaten. And each time he did, she became more and more familiar with his face. She saw that his beard hid a small scar near his chin and that he had more flecks of green in his right eye than his left. His scar revealed something as well. It was thin and straight which made Bliss think it was a quick slash to his face possibly from the tip of a dagger. It had healed fairly well, and while permanent, did not distract from his fine features. If anything, it added to them, giving him the distinction of a seasoned warrior.

Another thing she learned about him was that he did not talk much, but she was determined to change that—she needed to. She needed him to come to know her and maybe even like her at least a little bit. If he did, when he learned of her deceit, he would understand that she had kept the truth from him out of love for her sisters.

He placed her by a tree and walked a few steps away, turning his back to her.

She smiled as she watched a couple of squirrels. "It will be a cold winter. The squirrels are busy burying food."

"Aye, which is why you need to rest, heal, and leave here soon."

Bliss thought to speak up and tell him she had decided to remain for the winter with him, but now was not the right time.

She finished and took careful steps toward him. He turned before she reached him, he always did, but then her footfalls were not quiet in the woods. She was not surprised when he once again lifted her gently in his arms.

He said nothing until they were near the cottage. "You will rest. I will see about catching us fish for tonight."

"I could make a fish stew," she offered.

42

He turned his face to hers and for a moment she thought he looked startled, but it was so fast she could not be sure.

"Rest is all you will do," he ordered sternly and deposited her at the open doorway.

Without a word, he grabbed his shirt off the pile of stacked logs and disappeared around the corner of the cottage.

That he avoided her when possible was obvious. That he didn't want her here was also obvious, which was why she had no choice but to accept his offer of spending the winter with him. Otherwise, she feared he might physically send her on her way. But what if he had changed his mind about her remaining there?

She shook her head. She could not let that happen. She entered the cottage thinking that the sooner she informed him that she would accept his offer to spend the winter with him, the better. She also decided that it might help if he tasted her cooking. Her sisters would never speak about what a good cook Bliss was, for fear the chieftain would make her a cook in the keep.

She also needed to see if she could mend her shift that Rannick had been forced to cut off her. At least she had her tunic which she could wear over his shirt if necessary. She would get busy, glad to have a task or two to do, though she would stop if she grew tired. The sear that had closed her wound was healing nicely, and though she would be left with a scar, it was better than the alternative—death.

The thought faltered her steps as she entered the cottage and she leaned against the door once closed. When the branch had speared her side, she had thought the curse had struck her and she would die. She had been surprised that she had found her way back to Rannick at night in the storm. She had wondered if fate had somehow intervened, sending her the stark squawk of a raven that had seemed to guide her way. Then when the fever had struck her, she had worried

43

the curse had reached out again to claim her and when it didn't, she continued to wonder if fate and the curse battled.

There was another possibility that poked at her. Her sister Annis had been determined to find out how the curse could be broken and when she got an idea in her head, there was no stopping her. She wondered if Annis had set off on such a mission and had found a way to at least disrupt the curse.

She shook her head. Annis could be stubborn, but she supposed it would take a strong tenacity to go on a quest to find the one person who could possibly help with the curse—the witch in the hills. She did not like the thought that Annis would take such a risk, but just as she had taken a risk to protect her sisters, Annis would do the same for her.

Bliss hoped in the end that whatever risk any of the three of them took proved worth it. That meant she had to get busy and see her risk prove successful.

She slipped her tunic over Rannick's shirt to keep it clean since presently it was all she had to wear until she could get her shift repaired. It also provided more proper coverage for her legs, something she should not be showing, though Rannick was her husband and did have certain privileges, as did she. It made their situation easier for her, for if he was not her husband, she did not know how she would have been able to allow him to tend her as intimately as he had done.

"Set to your task, Bliss," she ordered herself. If she allowed herself to get lost in endless thoughts, she would forever question and doubt her decisions. And now was not the time to let doubt in.

She had searched the crocks and sacks earlier, and knowing where things were, she grabbed a wood bowl and went and scooped ground barley out of one of the sacks and after placing the bowl on the table, she finished gathering what else she needed, then got busy making bread.

***

Rannick had two fish gutted and prepared to cook on his return to the cottage. He had lingered by the stream as long as he could, not fishing, until he could linger no longer. His mind had been in turmoil since he had glanced at Bliss earlier when in his arms and saw a genuine trust and gentleness in her eyes that had startled him.

The fear he had first seen there when they had first laid eyes on each other had vanished and allowed him to see her true nature. She was a caring woman, and though he had found not all healers caring, Bliss cared down to her soul. Never had he expected to find that depth of compassion in a woman. Many women he had met through the years cared and thought for nothing but themselves, and he could not blame some of them, their families interested only in the benefits a female could bring them. But Bliss was a peasant, she could benefit no one, and her lot could not be an easy one. How then did she hold on to such kindness, to such strength, to such trust?

The curse had robbed him of any decency, any humanity he had once possessed. It had robbed his friends as well. He had watched his friend Brogan suffer wound after wound that would have killed most men, but he did not die, the curse condemning him to a life of pain and suffering. The curse had turned Odran silent after he killed his brother on the battlefield, though few understood he had had no choice. He buried himself in silence and solitude after that. After endless attempts to try and break the curse, they had come to an agreement. The curse had to end and the only way to do that was for it to end with them, the last heirs to each of their clans. The three would die childless, leaving the curse with no one left to feed on, leaving it to finally die.

It had been a desperate decision and a necessary one

45

and one that hurt more than any of them would admit. He was an only child and had hoped to have a large family. He had been happy, though worried, when his first wife, Cecilia, had announced she was with child. She had been a pleasant enough wife, undemanding and obedient, and they had gotten along well enough, but that could have been because they had spent little time together.

He tried to push the memory away, but it raged in him, and the blame grew each time he recalled the day he had lost Cecilia and their bairn in childbirth. He should have never wed, but his father had insisted, and he had surrendered to his command. Though, if he was truthful with himself, he had wanted to wed, had wanted a family, had wanted to believe the curse had no power over him.

How wrong he'd been.

Bliss is not your wife.

Would it matter? Would she fall to the power of the curse anyway?

She had survived her wound and the fever that had come with it. Didn't that prove that the curse would not touch her? With no vows, no caring, no love between them, and only the winter months to keep each other warm and satisfied, could he at least know the compassionate touch of a woman for a few months? Did he dare take such a chance?

He almost laughed. He was thinking she would agree to stay with him when she was probably already planning her escape after blatantly displaying his hard shaft the way he had. And she should escape. He was evil for even continuing to give it thought.

It was having a woman suddenly thrust upon him that caused the problem.

Thrust.

Damn but he could almost feel the pleasure of each thrust of his shaft into her, of getting lost with no thought of the curse, no thought of the guilt, no thought of the never-ending loneliness. He shook the disturbing thoughts away. It could never be. He would not chance another woman dying because of him.

Bliss is not your wife.

He intended to keep it that way.

He entered the cottage, to a scent that tempted his stomach. Bread sat on the table that was warm to the touch while Bliss slept peacefully in his bed. He set the fish to cooking in the hearth and after giving his hands a good washing in the bucket, he walked over to the bed.

Bliss laid on her side, facing him, wearing her tunic over his shirt, though it failed to cover her legs and bare feet. A faint touch to her leg warned she was cold, and he carefully covered her up over her shoulders since she had rolled the sleeves to his shirt up.

He smiled at the smudge of ground barley on her cheek and with a soft swipe of his finger, wiped it away. He could get used to coming home to her after fishing or hunting and joining her in bed.

Rannick shook his head and turned away abruptly. This had to stop. He had enough blood on his hands from the curse, from battles, and from endless fights that came about for no good reason. He had gone in search of what death would bring him—peace—and had not found it. When his father had forcibly returned him home, he had sworn to himself that here was where he would live out his days alone so that not one more person would suffer the curse because of him.

It was his penance, and he would serve it well.

He went to the table and broke off a piece of the bread. His eyes went wide at the first taste, and he finished the piece in two bites. It was the tastiest bread he'd ever eaten. He should keep Bliss for the taste of this bread alone and if she could make bland bread taste this good, what could she do with other food?

47

"Do you like it?"

He turned with a mouthful and watched Bliss stretch herself awake, her arms reaching back behind her head, forcing her chest out.

"Very much," he said, though he was not talking about the bread and realizing that hurried to add, "it's the tastiest bread I have ever had."

"Mint," Bliss said. "It gives the bread a nice flavor." She sat up and sniffed the air. "Fish. Next time you catch fish, I will make a fish stew. It is the least I can do after all you have done for me."

He did not need or want her gratitude. What he wanted, needed, was for her to leave sooner rather than later. It was no good for her to linger here. No good for him to grow accustomed to her. No good that he thought too often of coupling with her. He needed her gone.

She spoke before he could tell her that she would need to leave soon.

"I have been thinking hard on your offer of wintering here with you," Bliss said, keeping her hands folded tightly since they trembled.

He went to stop her and tell she had to leave, but his words stalled in his throat.

Bliss silently warned herself to hurry and be done with it before she lost her courage. "I would like to stay the winter with you."

Tell her no, now!

Met with silence, she continued talking. "I would be safe here with you."

Wrong. No woman is safe with me.

"You see I can cook, and I can mend, cloth as well as people, so I would serve you well." *And you do not know it yet, but I am your wife, and I must do this to save my two sisters.*

"And will you serve me well in bed?" he snapped,

48

hoping his blunt question would have her quickly rescinding her decision.

Ah, it is where I need you the most. I need you to get me with child. The words remained in her head as she said, "I have never been with a man, but I will do my best to please you."

A warning screamed in his head. *She is a virgin. Tell her no!*

She spoke what truth she could. "I fear my fate if I do not remain here."

A battle raged in him. Did he surrender to his loneliness and let her stay the winter or did he do the honorable thing and send her on her way.

He kept his mouth shut tightly, fearful of what might slip out, and did something he had never done before in battle, he retreated, walking out the door.

Chapter 6

Bliss's shoulders drooped and her stomach roiled with worry while she silently berated herself for letting him know she was a virgin. He had probably thought her an experienced woman since she was traveling on her own. Any decent woman would never travel alone. That had to be why he had made the offer in the first place.

How many times had she warned Annis to watch her tongue and think before she spoke? Why had she not heeded her own advice? She shook her head, disappointed in herself. What was done was done and she could not change it. Hopefully, though, she could rectify it.

How to rectify it was the question.

She thought to follow him outside and speak to him but decided against it. He needed time to think on it, as she did. Besides, what could she say? She certainly could not beg him to let her stay and she was not sure how to convince him to let her stay. She had accepted his offer. What more was there for her to do? He either agreed or would send her on her way. If she tried to convince him, he might become suspicious and that could make things worse.

There was no more that she could do but wait.

***

Rannick walked into the woods, not trusting himself to remain close to the cottage, close to Bliss. It was his own fault for shutting himself away as he had done, seeing no one. He had even refused to speak to the men who delivered the supplies his mother had sent to him. Though, they certainly hadn't minded. They would hastily drop the sacks of grain, barrels of ale, and whatever else his mum would send and be on their way. They wanted nothing to do with him and that was fine with him.

He needed no one, wanted no one… until Bliss. Her presence, her kindness, and her trust had made him realize how empty life had become for him. He had hoped for death in his travels and had returned home only to find a living death.

Suddenly, the lonely years stretched ahead of him, and he wanted to roar against the emptiness he would face. It was a living hell and Bliss could provide a reprieve from it if just for the winter.

Endless reasons of why he should send Bliss on her way filled his head while there was only one reason for her to stay—he wanted her there with him. He selfishly did not want to let go of her kindness and trust. His first wife had seen to her wifely duties with an unsettled nervousness. His second wife had been indifferent about her wifely duties, lying beneath him, not moving, her eyes shut until he finished. His third wife, he had refused to touch, and still she died.

Bliss was willing to try and please him even though she had no experience with coupling. That she was willing to do so made him think they would find pleasure in bed together and that was something that enticed him. It was also something he feared, for he worried that when winter faded away, he might not want to let her go.

He shook his head. How was it that he already thought that he might want to keep her beyond winter? How could that even be possible?

She was alone like him, two lost souls who needed someone. Nothing more.

The curse would have no interest in her for their agreement did nothing but fill a void in their empty lives. He would not love her. He was not capable of love, and she would not demand it of him since he would provide what she needed, shelter and safety.

It was a sensible agreement for them both. Why then did he question it?

Did he worry that his father might have had him wed against his will once again and sent Bliss here to trick him? Or had he sent Bliss to place her in a compromising position and, therefore, force a marriage? But she had left easily enough when he had sent her on her way. Though, he had not given her much of a choice.

But would his father wed him to a peasant? Who else could be so easily forced to wed the cursed lord?

One who would have no choice.

The answer was clear. If his father had forced Bliss to wed Rannick, she would be dead by now. The curse would have killed her.

He had a chance for a good winter with a kind and trusting woman. He would enjoy it, then he would see that she was taken care of after that.

With his mind made up, he headed back to the cottage.

***

Bliss tried to remain patient for Rannick to return but as time slipped away, her worry grew. He had had enough time to think it through. It was time for her to face him and her fate. She gathered her courage to confront him and stepped out of the cottage to find a man standing only a short distance away and Rannick nowhere in sight.

"Rannick's got himself a woman," the fellow said and approached Bliss on an angle.

She turned to keep an eye on him and realized too late his intention—to stop her from seeing the man who came up behind her.

He grabbed her arm, wrenching it with a sharp twist that sent a pain radiating up her arm and a painful stitch to her side that sent her to her knees.

The other fellow hurried to take a cautious peek in the cottage. "He's not there."

"Keep watch while I have some fun with her," the fellow who kept a tight hold on Bliss ordered.

"There's no time for that. Our orders are clear—kill Rannick," the other man argued.

"And we will, but there's always time for a quick poke," the fellow said.

"And if he comes back while—"

"Kill him, then you can give her a poke and maybe we'll take her along with us for the other men to enjoy," the fellow said.

Bliss was shocked at what she heard. They had been sent to kill Rannick, but why? Whatever reason, they had not known of her marriage to Rannick. That meant this had been planned before she had wed him.

The one who held her had a more unkempt appearance than the other and an unpleasant odor about him. She would think them common thugs, but the one's bravado spoke more of a mercenary confident in his skills. And that he thought to keep her and share her with the other men made it obvious they were part of a group of mercenaries. Yet only two had been sent or were there more waiting close by?

She was relieved to learn the answer without asking the question.

"Just think of the fun we can have with her in the three days it will take us to reach the others," the fellow said.

The man grinned at the suggestion, though it quickly faded. "You'll wait to poke her until we kill Rannick. You heard what a fierce warrior he is. It will take us both to see him dead."

"I will see him dead with no problem," the fellow

boasted.

Bliss listened, praying Rannick would return while trying desperately to think of how she could escape. She would fight if there was no choice left to her. But the odds of her defeating two men were not good. Even running if she got the chance would prove difficult with her side still healing. Rannick was her one sure chance of surviving.

"Good, then I'll hold the woman while you see to Rannick," the man said.

"I get first poke," the fellow ordered.

"That is if Rannick does not kill you and I am left to kill him, then she is all mine," the man said with a grin.

The fellow laughed. "Then I better poke her now since I wouldn't want to die without one last poke."

"TAKE YOUR HANDS OFF HER!"

Both men jumped and the fellow that was holding Bliss swung her around in front of him, positioning her like a shield. So much for his confidence.

"Or what?" the fellow bravely said from behind Bliss, his head moving from side to side as his eyes searched for Rannick.

"Or I'll see that you die painfully instead of swiftly," Rannick said as he stepped out from around a group of trees.

Bliss suddenly felt the point of a dagger at her neck.

"Come close and I will kill her," the fellow shouted.

"If you kill her, I will rip your limbs slowly from you one by one until you scream and beg for death," Rannick said, walking toward them. "I have seen it done to men and some actually survive the ordeal and if by chance you do, I will leave your torso in the forest for the animals to finish. They do like live, fresh meat."

The man paled and looked to the fellow holding Bliss. "He's the devil himself and I want nothing to do with the devil." He ran past Bliss, headed for the woods.

He fell just before the woods would have swallowed

him whole, a dagger protruding from his back.

"That leaves you without a weapon," the man said with a bravado that didn't match the way he trembled against Bliss.

Rannick held up his hands. "These are much more lethal and painful than a dagger. Now let her go."

"I let her go. You let me go," the fellow bargained.

Rannick nodded. "I will let you go."

The fellow kept the dagger near Bliss's neck as he forced her to walk with him to the edge of the woods, then he gave her a shove, sending her sprawling to the ground, and took off into the dense woods.

Rannick had her up on her feet so quickly her head spun. "Are you all right?"

"Aye," she said with a nod.

He dropped his hand off her arm and went to the dead man and slipped his dagger out of his back. "Get in the cottage and stay there until I return."

"Rannick," she said before he could turn away. "They were hired to kill you."

Fury raged across his fine features and his eyes scanned the area.

Knowing what he thought, since she had thought the same, she said, "They talked of it taking three days before they reached the others."

"In the cottage and do not dare come out. You're not going to want to see what I do to him," he said and disappeared into the woods.

Bliss knew she should wait in the cottage, but she feared being trapped in there if something should happen to Rannick. She remained outside pacing in front of the cottage, her mind churning with thought.

Who would want Rannick dead?

Who wouldn't?

Her sudden response disturbed her. He was a cursed

lord and blamed for the endless suffering of many in the area. The curse had been cast on the fathers, but it was the sons it had taken its toll on and spread to touch anything they touched. Had someone grown tired of the endless madness of the supposedly worst of the cursed clans and decided to end the curse with Rannick? And what would happen when it was discovered that she was his wife? Would her life be doubly in danger from the curse and these madmen?

Bliss jumped when she heard the scream that echoed through the woods and had the birds taking flight.

Rannick had caught him.

Try as she might, she could not bring herself to go inside the cottage. She waited, for what she wasn't sure, but she waited.

The fellow stumbled out of the woods, his face a bloody mess and clinging tightly to his right arm. He stumbled as Rannick appeared behind him, giving him a hard shove.

Rannick's eyes caught with Bliss. "IN! NOW!"

She jolted at the fierceness of his command and turned to hurry inside the cottage, though she kept the door ajar just enough for her to hear what was said, if anything.

"You said you would let me go?" the fellow pleaded and fell to his knee.

"Aye, but I didn't say how far I would let you go," Rannick said.

The man screamed in pain. "My ear! My ear!"

"You have another one," Rannick said. "Though I will cut that one off as well if you do not tell me what I want to know."

"Why should I tell you when you're going to kill me?" the man argued.

"As I told you before, you can have an easy death or a painful one. It is your choice."

"I do not want to die," the fellow pleaded.

"Pity since that is not a choice. You die either way,"

Rannick said.

Bliss shivered at the coldness of his voice. He did not care in the least that he was going to take this man's life, make him suffer. It was nothing more than a task that would be done, and he showed not an ounce of remorse for it.

"Who hired you to kill me?" Rannick demanded.

"I don't know." The man let out an agonizing scream. "My finger! My finger!"

"You have another nine more to go. How many are you willing to lose?"

Bliss shut her eyes tight, not that she could see what was happening, but it was easy to imagine and still Rannick remained impassive. How could a man that had tended her with such gentleness now be so cruel? Surely, he could get answers without cutting off the fellow's ear and fingers?

"I honestly don't know," the fellow said. "The leader of the mercenary troop I sometimes go on missions with approached me about the task and offered me a good sum. I didn't need to know where the coin came from as long as I got it. He gave me half to start, the other half to follow when the task was complete. He was confident I would not fail him, since I have never failed him."

"It looks like that's about to change," Rannick said.

"Please let me go. You will never see me again. I will tell him that I succeeded and killed you. I will take the money and go far away. Please, I beg you."

"I am to trust your word?" Rannick snarled.

"Never would I dare face you again," the fellow said.

"Not alone, you wouldn't," Rannick said. "I learned well about the burning hate that rots the soul until you would do anything—unimaginable—to stop it. Even beg the devil himself for help. I know the devil well and he will not help you… he would rather have your soul. And I will gladly send it to him."

"NO! NO!" the fellow screamed.

Bliss could tell that Rannick was dragging the man away from the cottage, his screams drifting off. Her heart thudded in her chest and her stomach churned. She had been warned about Rannick, and how evil he had become.

I know the devil well. He will not help you.

Had he asked the devil for help? Had the devil wanted his soul? Had he been wise enough not to give it to him? And who had she truly struck this bargain with, Rannick's father or the devil himself?

She stepped outside, needing air and space to breathe, the cottage suddenly feeling too confining. She tried to avoid the area where the other man had fallen dead, but her glance fell there anyway. She was surprised to see he was gone.

She went to the spot and saw a drag mark. Rannick must have dragged him into the woods. She shook her head trying not to think of their fate. They were not good men. They had meant Rannick harm and her as well. Rannick did what needed to be done.

Life in the Highlands could be brutal if one did not have the courage to do what was necessary to survive. Wasn't she doing just that… doing what was necessary to survive?

Bliss sat on a small bench near the cottage, dazed and confused. It had seemed so simple when she had presented her proposal to Lawler. After all, she was a healer and there had been a small hope in her that she could help heal Rannick even in some small way and perhaps even survive the curse. She supposed it was because she always believed that if she did not dwell on the good when treating someone, then bad would surely befall them.

She had to keep a good thought even if things seemed bleak.

"Bliss."

Her head shot up to see Rannick standing in front of her, his eyes narrowed, and his muscles tensed. It was obvious rage still raced through him.

He raised his hands, blood covering a good portion of both. "This blood is nothing to the blood of others that I have spilled. Think hard on spending the winter with me, for it is these hands that will touch you intimately." He paused a moment. "I will have a definite answer from you tomorrow."

Chapter 7

Rannick cleaned himself of all the blood and as he did, he recalled the endless blood that still stained him. He would never be rid of it. It would always be there on him, no matter how often he tried to wash it away. At least this blood would serve a better purpose. It would make Bliss open her eyes to the evil in him and he would not be surprised if she wished to leave this very moment.

He tossed the dirty water from the bucket and placed it by the rain barrel. He turned to the closed door and his stomach clenched. He had faced many a battle with less apprehension than he felt now. He wanted her to go, leave, save herself, and yet he desperately wanted her to stay. It made no sense. He had committed to living the rest of his life alone but after spending time with Bliss, caring for her, helping to heal her, something inside of him did not want to let her go.

"Selfish," he whispered.

Lonely, came the response.

He shook his head. "Punishment."

That was it—punishment—and he would suffer it again and again, the curse would make sure of it.

He shook his head, clearing his thoughts as he went to the door, opened it, and stepped in.

She stood by the fire, and he caught the slight tremble in her body. He had seen that in some men after battle, only realizing what they had been through and how close they had come to death. It bothered him no more since he would welcome death.

He noticed the scuff of dirt on one cheek and the way

her dark hair lay unkempt over her shoulders, but it was her dark eyes filled with anxious worry that got his full attention. The incident had taken a toll on her, and he steeled himself against the inevitable—she would leave him.

He almost laughed aloud.

Leave him.

They meant nothing to each other, which was the very reason she would be perfect for him, so she truly would not be leaving him, she would simply take her leave. Why then did it feel differently? And why did it disturb him so much? Anger poked at him for allowing it to bother him.

She spoke up, the tremble in her body reflected in her voice. "I have my answer now for you."

"It can wait," he snapped, not wanting to hear what he was sure she would say.

She rushed her words. "Nay, I have made up my mind and I will not change it. I will stay with you."

He could not hide his surprise, though he did question what he heard. "You will stay?"

"Aye, I will stay," she confirmed with a firm nod.

One word slipped out of his mouth. "Why?"

She spoke the truth. "I need you."

He could not keep the scrunch out of his brow as once again he asked, "Why?"

How could she be as truthful as possible with him without admitting the truth of why she was there and had no choice but to remain there?

A reasonable response came to her, "You offer me protection, which you proved more than capable of a short time ago, and a home, and I am in need of both."

"I offer you no home, only temporary shelter," he corrected, making it clear this would not be permanent.

"I understand," she said and was stabbed once again with a pain of guilt for the lies that kept mounting between them. And again, she tried to convince herself it was necessary if she was to accomplish the task agreed to. Otherwise, he would send her on her way.

Rannick walked over to her and even before he stood in front of her, he could see apprehension grow in her eyes. He raised his hand and was surprised and pleased she did not flinch. He cleaned the dirt off her cheek with a soft swipe of his thumb.

"You were not hurt?" he asked.

His touch was gentle. It had been since he had first tended her. It was in stark contrast to the brutality of the man who had not only killed two men but made one suffer.

"My shoulder hurts some from the way he yanked my arm, but otherwise I am good," she said, grateful to finally speak the truth. His next words surprised and worried her.

"We will not be intimate until you are well-healed."

Time was of the essence; she could not delay in trying to conceive. "I am not fragile," she said.

"I can be demanding in bed," he said as if that was explanation enough.

"I am not fragile," she repeated, not sure how else to respond and with a twinge of concern of what might await her in bed with him.

"We shall see," he said, his glance going to her lips. "I will bed you soon enough so if you find it distasteful, you may take your leave before winter sets in."

She would not leave. She was there to stay and far beyond winter, unless the curse thought otherwise, but she simply nodded in response.

He rested his hand at the back of her neck, his fingers rubbing there, and she closed her eyes for a moment relishing the ease it brought the taut muscles. As her eyes fluttered open, her lips parted slightly in surprise at how close his mouth was to hers and she felt as if her whole body gasped when his lips touched hers.

The kiss was soft and tentative, leaving her to respond,

and she did. She instinctively returned the kiss, welcomed it with the same softness and hesitancy. That she acquiesced made all the difference. His kiss turned powerful and commanding, shooting sensations through her that were far more pleasant than she had expected and made her respond in kind.

Her hands went instinctively to his arms, grabbing hold, finding herself not wanting to let go. That was until his tongue darted into her mouth and the shock of such an intimate invasion had her pulling her head back only to be stopped by the grip he had on the back of her neck. Her heart pounded against her chest as she realized at that moment she was trapped in his arms.

She was shocked even more when he eased his hold on her and ended the kiss.

"Think of what I will demand of you before you fully commit," he said and stepped away from her.

I demand so much more of you than you demand of me. Her thought startled her almost as much as his tongue had, but she had to face both. She had no choice.

Her decision was made. It had been made before she arrived, and she did not want to dwell on it. She did, however, have pertinent questions for him that she could not help but ask.

"Who would want you dead?" she asked.

Rannick had walked over to the bed and snatched up the blanket folded at the bottom. He returned to Bliss, his hands settling on her shoulders to move her away from the fire, then draped the soft wool blanket around her.

"Many people," he said as if it did not disturb him at all.

"Did the man tell you who hired him to kill you?"

That she even thought that he would ask told him that even while fearful; she had been observant.

"You ask many questions," he said, not sure how much he wanted her to know.

She tucked the blanket close across the front of her, glad for its warmth. "How else would I keep you safe?" His sudden burst of laughter surprised her and somehow made him seem less evil.

"You think you can keep me safe?" He slapped his hand against his chest. "Me, the cursed lord?"

She smiled softly. "I can try."

A slight smile remained on his face. That this woman would even think to do the unthinkable amazed him and while he did not want to admit it—let alone feel it—her sincere words touched his heart.

"You will not try," he snapped, the sudden thought of what might happen to her if she dared to try or dared to show any feelings for him.

Bliss thought to argue, but then thought better of it. It would make no difference. He could bluster and command all he wanted; she would still do what she needed to do to save her sisters.

She did, however, ask the question that seemed to hang over them. "If the two men had been hired to kill you, does that not mean more men will come in an attempt to do the same?"

"That is not for you to worry about. I will see to it," he said.

She turned a soft smile on him. "Please do not keep me ignorant of this. I prefer to know what is going on and if I can help in any way."

It surprised him that she was willing to help and not cower in fear, something most women would have done. But then most women would not involve themselves with the cursed lord.

"Are you sure of that?' Rannick asked, seeing if her bravado was just that.

"I am a healer, Rannick, and healing is much like a puzzle. I go through many questions and possibilities before deciding on how to treat the ailment successfully. That skill makes me good at deciphering problems."

He was intrigued not only with her interest but with her skill and her desire to help. As a woman and a peasant, she would observe things differently than he did and perhaps cast more light on the problem.

"Many want me dead for the curse alone. Kill me, the only heir to Clan MacClaren, and, in essence, you kill the curse. But I have made it clear that I have no intentions of producing an heir to the clan. This curse dies with me. I will have it no other way."

"What if fate thinks differently?" she asked since she was there to do the exact opposite of what he intended.

"Fate does not decide my destiny—I do!" he argued.

Life had taught Bliss differently. "I find that fate often has its way."

A snarl flared Rannick's lips. "Fate will rue the day it battled with me."

"What if fate is wiser than us?" she asked.

"Until fate can prove that to me, my life is mine to dictate," he said with a touch of anger.

She hugged the blanket close, almost like a shield. "But your life is not yours to dictate—the curse dictates it."

Anger sparked the green flecks in his eyes. "The curse does not dictate me—it dies with me."

Bliss thought of the tales that circulated about the curse, particularly the one she had thought might help, but had no time to pursue. "What if the curse could be broken?" He stared at her not saying a word for several moments and she waited.

Rannick shook his head, shaking away troubling memories before he responded. "You heard the tale of the witch in the hills. She does not exist. She is nothing more than a myth."

"How can you be sure?"

65

"I have searched along with the other two cursed lords, Brogan and Odran, then I searched alone and found nothing," he said, unable to hide his disappointment.

A heaviness settled in her heart hearing that. It meant her sister Annis's search would find the same, since she had no doubt Annis would attempt a search to find the witch powerful enough to break the curse. Although, with how tenacious Annis could be when she put her mind to something left a sliver of hope in Bliss that she might succeed where others had failed. Though, her discovery may come too late to help Bliss, it would at least bring peace to many.

"The curse will not touch you if that concerns you. You are not my wife, nor do I have any love for you, therefore, the curse has no interest in you. You are here to satisfy a need, nothing more."

Bliss could tell by the way the lines between his eyes drew deep that a worrisome thought had struck him.

He spoke his concern without hesitation. "You are a healer. You know what to do to prevent my seed from taking root in you."

"Aye, I do," she said, though made no commitment to do so.

"Good. Make sure you see it done, for I will not see you get with child."

She almost choked on her lie. "As you say."

"I will have your word on it," he insisted.

Her word.

How did she keep her word when she had already given her word to another? That question answered it for her.

"I will keep my word," she said.

He did not need to know that the word she kept was to his father. The weight of her guilt for keeping the truth from him grew heavier with her every lie and she wondered how long she would be able to carry it.

"You will not go wandering off on your own nor will you leave the cottage when I am gone. I will fashion a board to go across the door so no one can enter when you are here alone and at night." He did not bother to let her know that it was also to give him time to grab a weapon if someone should try to enter while they slept.

"You expect more men to come, don't you?"

"Aye," he said and turned to face her when he reached the door. "That curse brings its evil down on me, but I will not see it touch you."

She chanced to ask, "What if you begin to care for me?"

Rannick's response came easy. "My heart turned cold many years ago. It will never thaw."

She did not know what made her ask, the words rushing from her before she could stop them. "What if I begin to care for you?"

"As cold as my heart is... so is my touch," Rannick warned. "You will never warm to it and you will be only too glad to leave at spring's first bloom, if not before then."

The door closed behind him and Bliss went and sat on the bed, a shudder leaving her chilled and a tremble in her legs. His kiss had not been cold nor his touch. It had been gentle enough, but had it been empty? She had not noticed, but then she had been too weak to notice much of anything.

Warm or cold. It mattered not as long as she got with child. If all went well, she would be rounded nicely with child by spring. Unless, of course, the curse got her first or if Rannick was true to his word and would see any wife forced on him dead before the curse could claim her.

She shut her eyes against the dreadful thought. Had she been insane taking on this task? She had had no choice if she wanted to protect her two sisters. She might not survive, but at least they would.

Her mind was so heavy with thought that she stretched out on the bed and surrendered to sleep.

***

The crackle of the fire woke her, and she snuggled against the pleasant warmth wrapped around her. She did not want to leave it. It was much too comforting as was the potent scent that stirred her senses. There was something familiar about it.

Her eyes popped open against a naked, hard-muscled chest. Rannick was in bed with her, and she was cocooned in his powerful arms.

Where you need to be, she reminded herself. *But not yet.* She was not ready for this yet. He said himself that he would not touch her until she was fully healed. Her worry eased and she settled once again comfortably in his arms.

It was good he joined her in bed. It would allow her to get used to him there before they became intimate. She lay quietly, listening to his steady breathing and the steady beat of his heart. There was something soothing about both, a soft rhythm that calmed and a warmth that protected. She had never felt anything like it before and she cherished the peaceful moment.

She tried to drift back to sleep, but it had been too long since she had seen to her need, and she feared the morning was too long for her to wait. She did not want to wake him, but he had warned her about not going anywhere alone, though it was late and surely no one lurked about. She could hurry a short distance into the woods and be back in no time, that was if she could leave his arms without waking him. If she woke him, it would simply mean Fate did not intend her to go alone.

It was easier than she expected to slip out of bed without disturbing Rannick, though looking down as he slept, she could see a deep sleep had taken hold of him. He must have been exhausted after the strenuous day he had

had. That thought had her glad she had not disturbed his sleep. She would hurry and get done, then make herself a calming brew and return to sleep beside him.

A board sat braced against the door and she wondered if he had not completed the task so he would not disturb her sleep—a caring thought. Something he would not do—care for her.

She never expected that he would care for her. She had meant to survive him and the curse as best she could. Why then did the thought that he would never have any feelings for her upset her?

She shook her head, refusing to dwell on it.

Survive, Bliss, survive so you can see Elysia and Annis again.

It took effort to move the board since he had planted it firmly in the earth floor and braced against the door. There were a few times she thought her effort might wake him. But he slept soundly. When she finally got the door open, she slipped out soundlessly and closed it behind her.

She realized then that her feet were bare. She shrugged and shook her head. How had she not noticed that? How had Rannick gotten her boots off without waking her? She shook her head again and hurried to the closest entrance to the woods.

She could not help but notice the clear half-moon and the stars that lit up the night sky. It was the clearest night sky she had ever seen, not a single cloud disturbed it. It seemed more dreamlike than real it was so beautiful. She lingered a few moments after finishing, the surreal sky and the chilled night far too welcoming to hurry back to the cottage until… she heard a sound.

Bliss listened. Had she heard footfalls or was a nocturnal animal at play or hunting for food. That thought got her moving as quietly as possible. When she reached the edge of the woods, she peeked past the trees to see if anyone lurked about. When she didn't see or hear any movement, she stepped from behind the tree to hurry to the cottage.

She was snagged around the waist, hoisted off her feet, and a warm cheek was planted firmly against her cool one.

"What did I tell you about going anywhere without me?" Rannick demanded with a snarling anger.

He didn't give her a chance to respond. With a firm arm around her waist, he carted her back to the cottage and planted her on her feet once inside.

"Take off your garments and get in bed!" he ordered.

The fiery anger in his eyes alone warned her not to argue but fear had her hesitating.

"NOW!" he shouted and stripped off his plaid and boots, the only things he wore.

Bliss hurried out of her garments and into bed, not dare glancing his way.

He climbed in beside her, his arm snagging her around her waist once again and yanking her so that her back rested tightly against the front of him.

He rested his lips next to her ear. "You will sleep naked with me in this bed from now on and disobey me again, Bliss, and you will know the wrath of the devil himself!"

Chapter 8

Bliss sat on the bed with a blanket wrapped around her as Rannick worked on securing pins that would keep the board in place across the door. A chilled breeze swirled in from the open door, the reason Bliss hugged the blanket close. Though the chill she felt had started long before Rannick had opened the door.

He had said not a word to her this morning, not through the whole time she made a porridge for them or while they ate. She would have attempted to converse with him but the deep scowl on his face had her holding her tongue. It was easy to see he was still angry from last night and she thought it was best to let it be. He would speak to her when he was ready.

Now, though, after hours of silence from him, she found herself eager to speak. She and her sisters had talked endlessly, and she missed conversing with them. While Rannick was a man of few words, she missed those few words.

Once again, the blanket became her shield and she held tightly to it as she raised her chin with a courage she did not feel. "I am truly sorry about not paying heed to your word last night, but I did not want to disturb your sleep."

He turned his head, his scowl remaining. "That is a poor excuse for disobeying me."

"Aye, you are right, but I only have the truth to offer you and I truly am sorry."

"You'll sleep naked beside me from now on since it will hamper you from sneaking off again," he ordered.

At least he confirmed what she had thought was the

reason for him demanding she strip naked last night.

"And do not think to tell me you will leave," he said, anger in each word. "That chance is now gone. You made your decision, and you will abide by it."

"Aye, I have, and I will abide by it," she said relieved that that worry had been taken off her shoulders. She would go nowhere. This was her home now and he was her husband.

Rannick raised his hand to poke at one of his fingers, then brought it to his mouth to bite at it.

"Something is wrong with your finger?" she asked.

"A splinter," he said and bit at it again.

"Let me have a look and stop biting it," she ordered as she hurried off the bed, dropping the blanket as she went.

When she stepped close to him, he hooked her chin with his fingers. "Never tell me what to do, Bliss."

She eased her chin out of his grip. "I acquiesce to your skill as a warrior; I ask only that you grant me the same respect as a healer."

Rannick conceded to nothing, but he held his hand out to her.

Bliss scrunched her eyes trying to see. "Come closer to the hearth."

He did as she said, mesmerized by the gentleness of her touch, so when she pressed on his shoulder for him to sit on the bench, he did so without hesitation.

"This did not happen today," she said, seeing how the wound had swelled red. "You should have come to me as soon as this happened."

"Are you scolding me?" he asked.

She thought she detected a bit of humor in his voice.

"Advising," she said with a smile.

"Then I will defer to your knowledge."

Her smile grew. "A wise decision."

"I am not always wise." He didn't know why he told

her that, yet he did not regret it.

"Who is?" She chuckled.

There was something about her face when she smiled, something that revealed a goodness in her he had never seen in anyone. He wanted to lose himself in her goodness. Or was it that he hoped her goodness could conquer his evil?

"I am going to soak your finger in a brew that I will make, then I will remove the splinter," she explained.

"I should finish the door first," he said, though preferred that his hand remained in hers. It soothed and brought him a calm foreign to him.

"Finish it while I brew the leaves," she said and gave a nod to the open door. "The chill and gray skies promise rain."

"I will hunt or fish for supper when you are done," he said.

"Nay. I saw kale, cabbage, and wild onion in the garden. I can brew a hardy soup with that and bake bread as well. Your finger needs to stay clean if it is to heal well. Do you have honey?"

"Aye, my mum sent a crock with the last supply of food."

"She looks after you," Bliss said and let go of his hand to gather what she needed to make the brew.

The absence of her touch left him baffled. He liked how she had gently cradled his hand in hers and how she had probed his wound with a tenderness that sent a pleasant sensation racing through him.

Do not let her touch your heart!

The warning rang powerfully in his head. He could not care for her, not even a little. He had to keep his heart cold, or she would suffer for it.

"My mum is a good woman," he said and returned to finish the door.

Bliss recalled what his mum had begged of her. *Heal*

my son. His mum's heart hurt for her son, and she could only imagine the pain she suffered seeing her son suffer. Seeing how the curse had hurt so many lives, she wished there was a way to end it.

The brew was ready by the time Rannick placed the board across the door.

"Come sit and let me see to your finger, then I will go and collect what I need for supper," Bliss said.

"Not without me," he ordered sharply.

"Not without you," she confirmed.

Bliss placed his hand in the bowl with the brew she had cooled down enough for him to soak his finger and sat on a bench she had placed in front of him.

"What made you become a healer?" he asked.

She laughed softly. "It was forced on me. I was told by an old healer that I was a healer and had to follow the way." She dared not mention it was Kendesa for fear he would recognize the name from Clan Loudon. "Surprisingly, I found it came more naturally to me than I expected, so I guess the old healer was right."

Bliss lifted his hand out of the bowl and patted it partially dry, then she picked up the thinnest needle she had brought with her and set to work.

Rannick watched her work with interest. Her touch was gentle and instinctive. She did not hesitate in what she did, she did so with confidence and precision. He felt little pain, but then his thought was on how her hand held his with such firmness.

"Got it!" she said triumphantly and smiled wide when she raised her head.

"Will you see to the other ache that hardens me… with such ease?"

Bliss stopped her mouth from dropping open. He meant to shock her, but why? She might never have known a man intimately, but she was far from ignorant about men and their needs thanks to the endless women who sought her care.

"When I am healed, I will do my best," she said, scooping up a sizeable dab of honey and spreading it over the wound. "Until then, I am sure you can ease your ache yourself."

Her unexpected response surprised him, and he grinned. "Would you like to watch me?"

Bliss's heart thumped madly against her chest, but she kept a false smile on her face. "If you would like me to."

"Tonight, before we go to bed," he said.

How she managed to bandage his finger without trembling, she did not know, nor did she know how she kept a tremor out of her voice. "As you wish. Now I must clean the table then gather what is needed for supper."

Rannick remained where he was on the bench, leaving her to clean around him. It was easy to see that he had startled her, but she had not shied away from his remark. She had responded, showing him no fear, not a tremble escaped her, but he saw it in her eyes. Why he had remarked as he did, he couldn't say, but now that he had, the idea of pleasuring himself in front of her took root and wouldn't let go. She should see what she would face with him and what he would demand of her while she was with him. It was sure to make her dislike him, not favor him in the least, and keep her safe from the curse.

Rannick stood abruptly and Bliss jumped.

"I make you anxious?" he asked, knowing full well he did.

"You can be unsettling at times," she admitted.

"At least you are truthful." He grabbed a basket from the two by the door. "Come. I will stack the wood while you get what you want from the garden."

"Be cautious of your finger," she said and snatched the basket from his hand and was out the door as soon as he opened it. She needed the chilled air to cool her cheeks and the chore of harvesting to ease her mind.

She was relieved Rannick left her to herself while she saw to gathering what she needed. And she needed a separation from him if only briefly. She had worried how she would get him to couple with her and now she worried he would want to couple far too frequently. But wasn't that what she needed if she was sure to conceive?

"Survive," she whispered to herself. "Survive to see your sisters again."

"Stop where you are!"

Bliss turned, fear racing through her that more men had come for him and was relieved to see an old woman, stooped from age or exhaustion a short distance from the edge of the woods.

"Drink and food, I beg of you," the old woman managed to say.

"You will find drink at the stream beyond the cottage," Rannick said briskly.

Bliss hurried out of the garden. The old woman looked as if she could not take another step. Her long white hair fell loose from its braid and patches of dirt marred her face while a fine dust covered her cloak, signs she had traveled a distance.

"Stay where you are!" Rannick ordered, his hand shooting out to point at Bliss.

Bliss paid him no heed and she let Rannick know why. "She needs help."

"Bless you," the old woman said when Bliss's arm went firmly around her.

"Come sit and rest. I will bring you drink and food," Bliss offered.

The old woman looked to Rannick as she walked past him. "I mean you and your wife no harm."

"She is not my wife!" Rannick snapped.

Bliss helped the woman to sit on the bench beneath a tree. "Rest. I will be right back."

Rannick approached the woman. "Have your drink and food and be on your way."

"I mean you no harm," the old woman said again.

"And I mean you none," Rannick said. "Be wise and move on."

The old woman nodded. "As you say, Lord Rannick."

"You know who I am, yet you do not avoid me." His brow narrowed. "Why did you come here?"

"I had no choice," she said, licking her dry lips.

"Be on your way soon," he warned.

"She needs rest," Bliss said, having heard her husband when she stepped out of the cottage.

"Feed her and send her on her way," Rannick commanded and walked over to Bliss and grabbed her by the chin. "Do not disobey me on this." He released her and returned to stacking the logs.

Bliss handed the woman a tankard of cider and the bread left from the morning meal. "There is a stream not far beyond the cottage. It will provide you with drink and I will give you a blanket to keep you warm and some food to take on your journey."

"You are kind, but I do not have far to go. This drink and food will sustain me till then."

"You travel alone?" Bliss asked, worried for the woman.

"I have no choice, a loved one is in need," the old woman said and lowered her voice to a whisper. "What brought you here?"

"Necessity. Now let me get you food and drink to take with you," Bliss said before the old woman could ask any more questions and she would be forced to add to her mounting lies.

The old woman finished the last of the cider and rested

back against the tree, closing her eyes. When she opened them, it was to see Rannick standing in front of her.

"Do not return here," Rannick ordered.

"I mean you no—"

"I will have no more of your lies," he snapped, annoyed. "Bliss is a kindhearted woman and a skilled healer. She helps any in need without question."

"And I am grateful for her help and your generosity."

"You do not require her help or generosity. You hide good features behind the dirt on your face and your white hair has far too much of a shine to it while your cloak is covered in dust. Your stoop is forced, and your slim hands hold firm to the tankard. You present a false persona, which means you hide something."

"You are observant, my lord," the old woman said, her shoulders broadening.

"Did my father send you to spy on me?" he demanded.

"Nay, not your father."

"Then who?"

The old woman stood, her stance regal and commanding. "Fate!"

A swirling wind suddenly struck and disrupted the dirt at their feet, forcing Rannick to turn his head and shut his eyes for a moment. The wind settled as fast as it had appeared.

"Where is the old woman?" Bliss asked as she hurried to her husband.

He turned to see the woman had vanished. He glanced around, but she was nowhere to be seen and he wondered how she had vanished so fast?

"She took her leave," Rannick said, having no other explanation.

"But I had food and drink and a blanket for her," Bliss said, casting an anxious glance around.

Puzzled, Rannick said, "Evidently she was not in need

of them."

"There was something familiar about her," Bliss said.

"You have met her before?" Rannick asked, curious.

"Not that I recall and yet…" She shook her head. "Perhaps I treated her once in passing."

"She is gone. It matters not."

A sharp squawk had them both turning and Rannick wrapping himself around Bliss as a raven flew at them, the black bird's beak barely missing his head before it flew off into the woods.

"How odd for a raven to come at us like that," Bliss said after Rannick unshielded himself from around her. "I know they make their home in the woods but are rarely seen."

"And many prefer it that way," he said, his eyes intent on the sky.

Bliss understood what he meant. Most preferred not to lay eyes on a raven for it was an omen of something bad to come.

***

Supper was a quiet meal with the rain beating against the cottage the only sound heard. Few words had been exchanged between Rannick and Bliss after the incident with the old woman. He assumed it left Bliss wondering as it did him, yet neither of them gave voice to their thoughts. Or with it getting late was her mind on what he had remarked on earlier?

Whether she did or not, he decided to go there once again. "Has your hand ever held a man's shaft?"

It was rude of him to so blatantly ask an improper question, yet it was also good that he did. His inappropriate behavior would leave her to do no more than tolerate him out of necessity.

With her back to him, Bliss was able to hide her

surprise at his question. Not that it should surprise her, since she believed he intended to startle her with such outrageous questions. She just was not sure if taunting her rudely brought him enjoyment or if he had a specific purpose in doing so. But she was not about to let him know he unnerved her with such talk.

She turned around to face him. "Nay, I have never touched a man's shaft, but I have seen my share of them."

His eyes narrowed. "How so?"

"I have helped cleanse and prepare many a man for burial."

"So, you have seen only flaccid shafts, never one enlarged," he said and actually admired how she handled herself with such pretend calm.

"That's correct," she said with a nod and gathered all her strength to say what she had never dreamed of saying. "I do look forward to seeing yours enlarged. It will better help me to understand the workings of a man's shaft."

That she would view his shaft through the mind and eyes of a healer annoyed him.

"It might also better help me understand why some women find coupling pleasurable while others find it unpleasant, more a duty that is to be endured."

"You talk of a wife's duty. You are not my wife."

"I am free then to take pleasure in it or endure it," she said.

Did he chance her taking pleasure in their coupling? Or did he make certain she was eager to leave by winter's end?

"Your choice. Endure it or enjoy it. It matters not to me. I look only for relief to my own need," he said, reminding himself that was what she was there for, to keep him warm in bed and feed his need to couple. That she cooked tasty food was a plus and that she was a healer, another plus. That she was pleasant to look upon and easy to talk with helped as well.

She would serve him well for the winter then be gone.

He stood, shed his garments, and went to sit on the edge of the bed. "Take your garments off and come here."

Bliss told herself not to be nervous. He had seen her naked, and he had bathed most of her body with a cool cloth. And she had seen him naked as well. But this was different. This was intimacy.

Still though, she was apprehensive about shedding his shirt and her tunic so deliberately in front of him. She sought a shadowed corner to see the deed done and as she turned and walked toward him, she saw that his hand was already stroking his swelled shaft.

Chapter 9

Quick words came to Bliss as she sat on the bed beside him. "I do not know whether to be impressed by your size or not since I have seen no other shaft enlarged to compare it to. And some women say size matters, while others say if the man is talented size does not matter. Is that true?"

That she blatantly asked him such a question dumbfounded him for a moment and almost deflated him. "Woman should not be talking of such things," Rannick scolded.

"Why not? Men talk of their prowess with women, so why shouldn't women discuss such matters?" she argued, finding their discussion interesting.

"It is something that should be discussed between husband and wife," he argued.

"How could a husband answer such questions when he does not understand or often does not care how his wife feels when coupling?" she asked. "I have had women cry to me that they must be doing something wrong when coupling since they feel nothing and are glad when it is done. Then I have other women who tell me how wonderful it is. It makes me wonder, is it a woman's problem or a man's? As a healer it would help me to understand and see if there is anything I could do to help."

His hand had fallen off his now limp shaft. "That should not concern you."

"Why should it not concern me as a healer when it could relate to other problems in a woman or a man? How do I help them if I do not have the information I need to do so?" She went on, shaking her head. "A woman once complained to me that her husband had not touched her in over a month when he had rarely let a few days pass in doing so. She feared he might be seeking his pleasure elsewhere and asked me if there was anything I could give her that would amend the situation. If she had not come to me with her problem, her husband would probably be dead."

Rannick's brow scrunched in question. "How so?"

"I suggested it might not be her fault that there might be an issue with her husband. I advised her to talk with him about it. She told me they never talked of such things. I was surprised when she returned in two days in tears. She had gotten the courage to ask him if he was seeking another woman's bed. They argued and that was when the truth came out. Her husband's shaft had grown a large boil and coupling was painful for him. She cried while detailing it to me since he refused to come see me himself. I gave her what was needed and how she was to tend him and prayed he had not waited too long. Thankfully, all worked out well."

What she didn't tell him was that John had made sure that she and her sisters had wood aplenty for winter that year in appreciation for what she had done.

Bliss surprised herself and Rannick as well when she gently cupped his flaccid shaft in her hand and felt it stir. "So, you see I can learn much from your shaft and look forward to doing so."

Her words had helped calm her since it made her realize that if she approached coupling as a way of becoming a more skilled healer instead of trying desperately to conceive, then she might feel at least a little less guilty of deceiving him.

His shaft began to swell in her hand, and he quickly stood and walked to the hearth. She was giving him what he wanted, no attachment, no feelings, so why did it disturb him? They would couple and his need would be satisfied along with her curiosity. It was perfect. And yet, it annoyed him. Why? What did he truly want from her?

"I am sorry," she said. "I should have sought permission from you before touching you, my lord."

Rannick turned with an angry gait. "Do not call me my lord." He shocked himself with the words that followed. "And you do not need permission to touch me." He quickly added. "As I do not need permission to touch you."

Bliss was going to let it be and say no more, do no more, but she recalled why she was there and what she had to do. She patted the spot he had vacated beside her. "Then come sit and let me touch you."

Her voice was like a gentle whisper that stroked his shaft, and it didn't just stir, it saluted her, and it annoyed him that it responded so quickly and easily. But again, he should be happy that it did.

He walked over to her, thinking how quickly she had taken command of the situation and that did not set well with him. He was in command, not her. He came to a stop in front of her, his protruding shaft near her face.

"Touch all you want," he challenged.

Bliss could not help but admire his body when he walked toward her. His movements held power and confidence and his muscled form exuded strength, not to mention how large his shaft had grown in such a short time. That he stopped in front of her—his shaft so close to her face that she almost recoiled—made her realize that he challenged her.

She accepted the challenge without hesitation, her hand taking a gentle hold of his shaft. "How strange that it is soft to the touch and yet hard as well." Instinct had her begin to stroke it. "And powerful," she added with surprise, feeling as it came to life in her hand.

Her tender, tentative strokes coupled with her praise swelled him near to bursting. He silently cursed himself for not keeping control and taking a deep breath, he forced himself to do so.

For a moment he thought she would take him in her mouth, she got so close to his shaft, but he saw that she studied his swelled appendage with more interest than with passion and that annoyed him.

"Did you know you have a freckle on your shaft?" she asked, the flat spot drawing her eyes closer as she continued to stroke him.

Her soft breath fanned his stiff rod and he fought to keep the groan that rose up in his throat from escaping. This was not going at all as he had thought it would.

She drew her head back and she raised her other hand and with one finger gently swiped across the tip of his shaft, rubbing the wetness between her fingers.

Rannick groaned low and forced himself to remain standing, once again silently cursing himself.

"Interesting," she said and stroked his shaft harder. "It feels quite good. I do enjoy touching you." She tilted her head back as her free hand went to his testicles. "I can touch—"

That did it for him. He grabbed his shaft and turned just in time to catch his seed as it shot into his hand. He walked to the hearth with weak legs and more curses spilling muffled from his lips. He braced one hand on the stone that ran up the wall and rode out the climax that consumed him far more powerfully than he expected.

When it finally subsided, he got a cloth and cleaned himself off, went to the door, removed the board, and stepped out in the rain naked, closing the door behind him.

Bliss dropped back on the bed, her body more alive than she had ever felt it. The sensations had begun to spark in her shortly after touching him and they spiked in her the more she touched him and the harder he grew. She had had all she could do to keep herself from surrendering to the passion that had flourished and nearly consumed her. She had never expected that merely by touching him the way she had that it would send her burning with an overwhelming need and leave her with a wetness between her legs that shocked her.

She had talked with endless women but never, until this moment, understood the depths of their experience. It puzzled her but also made her think that perhaps it would not be as difficult to couple with him as she had feared it might be.

But what of the consequences?

That was a difficult question to answer. How did she couple with Rannick and then betray him? It was to save her sisters, but by doing so, what would happen to him? And what would her fate be?

She slipped under the blanket, curled into a tight ball and prayed for sleep, desperately needing a respite from her troubling thoughts.

***

Rannick entered the cottage relieved to see Bliss asleep. He secured the board in the latches and, soaked from the rain, dried himself with the cloths stacked on a chest. He watched her sleep as he rubbed himself dry. She was curled tight as if attempting to protect herself... from him?

He knew so little about her. She claimed to be a healer and from what he had seen so far that appeared to be true. But healers—good healers—were always welcome in a clan. And she had talked about speaking with many women, so why had she left her clan. Or had she no choice? That led to more questions. If the clan cast her out, then why?

Again, he was reminded of how little he knew about her. He had accepted her far too easily and quickly. He needed to learn more about her... and yet? He wanted her there with him. He did not want to let her go, especially after enjoying her touch so much. Never had he found such pleasure in a woman's touch as he had with Bliss, and he wanted more from her.

It was good that her only interest in him was that of a healer. It made things easier, and yet he could not help but think what it might be like if things were different and he could allow himself to care, to feel, to love.

He climbed into bed with her, eased himself around her, and settled peacefully. It would be a good winter with her to warm his bed and satisfy his needs and nothing beyond that. He closed his eyes waiting for sleep and as he drifted off, he wondered why a strange ache settled around his heart.

***

Though the sun sparkled in the sky, the air remained crisp. Bliss threaded a needle with the thread she had managed patiently to salvage from her torn shift as she sat enjoying the sun, that probably would not last long, while she attempted to mend the garment. She had worn Rannick's shirt and tunic long enough. She needed her shift repaired before winter set in. She wished Elysia was there or at least nearby. She would stitch it for her or stitch a whole new garment.

She wondered how Elysia was doing. Had she paid heed to her word and wed Saber, a bear of a man, but a gentle soul, who worked a croft not far from the village. She could tell by the way he had looked at Elysia that he cared for her, and she was sure Elysia felt the same about him. If she had wisely wed Saber, he would keep her safe and that was what Bliss wanted more than anything—her two sisters safe.

Rannick was busy sharpening his daggers with a rock not far from where she sat. He had made no mention of last night and either had she, and when she woke in his arms this morning, he had quickly left the bed, dressed, and left the cottage.

87

Her stomach churned when his silence ended, and he asked her an unexpected question.

"What clan were you a healer to?"

"I remained with no particular clan. I made my home in a lone cottage in the woods and people from different clans came to see me," she said, thinking of Cumina, the wise woman who women from all around visited when in need of a potion or charm.

That seemed reasonable enough to him, though he wondered, "Why did you leave?"

"It became unsafe," she said, recalling the stories Kendesa, the old healer she had replaced, told her about.

"How so?" Rannick asked, intending to learn all he could about her.

She repeated what Kendesa had told her. "When illness strikes a clan, the healer is usually blamed, and she is often driven off or killed. I learned from watching what happened to other healers and I have taken my leave when such times have threatened."

Bliss recalled how pleased Kendesa had been to remain with Clan Loudon for the last ten years of her life. She had learned much from the old healer.

It was easy for Rannick to believe that. He recalled his father sending their healer away because he felt she had failed the clan. He had thought differently but his father was too stubborn to listen, and he had not cared enough to argue with him.

He did not like to think of Bliss going off on her own to be left vulnerable once again. When winter was done, he would see what could be done to keep her safe.

Rannick's hand suddenly gripped the dagger he worked on and ordered, "In the cottage now!"

Bliss was about to rush to her feet when Lawler stepped hesitantly out of the woods with his horse tagging along behind him.

88

Lawler's eyes went to Bliss, and she felt a rush of panic seize her. How did she let him know that Rannick was not aware that she was his wife?

Relief washed over her when Rannick spoke, seeing it done for her.

"I warn you, Lawler, if you say a word to my father that a woman is here with me, you will rue the day. Do I make myself clear?" Rannick asked, though it was more a threat.

"I do, my lord," Lawler said with a nod.

"I will have your word on it," Rannick demanded.

Lawler nodded again. "You have my word. I will say nothing of the woman here with you."

He could easily keep his word since it would be Rannick's wife Lawler discussed with her husband's father. Bliss hoped to find a moment to speak with Lawler alone before he left and let him know things were going well, since no doubt that was what he was here to find out.

"Your mother was concerned that you might be in need of more supplies before winters sets in," Lawler said, pointing to the two sacks hanging from either side of his saddle. "Cloth, blankets, and other items she thought you might need."

"My mum does well?" Rannick asked.

Bliss heard the genuine concern in his voice for his mother. If he cared for his mom, he could not be all evil.

"She does and she told me to tell you she misses you and hopes you return home soon," Lawler said and gave a nod to Bliss. "Is there anything the woman is in need of that I may bring the next time I visit?"

"Find her some garments without anyone knowing of it," Rannick ordered. "And a fur-lined cloak for winter."

"I will see to it, my lord," Lawler said. "Would it be permissible for me to approach her and judge what garments might fit her?"

"See to it while I get the sacks you brought," Rannick

89

ordered. "And do not take long, since you will take your leave soon."

Lawler bobbed his head and went to Bliss.

Bliss stood and kept her voice to a mere whisper. "He does not know."

Lawler looked her up and down as if judging her frame. "Does all go well?"

"Aye," she said.

"Any news?"

"Too soon," she whispered.

Lawler nodded and smiled.

It would be good news he delivered to Rannick's father and that pleased the man, and Bliss felt the guilt weigh more heavily upon her.

"There is news, my lord, your father believes you should know," Lawler said when he walked toward Rannick."

"Tell me," Rannick said, wanting the man gone.

"Chieftain Gowan of the Clan MacFarden is giving Lord Fergus trouble. He believes battle is inevitable. Lord Fergus has already let other clans know he may need their help and your father believes he will reach out to his son, Odran, to return home and fight."

The news worried Bliss. Her clan—Clan Loudon—was one of the clans beholding to Clan MacBridan. That meant Saber could be called to fight. What then would happen to her sister Elysia?

"Odran is as tired of battle as I am and wants nothing but solitude and peace," Rannick said.

"Still, like you, he would not neglect his clan, if necessary," Lawler said.

"Keep me apprised of the situation," Rannick said.

"Aye, my lord," Lawler said with a nod and went to his horse.

"Lawler."

"My lord?" Lawler said, turning.

"Return with the garments for the woman as soon as you discreetly gather them," Rannick ordered.

"As you say, my lord," Lawler said and mounted his horse and rode off.

Bliss sat in silence as Rannick moved the two sacks inside the cottage, her thoughts on Elysia and Clan Loudon. She prayed her sister was safely wed to Saber, though she worried what might happen to him if he had to go fight. And what of the other men in the clan. She would not be there to tend them, to stitch their wounds, but Elysia would be. She had assisted Bliss many times and her skill with a needle would serve the wounded well.

She felt helpless, even more so for not knowing what truly was happening. She was glad Rannick had told Lawler to keep him apprised. She would be eager to hear more news on the possible battle and Clan Loudon's participation, if necessary.

Bliss raised her head, having been staring at the torn garment in her lap and realized that Rannick stood in front of her.

He glared at her. "Tell me what you and Lawler were whispering about."

Chapter 10

The question was not a surprise to Bliss, and she responded truthfully. "He asked if all was well, and I assured him it was."

"He inquired no further?" Rannick asked.

"We exchanged few words in our brief encounter."

"And you will exchange no more words when he returns," Rannick ordered. "Lawler is loyal to my father and if word reaches him that you are here with me, my father will force a marriage and I will not wed you."

Too late, she thought, but there was time for him to learn of that and she was fearful of how he would receive the news.

There was, however, a question that had her curious. "Why didn't you tell Lawler about the attempt on your life?"

"My father would send warriors to protect me, and I do not want the intrusion, not that any of that should concern you."

"I was but curious," Bliss said.

He ignored her response and asked, "Your side heals well?"

"A stitch in my side time and again, but the wound has healed well," she assured him knowing why he asked and eager herself to couple with him and hopefully conceive. Though once she did, she feared his reaction and she could not help but feel he would have every right to his anger.

"And you have been taking what you need to prevent a child?"

The lie slipped from her mouth. "Aye."

He gave a quick nod and went back to sharpening his daggers.

Bliss returned to her stitching, her hands busy and her mind wandering. She hoped she conceived quickly then her bargain would be fulfilled. It would mean no more worry for her sisters. They would be safe.

She had hoped to wed someday—nay—she had hoped to love someday. But the older she got the more her thought of finding love had slipped away. She had begun to resign herself to a future of a doting aunt to her two sisters' future children. This bargain with Rannick's father had changed that. She had a chance of having a child of her own, but she also had a good chance that the curse would strike her dead as it had done to Rannick's three previous wives.

"Something troubles you?"

She raised her head to find Rannick standing in front of her once again.

He pointed to her lap. "Your hands have stopped stitching. Do you regret our bargain?"

"Nay," she said, shaking her head. She would never regret saving her sisters and was glad this was one time she could speak the truth and that brought a smile to her face. "I am glad to be here."

He stared at her, a scrunch to his brow. "Make no mistake, Bliss, I am not a kind man."

That was debatable. She had seen a kind side to him and an unkind side. But the Highlands could be unforgiveable and sometimes what was unkindness to some was survival to another.

She thought to ask him of the possible battle that might affect Clan Loudon, but she feared raising suspicion, so she held her tongue. Surely, Lawler would find a way to let her know how her sisters were doing. And if not, then surely Annis would.

"Two days. You have two more days to rest and heal,

then we seal our bargain, and we see the winter out together. Two days," he repeated and walked away.

She watched him go and gave thought to what she was about to do to this man who had already suffered through no fault of his own. How did she continue to lie and deceive him?

Lies hurt, but so did the truth sometimes.

The question was, could she live with this lie and the lies that continued to build with it? And what if Elysia had wed Saber? It would mean she was already safe from a forced marriage. That still left Annis to protect. She had never intended to lie to Rannick, but when she first saw him, she feared telling him the truth, feared there was no other way to keep the bargain. Guilt and fear weighed heavily on her, and she did not know what to do.

Would he understand if she confessed all to him? Or would her sisters suffer unwanted marriages because it was too difficult for her to lie and save them?

Her stomach churned with worry, and she stuck the threaded needle in her torn garment, gathered it in her hands, and stood.

"Something wrong, Bliss?" he asked from where he worked on his daggers.

"I am suddenly tired," she said. "I am going to rest."

He nodded. "Rest will help heal you."

She entered the cottage, dropped her garment in a basket and discarded her cloak on a lone peg before going to the bed and sitting on the edge. She was overwrought with worry and the only thing that would help was sleep. She dropped on her side and closed her eyes, leaving her boot-covered feet to dangle off the bed. She had no strength or wont to remove her boots. She felt torn in what she should do and hoped with rest her head and worry would clear enough to let her see reason and find a clear solution to her problem.

"Let me see your wound."

Bliss's eyes flew open. She had been so engrossed in her thoughts that she hadn't heard Rannick enter the cottage. He stood near the bed, looking down at her. The way he towered over her, and his imposing stance, intimidated.

"My wound is good. I am just tired," she said.

"Show it to me or I will look myself," he ordered and stepped toward her.

Her hand quickly went to her side pulling his shirt she wore up and moving her tunic out of the way while keeping herself discreetly covered elsewhere.

He hunched down beside the bed and reached out to tenderly probe the area around the seared wound.

"It is still tender," he said, seeing her eyes wince.

"The outside heals well but the inside needs a bit more time," she said.

He eased his shirt down over her hip, then proceeded to remove her boots and place both her feet on the bed. He pulled a blanket up over her and tucked it around her.

"Sleep will help heal," he said, and his hand went to her face and brushed the few stray strands of hair off her cheek, then rested his hand there while he ran his thumb gently over her lips.

It felt like an intimate kiss and a tingle shot through Bliss, and she shuddered.

"Soon," he whispered. "Soon I will make you do more than shudder at my touch."

Her tears started as soon as the door closed behind him. She realized what disturbed her about the situation. It touched her heart the way he tended her as if he truly cared. Then there was his touch and his kiss. She had known neither from a man and it had surprised her that she found both pleasurable and from the cursed lord. She even, to her great surprise, favored sleeping naked in his arms as well as the warmth they shared wrapped snugly together.

He might think himself an unkind man but—in his own rough way—he had shown her kindness and what had she shown him—deceit.

This task had suddenly become far more difficult in a way she had never expected. Never did she think she would find herself caring for the cursed lord.

***

Rannick inhaled a deep breath after stepping outside. What was it about Bliss that so enticed him? His three wives had been appealing enough, his first wife the most attractive. Bliss's features were plain and yet he saw a beauty in her that he had never seen in any other woman.

He blamed her—unfairly—for disturbing his solitude and showing him what he had missed… the comforting companionship of a willing and compassionate woman.

He shook his head and returned to sharpening his daggers, annoyed at the lie he attempted to tell himself. He had never truly had the intimate companionship of a woman that he shared with Bliss, and they had not even coupled yet.

He and his first and second wife had never shared a bed nightly, nor had either woman ever slept naked in his arms or were bold enough to touch his shaft. And never did either of them stand naked in front of him. He had barely seen either throughout the day and once his first wife got with child, she had explained nervously that he need not make any more nightly visits to her bed until such a time he wished another child. He had not argued or demanded she see to her wifely duties, since that was all they ever were to her—duties.

Few willing women wanted to couple with the cursed lord, so he had turned to women who coupled for coins. Was it any different with Bliss? He provided her with food and shelter and in return she warmed his bed and would couple with him willingly.

He was an evil bastard for putting her in such a situation. With no place for her to winter, what else had he expected her to do? She had little choice but to remain with him.

"It was a fair bargain," he said to himself. She could have said no. Why hadn't she? Why take a chance of the curse touching her?

Those thoughts had disturbed him since she first agreed to his proposition. But she had explained it away and he had believed her. He wanted her to remain there with him. He wanted to feel her naked and snug in his arms each night, their bodies warming each other. He wanted to wake to her gentle smile she did not even realize she wore in the morning when she woke. And he wanted to lose himself deep inside her hoping that somehow, she could heal the endless pain that pounded at his heart.

He cursed himself. "Selfish bastard."

He should send her on her way, far away from him and the misery he would surely bring upon her and yet he didn't want to let her go. The thought of her leaving, not having her there in his bed, in his arms, feeling her gentle and inquisitive touch filled him with intense pain.

He needed her, though he had to be sure he did not care for her, have any feelings at all for her or she would suffer for it.

Distance. He had to make sure to keep an emotional distance from her. It shouldn't be difficult. He had felt nothing in so long… except. He could not deny the obvious. He had felt something stir deep inside him when she had freely touched his shaft and his intense climax had shocked him. Something had changed in him at that moment and had given him something he had thought long dead… hope.

Several oaths slipped out. He was a fool to feel even a speck of hope. Nothing would change and he would find no peace until he died, and the curse died with him.

"Do not be foolhardy," he warned himself, and yet that spark of hope continued to poke at his heart.

Chapter 11

Rannick took Bliss's hand after she stumbled briefly on their walk to the stream. He kept hold of it even when she remained steady on her feet, and she showed no objection. Her grip had actually grown tighter as if she did not want to let go.

How the act of simply holding her hand could bring such satisfaction, he didn't know since he had never experienced such a simple pleasure of a woman welcoming his hand when he reached for hers and gripping it firmly as if she was overjoyed to hold it. Annoyance poked at him and warned him to let go, release her hand, stop enjoying her so much.

He could not do it. He kept his hand firm around hers.

They walked in silence and that was fine with Rannick. Having her by his side was enough for him, though he was concerned. The last two days Bliss had been more quiet than usual, not engaging him in conversation as she usually did. He wondered if she regretted committing to spending the winter with him and did not know how to tell him that she had changed her mind. He would not force her to stay. He had three women too many who had been forced by marriage agreements and had wanted no part of him.

But the thought of her leaving actually pained him and that was not good. Maybe it would be better for them both if he let her go. The stab to his chest at the thought warned him that would not be easy to do.

He almost shook his head, not understanding why he felt this way. What did it matter? She was a woman like any other woman, except she was the one woman who chose to be with him of her own free will.

Once they arrived at the stream, Bliss released his hand and walked away from him. He had given her no choice but to come with him since he had refused to leave her alone at the cottage while he fished for supper. He could see now by the way she paced anxiously that something troubled her greatly.

"Have your say, Bliss, and be done with it," he said sharply, knowing what was to come. She would leave him, and he tried to keep his heart frozen against the hurt, but he feared it had already begun to melt.

"I cannot do this," she said, walking toward him.

His chest tightened so hard he thought it would squeeze the life from him.

"I cannot lie to you any longer," she said, stopping a short distance from him.

A scowl pinched his face tight. "Lie to me?"

"Aye," she said, not able to carry the burden of her deceit any longer. "Please forgive me. I truly did not mean to hurt you."

"What lie?" he demanded, turning his head slightly, suddenly picking up another sound not far from them.

Fearful she would lose her courage, she hurried to say, "We are wed. I am your wife."

Rannick's hand snatched his dagger out of its sheath as he lunged toward Bliss.

She gasped, frozen in fear, waiting for the dagger to plunge into her. Instead, he shoved her behind him as he flung his dagger, catching one of the two men in the chest, who rushed out of the woods. The other man ignored his fallen comrade and ran straight at Rannick, an axe gripped tight in his hand.

"Stay here," Rannick ordered Bliss and charged at the man.

Bliss watched startled as Rannick pulled the second dagger he kept tucked at his waist and flung it in a perfect arc, catching the man deep in his side before he had a chance to do anything. The man dropped to the ground, blood pooling beneath him.

"Who sent you?" Rannick demanded, staring down at the man once he reached him.

The man glared at him while he struggled with the pain. "I am not the first and not the last."

Rannick dropped down beside him and pulled the dagger from his side, causing the man to scream out in pain while Rannick calmly advised, "That's the first wound and it won't be the last. Now who sent you to kill me?"

Painful groans marked his words. "More will come for you and your wife."

Wife.

Fury raged through him at the shock that not only was Bliss his wife but that she now was in tremendous danger not only from whoever wanted to kill him but from the curse as well. One of those he could protect her from, the other he couldn't, and that infuriated him even more.

"WHO?" he demanded, knowing the man had little time left.

The man coughed, blood spewing from his mouth. "I know I am soon to be a dead man. You are a dead man and don't even know it." His laugh turned into a cough, then he gagged struggling to breathe until all breath finally left him.

Rannick looked the man over to see if there was anything that might hint at where he had come from, but he found nothing. He grabbed the man by the arm and dragged him into the woods. He retrieved his dagger from the other man's chest and dragged him into the woods as well. He returned to Bliss, gripped her by the arm and with strong steps, she hurried to keep up with, rushed her back to the cottage.

101

The sky turned bleak as if in response to the deadly incident and Bliss shivered from the sudden rush of cold air that hit her just as they reached the cottage. He shoved her through the door he kicked open and she stumbled and hurried to put the table between them as he shut the door tight.

"Please let me explain," Bliss said, hoping that somehow, she could make him understand and miraculously repair the damage her confession had caused.

He slammed his hands flat on the table and it trembled from his strength. "My father forced you to wed me?"

"Nay," she said, shaking her head. "I chose to wed you."

"In exchange for what?" he demanded. "Since no sane woman would do such an insane thing."

"To keep both my two sisters from being forced to wed. Lawler planned to wed my sister Annis to Lord Brogan. I offered to wed you," —she shut her eyes briefly— "and get with child in exchange for their freedom to choose their husbands." She continued, her stomach churning. "You frightened me so much when I first met you that I thought it was better I did not tell you the truth."

A fiery fury ran through him, and he had all he could do to contain it. "Instead, you lie and trick me into getting you with child?"

"That seemed to be the most sensible plan, otherwise you would have sent me away, and I would have failed, leaving my sisters vulnerable. But the burden of my lies has been far too heavy to bear. I could carry it no more, though my confession does not change the fact that I am your wife."

Rannick pushed himself away from the table. "Not one of my three wives, unlike the foolish fourth one, wed me of their own accord and for a good a reason—the curse."

"I wed you of my own accord knowing full well what marrying you meant," she insisted.

"You are willing to die for your sisters?" he asked, shaking his head in disbelief.

"Would you not die to protect those you love?" she asked.

"I have no love in me, just a cold, bitter heart."

"I do not believe that," Bliss said.

"More the fool you."

"Or are you the fool for refusing to admit the truth?" she accused and jumped back when he lunged forward and brought his fisted hand down on the table with tremendous force cracking one of the boards.

"Watch your tongue with me, woman, or you will lose it," he warned.

His threat came from anger, but she would not test her theory. She held her tongue.

"You did not think this through enough. If you do not keep your end of the bargain, my father will not keep his. He will see your sisters wed to men of his choosing, most likely Lord Brogan and Lord Odran, something neither of my friends want."

"I had little time to think on it with the impending nuptials of Lord Brogan and my sister, something she was not in favor of either. And I worried over my sister Elysia, she is too kind and sweet to be caught up in a marriage with one of the cursed lords."

"Yet you believed yourself capable of dealing with the worst cursed lord of the three?" He shook his head. "You are beyond foolish."

"I have hope of a better outcome for our union," she argued. "Without hope I could never heal. Sometimes it is the only thing left to me to offer someone or to cling to myself."

Hope. The very thing the curse had taken from him and the very thing he longed to feel again. But he knew the mistake in thinking that way.

103

"There is no hope where the curse is concerned. It commands and demands and strikes with a power that cannot be stopped."

Bliss reached for a sliver of hope. "The witch in the hills—"

His fist came down on the table again, though not as hard this time. "I told you there is no witch in the hills. She is a myth. She does not exist. I searched for her endlessly. I traveled to foreign shores to find witches, demons, anyone or thing that could end this misery and was told the same thing over and over. The curse could only be ended when it was fulfilled—when the wrong was made right." He shook his head. "How do you right the wrong of the murder of an innocent bairn barely a few days old?"

"Maybe we can figure that out," Bliss suggested.

"Before you die in my arms for no apparent reason like my last wife?" he asked the image his words evoked of Bliss lifeless in his arms tearing at his heart.

"Death does not consider age. I have seen young and old die like you say for no apparent reason. Your last wife could have been ill and not have known it or not told anyone about it," Bliss said, trying to make sense of a senseless death.

"Make no mistake, it was the curse… and now it will come for you."

"I do not fear it," Bliss said bravely.

"You should. It claimed all three of my wives," he warned.

She tried to make him see an alternative to the curse. "Your first wife died along with your bairn in childbirth. Unfortunately, that is something that happens far too frequently, no curse is the reason for it. Your second wife died from a riding accident, something else that commonly happens and should not be blamed on the curse. And as I said about your third wife, she could have been ill and not

104

have known it. None of their deaths can be positively blamed on the curse."

"And do you say this to make yourself feel good or for my benefit?"

She smiled softly. "I hoped it would benefit us both."

"You still cling to hope?" he asked, wishing he could feel a morsel of the hope that she did.

"As I said, sometimes it is the only thing I have to cling to."

"I am your husband. You will cling to me from now on," he ordered sternly.

"Then you accept me as your wife?" she asked, hope rising in her heart that this all might work out after all.

"What choice do I have?" he snapped. "But do not think I will get you with child... that will never happen."

She surprised herself, saying, "That disappoints in many ways. While the thought frightened me at first, after having spent time with you, I found myself favoring the thought of having a child with you. I had hoped to one day have one or more, but no man has ever shown interest in me. You are the first even though your interest is no more than for you to satisfy your needs. It is the comfort I feel with you that makes the difference. I never thought I would sleep naked with a man, let alone enjoy it, but I do like sleeping naked in your arms. You keep me so warm, and I feel so safe. Though you can be gruff at times, there is a tenderness about you. I could feel it in your touch when you tended me, and the strength of your kiss is quite pleasant. You are a better man than you think, and I believe you would make a good father."

He stared at her dumbfounded. He had wanted to be a father, had looked forward to it when his first wife had gotten pregnant, but the pain of losing them both had been far more difficult to bear than he had ever thought. And he had blamed himself for bringing the curse down upon her and his innocent son.

Rannick did not know how to respond. That she willingly wanted a bairn with him, that she enjoyed being naked in his arms and enjoyed his kisses, was something he never expected to hear from a woman. So, of course, he had to question it, especially since she had a bargain to keep with his father.

"I know what you think," she said with a sad smile. "That I say this to entice you to get me with child and keep the bargain I made with your father. I have given you little reason to trust my word after my many lies. I can only say that I speak the truth now and will continue to speak the truth to you from this day on. On that I give you my solemn word." She raised her chin. "Perhaps we can start over, and you can come to know me, and I can come to know you while we work together to find out who it is that wants you, and now me, dead."

He should deny her, send her to the keep where she could be kept safe but if he did that his father would believe his bargain with her a failure and issue orders for her sisters to wed, not that he should care. So why did he?

"We stay here until I say otherwise," he ordered. "My father can continue to believe that you are working to fulfill the bargain."

"I am grateful for that. Thank you. It will keep my sisters safe," Bliss said, relieved for at least a short reprieve.

"Now tell me what you truly told Lawler when he was here."

She kept her word, speaking only the truth to him. "I told him you did not know I was your wife, and he asked if there was any news, and I told him it was too soon."

"Meaning he wanted to know if at least there was a chance you were with child."

Bliss nodded, though it had not been a question.

"That is what you will continue to tell him when he

returns until I decide otherwise," he ordered with a firmness that left no room for debate.

"And will you confide in him the attempts on your life?" she asked.

"Not until the time is right."

She would ask what he meant by that, but she didn't think he would explain, so she said nothing… for now.

"It will be difficult for us to find out any information about who wishes you dead being secluded here," she said.

He disagreed. "Not so."

She went to dispute his response, then realized his intent. "You will wait for the next attack and—"

"Keep one of them alive long enough to convince him to tell me what I need to know," Rannick finished.

Giving it thought, she said, "By now surely whoever is responsible for the attacks will have learned that it will take more than two men to see the task done."

"Two men at a time tells me that whoever is responsible is having a difficult time getting not only a sufficient number of men to see to the task but proficient men as well. There are also two different reasons that the men who attacked agreed to the task. The first two men were mercenaries hired for coin. The man today said more would come, that he would not be the last. The mercenary was quick to bargain with me to save his life, not so the man today. He accepted he was dying and told me I was a dead man and did not know it. Each man attacked for a different reason; one for coin and one for a cause or belief."

"That cause or belief is what we need to find out," she said.

He glared at her. "I will not see you placed in harm's way." He shook his head. "Not that you aren't already in harm's way by simply being my wife." He shook his head again, still trying to comprehend that she was his wife.

She recalled how she had gone to Lawler with her

107

proposition, having considered all that went with it. "I was aware of that before I offered to be your wife."

"Yet you still followed through with it, and what has it gotten you?" he demanded. "Nothing but misery from the start and a certain early death. You were a fool, a complete and utter fool."

Bliss defended herself. "I have brought things to this marriage your other wives didn't."

"And what might they be?"

She squared her shoulders. "I brought a willingness to wed you, hope of a good marriage, the willingness to couple with you, and the pride to carry not only one child of yours but more if agreeable with you."

He would not let her know how her heartfelt words had impacted him, chiseled at his frozen heart, and tempted his passion. Instead, he told her what she needed to hear. "Give it time and the curse will destroy every one of them."

With that said, he had had enough and walked out of the cottage. His rage with the news that Bliss was his wife had abated, though it still rumbled around inside him. It shocked him to find out his father had arranged another marriage for him, though truth be told, it was Bliss who had proposed it. That had never happened with his other wives. He had learned that all three had protested the proposed union. But his father had offered a hefty sum to seal the marriage arrangements and the clans greedily accepted, selling their daughters to the cursed lord.

Bliss had been different. She had chosen to wed him out of love for her sisters. That said much about her nature and had made him admire her even more, though she still had been foolhardy to do such a thing.

Surprisingly while anger still lingered, so did a sense of relief he should not be feeling. Bliss belonged to him now and try as he might to understand it, he was glad that she did. A foolish thought on his part. She would only suffer being his wife and yet he selfishly wanted to keep her, though it was lost to him as to why.

He shook his head, growing tired of the heavy constant thoughts. He wished for a simple life like the last three weeks with Bliss, helping her heal, waking with her in his arms, catching her smiling, the feel of her soft skin, the gentleness of her touch and the willingness of her kiss. The pleasant memories haunted him, and he wanted to make more memories with her.

"You are a fool, Rannick, you will bring her nothing but pain," he warned himself.

Too late! You already care for her.

He nearly roared to the heavens at the thought. He did not care. He would not let himself care. She meant nothing to him and never would.

Why then did his own words bring such pain to his heart?

Chapter 12

Rannick watched his wife busily collecting greens in the garden to make a soup for supper and he looked forward to it. He had discovered that she could make any food taste good, an attribute that he had never considered necessary in a wife since the keep's cooks saw to that. Experiencing both, he much preferred the meals he and Bliss shared alone and the intimacy of the cottage. He would love to spend the winter here with her, but he did not think it wise to isolate them when they were being hunted. The keep would be a far better place to keep her safe.

He would see what information he got from the next attack and make his decision then. Until then, he kept himself alert to all around him. He had also set traps in the woods that would warn him to anyone's approach. For now, he was confident he could keep them safe. He would have to reconsider that thought if more than two men attacked.

He also needed to reconsider having them sleep naked together. He had fought the urge to couple with her over the last few days, worried that if he sealed their vows that it would make her more vulnerable to the curse, not to mention the chance of getting her with child. He had not even kissed her though he wanted to—ached to. He knew it would only flame his already heightened passion.

He shook his head, knowing it was one battle that would not see victory.

Rannick walked over to the garden to take the full basket from his wife, though healing well, she still caught a stitch in her side now and again when lifting anything too heavy.

"Leave the basket where it is," he ordered when he saw her ready to lift it. "I will get it for you."

"That is kind of you," Bliss said and smiled at the scowl he turned on her. She waited for his warning that was sure to follow.

His scowl deepened. "How many times must I warn that I am not kind?"

Her smile grew. "It is difficult for me to believe that when you show me differently."

"I want your wound to heal well so I do not have to tend you again," he said and snatched up the basket.

Bliss wanted to reach out and take his arm, but he had been keeping his distance from her except in bed at night. Though, she had not given him a choice. She had disrobed and slipped in bed before he could order her otherwise, though he never did. He seemed just as eager to have her naked in his arms as she was to be there.

She had thought to encourage him with intimate touches, but worried over his response. When she finally attempted, with great nervousness, to do so, he had pushed her hand away.

"You will not touch me without permission," he had warned and left their bed.

It had upset her and robbed her of some of the ease she had felt with him. She had not tried again, and she had no plans to do so. She would wait and see what time with him would bring.

She followed alongside him to the cottage and they both stopped when they heard the rattling of the cascade of sticks Rannick had hung with rope from several trees.

He placed the basket on the ground and grabbed Bliss by the arm. "You will go inside and secure the door and not come out until I come for you."

"If there are more than two you will need help," she protested.

111

"Do not even think it," he argued. "Now do as I say."

"Oh look, it is Lawler," she said, seeing the man emerge from the woods with his horse.

Rannick was furious and gripped her arm tighter. "Never again argue with me when I give you an order. If it was someone other than Lawler, we could both be dead by now."

"Aye, my lord," she said and winced, his grip far too tight.

He let go of her arm. "And do not call me my lord."

"Is all well, my lord?" Lawler asked as he drew closer, his glance going to Bliss.

"She is no concern of yours, Lawler," Rannick snapped.

Lawler bobbed his head. "As you say, my lord. I have brought what you requested, and news as well."

"Tell me," Rannick commanded.

"The disagreement between Clan MacBridan and Clan MacFarden escalates. Chieftain Emory has sent warriors to help Lord Fergus."

"Has Odran been informed about this?" Rannick asked.

"Aye, my lord, he has, but I do not know his response to the news," Lawler said.

"See what you can find out," Rannick ordered.

Lawler nodded. "Your father has a message."

"Of course, he does," Rannick said, annoyed.

"He says you are to come home before winter sets in," —Lawler hesitated— "or he will see you brought home." He stepped back a pace, waiting for Rannick's temper to flare and was shocked to hear the man laugh, though it was not a pleasant laugh.

"Let my father know that he would be unwise to do so and if he asks if it is a threat, let him know it is a promise. Anything else?"

"Your mother says she misses you," Lawler said.

"Her way of saying she wishes me to return home."

"Both your parents wish for your return," Lawler said.

"And what of the clan? Do they want the cursed lord to return home?" Rannick asked, though was aware of the answer. His clan feared him and with good reason. His presence always brought trouble or heartache. Rannick waved off Lawler's response. "I need not hear what I already know."

Lawler remained silent, waiting for any further orders as he snatched the sack he had brought with him off the horse.

Bliss stepped forward. "Let me fix you a hot brew to enjoy, Lawler, before you take your leave." Rannick had told her he would see that she had time alone with Lawler on his next visit. She hoped he remembered and would see it done.

"Have the brew and give Bliss what you brought for her. I will speak with you when you are done." Rannick walked off but as he did, he called out, "Do not lift that basket, Bliss."

Lawler snatched up the basket and whispered, "Are you—"

She shook her head and waved him to follow her into the cottage.

"Lord Lochlann is eager for news," Lawler said.

"There will be news soon," she said, though it was not news he would want to hear.

"You look well," Lawler said as if surprised. "He treats you well?"

Kind came immediately to mind, but Lawler was sure to think that she lied to him. "He treats me well enough."

"I am glad. You are a good, unselfish woman, Bliss. I would not want to see you harmed."

Bliss got busy fixing a brew. "That is kind of you to say so, but tell me, is there any news of my sisters?"

"I heard that Annis searches for the witch in the hills, but I cannot be sure if it is true," he said.

113

"Knowing my sister as I do, I would say the news is accurate. Annis did not take well to the news of my marriage to Lord Rannick. She blamed herself for not agreeing to wed Lord Brogan, which means the guilt she feels is urging her to make it right. Though it truly is no fault of hers, nothing anyone says to her will stop her. I only hope she keeps safe." Bliss smiled. "Though I do feel sorry for anyone who gets in her way. She can be an immovable force when she wants to be."

"From what I have seen of her, she can be a handful, though," —he shook his head— "I actually thought Lord Brogan and your sister would have made a good match. They somehow seemed right for each other. And it would have saved you from Lord Rannick."

Bliss did not realize she frowned as she handed him a tankard.

"Something troubles you?" Lawler asked, taking a seat at the table.

Something did trouble her but not what she expected. It troubled her to think of Rannick here alone while men hunted him. He would have no one to help him if he was wounded.

She responded truthfully as she lowered herself to the bench opposite him. "Just that none of this has been easy for anyone and now with the problem between the clans… it makes matters worse. Is there any chance of Clan Loudon being attacked?"

Lawler shrugged. "Where disputes are concerned you never know, though at this point it seems unlikely. I will find out what I can about both your sisters before I visit next. Lord Lochlann wants frequent updates about how things go with you, so it will not be long before he sends me here again." He gave a nod to the sack he had placed on a chest along with the basket after they had entered. "There are garments in there for you, Lord Rannick's orders. He told

114

me to be discreet in getting them, but since Lady Helice met you, I thought it more prudent I speak to her."

"Please extend my gratitude to her," Bliss said, relieved she would have proper garments to wear. The shift she had repaired was not wearing well. She recalled what Rannick's mother had asked of her and quickly asked, "Can you give Lady Helice a message for me?"

"Aye," Lawler said, surprised.

"Please tell her there is hope that she may get what she requested."

Lawler nodded and Bliss was glad he did not pry and ask her to explain. This was between Lady Helice and her. She had asked Bliss to heal her son and at that time, Bliss feared it was an impossible task. Now, however, she had hope that healing Rannick was at least possible. And being a healer, she could not help but try to see it done. Or was it also that she cared what happened to Rannick, the curse having robbed him of so much?

"I must say, Bliss, that when I left you here, I feared what I would find when I returned. I did not think you had a chance with Lord Rannick. But seeing how well you do, and that Lord Rannick did not want you to pick up that basket— an act of kindness, though gruff as he was—I now believe you just may succeed where so many have failed."

The door swung open startling them both.

"I will speak with you now, Lawler, then you will take your leave," Rannick ordered, remaining outside.

"Aye, my lord," Lawler said and gulped down the last of the brew and hurried outside.

Rannick poked his head back in. "You stay here."

Bliss winced when the door rattled, he closed it so hard, and eagerly opened the sack.

Rannick walked away from the cottage and Lawler followed. "Do you recall the rumors that have circulated that there was a group forming who wanted to see Brogan,

Odran, and me dead?"

"Aye, and rumors still circulate," Lawler informed him. "Your father believes that this battle with MacFarden over Clan MacBridan land, where the church was built, is but a poke at the true problem."

"That Odran, Brogan, and I will sire heirs and the curse will continue to plague the area," Rannick said.

Lawler nodded. "Your father grows frustrated, unable to discover who leads the group. He has come to believe it may just be some discontents stirring trouble."

Rannick said no more about it, not ready to tell him about the attacks and let him know that it was more than discontents.

"Return in a week with more provisions," Rannick ordered.

Lawler nodded, pleased he would need no excuse to return so soon. "Aye, my lord. Is there anything you would like me to bring?"

Rannick had given it thought. He knew what he wanted, what he needed. "Seek out a healer and tell her you want something for your woman so that your seed will not take root in her."

Lawler did not let his request worry him. Bliss would know what to do when he brought what Lord Rannick requested. That was if he brought the right ingredients.

"As you wish, my lord," Lawler said.

Rannick turned his back on Lawler and walked toward the cottage, his departure ending their talk, and Lawler taking his leave.

Rannick entered the cottage and was met with a hug and a kiss. He stiffened in response as did his manhood. Never had a woman hugged him or kissed him so spontaneously and with such enthusiasm. Her scent lingered on him when she hurried away from him. It was potent from being in the garden. She smelled of fresh earth and ripe plants and all he wanted to do was dig into her.

"I am so grateful," Bliss said, going to the table and waving her hand over the stack of garments. "I have never had so many lovely garments. The wool is so fine and soft to the touch and never have I felt linen as gentle. I cannot wait to feel them against me." She smiled as she lifted a folded garment and rubbed it gently against her cheek. "I have never felt a cloak as thick and warm as this one. It will serve me well this winter." She returned it to the pile and picked up a white one. "A nightdress. I have never had a nightdress."

"You slept naked?" he asked, annoyed, thinking she had only done that with him.

"Nay," she said, shaking her head. "In the winter I slept in my garments and in the warmer months, I slept in my shift and blanket. The bed was barely large enough for my two sisters, my bed was the earth floor.

The image of what she had endured bothered him. He had slept on the ground many times, but out of necessity. When he returned home, he had a good-sized bed waiting for him. The thought evoked an image in his head of the two of them curled naked around each other in his bed, which tormented his manhood even more.

"You will sleep in that tonight," he snapped, desperately needing a barrier between them. "I spoke with Lawler. He will bring what you need to prevent my seed from taking root in you when he returns in a week's time, since I do not trust you in taking the correct mixture."

The nightdress was not as appealing now that she saw it as a barrier that separated them. And she could not blame him for not trusting her when it came to taking what was needed to prevent her from conceiving. That Lawler would bring the mixture meant that her husband would not touch her until then. She could easily fake taking the brew, but she had given her word she would not lie to him. What then did she do?

"As you say, Rannick," she said and scooped up the bundle off the table and placed them on top of a chest not far from the foot of the bed.

"Remember that the next time I order you to do something. I will brook no disobedience from my wife."

She did not know what dared her to respond as she did, but the words came easily. "I am not your wife until our vows are sealed."

He was at her side in an instant, gripping her arm and releasing it as fast as he had gripped it when she winced in pain. He took hold of her wrist and pushed up the sleeve of his shirt, she had rolled back several times so it would not be in the way of her hand.

His anger flared, at himself, when he saw that his earlier grip had left a bruise, an imprint of his fingers on her upper arm.

"You are stronger than you know," she said, as if making an excuse for him.

"Don't disobey me and you won't suffer my strength," he argued when all he wanted to do was take her in his arms and tell her how sorry he was for hurting her, a senseless response. This might be the first time he hurt her, but he doubted it would be the last hurt he caused her, and it pained him to think that.

He gave her no chance to respond, leaving the cottage in a huff.

She kept herself busy, putting her garments away in a small, empty chest and hanging her new cloak on the lone peg. She did not slip into a new garment, not wanting to soil it while she prepared their meal. She kept her hands busy chopping, hoping her mind would concentrate on the task at hand and not wander. Unfortunately, she was not successful at it. It was as if she poked herself in the side, whispering, "*Do what you must. Do what you must.*"

Though her meeting with Rannick's father had been brief, it had been enough time for her to see that he was a man who stayed true to his word. Her sisters would surely be forced to wed if she did not keep her end of the bargain and with Rannick so adamant of not producing an heir... she shook her head exhausted from the endless thoughts that circled there.

If she could get him to couple with her just once, at least there would be a chance of her getting with child. And a slim chance was better than no chance at all. But how did she accomplish that when he refused to let her touch him, nor would he touch her and now he ordered her to sleep in the nightdress?

She struggled to think of something, but nothing came to her. She would let it rest and revisit it with a fresh mind tomorrow. She would think of something... she had to.

***

Later that evening after supper was done, little talk exchanged between them, he announced, "I will step outside while you slip into the nightdress."

Bliss said nothing, knowing he didn't expect a response and there was nothing for her to say. He would have his way. She hurried and slipped into the nightdress and got into bed. He returned a short time later and to her surprise shed his garments. She had expected him to leave at least his shirt on, but he didn't. He joined her in bed naked, though he didn't curl around her as usual.

She remained on her side, hugging close to the wall, and for the first time, feeling strange there. She was not close to sleep, and she feared she had a long sleepless night ahead of her. She shifted her bottom an itch scratching at her. The garment was uncomfortable, or had she grown accustomed to sleeping naked?

119

She shifted her bottom again, the itch more irritating.

"Lie still," he snapped, the sway of her bottom doing more than frustrating him.

She tried to do as he said, but the garment became increasingly more uncomfortable. It itched and poked, and she tried her best to ignore it, but it was impossible. She tried to move the least bit possible while attempting to ease the discomfort.

His arm suddenly snagged her around the middle and yanked her back against him. "Now keep still."

She heard the anger in his voice and froze, at least she tried to. The itch was too much, and his hard body was perfect to rub against and bring her some relief.

His shaft stiffened with every shift of her backside. Did it truly irritate her or was she trying to get him to couple with her?

He settled his lips near her ear, and with a growl he ordered, "Take the damn thing off before I rip it off you."

Bliss moved away from him, struggling to get out of the garment as she did.

His hand was suddenly at the neck of the nightdress and with one powerful yank he ripped it down the middle almost to the hem, pulling what was left of it off her and tossing it away.

"You will have no need for it anyway," he said and snagged her around the waist to yank her back against him once again.

She stiffened when his hard shaft poked at her bottom.

His lips settled by her ear once again. "If that was your attempt to seduce me, you succeeded in arousing me, but you will not feel me inside you until I am sure you will not grow heavy with my bairn. Now stay still and go to sleep."

"It itched," she said, wanting him to know the truth.

"Sleep," he ordered in her ear.

There was no point in arguing with him. She closed her

eyes, finally feeling comfortable, warm, and protected in his arms, and sleep came easily to her.

Not so, Rannick. He laid awake wondering how he was going to keep his hands off his wife for a week.

Chapter 13

Bliss was tired of the silence between them the next day. The rain had forced them to remain in the cottage together since shortly after mid-day. He had spoken not a word to her, keeping himself busy with cleaning his sword that needed no cleaning. That he purposely ignored her was obvious.

Her husband might be accustomed to silence, but she wasn't. She and her two sisters would talk non-stop, sharing news, concerns, or recent gossip that usually had them laughing. She missed those times together, the pleasant memories being the reason for her finally speaking up.

"Tell me about your search for the witch in the hills," she said.

"Why? Nothing came of it," he said without looking at her.

She cared not about that, only that she could get him talking. "I am curious why you even tried if you believe the witch does not exist."

"When you are desperate, you try anything," he said, his focus remaining steady on cleaning his sword.

She was not ready to cease conversation with him. "When did this rumor about the witch in the hills begin?"

He stopped cleaning his sword and his brow crinkled. "I believe it was shortly after Lord Brochan and Lady Aila died. I was young, but I do recall my father telling me about it and how it was nonsense. That there was not a bit of truth to it. But through the years, I discovered that many thought differently than he did. After hearing endless tales, I decided to find out for myself." He shrugged. "I found nothing. My father was right. It was nothing but nonsense."

"But Lady Aila had to have gotten the curse from someone," Bliss said, curious as to how the curse actually came to be.

"There is always a peasant somewhere offering spells, amulets, and more. It was one of the reasons he and others had warned Lord Brochan not to get involved with Aila, that she was a peasant and not worthy of being his wife." He turned silent for a moment; his eyes fixed on Bliss. "I wonder how he feels now having been forced to marry his son to a peasant since no noble family would have him."

Bliss's chin went up. "I will remind you again. I chose to wed you."

"You bargained to wed me," he corrected.

"Of my own choosing," she said. "No one coerced me. It was my choice and my choice alone."

"You bargained from your heart instead of your head and sound reason. My father was desperate to get me wed. You could have struck a better bargain for yourself since you were willing to wed me."

"I was not thinking of myself. I was thinking of protecting my sisters." She smiled. "Finally, you accept that I wed you willingly."

"Foolishly," he corrected.

"Out of love," she said and realizing it made it sound as if it was out of love for him quickly added, "for my sisters." She caught the spark of anger in his eyes before he spoke.

"I am not looking for love from you or for you to even like me. You will provide me with what I need, and I will provide you with what you need."

"But you don't provide me with what I need," she said.

The spark of anger in his eyes flared. "I will not get you with child."

"Then if you do not give me what I need, why should I provide you with what you need?" she challenged.

"Be careful with your words, wife. I will only tolerate so much from you," he warned.

"It is a fair question," she argued.

Rannick laughed. "You think this marriage of ours will be a fair one? I did not ask for it. I did not want it. But it is upon me, and you will follow what I dictate." He returned to cleaning his sword.

He angered her and she rarely if ever got angry, but then her life had been hers. Now that she was his wife, it was no more. At that moment, she realized how much she had sacrificed for her sisters and how she might fail them. It had her speaking up.

"You may think you dictate, but it will be the curse who that has the final say."

Rannick got to his feet so fast that the bench he was sitting on fell over. He reached her in an instant, his hand rushing out to capture her chin. "You made your choice. You not only chose me... you chose death." He didn't expect the words she threw back at him.

"Then honor my bargain and let me give you a bairn before the curse claims me."

He shoved her away from him, fury racing through him. "I may not have loved my first wife but seeing the agony she suffered in childbirth only to die, and my son not even take a breath is something I will never see happen again. If the curse wants you, it will have to take you another way." He stormed out of the cottage into the rain.

Bliss went to the door he had left open and stared after him. He stopped before he reached the woods, threw his head back and roared like a mighty beast. She could not help but think there were two men in Rannick, one a good man and one so fraught with so much pain that it turned his heart cold making him appear evil. His heart needed to heal so that the good man could finally be free. She hoped she was strong enough to help heal him and brave enough to challenge the curse and survive.

***

Bliss avoided speaking about the witch or the curse the next day, realizing it would do little good. He had suffered enough due to both, and it would serve no good purpose to dwell on it. It was more important to focus on the present and what could be done from here on.

It had been a busy morning. With the clouds gone and a clear sky overhead, she had gotten busy washing his shirt she had worn, another shirt of his, and her tunic. She had hung them on branches to dry since early morning, and she would move them before nightfall to finish hanging in front of the hearth.

She watched as he stood scanning the edge of the woods as if he expected someone to emerge from there. But if he thought that imminent, he would have sent her in the cottage. She could understand why people feared him. He was a formidable warrior, his confident stance alone a warning and his cold, scowl threatening. There was no joy in his laughter, as rare as it was, it more scorned. She wished she could have seen the man he had been before the curse had inflicted such pain on him.

It was not always easy to determine how to treat an illness. Kendesa had told her that wounds on the outside were easier to treat than wounds on the inside. Outside wounds you could clearly see, not so inside ones. The most difficult wounds, she had warned, were the wounds that damaged the soul. Those wounds, Kendesa had said, required patience, a kind heart, and endless love, and still, she had warned, the person might not heal.

He turned to completely face her, and Bliss thought she caught a slight lift of his lips as if a smile tried desperately to escape, but it was so quick she couldn't be sure. It did not matter since her smile came easily and quickly.

She walked over to him. "Would you take me into the woods today? It is a good time to collect some roots of healing plants."

"Aye, get a basket and we will go now while the sky remains clear," he said and followed behind her into the cottage.

She grabbed a basket and dropped two clean cloths in it, then she slipped her healing pouch onto her cloth belt. A healer never went anywhere without it, and it was time she began wearing it again. Watching Rannick slip daggers into the sheaths inside each of his boots and add one more to the one already at his waist and one in the back of his waist, made her realize that he was prepared for any attack. That knowledge put her at ease, though she worried what would happen if more than two men attacked.

"You will not dally. You will get what you need, and we will be on our way," he ordered.

"As you say, husband," she said with a nod and a smile, and out the door she went.

Rannick grumbled to himself, little good that it did, annoyed that his wife had almost forced a smile from him when he had turned to see her simply standing there. He had been struck with a moment of joy and it had almost forced a smile, but he had stopped it as he did just now when he wanted to return her smile that seemed filled with happiness. How could she find any joy with him at all? She was a fool, but she was his fool, and he foolishly found the thought pleasing.

He grumbled some more as he shut the door. This was not good. He could not let himself care. In the end, she would suffer for it and his heart would suffer for it far worse than it ever had, for try as he might, he could not stop Bliss from touching his heart and he was powerless at stopping the curse from claiming her.

***

Rannick actually enjoyed watching the pleasure Bliss got from digging in the soil and the way she handled each rooted plant with such gentle care. He had not found such contentment as he did this day with his wife and all he had done was lean against the tree and watch her. It was a simple pleasure and simple pleasures had long been denied to him.

She stood from where she had squatted down to dig at a plant and wiped her hands free of the dirt on one of the cloths she had brought along. She stretched out her back and winced when a stitch caught her in the side.

Rannick pushed himself away from the tree and went to her. "You have done enough for today." He reached for her basket and her hand on his arm stilled him.

"I have one more root to harvest and then I am done." Seeing a slight scowl wrinkle his brow, she said, "Just one more if you do not mind."

"Show me which plant and I will see it done while you go rest against that boulder over there," he said with a nod to a large stone while keeping his scowl at bay.

He was not annoyed at her. He was annoyed with himself for letting the simple touch of her hand on his arm spark such an urgent desire in him. He wished he had told Lawler to return sooner than a week.

"Rannick," she said softly, her finger pointing to the plant she wanted dug up.

He shook his head, annoyed his mind had wandered where it should not have gone.

"Go rest while I see to this," he said more abruptly than he intended.

"You must tend the root as gently as you tended me," she advised and without thought she quickly stretched up to kiss his cheek.

127

It was too much for him to ignore, instinct had his arm shooting out to hook her around the waist and yank her against him. His lips came down on hers and he kissed her with a need that he feared would never be satisfied.

Bliss was so shocked that for a moment she froze, then she freed her own desire and returned his kiss.

His other hand went to the back of her head to hold it tight, fearful she would slip away from him or somehow disappear. He could not let her go, he needed her in so many different ways and the eagerness in which she returned his kiss told him she felt the same.

It was almost as if with each kiss she restored a part of him, a good part, and he hungered to have not only that goodness in him restored, but to once again feel whole. His hand roamed down over her backside, and he pressed her hard against him. He wanted badly to do more than just kiss her, so much more.

He lingered in the kiss until it grew too dangerous to continue, then he wisely ended it and eased her away from him.

"Go rest," he ordered, releasing her only to grab hold of her arm again when she swayed ready to fall.

Her befuddled look told him much. This was all new to her. She was feeling things she had never felt, and she did not know what to make of it. She would learn soon enough.

She stepped back and he let her go, his hand falling off her, though the confused look on her face made him want to take her in his arms once again. Wisely, he kept his hands at his sides and when she reached the boulder, he quickly turned his back to her and his attention to the plant, dropping down to start digging.

Bliss leaned against the boulder, her hand going to her mouth and her fingers faintly touching her lips. She could still feel the strength of his lips upon hers. It lingered there, tempting and confusing. His desire for her was palpable but it was her own intense desire for him that confused her. She had hoped intimacy with her husband would be something she would enjoy rather than tolerate. She realized now she would more than enjoy intimacy with him, she actually hungered for it.

Consumed by her unexpected thoughts it took her a moment to hear a soft whimper. She turned her head and saw two eyes that looked as if they glowed red staring at her. Slowly, they approached until Bliss saw they were the eyes of a sizeable wolf. But what she noticed most was that the animal held his one paw up. He was hurt and looking for help.

Her healing instincts had her walk slowly toward the wolf as she spoke gently to him. "You are hurt. Let me help you." She held her hand out to him and the wolf took a step toward her.

"Bliss, stop and back away slowly," Rannick ordered, fear for his wife's safety turning his stomach when he had turned and saw what she was about to do.

Bliss turned and saw her husband's hand on his dagger, and she quickly moved in front of the wolf, shielding him. "He is hurt and seeks help."

"He is a wolf who will tear you apart," he warned.

"Nay," she argued, shaking her head. "He seeks help and will not harm me."

"Do not be foolish!" Rannick snapped and the wolf growled.

"Your anger upsets him," Bliss scolded.

"And his presence upsets me," Rannick shot back.

"Then take your presence elsewhere because I intend to help him," Bliss said defiantly.

His eyes went wide. "You disobey me?"

"I am a healer and I help those who seek my skill whether humankind or animal," she informed him and turned her attention to the wolf.

"BLISS!"

The wolf growled again.

"Go away, Rannick, if you intend to make this more difficult for me, since I intend to help the wolf no matter your objection."

"You will suffer for disobeying me," he warned.

"I have been threatened several times by those who thought they knew better than me and it did not stop me then from healing, and it will not stop me now." She continued to approach the wolf.

Rannick's stomach tightened in an agonizing knot. He could rush the wolf, but he could easily attack Bliss before he reached her. If he could get closer, he might have a chance. He took a careful step forward and the wolf growled.

"Stay where you are!" Bliss ordered, seeing the wolf's eyes looking past her.

Rannick stopped, muttering several oaths.

"His instincts tell him I will help him while your foolish actions warn him of an approaching prey," Bliss said, trying to make her husband understand.

"The curse," he reminded not only himself but his wife as well and hoped it would help her see reason.

"The curse has no place here today," she said confidently. "Now be still and let me help this beautiful animal."

He hoped she was right, but hope had failed him each and every time, only this time if the beast killed his wife, he would follow her into the death and take the wolf with him.

"I see you are in pain, my friend. I am a healer, and I will help you," Bliss said, gently getting closer to the magnificent animal.

His fur was a mixture of gray and white and he was large with powerful muscles. His eyes, which now appeared dark, were cautious and he showed just enough of his sharp fangs to intimidate.

When she was nearly on top of him, she held out her hand. "I mean you no harm. I am here to help you. May I see your paw that pains you?"

The wolf stepped forward without hesitation, though his eyes darted past her to Rannick as he sat in front of Bliss and offered his paw to her.

Rannick watched amazed. It was as if the wolf understood her every word.

Bliss tenderly slipped her hand under the offered paw. She carefully examined it. She was relieved to see the problem would be easy to fix. A small stone had embedded itself in between two of his paw pads.

"A stone," she said softly, pointing to the object of his pain. "I am going to remove it. I will try not to hurt you but there may be some pain."

Rannick did not like hearing that, but he remained silent, realizing it was not only the best thing for him to do right now but the only thing left for him to do.

Bliss released his paw and dug into her healing pouch for the cloth that contained different sized needles. She chose one of the thicker ones, knowing a thin one would snap too easily with the stone dug in deep.

"I need your paw again," she said softly, reaching out to him, and the wolf held it up to her.

Rannick had managed to position himself to be able to see better. He still could not fathom what he was seeing, a wild beast seeking help from a healer. Which begged the question, did the animal instinctively know she was a healer?

Bliss bent her head close to the wolf's paw and the animal did the same, watching her every move. She dug as gently as she could, prodding the stone to move and it finally did. A few more prods and it surfaced enough for Bliss to pluck it out. She tossed the offending stone behind her.

"Wait," she cautioned when the wolf moved his paw away, holding her hand out to him. "I must make certain it has not turned putrid."

The beast returned his paw to her without hesitation.

She examined it closely. "It looks good and no doubt you will see it healed with a few licks." She smiled and released his paw.

The wolf stared at her a moment, then moved closer to Bliss.

Fear clenched every muscle in Rannick, and he was ready to charge the beast, but shock froze him as he watched the wolf rub the side of his face against her leg several times.

Bliss understood the wolf was thanking her, and she rested a gentle hand on his head. "You are most welcome, my friend."

The wolf backed slowly away, not taking his eyes off Rannick and soon disappeared into the woods.

Bliss turned and went to Rannick, who stood shaking his head. "I cannot believe the wolf let you tend him let alone that he sought your help, and that he thanked you."

"Most animals instinctively know when a human will offer help rather than harm them," Bliss said. "I was startled when I first saw an injured squirrel go to the healer I learned from while we were collecting plants in the woods. She helped him. I watched time and again her tend different animals and birds as well. They knew her hands healed and that her heart was kind."

"Still, you not only took a chance with your life, but you disobeyed me," he reminded.

Bliss placed her hand on his chest. "When it comes to healing, Rannick, I ask that you trust me. I know when I can help someone and when I cannot."

He rested his hand over hers. "As long as healing does not put you in harm's way, I will trust you and allow you to heal."

Her smile bordered on a laugh. "You cannot stop a healer from healing."

He leaned his head down until his forehead almost touched her. "Maybe not, but I can stop my wife from healing."

Arguing with him would prove senseless, so she slipped her hand from beneath his.

Rannick felt a jolt to his heart, as if she had torn herself away from him. It eased when she took his hand and locked her fingers with his and he wasted no time in closing his firmly around hers. He wanted to hold on to her, keep her close, and never let her go. He was insane to think that way, insane to think the curse would not recognize that he cared for his wife and purposely yank her away from him. The thought troubled him, but he refused to let go of her hand, let go of her.

Rannick scooped the basket up and they made their way back to the cottage as clouds rolled in overhead.

Bliss was quick to gather the damp garments off the tree branches and place them over the benches in front of the fire to dry. She placed the roots she had collected on top of a chest to dry, then giving her hands a quick wash in the bucket of water near the hearth, got busy fixing supper.

Rannick sat on the bed watching her. After a several minutes, it struck him how graceful her movements were, more like a noblewoman than a peasant whose endless toil produced aching and gnarled fingers at a far too young age. Each day he saw more beauty in her face. He caught it in the corner of her eyes as they wrinkled when she smiled and the way her face brightened when something caught her interest and the scrunch of her brow when deep in thought and the contentment when she slept in his arms. Of course, a troublesome thought had to interfere… she was his wife, and the curse would eventually strike her.

He recalled something she had said, and his protective instincts reared up in him. "You mentioned something about being threatened before when healing. Who threatened you?"

133

"Men who had more to drink than they should have and some who believed themselves more knowledgeable than me because they tended men on the battlefield."

"Did any of them harm you?" he asked, his tone sharp.

She stared at him a moment and he could tell by the sudden worry on her face that she had recalled a disturbing memory.

Rannick stood and went to her. "Tell me."

"One man frightened me."

"Who?" Rannick demanded.

She shook her head. "I do not know his name. It was shortly after Kendesa died. I was called to the keep at night to tend a visitor. He had broken his finger badly and he ordered me to heal it. I warned him that the break was bad and that the finger might not heal properly." Her hand went to her throat.

"He grabbed you by the throat?" he asked, and gently moved her hand away.

She nodded. "Aye, he did. He was a big, bald man with a scar under one eye and an ugliness to him that otherwise would have been good features. He warned me he would enjoy seeing me punished if his finger did not heal well." She shook her head. "The finger was too severely broken. It would never heal well. I did what I could and told him to limit the use of his hand for several weeks. He laughed at me, and Chieftain Emory stepped in and sent me on my way. He left the next day and thankfully I never saw him again."

"Did he have a thick dark beard and a thick body?" Rannick asked.

Bliss's eyes went wide. "How did you know?"

"His name is Jaffee He's the one who gave me the scar on my face."

Chapter 14

Bliss ran her finger gently over his scar. "What happened?"

Rannick nearly shut his eyes against the enticing pleasure of her faint touch as it spread slowly through him alerting all his senses.

He quickly recovered seeing how she patiently waited for him to explain. "Jaffee caught me off guard. I was lucky it was only the tip of his blade that caught my face or else there would be little left of it. He is a wicked warrior to fight, unfair in battle. Though I will say, you had a hand in his hasty departure from our encounter."

"Me?" she asked, lowering her hand.

He wished her hand had remained, warm and tender, on his face, though he was glad when she rested it on his chest.

"He paid no heed to your warning about his finger and had a difficult time fighting with the painfully crooked appendage. When I spotted the weakness, I took advantage of it, and he soon abandoned the fight."

"Why did he attack you?" she asked.

"Jaffee is known to do anything for substantial coin."

Her brow drew together tightly. "Then an attempt on your life was made before the ones that took place here?"

"Gossip spreads about a group that wishes to see me, Brogan, and Odran dead so that the curse dies with us and puts an end to the pain and suffering of so many. I assumed someone paid Jaffee to see it done."

"And you waited to tell me this?" she asked. Her scrunched brow suddenly disappeared with the widening of her eyes. "You do not trust me."

135

She went to move away from him, and he caught her arm in a tender grip. "This is not your fight."

"You are my husband. Your fight is my fight but that does not answer my question," she said. "Do you trust me?"

He wanted to trust her, but her priority was for her sisters. "Your love is for your sisters and their safety, and you will put them before anyone else. Does that answer it for you?"

She lifted a stubborn chin to him. "You are right. I wed you to protect them, but what good are you to me dead? I need you to fulfill my bargain with your father. So, I will fight by your side whether you trust me or not and hope that you will fight this curse rather than surrender to it."

"I never surrender," he snapped and released her arm and returned to sit on the edge of the bed, her remark annoying him.

"Rannick."

"What?" he barked.

"There is something we did not consider," she said, her brow once again pinched.

"What is that?" he asked, unable to keep the annoyance out of his voice.

"If Jaffee was paid coin for his services, what was he doing with Chieftain Emory at Clan Loudon?"

***

Bliss's question continued to haunt Rannick the next day. He had laid awake thinking on it while his wife slept peacefully in his arms last night. He had grown more and more content with her in his bed. She had restored an ease in him he thought forever lost. Oddly enough, he was glad he had gotten this time with her without being completely intimate. When they coupled, they would not be strangers to each other. She would show no reluctance to stand naked in front of him or shy away when he was naked. They had grown and continued to grow comfortable with each other. He was counting the days, anxious for Lawler's return.

He shook his head realizing he was growing aroused at just the thought of coupling with Bliss. He turned his attention back to her question.

What had Jaffee been doing at Clan Loudon?

Had he gone to meet and plot with Chieftain Emory? Or had his visit been brought on out of necessity of his injured finger?

"I was thinking," Bliss said after stepping out of the cottage and walking toward her husband, sitting on the bench at a small table where his axe and sharpening stone waited.

One thing he favored about Bliss was that she did not let his all too often surly way bother her. She kept a pleasant smile on her face more often than not and even though he would turn silent on her, she would talk to him anyway and often draw him into conversation. She truly did have a healing way about her.

She stopped in front of him, and he frowned. "You should wear your cloak. The air is colder today."

"I will only be a moment. Share yours with me," she said and set herself in his lap, tucking herself in the crook of his arm and pulling his cloak around her to share as if it was the most natural thing to do.

His arm instinctively circled her waist to keep her steady and her backside safely away from tempting his manhood. Though he had to admit to himself that he favored that she was comfortable enough with him to sit without invitation on his lap. And, of course, his thought had to turn wicked and think of her sitting naked on his lap, something he intended to see happen.

Four more days, just four more days, and Lawler damn well better be on time.

"If Jaffee simply stopped at Clan Loudon to get help with his injured finger, it would still beg the question what had he been doing in the area?"

How was it that she always smelled so good? He would catch the scent of mint on her one day and another day it would be a sweet scent that caught his attention.

"Rannick, are you paying attention?" she asked.

"Aye. Aye," he said and was glad he recalled her question. "I was thinking the same myself. Why would Jaffee be in the area? Someone had to be looking to hire him."

"But for what?" she asked, nipping at her lower lip in thought.

Her lip grew plump, and he had the overwhelming urge to nip at it himself and grow it plumper before he kissed her.

"If Jaffee's intention was to kill the day he attacked you, why hasn't he tried again? He must know you have returned home by now."

Rannick chased the wicked, distracting thoughts from his head. "I would assume that since he failed to succeed in his first attempt, the person who hired him no longer has any confidence in him."

"The reason why others hunt you," she said.

Try as he might, he could not take his eyes off her lips. The urge to kiss her was tearing at his gut and he feared he would surrender to it. His own words came back to taunt him.

I never surrender.

This just might make a liar out of him.

She licked her lower, plumped lip and a low groan rumbled deep inside him.

"Rannick," she said softly.

His eyes went to hers and he saw the flare of passion there. She felt the same as he did. She wanted him to kiss her as much as he wanted to kiss her. Seeing his own desire reflected in her eyes made all the difference. He went to claim her lips when the clatter of the wood sticks that he'd hung in the trees reached his ears.

He stood, his arm strong around her, grabbed his axe with his other hand, and rushed her to the cottage. "Secure the plank across the door and open it only for me." He shoved her inside.

He shut the door on her, but she did not fasten the plank. She had to know if more than two men had come for him. If so, he would need help. She did not want to take a chance and open the door in case she had to secure the plank. She pressed her ear to where the door met the frame and felt the cold air seep through it and waited.

"Surrender and we will give you a swift and painless death," a man yelled.

"You cannot take down five of us," another cried out.

Bliss's eyes shut with fear for a moment. *Five.* He could not defend against five warriors. And only one needed to get past him to reach her. She spotted Rannick's sword but knew it was not only too heavy for her to wield, but she had no skill with the weapon. She had little skill with any weapon, especially against adept warriors.

What skills did she have that could help?

Her eyes went quickly to the crock of bubbling soup that sat on the hearth's stone a breath away from the flames.

"SURRENDER!" a man roared.

Another called out, "You cannot stop all of us at once. One of us will reach your wife and give the curse what it craves."

"DEATH!" a man bellowed.

I never surrender.

That is what her husband had said to her. He would die trying to protect her and the thought sent a horrible ache through her. She hurried and with a slim log pushed the crock farther away from the flames. She padded her hands with wads of cloths and used them to lift the hot crock, wincing as she felt a sear to her wrist, but she did not let it stop her. She got the crock to the table, sat it down and waited.

"YOU KNOW WHAT TO DO!" one man yelled.

A roar split the air that shivered Bliss and fear had her heart beating wildly but determination kept her hands from shaking.

She heard the clash of metal and a painful scream ripped through the air. Her husband had taken down one man. A few moments later the door crashed opened, and a man rushed in. Bliss didn't hesitate, she heaved the contents of the crock at him, the boiling soup catching him in the face and neck. He stumbled back screaming and grabbed at his scorched face, then passed out, collapsing outside the door.

She hurried to shut the door and secure it; confident her husband could easily handle the three men left. Before she could get it closed another man shoved it open sending her tumbling back, but she managed to stay on her feet.

The man laughed. "No place to hide."

His smug laugh and pause gave her just enough time to grab the crock and fling it at him. It caught his forehead high up and as he stumbled she grabbed a log.

"You witch," the man yelled, as he steadied himself and swiped his sleeve-covered arm across his brow several times to clear away the blood spilling down to pool in one eye. He threw curses at her, the bleeding growing worse, and lunged at her once again.

She threw the log and caught his head again and he fell back against the wall.

Anger got him to his feet fast and she reached for another log, but she wasn't fast enough. His hands caught around her throat tight and squeezed.

She clawed at his hands, but his strength was too much for her, she couldn't budge them. She tried for his gut and hit solid muscle and he laughed.

He yanked her close to him and he whispered harshly, "You're going to die."

He was right, life was draining out of her when suddenly he loosened his hold and dragged her across the room to slam her down on the bed.

"I will make you suffer before I squeeze the last breath from you," he said with a sneer and tightened his hands at her throat.

She pushed at him, but her strength was waning, and her vision blurring, and her hands fell off him. She gasped as breath returned to her and she heard him laugh.

"Soon you will breathe no more," he said and squeezed her throat again.

The slight reprieve returned a modicum of strength to her, and she did not waste what little time she had. With her hand dangling off the side of the bed she was able to grab the small, empty bucket and fling it at his head.

It caught the open wound on his head, and he fell off her with a yell, stumbling to stay on his feet, then with fury molting his face red, he launched himself at her.

He didn't get far before he was yanked back and spun around to face the raging cursed lord.

Bliss cringed; her husband's face twisted with such savagery that she thought she was looking upon the devil himself.

Rannick dragged the man outside and soon after, horrifying screams filled the air.

Bliss struggled a bit to sit up, her strength not having fully returned to her. She took low steady breaths, working sufficient air back into her body. She had come close to losing her life—her hand went to rest at her neck—and now thinking on it, she realized that the men had come after Rannick and her with a vengeance. They would not stop. More would come. They could not remain here alone.

"BLISS!"

She raised her head, not realizing she'd been staring at the floor. Her husband stood, as if frozen, in the doorway. She didn't hesitate, she bolted off the bed and ran straight for him.

Rannick caught her around the waist with one arm, and her arms rushed around his neck to cling tightly to him. He kept his bloody axe clasped in his other hand, not ready to let go of it just yet. He hugged her tightly against him, relieved he had gotten to her in time. His heart nearly failing him when he saw the man easily fling open the cottage door as he fought the other men. But his fury knew no bounds when he had entered the cottage and saw the man lunge at his wife.

Never had he wanted to kill a man as badly as he did at that moment.

"You're not hurt, are you?" she asked and before he could respond, she kissed him quick, then her hands roamed over his face to make sure the blood there was not his.

"None of the blood is mine, and you?" he asked, amazed that she thought of his well-being after what she had gone through.

"I am unharmed. You saved me before he could choke me to death." She kissed him again.

"From the looks of what I saw upon entering the cottage, you did a fine job of protecting yourself," he said, admiring her courage.

"Until you could get to me," she said. "The painful scream alerted me to how many men were left. I knew it would not take you long to reach me."

"There would have been no problem if you obeyed me and secured the door," he reminded.

"I misjudged," she confessed with a cringe. "I thought I could at least get one, then secure the door and at least favor the odds for you. Unfortunately, the other fellow was too quick."

"You should not have taken the chance," he scolded, the fear he had felt for what might have happened to her finally fading now that she was safe in his arms.

Disbelief filled her face. "I would never desert you when you need help." She kissed him before he could respond.

He cherished that she kissed him so freely and went to return the kiss, needing more than a quick kiss from her, when they heard a groan.

"One lives?" he asked, surprised.

"The soup burned his face and neck badly but did not kill him," Bliss said.

"You did well, wife," he said and reluctantly stepped away from her. "You will remain here while I question him."

"Nay," she said, reaching out to grab his arm. "We do this together."

"I will not have you see what I do to him to get answers, nor will I allow you to see what I did to the man who I dragged out of here," he argued.

"I will not be left out of this or be left alone again. I will remain by your side, husband—no matter what."

No matter what.

Never had he had such a strong commitment from any of his wives. That she would stand by his side no matter the circumstances left him feeling that she actually cared for him.

"You will leave when I tell you to," he ordered.

She agreed with a nod and a promise. "Aye, you have my word on it."

He took her hand, and they left the cottage.

Rannick dragged the injured man away from the cottage.

"Please help me. Please, I beg of you. My face is on fire. Help me," he pleaded.

Bliss glanced at the burn on her wrist and how it stung

and felt like it still burned. She could only imagine how he felt, blisters already starting to form on his face and unable to open his eyes. She had to remind herself that he had intended to kill her, yet the healer in her ached to help him, though there was little she could do for him.

Rannick stepped closer to the man writhing in pain on the ground. "Tell me what I want to know, and I will end your life quickly."

The man groaned. "I know little."

"You must know who sent you?" Rannick demanded.

"Nay," the man moaned. "Please, I beg of you, help me."

"Who sent you?" Rannick asked, ignoring the man's pleas.

The man struggled to speak. "I do not know." A single tear slipped from one eye, and he cried out when it touched his burned skin.

"Are you a mercenary?" Bliss asked.

"Nay," he whimpered.

"You are part of the group who believes the cursed lords must die along with their clans so the curse will end?" Bliss asked.

The man continued to groan. "Must end, no choice."

Bliss had difficulty not stepping forward and doing what she could for the man. The numerous and severe burns would be difficult to survive, and the pain would grow much worse. He could linger for days as blisters continued to form and the skin began to peel, and fever could set in. It would not be an easy death.

She looked to her husband. "I should help him."

"You will not help him," Rannick ordered firmly. "Did you not hear him? It must end. He would use his last breath to see his task done. They all came here to die if necessary." Rannick nudged the man hard in the leg with his booted foot. "Isn't that right? You will die for the cause."

144

The man shook his head, then moaned from the pain. "Not slow and tortuous like this."

"Then provide me with information or I will let you linger in your suffering," Rannick said with another kick to his leg.

The man struggled to speak. "I know nothing."

"Liar!" Rannick snapped. "You came here to die, if necessary, that tells me you know much more than you claim. One last chance. Provide me with some information or I will place you in the woods to linger and die."

"You cannot, the animals will feast on him," Bliss said, the thought turning her stomach.

His wife did not disappoint. She did exactly as he expected... help put fear in the man.

"Nay, I beg," the man cried.

Rannick grabbed his arm and began to drag him.

"Nay! Nay! Poison! Poison!" the man shouted.

Rannick stopped, a wrinkle in his brow as he asked, "What about poison?"

The man struggled with each word. "Poison... claimed... your last wife."

Chapter 15

Rannick clenched his fist, angry to learn his last wife, Shona, had been poisoned and angry at himself for blaming the curse for her death and not even thinking someone may have actually harmed her.

He bent down and grabbed the man by his shirt and shook him. "Who? Who killed my wife?" he demanded.

The man's eyes turned wide, and his hand clutched at his chest and before he could take a breath, death swiftly claimed him.

Rannick shook the man, thinking he may have fainted.

"He's gone," Bliss said.

Rannick stood and turned to face his wife.

Bliss almost jumped back, not recognizing him, the mask of fury making him appear diabolical. Normally, she would avoid a man when anger corrupted him, but Rannick had just learned his last wife had been poisoned and that would enrage any decent husband.

She approached him slowly and cautiously reached out to rest her hand on his chest, hoping to provide a small bit of comfort. "I am so sorry about Shona, though I am glad you have learned the truth and you no longer have to wonder what took her from you."

Her words penetrated his anger, and his hideous mask began to fade away to her relief.

He raised his hand to gently stroke her throat. "He left you bruised."

"I survived and the bruise will fade, that is all that matters," she said softly.

His hand fell off her throat and he tilted his head back

slightly as he took a deep breath, then his eyes met hers. "Go inside while I dispose of these men."

She hesitated, worried over him and not wanting to leave him alone.

"Do as I say," he ordered curtly.

She nodded, understanding it was not only about ridding them of the dead men, but him needing time to himself to digest the unexpected news.

Bliss leaned back against the closed door after she entered the cottage. She had done her best not to worry over the curse claiming her life. She had been more concerned about keeping her sisters safe. After all, she had promised her mother just that… to keep her sisters safe. But that had not been the only promise she had made to her mother on her death bed. She had vowed to keep a secret her mother had revealed to her, a startling one, but one that had made no difference to her. She had managed to do both even with the threat of the curse hanging over her.

If that was not enough, she now had to contend with someone attempting to kill her.

***

Bliss left Rannick to his silence that had lingered since he had returned to the cottage. It had continued all through supper even though she tried to engage him in conversation and failed to get nothing more than a few grunts from him. She wondered over his thoughts and would have preferred he discussed them with her since no doubt she was part of them. It was difficult after so many years of living freely, as much as a woman could, to wed and have decisions made for her. She feared that was what her husband was presently considering. What would he do with her?

After what seemed like hours or more, but probably far less, Bliss spoke up. "I go where you go."

147

Rannick's head shot up and his eyes narrowed as they settled on her. "You go where I tell you to go."

Her chin went up with a stubborn toss. "I stay with you."

Rannick glared at her, annoyed with her defiance and yet pleased that she insisted on remaining by his side like a loving wife.

Loving?

Where had that thought come from? Bliss did not love him. She cared for his well-being because he was the key to her sisters' fate. Had she given no thought to her own? Would she surrender so easily to protect those she loved? He could not imagine a love as strong as that. His mother and father had had an arranged marriage and while his father treated his mother well and they cared somewhat for each other, he did not believe they loved deeply. Duty kept them together, nothing more.

He wished for something more, something stronger, more enduring, something he would never find. Something the curse would never allow.

"Argue with me all you want, I will remain with you," she said.

"Of course, you will," he said with an angry laugh. "You need me to get you with child to keep your sisters safe."

I want you safe as well.

The thought caught her by surprise. Never did she suspect that she would care for the cursed lord. All the gossip and tales had warned her of an evil man or a madman. Never had she thought she would find a scarred and injured man in need of healing, and it was not the prominent scar on his face that concerned her, but the scars on his heart and soul.

"I won't deny that is true, but I care what happens to you," she said.

148

She cared?

No woman ever cared what happened to him, not one of his wives or the women who took coin to couple with him.

Rannick stood and went to step in front of her. "Why? Why care what happens to me?'

"You are my husband," she said as if that explained it.

"So, you care for me out of duty of a wife for her husband," he said, sounding as if he accused her of something troublesome.

"Nay," she was quick to say. "I care for a man who tended me when in need, protects me, has been kind to me—"

"There you go again, Bliss, thinking me kind."

"Deny it all you want," she said. "I have seen and continue to see the truth of my words."

"Then it is kind of me to send you to live out your days safely in the keep," he said with a smile that was far from pleasant.

Bliss stepped closer to him, so close their garments brushed. "You think to send me where Shona was poisoned?" She did not give him a chance to respond. "And what of your other two wives? Was someone instrumental in their deaths as well rather than the curse? I would be far safer by your side, and by your side is where I wish to be." Her hand went to rest on his cheek, her fingers gently stroking his scar. "You cannot get rid of me, husband, I am here to stay."

"You condemn yourself to death remaining with me," he said, a creeping dread crawling over him. The curse would eventually take her from him, and he could not bear that thought. He cared far too much for this woman who had forced herself into his life and refused to leave.

"Healing has taught me that death is inevitable. That no one can escape it. That we must live and embrace each day. We can do that together if you will let us."

It appealed to Rannick more than he cared to admit, but a barrier still existed between them. "And how will you feel when you are forced to remain my wife after failing to get with child and your sisters forced to wed? Will you embrace each day with me then with joy or with hatred?"

"I cannot speculate on what may or may not come to pass. I protected my sisters when necessary. Who knows if it is any longer a worry? Elysia may have wed Saber and is now safe, and Annis," —Bliss smiled— "Annis may just save us all. Whatever the outcome, I am your wife and will remain so until I am laid to rest."

Her last few words evoked a vision of her being swathed in cloth prepared for burial and it tore a pain through his heart he feared might take him to his knees. He could not lose her. He would not lose her.

His arm instinctively went around her waist to tug her close and he lowered his brow to rest on hers. "You are bound to me now and forever."

"Not until our vows are sealed," she reminded.

"Vows or not, you belong to me, and I have no intention of letting you go." His declaration brought a sense of relief to him.

"Say that all you wish, but it does not make it true until our vows are sealed," she said.

Rannick released her and stepped away. "Still, you attempt to fulfill your end of the bargain."

"I bargained in good faith and for good reason. Would you expect anything less from me? Besides, I can speak the truth to your father when he questions why I failed." She smiled. "I can tell him that I tried my best, but his son is far too stubborn for his own good."

A smile tickled the corners of Rannick's mouth. "You think me stubborn, wife?"

Bliss laughed lightly. "I know you are stubborn, husband."

"You are wrong. I am not stubborn. I am determined."

Bliss hurried her arms around herself, his eyes roaming over her in such an intimate way that it left her feeling naked and vulnerable.

"Take your garments off, Bliss," he ordered.

There was tenderness in his tone but also a sternness that left no room for her to deny him, but why should she? Wasn't this what she wanted, at least a chance to get with child?

She began to disrobe and when she saw her husband doing the same, her hands began to tremble. It was not being naked in front of each other that caused her anxiousness, it was the possibility of what may come of it.

"Get in bed," he said as he walked toward her.

She hurried into bed, pulling the blanket over herself, only to have it yanked off when he joined her. She shivered at the chilled air that rushed over her and sent gooseflesh tingling along her skin and shriveled her nipples hard.

He turned on his side, to face her, cushioning his head with his hand. "I am going to touch all of you, wife."

"You've done that before," she reminded.

He smiled, a wickedly sinful smile. "This time it will be much different."

"Then I will touch you as well," she said, her hand drifting down along his side.

He grabbed her wrist. "I gave you no permission to touch me."

"It is only fair," she challenged.

His wicked smile returned and as he lowered his lips toward hers, and whispered, "I never play fair, wife."

She tensed not at his kiss that was most welcome, but at his hand on her breast, his fingers, gently squeezing her nipple. His kiss was tender yet powerful and aroused an equal response from her. She soon was lost in their kiss, the sensations it evoked firing her passion.

Donna Fletcher

When he moved his lips to her nipple, her body arched
in response, and he splayed his hand on her stomach to ease
her down. Having watched many a mother nurse her bairn,
Bliss wondered how it would feel for a newborn to suckle
her breast. Never had she thought a man would be the one to
suckle there first, nor that she would enjoy it so much.

A soft moan escaped her lips as his hand moved off her
stomach to caress the slight curve of her waist before drifting
down over her slim hip. When his lips moved to her other
nipple her moan was not as soft. But when his fingers
brushed the hair between her legs, she gasped.

He lifted his head, the intensity of his passion-filled
eyes sending a shiver through her.

"You are mine, *mo ghràdh*, there is no changing that
now... not ever."

She gasped when his fingers brushed her intimately and
by the time his fingers slipped into her, she had lost all sense
of reason. The pleasure was intense, and it grew with his
every intimate touch and kiss. She grabbed the bedding at
her sides, gripping it tight as her passion soared to
overpowering heights.

Rannick brought his lips near her ear and whispered,
"Let go, wife, I will catch you."

Bliss turned her head and gazed into his heated eyes, the
green flecks sparking wildly.

"Let go," he whispered again and left her no choice as
his fingers brought her to climax.

Bliss cried out as she burst with pleasure that raced
through her until she thought she would die from the
incredibly satisfying sensation. And the ripple that followed
slow and easy until coming to an end left her completely
satiated.

"It is but a taste of what we will share," Rannick said
when he saw she was able to focus. "You will feel far more
pleasure when I am inside you."

She shuddered not only from his remark, but the chill that slipped over her when he left the bed. He tossed the blanket over her before he grabbed his plaid off the bench, donned it, and left the cottage.

Bliss pulled the blanket up over her shoulders as she stared at the closed door. The urge to cry poked at her, but she refused to let tears fall. She arrived here fearful of what she would find, and now she believed she may have found something she thought she never would—love.

She could tell herself repeatedly that she simply cared for Rannick, that he was a good man despite what many believed or, at times, his actions. But how did she ignore what she had been feeling of late? How did she ignore that she actually favored her time spent with him or the way they talked easily with each other? Or the joy and satisfaction of sleeping in his arms. And never had she suspected to not only favor his kisses but to yearn for them. Then there was his touch, intimate or not, she loved the feel of his hands on her. Whether powerful or gentle, both made her feel safe, protected, and she did not know why, but his touch felt as if he actually cared for her.

A tear fell from one eye. She felt foolish to think she loved him. He had no thoughts of love for her. Did it matter? At least if her heart felt for him, it would make their marriage more bearable. And maybe, just maybe, her love could help heal his heart enough for him to truly care for her for the time left to them. Another tear fell and another. What did love matter when the curse hung over them, threatening every day?

She let herself cry for the love she finally found and the curse that would rob her of seeing what might come of it.

***

Rannick walked around to the side of the cottage trying

to rid himself of the passion that had his shaft so hard it ached something awful. Never had he the intense desire to bed a woman as he did Bliss. At one point he had feared losing control and slipping into her. The thought alone grew him harder. How did he return to her naked in bed when he wanted her so badly?

What troubled him even more was that it wasn't only his shaft that ached for her, it was his heart. He loved taking her in his arms and holding her close, feeling her warmth and the gentle way she would snuggle against him as if she wanted to be there, enjoyed his embrace. And he wanted her there, ached for her to be there. It had become more and more second nature to him to hold her in his arms, or to catch hold of her hand and cherish the feel of her fingers closing around his.

He had never given much thought to holding a woman's hand, since he rarely had, there had been no reason to. It was more an intimate act shared by a husband and wife. He could understand why now. When their hands joined, it felt to him as if they were one and that nothing could separate them.

"Damn," he whispered. He was falling in love with his wife. He almost laughed. Who was he kidding? He had already fallen in love with her. How and when he couldn't say, and it made no difference. Love had gotten hold of him, and it wasn't going away, and he didn't want it to. But what of Bliss? Could she ever love him?

He shook his head. Why was he being so foolish? He was thinking of love when he had the curse to contend with. Loving his wife only made the whole situation worse. He couldn't love her. He wouldn't love her. Love had no place in their marriage. He would ignore it, give it not a moment's thought and it would die as all things did when left untended.

"It is for the best," he said, glad he had taken command of the problem, and with his ardor faded, he returned to the cottage.

He disrobed, dropping his plaid on the bench and, seeing his wife turned on her side away from him, was ready to slip in beside her and take her in his arms.

He heard her sniffle as he got into bed, and she sniffled again as he inched closer to her. He lay quiet a moment, not touching her, simply listening and it did not take long for him to realize she was crying.

He did not hesitate. His hands were at her waist, turning her to face him, fearing he had somehow hurt her. "What is wrong, Bliss?"

She almost smiled hearing the concern in his demanding tone. He cared how she felt and that touched her heart. But how foolish it would be of her to tell him she believed she loved him. Instead, she found a truth she could speak.

"All that has happened has taken its toll," she said with a sniffle. "I could contain the tears no more."

Rannick eased her snug against him, and her arm went around his waist and her head to rest on his shoulder as her body relaxed against his. His body relaxed as well with her there in his arms where she belonged and where he intended to keep her.

Bliss kept her arm snug around him as if her meager hold on him could keep him there and she sniffled away the last of her tears before she said, "We stay together."

Damn but the woman could squeeze at his heart. "Aye, wife, we stay together."

Soon after, Bliss fell asleep, not so Rannick. His mind was much too busy to sleep. His thoughts were on all that needed to be done if he was to keep his wife safe from those trying to kill her as well as him. The keep would make that easier to do. The curse was another matter.

How did he keep her safe from that?

Chapter 16

Bliss stepped out of the cottage the next day and seeing her husband standing and glancing off into the woods, went to him. "You have been silent, dwelling in thought since you woke and all through the meal. What troubles your mind?"

"Keeping you safe, since you foolishly wed me," he said.

"You could send me to a convent," she said teasingly.

"I would if I thought it would save you," he snapped, though there was no way that would ever happen. They would remain together just as he had told her last night and just as he expected, she reminded him.

"You said we would stay together."

"And we will," he said, a spark of relief catching in her eyes and feeling it himself.

Her relief faded a moment when she asked, "Your word on it?"

Rannick gave it easily. "You have my word."

Bliss revisited what had been mentioned yesterday but they had not discussed. "Have you given any thought to the possibility that your other two wives may have met the same fate as Shona?"

"The thought has been on my mind. A riding accident can easily be arranged, but what of a woman delivering a child?" he asked, seeking her knowledge.

"Do you know if there was much blood?" Bliss asked, having given thought to what may have happened.

"Aye, there was," he said, the image of that day branded into his mind.

"Then it is possible that someone gave your wife a

mixture of plants that would cause excess bleeding and certain death," Bliss explained.

"I would be a fool to entirely dismiss the possibility of it being the curse," Rannick said, though felt a twinge of hope that with the possibility that the curse had nothing to do with his wives' deaths that Bliss had a chance to survive.

"The curse does not concern me as much as the fact that the demise of your clan has been in the making for some time," Bliss said, her mind stirring with a possibility.

"I can tell you have a thought on that—share it," he urged.

"What if those who supported the Clan MacWilliam gathered secretly and in strength and now seek revenge against those clans responsible for the massacre of the Clan MacWilliam?"

"I never gave that thought since the Clan MacWilliam was decimated. Not one MacWilliam survived." His brow wrinkled seeing the urgency in her eyes to say more. "I think there is more to your theory than you say."

She continued cautiously. "There had to have been clans who sided with the Clan MacWilliam but held their tongues for fear of what they would suffer. What if it was discovered that the MacWilliam bairn lived? Would those who once secretly supported the Clan MacWilliam wish not only to protect her but to seek some form of retribution?"

"The MacWilliam bairn is dead. My father saw to her demise, having little choice but to obey the King's edict, or lose his family as well," Rannick said.

"What if your father tired of the King's command, wanted the killing to end, and thus told the King what he wanted to hear?" Bliss asked carefully, not wanting it to sound as though she called his father a liar.

"My father is a man of his word," Rannick said, his father reminding him of it throughout the years.

"If your father is a man of his word, then why did he

157

turn against a man he had called a friend for many years?"

"They disagreed on what the King intended for the Highlands and that meant war was inevitable unless the unrest could be stopped."

"Would you turn against Lord Brogan or Lord Odran as your father turned against his friend Lord Brochan?" she asked.

Rannick stared at her. He would defend both his friends without question, but if it meant his actions would risk his wife's life, he was not sure if the decision would be as easy.

"I believe your honor, your friendship, would have you taking up arms beside them and I would be proud that you did regardless of what we might suffer. I would do the same for my sisters."

He had thought her foolish for marrying him, but at that moment he realized the self-sacrifice she had made to keep her sisters safe from forced marriages that could have seen them wed to men who could have harmed them.

He, Brogan, and Odran had remained steadfast friends through the years, had fought beside one another, had been there to help one another when no other would, and had chased after a myth together without question. They were like brothers and, like Bliss with her sisters, he would defend them without question. And he was proud that his wife would stand by him if necessary.

At that moment, he realized that it was going to be difficult if not impossible to stop his heart from loving his wife.

Rannick reached out and took her in his arms and she swung her arms up around his neck and lifted her head for her lips to meet his. His lips joined hers for a kiss that was far different than they had ever shared. It was a kiss of commitment that they would see this thing through together.

The sound of rustling leaves followed by horses' hooves had Rannick shoving his wife behind him and reaching for the axe that laid against the bench. He would fight as many as they sent to keep her safe, but the slow approach of the horses told him he had nothing to fear. Still, he kept the axe firm in his hand.

"I am pleased to see that you have accepted this wife and pleased with Bliss for honoring our agreement," Rannick's father said, smiling as he walked out of the woods, his horse following beside him and Lawler behind him.

A few weeks ago, Rannick would not have been pleased with his father's presence or that he brought warriors with him, several making their way out of the woods to flank his father's sides. However, now with the threat to his wife's life, he was glad to see them there.

Bliss stepped out from behind her husband, fearful of what Lord Lochlann would do when he discovered that his son continued to refuse to produce an heir. She took hold of her husband's hand not realizing how tightly she gripped it.

Rannick saw the worry in his wife's eyes and felt it in her tight grip. He slipped his hand out of hers and the worry on her face twisted at his gut, but she relaxed some when his arm went around her waist to ease her against him.

"You made a fine choice, Da, and it will not be long before you have an heir to the Clan MacClaren," Rannick said and felt his wife go limp against him in relief.

Bliss rested her head on his chest and whispered, "I am grateful."

Rannick returned the whisper, "Aye, so am I."

Her head shot up, wondering what he meant, but his eyes told her nothing. They were focused intently on his father. Still, she wondered what he meant. What was it he was grateful for?

His father approached, Lawler following at his side and his warriors fanning out along the edge of the woods their eyes as intent on their surroundings as Rannick's were on his father.

"When Lawler told me how well things were going with you and Bliss, I did not believe him and had to come see for myself," his father said, his voice strong with authority.

"It is good that you did, Da," Rannick said. "There have been several attempts made on my and Bliss's life and it is imperative that we return to the safety of the keep."

His father faltered in his steps as he drew closer. "Attempts on *both* your lives?"

Rannick explained. "Not at first, but that changed quickly enough. I assumed the news that I had taken another wife spread rapidly."

His father stopped in front of his son. "I thought the nonsensical talk that the cursed clans must be brought to an end had stopped."

"There is more for us to discuss," Rannick said.

"We can discuss everything once we return to the keep and you and your wife are safe," his father commanded.

"This cannot wait," Rannick said. "Lawler, go help my wife gather her things."

Lawler nodded and stepped forward.

Rannick's arm reluctantly left his wife's waist. "Go and make ready for our departure."

Bliss nodded, though wished it was not necessary for them to leave here. She liked their time alone together. Once at the keep, she would be Lady Bliss and she was not ready for that role.

Rannick waited until his wife entered the cottage before saying, "Walk with me, Da, there is something you need to know."

***

"I am glad to see all goes well," Lawler said once Bliss shut the door.

Not knowing what to say to him, she chose something that would make him understand the situation. "Did you bring what he asked?"

Lawler stared at her a moment, then nodded. "He says what his father wishes to hear?"

"He does so to protect me," she corrected.

A smile touched his lips as he nodded. "That is a start."

"He is adamant," she said.

"You have made a difference in him. He said more words to his father today than the whole time since his return home. And that he wishes to return to the keep, to see you kept safe and protected, means one thing—he cares for you. You have miraculously touched his heart."

If only that were true. She would like to think it was, but she was doubtful. Maybe in time...

She shook her head. "His heart needs to heal."

"And you are a healer," he reminded, "an exceptional healer to have warmed his heart that had turned cold. Now let me help you gather what you need so we may be on our way."

Bliss glanced around the cottage as Lawler set to work arranging the logs so the flames and heat would die off. It hurt her to see it. She had planned to make soup for the evening meal and spend a quiet evening with her husband. She even hoped, foolish as it was, that he would tease her alive with passion and in so doing lose his own to her and consummate their marriage, leaving her with a chance she could get with child.

She had struck a bargain and wished to keep her word, not let the lie continue and worry about her sisters' fate. Yet another part of her found that she wanted to defy the curse and everyone who condemned her husband to a loveless life and bear Rannick a child. Or was it just that she wanted desperately to make love with her husband?

"You care for him."

Lawler's words startled her because they were true. It was madness but somehow, she had fallen in love with the cursed lord, not that she would dare tell anyone. It would be a secret she would keep tucked in her heart.

"I do care for him," she admitted. "He has a far more caring soul than people think. They only see the curse when they look at him and nothing else. I am glad I got this time alone with him. I have learned much." She took a much-needed deep breath and set to work.

***

"Poisoned?" Rannick's father asked, shaking his head as if he had not heard his son correctly. "Shona was poisoned?"

"That is what the man said and under the circumstances I believe he spoke the truth," Rannick said. "It leaves the possibility that Cecilia and Phedra may have suffered the same fate."

Lord Lochlann's face scrunched in anger. "Someone does not want the Clan MacClaren to live on. It is that crazy bunch who believe the curse must die with you, Brogan, and Odran. Though, I do wonder who is behind them. Who has convinced them of this madness? At first, I thought it was only a few miscreants, dissatisfied with their lot. Then you, Brogan, and Odran made it known that not one of you intended to produce an heir and all turned quiet. Now that you are wed, it has stirred their ire and they are at it once again. And with much vigor from what you have told me. It is wise of you to return to the keep. You and Bliss will be safe there and we will see an end put to this madness."

"That is something I definitely intend to do, Da," Rannick said, a look so lethal in his eyes that it shivered his father.

"Hurry your wife along," his father said. "A good meal

162

and your bedchamber await at home. Your mum has kept it ready, hoping each day for your return. Of course, she also keeps your wife's bedchamber prepared where you can visit her often and where she will birth your bairn as Cecilia did."

Rannick recalled his bedchamber tucked away nearly at the top of the keep. He had forbidden his previous wife, Shona, from joining him there and Cecilia preferred visits to her bedchamber. Phedra visited on occasion but never spent the night. When they finished coupling, she got out of bed and retreated to the chamber kept for his wife on the second floor, one he had never been welcomed to visit.

"Bliss will remain with me in my bedchamber and also when she is with child," Rannick said, not that that would ever happen, though the thought of her growing round with his bairn was something he would love to see. Regardless, she would not leave his bed like his other wives had done. He and Bliss would sleep together each night until death took one of them.

His father opened his mouth to debate the issue.

"I will have it no other way, Da. Bliss and I remain together."

His terse response had his father nodding. "As you wish, son."

Rannick left his father to see if his wife was done gathering her things. He did not want to leave this place or the time alone he had with Bliss, but the last attack made it clear they could not stay here, not if he wanted to keep her safe. If not for Bliss, he would have stayed and fought the endless attacks and probably died. Death had been preferable to the life he had been living.

Bliss had changed all that and now all he wanted was her.

He entered the cottage to find Lawler ready to haul the two sacks in his hands out of the cottage.

"Did you bring what I told you?" Rannick asked.

163

"Aye," Lawler said, and nodded as his eyes went to the pouch on the table.

"Leave us, and as I said before, say nothing to my father about this," Rannick warned.

"Aye, my lord," Lawler said and left.

"Take some now," Rannick ordered, nodding to the pouch.

"There is no fire. I need to brew the leaves, and I need to see how strong a mixture it is to know if it needs a day or more to take effect," she explained.

Rannick picked up the pouch and held it out to her. "See to that now."

Bliss took it from him, having ignored the pouch when Lawler had placed it on the table. She knew paying it no heed would change nothing, but she had done so anyway. She opened the pouch and poured a sufficient amount in her hand to examine.

She pushed the dried leaves around and brought her cupped hand to her nose to sniff. She pushed the dried leaves around again, examining them more closely, then sniffed at them once again.

"This mixture will not prevent your seed from taking root," she said.

"You lie," he accused, thinking she made an excuse not to take it.

A soft laugh escaped her. "Do you hear what you imply? If that was so, I would say nothing and take the mixture and get with child."

Rannick went to the door. "LAWLER!"

The man hurried into the cottage at the commanding shout of his name, Rannick closing the door behind him and planting himself in front of it.

"Who gave you that mixture?" Rannick demanded.

Lawler appeared reluctant to answer.

"Tell me," Rannick snapped harshly.

Lawler hurried to say, "Your mother."

Rannick's annoyance showed in his sudden glare. "You went to my mother?"

"We have no healer. Who else was I to go to? Your mother has knowledge of such things and was willing to do as you requested."

"Start a small fire and bring water from the barrel outside," Rannick ordered.

Lawler nodded and grabbed a bucket to do Rannick's bidding.

Rannick turned a deeper glare on his wife. "You will take the mixture."

"I do not know if your mother does this on purpose or she is not knowledgeable, but this mixture is worthless against your seed."

"My mother made sure not to get with child after she miscarried two bairns. She knows what she does. And I am disappointed that you lie to me and still try to get with child."

"I told you I would speak the truth to you, and that is what I have done. This," —she held up her hand with the mixture cupped in it— "is worthless." She tossed the mixture on the floor.

Rannick slammed his hands flat on the table, causing his wife to jump. "You will take it and I will speak with my mother when we arrive home."

"And if it is your mother's word against mine?" she asked.

"Drink it," was all Rannick said before he walked out of the cottage.

Chapter 17

"You will ride with me," Rannick ordered when all was ready for departure.

"I prefer to walk," Bliss said and turned away from her husband.

She gasped when his hands settled tightly at her waist.

"That was not a request, wife," he whispered harshly near her ear. "And defy me in front of everyone and you will discover what I have repeatedly told you... how unkind I truly am."

Bliss was more annoyed with herself than she was with her husband. She rarely, if ever, got angry. As a healer, she needed a clear head and heart to do her best to help others. Anger clouded both. The walk to the keep would have served her well, clearing her head and heart from the annoyance she felt at her husband.

She remained silent when he lifted her and placed her on the horse.

"Be angry with me all you want," Rannick said after mounting and tucking her back against him to take the reins and direct the horse. "But you will obey me."

Bliss sagged against him. "I am not angry with you. I am disappointed in you. I thought you trusted me, and, of course, I will obey you, what other choice do I have?"

That he would have preferred her anger to disappointment stabbed at his heart and that she would obey because there was nothing else left to her did not set well with him. And that he lacked a response frustrated him beyond measure, but then what could he say?

"I wish we could have stayed here just you and me and

have grown to know each other better, then neither of us would ever question what the other said since trust would have been established between us and neither of us would ever doubt the other's word." She rested her head on his chest.

Again, he was at a loss for words. What was there to say to her when she was right? He would have preferred to remain there alone with her, grow to know her, trust her without a doubt, make love to her, and fall more deeply in love with her.

He should have known her anger was fleeting and how could he blame her? His father's arrival had changed everything, and he had expected her to accept it all without question. She had taken the time to discuss things with him, share opinions, see what came of both their thoughts, but most importantly she had told him she would speak truthfully with him, and he had accused her of lying.

The problem was he could not be sure if she had lied. Did he believe his mother, who had always kept an honest word with him even if he had disagreed with her or his wife, who he had only come to know and who had already lied to him once?

Regardless, she had done what he had ordered and drank the brew, but how could he be sure if it would work.

Rannick glanced down to see his wife had fallen asleep. He pulled his cloak to tuck around her and keep her warm against the cold that stung the air. Too much had happened in a short period of time. One day he was alone, content or so he thought, in his solitude, then Bliss had appeared, and it all changed. He could curse her for disrupting his plans or he could be grateful that she had rescued him from them. He believed the latter was a much better choice.

Having Bliss in his life had turned death from friend to foe. He had never had the burning urge to live as he now did since Bliss entered his life. Never had he wanted to share his life with someone as he did now with Bliss. Never had he thought he could love with such an intensity as he loved Bliss.

She may have been a fool for marrying him, but he was probably the bigger fool for not only falling in love with her but hoping for the impossible—that she would love him in return.

It was not a long way to the keep when on horses and though warriors rode along with them, Rannick still kept a keen eye on his surroundings.

"You favor this wife," his father said, after bringing his horse alongside Rannick's horse.

Rannick had no trouble admitting it. "I do favor her. She is a good woman with a kind heart."

"She is also courageous for marrying you and for standing up to me when I questioned her ability to bear a child."

Rannick turned ready to defend his wife.

His father held up his hand as if in surrender. "Save your reprimand, she was more than capable of correcting me. She told me large, small, thin, plump, it did not matter when it came to delivering a bairn. It is good she has delivered many bairns. Her knowledge will help her when her time comes."

"I will not let what happened to Cecilia happen to Bliss," Rannick said.

His father took on an angry tone. "It infuriates me to think we had or could still have a traitor among us."

"Not for long," Rannick said, his anger far outweighing his father's.

"I have news for your wife that I am sure will please her to hear," his father said.

"Good news would be more than welcomed for a change," Rannick said.

"Share it with her when she wakes. Her sister Elysia has

wed a farmer, though remind her that her sister Annis could still be forced to wed if Bliss fails to keep her end of the bargain." His father grinned. "Though, somehow I do not think that will be a problem and that pleases me."

"Unless, of course, Annis finds her own husband as Elysia has, then the bargain no longer holds any worth," Rannick said, deflating his father's grin, though laughter replaced it.

"From what I hear about Annis and her stubborn nature, I doubt that is even a possibility."

Rannick ignored his father's smug laugh. "How do things go with Clan MacBridan?"

His father's grin vanished. "I am afraid things worsen with Clan MacBridan and battle is on the horizon for your friend Odran, though I do not know how any sane person would go against his infamous warrior skills."

"I do believe there are more insane people in the world than sane people, Da," Rannick said. "Odran will reach out to me if necessary."

"And you will go?"

Rannick thought of his conversation with Bliss and his answer came easily. "My wife would be disappointed in me if I did not help my friend."

His father turned his head, looking off in the distance. "Sometimes we have no choice."

Rannick seized on the moment. "Did you kill the MacWilliam bairn?" He caught the surprised look on his father's face and thought he might not answer the question. Rannick was pleased to learn otherwise.

"Wagging tongues spread that news and I saw no reason to stop it since the King would be pleased to hear it. However, the bairn was already dead, an illness having taken her, when we finally found out her whereabouts."

"How could you be sure it was the MacWilliam bairn?" Rannick asked.

169

"We discovered where Gunna had gone and that led us to the bairn."

Bliss did not stir, feigning sleep when she had woken and heard her husband ask his father about the MacWilliam bairn. She had wanted to hear what he had to say and being she had, she began to shift gently in her husband's arms.

"We will talk more at home," his father said when he saw Bliss waking, and rode off.

"How much did you hear?" Rannick asked, having felt the change in his wife's body before she visibly stirred.

Bliss wasn't surprised her husband was aware that she had woken. After all, he was accustomed to her slightest movements from the time she spent in his arms each night.

"From when you asked him about the MacWilliam bairn," she said, sitting up straighter so she could look upon his face. Most would think a person's eyes would be drawn to his scar, but hers were always drawn to his eyes. They were expressive eyes, letting her see bits of him now and again that he thought he hid, other times they warned to keep a distance, and yet other times one shivered from the empty coldness that nestled in them. At the moment, his eyes were warm and attentive, drawing her in like a comforting embrace.

"There is good news to share with you," Rannick said and hurried to tell her knowing it would bring her great relief. "Your sister Elysia married a farmer from what my father said.

A smile captured Bliss's entire face. "I am so happy. Now Elysia is safe, Saber will see to it. I was so worried about her. She is a kind, sweet soul and wanted no warrior as husband, but a man gentle in nature."

"One less sister to worry about," he said.

Bliss ventured to ask, "Perhaps one day, she and her husband can make their home at Clan MacClaren."

"Perhaps," he said, though knowing what he did, that

170

would never happen.

"Thank you for that wonderful news, but you used it to avoid speaking about the MacWilliam bairn. There is a chance she could still be alive," Bliss suggested.

Rannick thought otherwise. "It is unlikely my father would make such a mistake."

"It would be easy and wise to convince someone that an already deceased bairn was the MacWilliam lass, giving time to the one who protects her to seek a safe place."

"You speak of Gunna, the servant who Lady Aila entrusted her daughter to," Rannick said, giving her suggestion thought.

"Who better?" Bliss said. "And does anyone know what happened to her? Can it be confirmed she died, or did she simply disappear? And if she did, did she take the MacWilliam bairn with her? If so, that means the bairn lives and that also means there is a chance to end the curse."

***

It did not take long for them to reach the village. Rannick had remained silent after she had mentioned there was a chance to end the curse if the MacWilliam bairn actually survived. And that returned something to him that had long been lost... a shred of hope.

He watched as his wife looked with a mixture of worry and annoyance at the way some people turned their backs on him as he directed his horse slowly through the village. Others showed their disgust with his presence by spitting at the ground as he neared them and still others gripped at crude amulets that hung at their neck in protection against evil.

Bliss's stomach churned with concern, and she voiced her worries. "How can this place be safe for you and me with the way so many look at you with such hatred? They would be relieved to see you dead. Who then can we trust?"

"They have a right to hate me," Rannick said. "I am heir to the clan as well as the curse as would be any bairn I sire, which makes the curse and their suffering never-ending."

"They look well-fed, their homes well-maintained, their garments in good condition. What is there for them to hate?" she asked.

"Illness and death."

"Both are part of life. No one escapes them," she argued.

"The clan has seen more than its share."

Bliss was uncertain what to do, but she was a healer so she would see if she could heal the troubles here. "I will see what I can do to help the people."

"NAY!" his stern shout had people turning away and scurrying off in fright. "You will go nowhere without my permission—without me."

Bliss would miss her freedom of doing as she pleased, but she understood her husband's reluctance to let her wander on her own. After the attacks they had survived, he would not want to return home only to lose her here among his clan. Especially since it was possible that whoever was responsible for Shona's death and possibly Rannick's other two wives as well could still live among them. So, she held her tongue—for now.

"Look at me, wife," Rannick ordered when she failed to respond.

Bliss turned her eyes on his and was not surprised to see anger sparking in them.

"You will give me your word that you will go nowhere without my permission," he demanded, just the thought of her doing so sending a fear through him that chilled him to the bone.

"I cannot do that, Rannick."

Her gentle response, not a bit of anger to it, caught him

off guard.

Bliss continued before he could argue further with her. "I am a healer, a reluctant one at first, thinking I had no skill for it until Kendesa showed me otherwise. Now that I know differently, I cannot turn away when someone is in need of healing or if a bairn needs to be delivered. If I should be called upon to help anyone in your clan, I will gladly do so. While I will keep you apprised of my whereabouts, there may come a time when that is not possible, thus I will not give you my word when I know I may not be able to keep it."

Her truthfulness was admirable but... "I care not if you should be needed, I will know where you are at all times, or you go nowhere." He pressed his finger to her lips before she could respond. "All I will hear from you is... aye, my lord."

Was that what he was now—not Rannick, but my lord? The thought troubled her. Had their arrival here changed things far more than she had anticipated?

"Aye, my lord," Bliss said.

Once in front of the keep and dismounted, Rannick took her arm to climb the few steps.

"Your mother will see your wife settled while we talk," his father said, dismounting his horse.

"I will see my wife settled, and we will talk later, Da," Rannick said and hurried Bliss up the steps.

"Rannick!" his mum cried out when they entered the Great Hall, and she ran to him.

He released his wife to take hold of his mum, hugging her close, and realized it was the first time he had hugged his mum in years, and it felt good to have her arms around him again. Memories returned of his father admonishing his mum for hugging him too much and her ignoring his da completely. As he grew older, he would protest, as a show for others, when he actually enjoyed his mum's loving hugs. Then one day came when he had stepped away from her when she went to hug him. He could still see the hurt on her face and the tears that had gathered in her eyes before she turned and hurried away. He had done it for her own good, fearful if the curse realized how much his mum meant to him, death would claim her.

"I am delighted and full of joy that you have returned home and with your wife," his mum said, her heart swelling with delight that he hugged her.

"It was necessary," he said.

His mum's brow scrunched as she asked, "Necessary?"

"Do not bother your mother with nonsense, son," his father said, his strides strong as he approached his wife. "We really should speak now, Rannick. Let your mum see to your wife."

"Lord Lochlann!"

Lochlann turned ready to reprimand whoever disturbed him.

"News that cannot wait," Lawler said.

"Go, Da, I will find you when I am done," Rannick said.

"See that you do," his father ordered and left the keep with Lawler.

"Something troubles you, Rannick, what is it?" his mum asked, sudden worry deepening her scrunched brow.

"There is much that troubles me, Mum, but one more immediate problem than the others at the moment. We will talk in my bedchamber," he said and stepped aside for his mum to precede him.

Bliss was impressed that Rannick allowed his mum to take the lead. Most men would have expected the woman to follow behind him and it reminded her just how right she was about her husband having a kind and also thoughtful heart and soul.

It was a climb to the third floor and Bliss was shocked at the size of Rannick's bedchamber and his bed. It could

174

sleep three people easily. The stone fireplace was sizeable enough to heat the room comfortably. Chests sat stacked on top of one another and a long bench sat in front of the hearth with small stools tucked beneath. A table that would have easily accommodated her and her sisters rested against one wall, benches shoved beneath. And the lone window's heavy wood shutters were closed tight. Thankfully, with the fire burning brightly in the hearth and the many lit candles, the room held sufficient light.

"There is a room across from this one, small but sufficient for a lady's solar unless," —Rannick's mum turned to him— "you wish it for yourself."

"Bliss is welcomed to it," Rannick said and wasted no time seeing that he got an answer to the question that had gnawed at him. "Lawler came to you with a request of mine, who did you go to for the mixture?"

"Is there a problem with the potion?" his mum asked.

Bliss went to explain.

"Hold your tongue, wife. I will have my mum answer," Rannick commanded.

"Really, Rannick, this is not appropriate talk for a mother and son," his mum scolded.

"You will answer me, Mum," Rannick ordered.

His mum's cheeks blossomed red. "It was given to me by our healer who your father sent away," his mum said with a sense of regret.

"The mixture could have lost its potency," Bliss said, though she did not believe that, but she did not wish to claim Rannick's mum a liar.

His mum's cheeks bloomed red once again.

Rannick's brow shot up in question.

"I will say that I know for a fact the mixture remains potent," his mum said. "Now I will leave you to yourselves. There will be food and drink waiting for you in the Great Hall." She left in a flurry, her cheeks stinging red.

Bliss went to speak after Rannick's mum shut the door, but his hand went up and he shook his head, stopping her. "I will give you the benefit of the doubt on this, wife. That you were mistaken in your judgment. And I will have your word that you will continue to take the mixture."

"I give you my word, Rannick, but I do so under protest. And I will have your word that if I get with child, the blame will rest on your shoulders not mine."

"I have no worry of that happening, so I give you my word, as unnecessary as it is, that you will not be blamed," he said. "Now I must go see what news was brought to my father that could not wait while you wait here for me."

Bliss dropped down to sit on the bench in front of the hearth. She shook her head perplexed. Something was wrong somewhere. The mixture she had received was worthless. Why then did it work for Rannick's mum? Unless she needed it no more and had not realized it.

There was another explanation, though it did not seem plausible. Someone changed the pouches and gave Bliss a worthless potion. But that made absolutely no sense. People wanted her and Rannick dead. This was just the opposite. Someone wished an heir to Clan MacClaren. Could Lawler have switched pouches? He was loyal to Lord Lochlann.

Bliss intended to find out and she intended to hold her husband to his word when she got with child, for there was no doubt she would get with child, and that brought a smile to her face.

Chapter 18

Rannick sat in silence during supper, his thoughts lingering on the news that he had learned earlier. They had been followed after leaving the cottage by a group of about eight, possibly more men from what the tracker had found. His father had arrived just in time or else…

He stabbed at the piece of meat in the wooden bowl with his knife, his anger just as volatile now as it had been when he had learned the news. He would have never been able to keep his wife safe against a group that size. And his fury at what she might have suffered angered him all the more. The tracker who had discovered the tracks told Lawler that the group had turned off in a different direction, after following at a brief distance, no doubt realizing Rannick was returning to the keep. They probably did not have sufficient men to go against his father's numerous and highly skilled warriors.

As much as he had not wanted to return home, he was grateful he had. Here he could keep his wife well-protected while he searched for the culprit responsible for it all. He would also reach out to Odran and Brogan and let them know what had happened and warn them to be careful.

"No need for worry, son," his father said, sitting next to him on the dais. "You and Bliss are safe here. No harm will come to either of you."

"I cannot believe someone wishes death upon the both of you," Helice said, shaking her head. "Everyone suffers enough. Why inflict more on us?" Her face pinched in annoyance. "It is that curse. It will never let us know peace."

Bliss remained as silent as her husband. She barely ate,

177

finding her surroundings far too uncomfortable. Warriors filled many of the tables and indulged in loud talk and spats of laughter. The long table on the dais was made for limited conversation to the person next to you and Bliss was relieved that her husband was the only one who she sat beside.

She much preferred the simple days she had spent with him alone in the confines of the cottage compared to the large keep. It felt like a home, and a home was something she had never thought she would find with Rannick.

"You need to eat."

Bliss raised her head, turning to respond and was surprised to find he had lowered his head down, his face close to hers. Instinctively, her hand moved to touch his face, the way she had grown accustomed to doing when they had been alone but stopped herself. It would not be appropriate here.

She rested her hands in her lap. "I am not hungry."

"Eat anyway and that is not a request, wife," he said. "You have not eaten since early this morning."

"My stomach churns. Food will not sit well," she said, her stomach uneasy since their arrival there.

Concern tightened the lines in his brow. "Is there something that can ease it?"

"I can make a brew that may offer some relief," she said and went to slip off her chair, eager to get away.

Rannick's hand quickly went to her shoulder. "Stay where you are, a servant will see to the brew according to your directions."

She did not trust anyone to brew what she needed, especially with what happened to Shona, and she reminded him of that. "It is best I see for myself what goes in it."

Rannick immediately understood and it reminded him that more precautions were necessary.

A rush of cold air sent the fire's flames dancing wildly and all heads turned to the door and hands went to daggers at

178

the warriors' waists when it swung open wide, a strong wind ushering in a warrior and a young man.

The warrior escorted the young man to the dais and all eyes followed them.

"This one insists his wife needs help," the warrior said, keeping close to the young man's side.

The young man hurried to speak, looking directly at Lord Lochlann. "I am Owen. It is my wife, Maura, my lord. Her time has come to deliver our bairn, but she is having much difficulty. She needs help. Please, my lord, send help."

"Does anyone know this man?" Lord Lochlann called out. "He is unfamiliar to me."

"I am busy working the farm, my lord, and rarely visit the village," Owen said, twisting his hands nervously.

"I stopped by his croft once. He is the size of the man I spoke to, and his hair was dark like this one. His wife was also round with child," a warrior confirmed.

Bliss hurried to her feet. "I can help your wife."

Rannick stood and sent his wife a heated glare. "I forbid you to go. It is not safe."

Bliss remained calm, understanding her husband's concern and worried herself, but there was someone in need of her skills. "I cannot leave a woman to suffer and possibly die when I can help her."

"It is a trap!" Lord Lochlann claimed loudly. "We cannot know for sure who this man is."

Silence fell over the Great Hall and the young man visibly trembled.

"Take him and beat the truth out of him," Lord Lochlann ordered.

"Nay!" Bliss shouted.

"Hold your tongue, woman, or suffer for it," Lord Lochlann threatened.

Rannick turned, grabbed his father by his shirt, and yanked him toward him. "Threaten my wife again and you

179

will be the one to suffer for it." He released him sending him tumbling back.

Lord Lochlann's face turned a molten red and he took a step toward his son.

"One word, Da, just one word and you will see for yourself the evil that exists in me," Rannick warned and turned to his wife. "Stay put." He did not wait for her response, the shocked look on her face telling him she was too stunned to do anything.

Bliss's eyes followed him along with the dead silence as he walked around the dais to come to a stop in front of Owen, whose trembling had worsened. For a moment, she had feared he would strike his father and she worried what his warriors would do, though seeing them look upon her husband with intense fear she doubted they would have lifted a hand to help Lord Lochlann.

"Do you know who I am, Owen?" Rannick asked.

Owen nodded, tears pooling in his eyes. "Aye, Lord Rannick."

"Then you know there is nothing I will not do to you to learn the truth. So, save me the time and you the pain and suffering and tell me the truth. Is it a trap you come to lead me and my wife to?"

Tears started running down Owen's cheeks. "It is a trap, my lord. Three men burst into our home, threatened my wife, Maura, hit her several times to tell me that she would suffer far worse if I did not do as they said. And the truth is that she is in labor and having a difficult time. I do not want to lose my wife and bairn, my lord."

"Are there more than three men?" Rannick asked, realizing that if he did not have Bliss in his life, he would have little sympathy for the man. That realization struck him like a punch to the gut. He had truly lost his humanity and if it had not been for Bliss, he would have lost it forever. He owed his wife much.

"I only saw three," Owen said, brushing away his tears.

"What croft do you work, and did you come on foot or by horse, and did anyone follow you?" Rannick asked.

"Wilkins's croft and by horse, though I do not know if anyone followed me. I was so worried for my wife that all I could think about was getting here and getting the healer's help."

"Not even the consequences of your lies?" Rannick asked.

"I will suffer what I must as long as my wife and bairn survive, my lord," Owen said with a bob of his head.

"That is admirable of you, Owen," Rannick said.

Owen shook his head. "Nay, my lord, it is what a man does for the woman he loves."

There was truth to that since Rannick would do the same for Bliss. "We will go rescue your wife and return her here so my wife can help her."

"NAY!" Bliss called out. "I go with you. Maura may not be able to travel."

Rannick turned and pointed a finger at her. "You are not going."

"I am going," Bliss said with a stubborn tilt of her chin.

"You will obey your husband!" Lord Lochlann shouted at Bliss.

"Stay out of this, Da!" Rannick warned.

Helice laid her hand on her husband's arm. "Let them be, Lochlann."

He went to argue with her, his face turning red once again.

"Do you wish to fight our son or have him take his leave and never see our grandchild?" Helice asked in a whisper, though she knew that was unlikely with Bliss taking the brew.

Lord Lochlann clamped his mouth shut and it took great effort for him to keep it that way.

"You are not going," Rannick reiterated tersely.

Bliss knew arguing with him would do no good, but how did she make him understand the importance that she went with him? She walked around the dais and did the only thing she could think of—she pleaded with him for the safety of the woman and bairn.

"Please, Rannick, the woman is in need. I cannot bear the thought that she and her bairn could die because my life is considered more important than hers. You protect me and keep me safe, and I have no doubt you will continue to do so no matter the circumstances." She felt a bit guilty because no doubt this situation brought back memories of losing his first wife in childbirth and that could possibly be a deciding factor for him.

"Your promise that you will obey my every word," he demanded, silently admonishing himself for allowing her to convince him.

"Aye, husband, I will obey your every word," she agreed.

"Then gather what you need, we leave shortly," he said, a scowl settling over him since he knew he would regret his decision.

Bliss broke out in a huge smile and without thought, kissed his cheek, then said, "I am grateful, husband. You are a good man and I love you so very much."

Rannick stood there too shocked to speak along with everyone else, the only sound heard was that of the crackling fire. Had she meant it? Did she truly love him? She had told him she would be honest with him or was this for the benefit of others? This was going to torment him until he could speak with her alone. What then? Did he come right out and ask?

The continued silence penetrated his confused thought and he turned to Lawler, seated at one of the tables, and ordered, "Ready thirty men."

Lawler nodded and before he could order the warriors present to follow him, they all stood and waited to follow him out.

Once the Great Hall emptied of warriors, Rannick placed a strong hand on Owen's shoulder. "Tell me now if there is anything else I should know."

"I wish there was more I could tell you that would help. As I said, my only thought was to fetch the healer to help my wife."

"You did not know my wife and I only arrived here today, did you?" Rannick asked.

"No, my lord, that news had not yet reached the croft."

Rannick gave his shoulder a squeeze. "You will obey my commands, Owen."

Owen bobbed his head. "Aye, my lord."

"Go wait with the warriors."

Owen turned and walked only a short distance before he stopped and turned around. "It may not be important, my lord, but I heard the howl of a wolf when I left the cottage. I have not heard a wolf's cry since I was very young."

"A bad omen," his mum said after Owen hurried off.

"Foolish superstition," Lord Lochlann admonished.

Rannick said nothing, his thoughts on some of the things Owen had said.

"I am ready," Bliss announced entering the room, the hood of her cloak pulled up on her head, her healing pouch attached at her waist, and a small sack in hand.

Do you truly love me? He wished he could voice his thought, but now was not the time. He held his hand out to her and she hurried to take it.

"Every word, wife," he reminded.

"Aye, I will obey your every word, husband," she confirmed.

Rannick looked to his father. "You need to post more warriors. This could also be a diversion so an attack could more easily be made on the village and keep."

"The thought crossed my mind as well. I will see it done," his father said. "And you and Bliss return home safely."

"You ride with me," Rannick said as he left the Great Hall with his wife. "I will not have your horse spooked or separated from me if attacked on the way there."

"As you say, husband," she said.

"That is the only response I will hear from you this night," he reminded and turned away to speak with Lawler.

Bliss hugged the sack to her chest, relieved he had said nothing about her declaration of love. She did not know from where it had come. It had slipped out of her mouth of its own accord, or had it been the love in her heart that had made it so easy to say? She had to admit that it had left her feeling more gleeful than regretful, which made her believe it had been the right thing to do. She did not think she would ever have had the courage to tell him how she felt. And yet, the words had come naturally, as if it was something she had said every day to him.

She sighed softly. It was done and could not be undone, and she would not take the words back if she could.

Rannick heard his wife sigh even as soft as it was and watched as her head lowered, her eyes focused on the ground.

He went to her and lifted her chin with one finger. "Regrets, wife?"

"Not one regret, husband," she said.

Did he have his answer? Was she telling him that she did not regret a thing she had said? Did she truly love him? There was no time to find out. Or did he fear what she might say?

He lifted her onto the horse and mounted afterwards. His arms went around her to take the reins and he whispered in her ear, "Silence. No talk so we may listen for what awaits us."

Bliss nodded and her stomach churned since there was a good chance they were riding into a possible ambush.

***

They rode more slowly than Bliss would have liked, but she remained silent as her husband had ordered. Though, it did seem to her that he was taking his time getting there. She grew more impatient when they stopped after a while and simply remained as they were... waiting, but for what?

Lawler approached. "It is how you thought, my lord."

"Bring me, Owen," Rannick ordered and dismounted, then reached up and lifted his wife off the horse. He shook his head at her when she looked ready to speak and he was glad she kept her word and remained silent and that she nodded when he ordered her to remain by the horse.

He walked only a short distance away when he saw Lawler, Owen in front of him.

"Is there a problem, my lord?" Owen asked. "We go so slow, and I am eager to return to Maura."

"I'm afraid there is a problem," Rannick said.

"What is it?" Owen asked anxiously.

A sudden scowl captured Rannick's face. "You lied to me, though at first you were convincing which is why I kept you talking. The more a liar talks, the more easily you can catch the lies."

"I swear, my lord, I have not lied, Maura—"

"I believe that part about Maura needing help, pleading for it, but the words were not yours. They belonged to Maura's husband, who begged you not to hurt his wife. And I am telling you now, if you or any of the other men have hurt Owen and Maura, you will suffer greatly," Rannick threatened.

"I have no worry, my lord, since I speak the truth,"

185

Owen insisted.

"You rushed to the keep looking for the healer—my wife—who you did not know had arrived there just today."

"Nay, I did not know your wife was there or that she was a healer," Owen said quickly.

"Then what healer did you expect to find?" Rannick asked.

"The one my wife told me to find, Berdina," Owen said, "though I would take any healer who can help my Maura."

"The problem with that, Owen, is that Berdina left the clan months ago," Rannick said, "and you would have known that if you were actually Owen."

The young man drew his shoulders back and his demeanor turned defiant. "Do what you will with me. I will tell you nothing."

"That is where you are wrong. You are going to tell me everything," Rannick said and gave a nod to Lawler.

The two warriors behind him grabbed his arms to hold behind his back while Lawler shoved a rag into the young man's mouth.

"I see in your eyes that you laugh thinking… how can you tell me anything with a rag stuffed in your mouth?" A malicious grin settled along Rannick's mouth. "You see, I don't want your friends to hear you scream when I cut off one of your fingers, though I may take two to show you I will keep going until you have nothing but nubs left, unless you want to save yourself the pain and suffering and tell me what I want to know and thus keep all your fingers."

The young man stuck his chin up in defiance.

"That insolence will cost you three fingers," Rannick said and nodded to Lawler.

The young man fought the two warriors who yanked his arm from behind his back, but in the end, he lost three fingers, though after he lost the first one his eyes pleaded with Rannick to stop.

186

"You made your choice," Rannick said and lopped off two more.

The young man could not talk fast enough. He told them how many men waited and that they were sent from different clans to see the task done, once it was learned that Rannick had taken a fourth wife. The last failed attempt had seen six men sent ahead to see it done. One had waited in the woods to report back if the others all failed. When the lone man returned with the news that all five men were dead, the group hurried to the cottage, fearing Rannick would return to the keep before they could stop him. They arrived too late. They followed to see that Rannick was returning home but to be sure they sent one man to confirm it.

Three of them stopped at Owen's croft to see if they could learn anything more and stumbled upon the woman in labor. They devised a quick plan. The others were fetched, twenty men waited in the woods surrounding the cottage and two waited inside to kill Rannick's wife when she entered. They had not been sure it would work, but they had been willing to take the chance, since they were committed to seeing the curse finally brought to an end.

Rannick kept his fury contained as he asked, "Has Owen and Maura been harmed?"

"The man suffered a beating trying to protect his wife and the woman suffered some bruises trying to stop the men from hurting her husband," the young man said.

"While she labored in pain?" Rannick snapped.

"Aye," the young man admitted as he agonized in his own pain. "Please. Please allow your healer to help me."

"My wife will help you," Rannick said, "after she helps the woman who labors in pain." He turned to Lawler. "Secure him and his mouth and leave him. We will pick him up on our return."

"The blood, my lord, the wolf I heard will smell it," the young man pleaded.

187

"Then he is welcomed to you," Rannick said and walked away, the man having no chance to plead for mercy, a rag once again shoved into his mouth.

Bliss had heard it all. "I could wrap his hand," she offered when her husband approached.

"He came here to see us dead, and you wish to help him?" Rannick asked, shaking his head.

"It would help keep him alive so that you can question him more," she said.

Rannick capitulated. "A warrior will see to his hand while other warriors will see to the men in the woods before they can raise their weapons. That leaves the men in the cottage."

"They may attempt to hurt the couple once a warrior enters," she said, worried for both.

"I will not give them the chance," Rannick said and took her hand in his. "We walk from here."

"You will be careful," she said.

"Keep silent," Rannick ordered.

"That was not a request, husband," Bliss said in a hushed whisper.

Rannick turned a scowl on her when he spotted the touch of a smile on her lips and at that moment, he wanted desperately to kiss her. To make matters worse, he could see that she felt the same.

"Tonight, wife, tonight our vows get sealed," he whispered.

Chapter 19

"Maura, it is Lady Bliss, I am here to help you," Bliss called out, standing a short distance away from the cottage door.

The door barely squeaked open when her husband stepped in front of her, and three warriors rushed in one right after the other. Bliss waited anxiously, worried for the woman inside. It wasn't long before two men were dragged out of the cottage, still Rannick would not let her enter until he saw for himself that it was safe.

"Please… help my husband," Maura pleaded, sitting on the floor, her husband's bloody head resting in her lap.

"Nay, my wife. Help my wife," Owen said, his one eye badly bruised and swollen shut.

Bliss took charge and silently blessed her husband for following her instructions without question. He helped Owen up to sit in a chair while she got Maura to her feet and to the bed, the woman pleading the whole time for Bliss to tend Owen.

"I promise I will tend your husband, but first I must see to you," Bliss said gently and turned to her husband. "I need water at least three bucketsful."

Rannick had a warrior fetch them, having no intentions of leaving his wife alone.

It didn't take long to ascertain that Maura was doing all right, having suffered a bruise or two to her face and her labor having progressed without incident through the ordeal.

Once Bliss had Maura settled comfortably, she turned to Owen and was surprised to see that her husband had already cleaned the head wound, though blood still lingered on the

189

young man's face.

"All the blood is from the head wound," Rannick informed her.

"Thank you for helping me," Bliss said and examined Owen's wounds.

It did not take long to let Owen and his wife know that he would be fine. The bruises would heal, as would the wound. Afterward, she sent both men outside, though both men were reluctant to leave.

"Maura needs her privacy, and you will be right outside if I should need you," Bliss said to her husband, her hand on his upper arm as she escorted him to the door.

Rannick turned to her when they reached the door. "I will not move from outside this door."

"You have responsibilities out there as I do in here. See to them so we may return home as soon as this is done," she said with a soft smile.

He thought about the night ahead. "Aye, there is a responsibility I must see to this night." He looked to Owen, who stood by the bed holding his wife's hand. "Let's go, Owen."

Owen looked torn between leaving his wife and obeying Lord Rannick's command. Maura settled his dilemma, urging him to go.

Rannick clamped his hand down on Owen's shoulder before walking out and the man stiffened in fear. "You are a brave man, Owen, and did well by your wife and the clan. I am proud of you."

Bliss closed the door on a stunned Owen and her husband, her smile spreading as she turned and went to Maura.

***

Bliss relaxed against her husband as he directed his

horse away from the cottage. Ten MacClaren warriors had escorted the defeated warriors to the keep, their skills no match for MacClaren warriors. They would be questioned there, and their fate decided by Rannick and his father. Two warriors had fled and ten MacClaren warriors were in pursuit of them. Five warriors remained at the croft to make sure Owen and Maura were safe and five were returning with Bliss and Rannick.

"The bairn was so tiny," Rannick said as they rode toward home, two warriors leading the way with torches, a mass of clouds churning across the night sky.

"Most are," she said with a brief chuckle. "But he and his mum are good, the birth easier than I anticipated, and all is well with the family." She reached up and ran her hand gently across his cheek. "Are you all right, Rannick? I worried the birth might stir painful memories for you."

He leaned his face into her touch, her hand surprisingly warm on such a cold night. "My only thoughts were for your safety." Now that she had mentioned it to him, he was surprised he had had no thought of the loss of his first wife and bairn. The only thing that had mattered to him was keeping his wife safe.

"And my safety was not a worry to me with you by my side," she said.

There was something that he had given thought to with having seen his wife cradle the bairn. "Will it upset you to deliver bairn after bairn and have none of your own?"

"Nay, since fate will decide that," Bliss said, aware that tonight would be the start of the possibility that she would get with child.

"Fate has no say in it. You will carry no bairn of mine and you damn well will never carry another man's bairn," he said, angry at the thought of some other man touching her intimately.

"Aye, you are right about that. I will have no other man

191

touch me but you," she said and shuddered at the thought.

The words rushed out of his mouth, not able to hold them back any longer. "Why did you claim you loved me?" His body grew taut as her body stiffened against him and he waited for her to tell him it was for the benefit of those in the Great Hall. Surprisingly, her body suddenly relaxed once again, leaning comfortably against him.

"I promised you the truth and I spoke it when I said I love you very much. I cannot say when I realized that I love you. It just seemed like I always did, as if we were meant to be." She gave a tender laugh. "Of course, I had to get over being frightened of you first, not that you still don't frighten me at times, but nothing like when I first laid eyes on you—thankfully." She sighed. "I never thought I would ever find love, nor do I expect you to love me in return, but that will not change how I feel about you. My love for you is deep in my heart and there is where it will stay always, no matter how you feel about me."

Rannick stared at her baffled. She loved him. She honestly loved him. His heart swelled with a joy he had never known in his entire life, and he was about to tell her the same when he caught a sudden movement out of the corner of his eye. He didn't hesitate. He clamped his arm around his wife tight and threw them both off the horse. He felt something slash at his shoulder just before they hit the ground.

He feared for Bliss, having wrapped himself around her to shield her and they hit the ground hard. He couldn't take the chance of seeing to her first. He, first, had to see to the man who had attacked them.

He swiped his dagger from its sheath and tossed his cloak off as he bolted to his feet and just in time. The man was nearly on top of him, his only weapon a knife. He ran straight at Rannick, a foolish move. It took all of two moves to fell the man and by then the warriors with him were on top of the culprit.

Rannick hurried to his wife struggling to sit up. "Slow and easy," he said, crouching down to slip his arm beneath her back to help ease her up.

Bliss grabbed his arm to rest her head against it and steady herself. "What happened?"

"One of the two men we failed to capture attacked. I caught a glimpse of him as he lunged for us from a low hanging branch and threw us off the horse."

Bliss felt something sticky on her face and her nose gave a sniff. She was familiar with the scent. "Blood."

"What?" Rannick said, easing her away from him and his gut twisted when he saw the blood on her cheek. "You've been hurt."

"Nay, you have," she said, her eyes following the trail of blood up his sleeve to the larger pool of blood on his shoulder. "Let me see," she urged, trying to hurry to her feet and being struck fast and hard with dizziness that sent her falling back against her husband.

"You will stay put," he ordered. "You took a hard hit."

"But you're bleeding," she argued.

"It is a scratch, nothing more," he insisted.

"The blood tells me differently," she continued to argue as the dizziness faded.

"You can look at it once we're home," he said. "I am going to ease you up in my arms."

"To my feet," she corrected, but of course he did as he pleased, and she found herself snug in his arms.

She was relieved when they were traveling once again, anxious to get home and tend his shoulder. She reassured him repeatedly that she felt much better when he asked how she was feeling.

"I will take you at your word, wife, since you promised to be truthful to me," he said.

"I am glad you believe me, for I speak the truth to you,"

she said and was relieved to see the village come into sight.

Torches were lit throughout the village and people mulled about, whispers circulating, and surprised eyes greeting Rannick and Bliss as they rode to the keep.

Rannick knew why they lingered and what they thought. They expected him to return home with a dead wife. They believed it was only a matter time before the curse claimed her and he feared the same.

"I am good to walk on my own," Bliss said when they stopped in front of the keep. "And I will see to that wound of yours right away and do not try to dissuade me."

He rubbed at the blood that had dried on her face, but it stubbornly refused to come off. "Giving orders, wife?"

"Aye, when it comes to wounds, I know best, and you will pay heed."

He lowered his head bringing his lips close to hers. "I will give you this one, wife, but be warned I do not take well to orders."

"Even orders given out of love?" she asked and kissed his lips lightly.

It was on his lips to tell her that he loved her, but not here on the horse with others about. He not only wanted to tell her, but also show her how much he loved her.

While Rannick wanted to rush her off the horse, into the keep, and up to their bedchamber, he managed to contain his impatience and tempered their steps worried Bliss might grow dizzy again.

"Oh, my lord!" Helice cried out upon seeing them. "You have both been injured."

"Nay, Mum," Rannick was quick to explain. "The blood on Bliss's face is from the small wound on my shoulder."

"Which I intend to see to right away," Bliss said.

"Have whatever Bliss needs sent to our bedchamber, Mum, while I take a moment to speak with Da," he ordered, giving no one a chance to say otherwise and, leaving his wife's side, followed his father to the hearth where they could talk more privately.

"The warriors are being held in a pen behind the keep," his father informed him.

"They are from various small clans," Rannick said, "though I cannot say for sure if their clan chieftains ordered them to gather. There is more we need to find out from those we imprisoned."

"It will do them good to worry what awaits them. Now go and let your wife tend your wound and get some rest. You both have had a long, tiring day," his father ordered with concern.

Rannick nodded and went to turn away.

"Rannick," his father said gently and Rannick looked back at him. "I am glad you both returned home safely, and your wife is far more courageous than I had thought. She does the clan proud."

Rannick smiled. "Did Mum have a talk with you?"

His father's eyes went wide, startled at seeing his son smile, then he smiled himself. "She made me see reason as she usually does but no one had to tell me how courageous your wife is, that is there for all to see."

"That it is, Da," he agreed with pride. "I will see you in the morning."

Rannick hurried his steps to his wife.

"Do not worry, my order trumps his when it comes to healing."

Rannick almost laughed upon hearing his wife's remark to his mum, though he saw how his mum's worry eased upon Bliss's reassurance and he was grateful to her for calming his mum's concern. He decided he would ease her worries even more.

He wrapped his arm around his mum's shoulders, and he kissed her temple. "No worries, Mum, my wife is a tyrant when it comes to healing."

Helice's mouth would have fallen open if she did not hurry and close it shut. Her son had not hugged and kissed her like that in… she could not recall when. Tears rushed to pool in her eyes. She pressed her face against his chest, relishing the moment and silently blessing Bliss for healing her son.

Lochlann walked over to his wife and slipped his arm around her as Rannick and Bliss walked off, and she rested her head on his chest.

"Pray, Lochlann, pray hard that the curse does not take Bliss, for I do not think our son will survive such a loss."

Chapter 20

The servant rushed out of the bedchamber almost bumping into Bliss. Her eyes went wide seeing Rannick's scowling face and she quickly lowered her head and apologized, "Forgive me, my lady."

"Worry not, there is nothing to forgive," Bliss assured her, seeing that the young woman made sure to keep her head turned away from Rannick even though her eyes were focused on the floor. She did not blame her. Her husband could be far too intimidating. She offered the woman comfort, recalling her own fear when she had first met her husband. "I nearly collide with others when I rush around myself."

"Still, you should watch where you go," Rannick scolded.

"Please forgive me, my lord, I will do better," the young woman begged.

"Nonsense," Bliss said, seeing the woman's hands tremble and hurried to dismiss her and save her from more fear and worry. "You have done well, and we have no more need of your help tonight."

"Make sure all the servants know not to approach our bedchamber tonight unless I give permission," Rannick ordered.

The young woman's eyes burst wide and looked with fright at Rannick, then looked with pity on Bliss and, after a quick nod, rushed off.

Bliss frowned as she entered the room before her husband worried over the gossip the young servant's tongue would spread throughout the keep and the village. Did she

197

think Lord Rannick would ravage his wife with no care to her well-being? She almost shook her head at the thought but stopped. If she had not come to know better of her husband, she might have thought that herself upon first meeting him. Not now, though, not after experiencing his tender touch. She wished others knew he was not the monster they thought him to be.

She turned, a soft smile on her face. "Sit so I can see to your wound."

Before he did so, he removed his shirt, then sat on the bench at the table where two buckets of water and a stack of clean cloths sat. He spread his legs and with a snap of his hand ordered, "Come here."

For a moment, she hesitated. His narrowed, intense brown eyes igniting a bit of fright in her. Or was it her own apprehension about tonight that did that? It wasn't that she was not eager to seal their vows, it was what would eventually come of it and her husband's reaction to the consequences. She went to him and when she got close enough, his hands reached out to lock at her waist and tuck her close.

What he did next startled her. He grabbed one of the cloths, rinsed it in one of the buckets of water and gently wiped his blood off her face.

She thought to stop him, the care of his wound more important than the blood on her face, but it would be senseless. He would have it his way. Besides, his caring touch reminded her of how he had tended her with such gentleness when she had been wounded. She would have never expected that of him and thinking on it now, she wondered if it was one of the reasons she had fallen in love with him.

"You are feeling well?" he asked. "That was a hard fall you took off the horse."

"You fell as well," she reminded and closed her eyes a

198

moment when he gently rubbed near the corner of her eye with his thumb. His tender touch definitely was one of the reasons that she had fallen in love with him.

"Aye, but I am used to taking blunt hits like that. I doubt you are."

"You protected me," she said softly.

"Always," he whispered and drew her closer against him.

She backed away from him so quickly that he had no time to stop her, and his heated glare made her catch her breath, he looked so angry. She kept the tremble out of her voice that slowly spread through her body as she spoke. "You will not touch me or kiss me," —her shiver grew as his glare fired hotter— "until I see to your wound."

"And if I do not want to wait?" he challenged.

She bravely stepped between his legs, to gently lay her finger near his wound. "I will find no pleasure until your wound has been tended."

"Then see it done, wife, for I grow impatient," he ordered, relieved, since having foolishly thought her sudden step away from him a rejection.

Bliss got busy cleaning his wound, realizing she was just as eager as he was to seal their vows. She was careful with her touch, not wanting to hurt him.

"I am not delicate, Bliss," he said and slid his hands beneath her tunic to grip her backside, though he much preferred to feel her silky flesh rather than the soft wool of her underdress.

She caught the gasp in her throat when his hands squeezed her bottom. She had grown familiar with his touch, had enjoyed it, to her delight, and looked forward to more of it. Realizing that she loved him made it easier to enjoy intimacy with him, to welcome it instead of fear it as she had at the mere thought when she had struck the bargain with Lawler.

199

The only troubling thought that continued to plague her was that she knew the brew she drank did nothing to prevent her from getting with child. What would he do when his seed took root?

It didn't take long to tend his wound, though it could barely be called that. His shirt had done a good job of stopping the bleeding. It was more a surface wound, like a deep scratch, than a wound that could prove troublesome.

"It's nothing," he said when she looked about finished.

"You're right," she admitted, relieved. "You know about wounds?"

"Anyone who has been in battle knows wounds. One glance, and one knows the odds."

He took the cloth from her hand and dropped it in the bucket. Then his hands went to her tunic and slipped it off her before going to her hips and gathering her underdress up in his hands until he was easily able to slip his hands beneath and give her warm backside a squeeze.

"I need to tell you something," he said and rested his head between her breasts for a moment, but her hands raked their way through his hair to hug his head tight against her as if she did not want to let him go. He lingered there, her womanly scent drifting over him, his passion mounting, and his heart bursting with a depth of feeling that he never thought possible.

He stroked her backside and lost himself in her warmth, in her intoxicating scent, and he let his fingers roam slipping between her legs and when her legs separated just a bit, his hands rushed between them, and he slipped his fingers into her wetness.

She groaned and he did as well.

"Rannick," she whispered with a hungry desire he had never heard slip from a woman's lips.

"Look at me, Bliss," he demanded, and her eyes that had closed fluttered open and he reluctantly slipped his fingers out of her. "I need you to know something."

She cupped his face in her hands, his beard soft against her warm palms. "I need you. I love you."

"And I love you with all my heart and down to the depths of my soul," he confessed and watched her eyes spring open wide. "Like you, I do not know when love struck me, nor do I care. I only know that you brought me to life, started my heart beating again, caring again, wanting to live once again... to live and love with you. You are everything to me, Bliss, and if the curse should take you, I will follow wherever you go, for my heart would stop beating and I would not want to live life without you... I love you that deeply, that strongly, that fully. You have my love, Bliss, forever and always."

Tears trickled from Bliss's eyes, and she was suddenly swept up in his arms and carried to the bed. He placed her on her feet and had her naked soon enough, then swept her up again to deposit her on the bed. She had never seen him disrobe as fast as he did and in the next moment, he was in bed beside her, and she rushed into his arms as he turned to her.

She rested her brow to his, and whispered, "To love you and be loved by you is all I want."

"You ask for little, wife."

"Nay, what I ask for is the most precious thing a man and woman can give each other. And I am forever grateful we share it."

"Promise me, wife," he said, easing her hair away from her face as his eyes settled on hers. "Promise me that you will love me even when I am least loveable."

Bliss laughed softly. "That is easy to promise since I have already done so."

He silently thanked the heavens he had long thought abandoned him for his good fortune in finding Bliss and blessed fate for seeing them brought together. He also warned both of the havoc and pain he would rain done upon them if either should take her from him.

A sudden rapid pounding on the door had Rannick's heart slam against his chest as he bolted out of bed and reached for his sword.

"A troop of warriors try to free the prisoners!" Lawler shouted.

"I will be right there. Post two guards at this door," Rannick shouted back.

"Already done," Lawler called out.

While her husband hurried into his garments, Bliss threw her shift on after scurrying out of bed.

"You will be safe here. Do not leave this room," Rannick ordered.

"Nay, my skills may be needed," she argued.

"Not this time. You are to stay safe," he said and swung the door open and quickly addressed the guards. "Do not let her out of this room and let no one in."

He was gone before she could make him see reason. The clan had no healer. Who would see to the wounded? Her answer came unbidden... other warriors accustomed to tending the fallen. She shook her head and began to pace, wondering if this madness would ever stop.

Until the wrong is made right.

How could the wrong be made right when no MacWilliam lived? The possibility that the MacWilliam bairn may have lived still poked at her. And she wondered once again if this could be all the bairn's, now grown lass, doing? Was the bairn, now a grown woman seeing that the wrong was finally made right? But would that mean her husband's death?

She shook her head as her heart squeezed with fright. Never would she have thought of protecting the cursed lord, but that was her thought now... how to keep her husband safe.

Her worry deepened when she had to add logs to the dying fire, meaning more time than she would have liked had passed. This was more than a skirmish and why hadn't this group of warriors been spotted? Unless... she did not like to think that someone in the Clan MacClaren had joined ranks with them. Or was it more than one person?

She continued pacing unable to sit, her mind overrun with worry until a sudden shout halted her steps.

"GO! It is done!"

Her heart beat heavily against her chest at the sound of her husband's commanding voice.

The door flung open and Rannick stood in the doorway. Water drops glistened on his beard and his wet hair, as well as a few on his naked chest. He had made the effort to rid himself of all blood and she feared the fight had not been an easy one.

He clutched his hands at his sides. "Go to bed, wife, I will see you in the morning."

Bliss understood then, had seen it in some men after battle, the need to release the overpowering rage and courage it took to fight not only the enemy, but the fear of death itself stalking the battlefield, ready to whisk your life away.

He turned to leave.

"Rannick!" she cried out and he turned quickly. She didn't hesitate, she ran to him.

His arm caught her around the waist and her arms circled his neck. He lowered his brow to hers before she could kiss him. "My need is too great."

"So is mine," she said and stretched her hand out behind him to hurry the door shut as if that could stop him from leaving.

"You are playing with danger, Bliss," he warned.

"There is no danger here, only love," she said and slowly brought her lips to his.

His hand gripped the back of her head, holding it tight,

as his lips claimed hers and none too gently. His hunger and need were powerful, and a spark of fright mixed with her own raging passion.

Their lips remained locked in the kiss as he hurried her to the bed and when he released her, she rushed out of her shift and went to help him out of his plaid. He stopped her, giving her a gentle shove to land on the bed.

He was soon naked and fell down on the bed nearly on top of her but stopped himself before their bodies touched. He slipped his arm under her waist and with a quick lift had her head on the pillow and her body positioned perfectly beneath him.

He nudged at her legs with his knee. "Spread them."

She quickly obliged.

He squeezed his eyes shut tightly and grimaced.

"Rannick?" she questioned softly.

"I should go slow, easy," he said as if warning himself.

She grabbed his arms, taut at both sides of her as he hovered slightly above her. "Nay! Nay! I cannot wait. I will not wait another moment." She arched her body against his and gasped when she felt the size of him poke against her.

"I do not want to hurt you," he said.

"You hurt me more by delaying, my need for you as great as yours," she argued.

He kissed her quickly and roughly, her words encouraging him and as he moved his lips off hers, he slipped into her.

She welcomed him with a soft moan and squeezed his arms, then her head shot back, and she cried out as he plunged fully into her.

He tried to slow and ease his thrusts not wanting to hurt her, but it was more than a need he felt… he felt as if he had found a piece of himself that had been missing. He felt whole joined with her.

Bliss soon matched his powerful rhythm. It came

naturally and was filled with an intense passion that had waves of pleasure flowing through her. But then she loved her husband and she believed that made all the difference.

Rannick always kept in control when he coupled, but not this time. Passion overpowered him or maybe it was love that made him lose control, either way he could not contain his need. He was close to bursting.

"Rannick!"

He was relieved and pleased to hear the pleading in her voice and he urged, "Hold on tight, *mo ghràdh*." He moved rapidly taking them over the edge and into the oblivion of pure pleasure.

Bliss let out a scream as the world exploded around her with such intensity that she feared she might faint from the endless bursting pleasure. She shivered when her husband let out a roar, sounding more like a majestic beast than a man, and she feared it echoed throughout the keep.

Rannick collapsed on top of his wife, his arms unable to sustain his weight. Never had he had that happen to him, but then never had he had experienced such extreme pleasure and never had he been in love.

He rolled off her, giving her room to breathe, having felt her chest heave against him. He hadn't wanted to return to their bedchamber after the skirmish that had become more of a battle. Anger had ruled him. Anger that the night with his wife had been disturbed, anger that someone dared attack on clan land, anger that more than one clan plotted against him and now his wife. With anger ruling and the aftermath of battle prevailing, he should have dismissed any thought of returning to his wife, let alone making love with her. Yet he could not stay away, and he was glad he hadn't.

Rannick turned on his side to face her, slipping his arm across her middle to hook his hand at her side. "I did not hurt you, did I?" Her soft laughter was like a gentle melody, and it relieved his worry as did her response.

"Hurt me? You made me feel the best I have ever felt. It was simply magnificent." She turned on her side and he inched closer to her, and she eagerly snuggled against him. "I am so glad I took the chance and wed you. I not only found love," —she chuckled— "I found a husband who knows how to make me scream with complete satisfaction."

"I can make certain you do that often," he said with a brief chuckle of his own.

"Promise?" she asked after a quick kiss to his lips.

"You have my word on it."

His lightheartedness began to fade, and she hastily rubbed at the lines deepening between his eyes. "No worries or serious thoughts. The rest of the night is ours to enjoy. Morning will come soon enough, and we will face whatever is needed then, but tonight is solely ours and it is filled with love."

Rannick tucked his wife against him, resting his brow to hers. "I do not think I will ever be able to tell you enough how much I love you."

She grinned. "But you can try."

"I do not have to try, saying I love you comes easily, naturally, truthfully. I am grateful you had the courage to marry me, and I hope you never regret it."

She pressed her finger to his lips and repeated, "No worries or serious thoughts. And never, ever will I regret marrying you or loving you. You have my love and my heart forever." She grinned again. "Though perhaps you will regret marrying me."

"Only those times you disobey me," he said teasingly.

She poked him playfully in the chest. "We can talk about that another time." Her poking turned to a caress, and she reminded, "Tonight is for us."

With a faint brush of his thumb over her lips, he whispered, "And I intend to make it memorable."

Chapter 21

Bliss glanced with disbelief at the wounded men enclosed in a pen behind the keep. Blood-soaked garments and makeshift bandages covered most of them. Death appeared near for a few, and she ached to rush into the pen and help those she could. Unfortunately, guards stood everywhere, their eyes on the prisoners and the surrounding area. She knew without asking that she would not be permitted to enter.

She also had to remind herself that these men had come here with the sole intent of seeing her and Rannick dead. Still, it was difficult to look upon such suffering and not want to help. Her husband had made no mention of the wounded last night or this morning before he left their bedchamber to speak with his father before breakfast. Of course, they had been otherwise occupied both times giving no thought to anything beyond making love. They had been of one mind, one purpose last night and had blotted out the horrors of the day by ending it with a night that would forever live in their memories. Today, though, she stood seeing the cold truth of what her husband had been forced to face and had gratefully survived.

The healer in her had brought her here this morning as had the emptiness of the Great Hall as well as curiosity. However, she had not expected to find the suffering and misery in front of her.

"Are you a fool that you cannot see his evil?"

The young man who had assumed Owen's name last night stood near a section of the wood enclosure that kept the men caged. He cradled his arm of the hand he had lost three fingers on, the bandage bloody and dirty.

Bliss had no chance to respond, and she did not think he cared if she did, he went right on speaking.

"Why do you think so many," —he turned to cast a glance over the wounded men— "would sacrifice their lives to see him dead?"

"And me as well?" she asked.

"You could spawn another to take his place and give the curse continuous power," he said as if his excuse made perfect sense. "There is a grander plan that will finally bring the endless suffering this curse has caused to an end."

"From what I see, you follow blindly, not knowing who leads the ragtag group," Bliss argued.

"Righteous group and the righteous will prevail against evil," he claimed with conviction. "We have stopped Lord Rannick's evil from spreading and we will do so again."

"You killed his three wives," she said, and his brow shot up in surprise that it was finally known.

"I wish I had had the pleasure of claiming such victory, but I did not do the deed. Evil has no right to seed a bairn. The devil has enough servants." His face scrunched in a sneer. "Pray the curse gets you before we do."

"The curse did not claim Lord Rannick's wives, selfish, ignorant men did," she said unable to keep the anger from her voice.

"Call us what you will." His sneer grew ugly. "We are among you, and we will know victory."

"You will see no victory! Though be certain, you will suffer for what you have done."

Bliss turned along with the young man to see her husband approach.

"We will be victorious!" the young man proclaimed, raising his chin defiantly.

Rannick's arm went around his wife's waist in a protective embrace after he stopped beside her. "We will see how long you continue to feel that way when your torture starts."

"I am not afraid," he boasted for all to hear.

"You thought differently last night after losing a few fingers," Rannick reminded. "I wonder how you will feel losing a limb or two."

The image her husband's remark brought to mind had Bliss cringing and the young man paled and wobbled as if at any moment he would faint, but he managed to stay on his feet.

"You can choose your death, fast and painless or agonizingly slow," Rannick said. "I will give you and the others time to think it over."

"I do not want to die," a man said, approaching the fence with a limp, a bloody soiled bandage wrapped around his right leg. "I will tell you all I know."

"You would betray us, Yester?"

"You fight for a belief. I fight for coin, Sheed," Yester said.

Rannick signaled several guards. They entered the pen and approached Yester.

"You will pay dearly for this," Yester," Sheed said, spit flying with his angry threat.

"Not as dearly as you," Yester said and limped his way out of the pen, the guards flanking him.

"I should see to his wound," Bliss said.

"Not until after he tells me what he knows and not without me present," Rannick said and looked to the guards. "Take him to the healer's cottage." He turned to Sheed. "Think over what I offered. I will not make the offer again."

"What if I decide like Yester, that I do not want to die?" Sheed challenged.

"That is not an option for you," Rannick said and took his wife's hand to walk away.

"SEE! SEE HOW EVIL HE IS!" Sheed yelled. "HE

WILL KILL ALL HERE AND NOT CARE. WE WILL STAND TOGETHER PROUDLY AGAINST EVIL AND DIE!"

Rannick let go of his wife's hand and went to the fence to shout, "SPARE YOURSELF SUFFERING AND TELL ME ALL YOU KNOW!"

Not one man spoke up.

Sheed remained defiant. "OUR SCARIFICE WILL NOT BE IN VAIN. OTHERS WILL FOLLOW AND YOU WILL DIE AND THE RIGHTEOUS WILL LIVE AND RULE!"

"We will see how many feel that way when the torture begins," Rannick said and walked away.

"You will torture him?" Bliss asked after they were a distance away.

"He already gave me what I need to know," Rannick said, and Bliss wondered what that was. "He and the others will spend the winter penned like animals waiting and worrying over their fate until each break one by one and we learn all we can from them."

It did not take them long to reach the healer's cottage, sitting almost in the middle of the village. Yester trailed a distance behind them, his gait slow due to his wound.

"I will question him before you tend him," Rannick said, entering the cottage with her. "You will wait outside until I am done."

"I would prefer to stay and hear for myself what he has to say, so that we may see this problem solved together," she said, her glance lingering around the room.

Rannick gave it thought before saying, "You will keep your distance from him until I allow otherwise, and you will hold your tongue and not interfere with my questions."

"What if I have a relevant question?" she asked, going to inspect several crocks on top of a narrow table against one wall.

That she didn't fear to ask him made him realize how comfortable she had grown with him, how much she trusted him, but mostly how much she loved him. He also realized the pleasure it brought her to be here in the healer's cottage. He would have to do something about that since when the clan discovered what an exceptionally skilled healer she was, they would seek her help. And he would not have her this far from the keep tending people. There was a place he thought might work well for her, though what mattered more was that it was located close to the keep where he could see her kept safe and reach her quickly if necessary.

"As long as it does not interfere with mine," he said.

She nodded, then sniffed at a crock she had opened. "From what I see here, your healer was knowledgeable."

"Berdina was a good healer. My father should have never banished her for something she had no control over, but I suppose he thought it was better to blame her than have the curse blamed for the illness that struck."

"I think I could work well here," Bliss said, her eyes filled with delight at the prospect.

"Nay," he snapped far too harshly and got annoyed at himself for seeing the joy fade from her eyes. He quickly sought to correct it. "There is a larger cottage near the keep that will serve you better."

The joy returned to her eyes. "That would be wonderful. I would prefer being closer to you in case I had a need to see you, then I would not have far to go."

His arm whipped around her to bring her against him in a firm hug. "Will you need me often?"

"Aye, very much so," she whispered and kissed him again, though Rannick did not let it end quickly. He lingered, savoring her sweet taste, her love.

She shuddered when the kiss ended. "You more than stir me when you kiss me. I fear you will tire of my endless desire for you."

Rannick laughed. "That is something you never need to fear."

She ran her hand over his beard. "I am so glad I wed you."

"I am so glad you had the courage to do so," he said and went to kiss her when a shout came from outside.

"Lord Rannick!"

He rested his brow to hers. "I am going to sneak you away to our bedchamber before supper."

"We can sup there alone tonight," she whispered as if planning a liaison. "I will feign exhaustion."

"I look forward to it," he said, images of the night ahead stirring his loins.

Rannick's thought swiftly shifted when Yester was brought into the cottage and seated on a bench by the table.

"Tell me what you know," Rannick ordered, his hand on the hilt of his dagger at his waist.

"I was sent to join these men to see the task done, but I could tell upon meeting the group that they had no fighting skills. They were thrown together, as if in haste, and I feared they were doomed to fail."

"Who sent them?" Rannick demanded.

"I do not know. I can only tell you who sent me," Yester offered.

"Who was that?" Rannick asked.

"An acquaintance I had not seen in a while and was surprised to see here on these shores, a fellow called Jaffee."

Rannick's skin prickled at the man's name. "How do you know him?"

"I fought in a battle with him, and once was enough. I kept out of his way after that, and I was not happy about running into him here. He is a vicious man. I thought to see this done and be on my way. He said it would be quick and easy and paid me good coin that will keep my family fed for the winter and beyond. I couldn't refuse him. He would have seen me dead if I did. I was to help these men complete the task and was free to go afterwards. I warned them not to follow you from the cottage, after the small group they sent to kill you failed to return. I also warned them that they were no match for your skilled warriors. I even tried to stop Sheed's foolishness to pose as that fellow Owen, but he refused to see reason. All he saw was victory and impressing whoever it is who is behind seeing the cursed lords and any wife, one of them may have, dead."

"You have no knowledge of who that might be?" Rannick asked.

Yester shook his head. "None. Whoever it is keeps his identity well hidden."

"Someone must connect them," Bliss said.

"It would seem logical, but I spent little time with Jaffee to learn anything more and to be truthful, I did not want to know more. I fear it would be the death of me if I did. Even now I worry that word will reach him that I betrayed the troop, and he will hunt me down."

"Are the various clans these men are from involved in this mission?" Rannick asked.

"I do not know for sure, but I did hear a few say that their clan would not condone their participation, too fearful that Clan MacClaren would retaliate. That is all I know, my lord, after my wound is tended, I will be on my way, and you will never see my face again."

"You really expect me to believe that?" Rannick asked.

"You have my word on it, my lord."

"How do I believe the word of a liar?" Rannick challenged and pulled his dagger from its sheath.

"I tell you the truth," Yester insisted.

"Some perhaps, since your surrender and sharing what you know would not only get me to trust you but would provide you with the opportunity to kill me. You are not truly part of this group. You surrender while the others stand for what they believe and you by no means battled alongside Jaffee. The men he fights alongside have neither family nor a home. They desire only battle and coin."

"Nay, my lord, I speak the truth," Yester protested, shaking his head, then cringing and reaching down at his wounded leg.

Rannick grabbed the man's hair and yanked his head back, his dagger's point scratching the surface of his throat. "Move and I will slice you from ear to ear."

"I swear," my lord, I mean you no harm," Yester pleaded.

"GUARDS!" Rannick yelled and the two warriors rushed in. He looked to the shorter of the two. "Unwrap the cloth around his wound and be careful, a dagger is tucked in there somewhere."

The guard did as he said and as Rannick predicted, a dagger was found.

"How could you know for sure that I lied?" Yester asked, his compliant demeanor gone.

"Jaffee would have never sent you to kill me. He wants that pleasure for himself. So, who is it who sent you, since you are not part of the righteous?"

Yester grinned and suddenly lunged forward straight into the blade Rannick held at his throat.

Bliss stepped forward ready to help the man.

"Stay where you are," Rannick ordered. "He is beyond help." He looked to the other guard who had hurried to his side. "Take Lady Bliss outside and let no one approach her." He then looked to his wife and warned, "Not one word of protest. I will join you shortly."

Bliss stepped outside, her mind a jumble of thoughts. She now understood what her husband had meant when he had said he already got what he needed from Sheed. The man had made it clear that all would die for their belief so when Yester chose differently it meant he was not truly part

214

of Sheed's group so who did he serve?

Her husband stepped out of the cottage, a wood bucket in hand. The guard quickly took it from him and filled it with water from the rain barrel. Rannick then proceeded to wash his hands clean of the blood. He wiped them dry on his cloak before he approached her.

Rannick issued orders to the guard. "See it all cleaned away."

Bliss walked with her husband, his hand reaching for hers to clench it tightly, as if needing to reaffirm that she was safe there beside him. She reassured him, giving his hand a tight squeeze.

She waited until they were clear of others to speak. "I am a bit confused. If Yester is not part of the group Sheed belongs to, what is he doing with them and why did he sacrifice himself?"

"Yester knew something important and feared revealing it under torture. Death was inevitable for him, so he chose to hasten his demise. What happened here confirms that we are dealing with two separate groups with two separate intentions. The one uses the other to hide its true purpose."

"If the righteous group believes they fight against evil, then what does this other group fight for?" Bliss asked.

"There is only one reason men and countries war... power. Someone wants power."

"How does killing the three cursed lords gain this person power?" Bliss asked.

"When we find the answer to that question... we find who is behind it all."

Chapter 22

Things had been quiet, no attempts made on Rannick's and his wife's lives since they first arrived over two months ago, but Odran's message that arrived this morning explained why. The group had turned their focus on Odran and his wife.

Rannick worried how Bliss would take the news and he saw no reason to delay telling her. He found her in the Great Hall, seeing to a wound on the hand of one of the servants.

"Keep it wrapped and dry and let me have another look at it in two days," Bliss said, and finished wrapping the bandage around the servant's forearm.

"I am most grateful, my lady, as are many in the clan you have helped. We are happy to have you here," the young servant lass said with a smile that faded rapidly when she spotted Rannick.

"You frighten the servants," Bliss scolded as her husband approached and the young lass rushed off.

"They all should have your courage," he said and reached out to ease his wife into his arms. She always drifted into his embrace eagerly, and with a smile, as if she had missed him no matter how long they had been apart... minutes or hours. He rarely let too much time pass without finding her to hug and kiss, and with the news he had to tell her, he preferred her snug in his arms.

"It is difficult to have courage against that scowl you wear all too often," she chided.

"My smiles are for you."

"I suggest you spread your smiles out and share them with others," she advised, her own smile fading some. "You are concerned about something. What troubles you?"

More and more she grew to sense when something was amiss with him or when he had need of her and not a passionate need, but simply a need to have her close. It would creep over him slowly at first, a fear of sorts that tingled his flesh, and he would have to hurry and find her to make sure she was all right, that no one had taken her from him. She would hurry into his arms as if she understood or as though she felt the same.

"Rannick?" she said softly when he did not respond.

He shook his head and reminded himself of why he had come to find her. "I have news of Elysia."

Bliss gasped. "Troubling news."

"I do not believe so."

"Tell me, please," she pleaded, concern churning her stomach.

"First, you must understand that I gave my word to Odran when after his brother's death he chose to seek solace in his silence and to protect others from the curse touching them as it had him. He never expected to fall in love, and he did all he could to avoid wedding her."

Bliss paled. "Saber is Odran? Elysia is wed to the lord that was cursed silent?"

"Aye, but Odran is a good man and will be good to your sister, especially with her being with child."

Bliss stared at him in shock, then hurried to ask, to make sure she heard him correctly. "Elysia is with child?"

"Aye, unexpectedly from what I am to understand, since we had pledged not to father any bairns."

Bliss shook her head wishing she could have been there when Elysia had found out about Saber and to provide her with what she needed to keep from getting with child. Although Elysia wanted bairns and many of them. She certainly was full of enough love for a large brood. She could only imagine how happy her sister was and also how worried she might be.

"I need to go see my sister," Bliss said.

Rannick knew she would not like his reply, but it was necessary. "Not at the moment."

Bliss was ready to argue with him when it struck her. "That is why there have been no attempts on our lives." She grabbed her husband's arm. "The group focuses on Lord Odran and my sister because she is with child."

He hated to agree with her since it would worry her all the more. "I have surmised the same, though Odran assures me Elysia is safe, and he intends to keep her that way."

"I must be there to deliver the bairn," Bliss insisted.

Again, he knew his reply would not please her. "That will depend on how safe it is for you and Elysia."

"I will not argue with you on this, Rannick. I will deliver Elysia's bairn no matter the circumstances," she said with such strong conviction that it returned his scowl that had faded. "You can scowl all you want. On this I will have my way."

Rannick grabbed her chin to squeeze lightly. "Think again on challenging me, wife, for you will not know victory. You will do as I say and not stubbornly chance losing your life running off to deliver your sister's bairn. If it is safe, I will take you, if not? You remain here."

Bliss had to temper her anger. It would do no good to argue with her husband. She had time yet to have her way and if not… she would find a way to get to Elysia by herself. But there was no way, absolutely no way that she would not help her sister through the birth of her first bairn.

"Do you know if my sister is happy living at Clan MacBridan?" she asked.

"I do not see why she wouldn't be—" Rannick stopped abruptly, his scowl deepening. "Bloody hell, wife, you tricked me into letting you know where Elysia now resides."

"I wanted to make sure that is where Lord Odran took

her," she said.

"So, you would know where to find her," he accused. "And sneak off to her."

"If I must," she argued. "I have looked after my two sisters, taken care of them, provided for them. I will not abandon either of them in a time of need... not ever. Elysia will expect me to be there to deliver her bairn and I will be there, on that you can be sure."

Bliss rushed past her husband before he could stop her and she struggled with the door, the cold wind fighting her as she tried to close it. An outside guard rushed to help her, and she hurried off, leaving the door for him to close.

Rannick cursed beneath his breath, feeling the rush of cold air and annoyed that his wife had failed to slip on her cloak, thanks to her anger at him. Her stubbornness fueled his anger as well at the thought that she would put her sister before her own safety and before any thought of him. He snatched up her cloak off the bench and took strong strides out of the keep.

Bliss brushed the tears off her cheeks and shivered after entering the dwelling that now served as her healing cottage. It brought her pleasure to be here and be able to work her skills, but not today. Today she was far too concerned about Elysia and Annis as well. She had wed Rannick to keep both her sisters safe and now Elysia, who she had believed safe, was wed to one of the cursed lords and she did not know anything about Annis's whereabouts.

After always being there to help her two sisters, she now felt helpless not knowing how they were truly doing. She shivered at the thought or the chill in the cottage, she was not certain, but at least she could see to getting warm if nothing else.

She went to the hearth and was just bending down to add more logs to the fire when the door opened quickly and shut just as quickly. She did not have to see who it was; she knew her husband would follow her. She did not turn around. She continued to tend the fire.

"Do not go out on such a cold day without your cloak," he ordered. "And do not defy me!"

Bliss got annoyed at the tears that trickled down her cheeks. She did not want her husband to see her crying. She was not one to give in to tears easily, the strength of not doing so born from making sure she remained strong for her sisters. She did not even know why she cried now when she was more angry than sad.

"Bliss!" he snapped, wanting her to turn around.

"Go away!" she snapped back.

That did it. He flung her cloak aside and went and grabbed her by the arm yanking her up.

Bliss gasped and turned startled, wet eyes on him.

Her tears weren't the only thing that tore at his heart, it was the hurt he saw there that shattered his heart completely and he realized her gasp had been touched with pain. He had hurt her when he yanked her to her feet.

He released her and before she could flee, he snatched her up into his arms and walked to the bed tucked in the corner of the room and sat down, cradling her in his lap. He wiped at her wet cheeks with his thumb.

"I allowed my anger to rule. I did not mean to hurt you. I was jealous that you would go to your sister with no thought of me. I have had you to myself and I selfishly do not want to share you or your love with anyone."

Laying a hand on his cheek, she said, "It is the love I have for my sisters, my family that allows me to love you so generously. I would do anything for those I love."

"That is what frightens me. That you would take a chance with your life for your sisters, for me… puts a fear in me I have never known. I cannot lose you, Bliss. I will not. You must obey me on this. I will have it no other way." He brushed his lips faintly over hers as if by not letting her speak she acquiesced.

But Bliss would not be silent. "I will have your word that you will take me to Elysia when her time comes, no matter what, and I will worry you no more."

"I can only hope that by that time this madness is at an end, but if it is not, know your safety comes first to me as would Elysia's safety be to Odran." Once again, he refused to let her respond, kissing her as she opened her mouth to speak.

She pushed at his chest and wiggled off his lap and out of his arms. "That is no answer, Rannick. You order me to obey to ease your fears while escalating mine. That is not fair."

"Fair or not, it is the way it will be," Rannick said, getting to his feet.

"Nay, it will not," Bliss said defiantly and grabbed her cloak as she went to the door.

"Do not walk away from me," he ordered curtly.

Bliss flung open the door, paying him no heed, and hurried toward the keep.

"BLISS!" Rannick shouted from the open doorway.

She ignored him and kept going.

That his wife refused to see reason gripped Rannick with anger and he rushed after her. He heard the close cry of a raven before he felt the sharp peck on his head. He looked to see the blackbird circle overhead and dive at him once more. He swatted at the feathered menace, but it did little good. The raven kept diving at him and squawking loudly.

Bliss turned when she heard her husband swear out loud and seeing him trying to swat the determined raven away, she ran to him.

"Begone with you!" she commanded, waving her hand at the sizeable black bird and the raven flew off after one last, loud squawk.

Rannick's eyes narrowed, annoyed that his wife

commanded the raven with such ease and order, "Stay where you are!"

Bliss tossed her chin up defiantly, hiked up the hem of her garments, and took off running for the keep. She cried out when she was suddenly scooped up off her feet and flung over her husband's shoulder. She should have known that she could not outrun him.

"Put me down!" she demanded, humiliation flaming her cheeks. What must the people think? If it was anything like the two guards at the keep door, they were finding it amusing.

"Rannick, whatever are you doing?" his mum asked when he entered the Great Hall.

"It is no concern of yours, Mum," he said and kept walking.

"You humiliate me," Bliss accused as he climbed the stairs.

"You did that yourself when you refused to obey me… *more than once*," Rannick emphasized.

He deposited her on her feet once in their bedchamber.

"I thought you would understand," she said.

"And I assumed you would see reason," he countered.

"I do not wish to see or speak with you right now… leave," she ordered, knowing any further discussion would only make the matter worse.

He grabbed her chin. "Do not ever make the mistake of ordering me from our bedchamber."

For a moment, she caught a glimpse in his eyes of the cold, unfeeling man she had first met at the cottage in the woods, the one she had feared meeting. The man who had isolated himself to keep others safe. The man who had killed to keep her safe. The man who worried over her and loved her.

Bliss stepped away from him to gather her senses and he did not stop her. She went to the hearth to stare down at the flames, the heat reddening her cheeks. She had foolishly argued with him and lost her temper, and for what? Time and patience would have taken care of it, so why let her temper flare? Why cry? She had always remained calm in difficult times and handled troubling situations calmly as well. Whatever was the matter with her?

His arms came around her, his hands locking at her sides, and she leaned back against him.

"I only want to keep you safe, Bliss."

His beard tickled her temple where he rested his cheek, and his warm breath fanned her already heated cheek.

"I do not wish to argue with you, wife. It hurts my heart and, therefore, it must hurt yours, for we are joined you and me, and nothing will change that, not even a foolish argument."

She turned in his arms, tears once again gathering in her eyes. A quick finger at her lips prevented her from speaking.

"We both want the same… to keep the ones we love safe. We will find a way to see it done." He wiped away her tears. "It breaks my heart that I made you cry, though I fear while it is the first time, it probably will not be the last."

"You can be difficult," she said on an exaggerated sigh.

"Life is difficult, but I do not want it to be difficult between us."

"On that I agree."

He kissed her gently, though not for long. It turned demanding soon enough, their fight leaving him with a churning passion. When she responded in kind, demanding of him as much as he did of her, he scooped her up in his arms and walked to the bed.

"The servants will talk of how much time we spend in our bedchamber during the day," she whispered.

"And they will know it's all your fault," he teased.

"How is it my fault?" she asked, startled by the accusation.

"You lead me into temptation when I find you here during the day," he whispered in her ear in between nibbling along it.

A sensual shudder ran through her. "You tell me to meet you here."

"And you do not deny me... that is temptation." He placed her on her feet. "Disrobe."

She looked at him aghast. "It is always a quick joining we share during the middle of the day with no removal of garments."

He leaned his head down to whisper in her ear. "Not today, wife. Today I take my time with you. Now off with your garments." And once again he sent a tingling shudder through her body.

Her hands trembled with anticipation as she disrobed. "What if a servant should appear?"

"They are too fearful to come here," he said, his hands busy with his own garments.

He was right about that. The servants always asked her permission to see to the bedchamber. None would dare come here unless given permission.

She got into bed once naked and pulled the blanket over her.

Rannick threw it off her before getting in beside her. "I want to see all of you, touch all of you, kiss all of you."

It was as if his words caressed her most intimate parts and she feared her passion would burst there and then.

"I fear I will not last long," she confessed.

"Good, then I can see you pleasured again."

Bliss moaned and he had not even touched her yet, and when he did, his fingers trailing faintly over her breasts, she knew it would not be long for her.

"I love the soft feel of you," he whispered, his fingers roaming over her in no particular pattern, simply freely and lovingly.

224

Not knowing where his hand would touch next excited her all the more. One moment his fingers faintly tormented her breasts, the next they dipped down between her legs to brush teasingly across her sensitive area and tingle her senseless, then they would move to her nipples to tease with the faintest touch until finally his lips replaced his fingers.

She heard the plea in her voice when she said his name. "Rannick."

He lingered, kissing her stomach as his fingers teased between her legs.

"Rannick!" she gasped, mindless with a passion that begged for release.

He raised his head and brought his lips to settle on hers with a gentle kiss. "Let go so I can bring you to pleasure again."

He gave her no choice, his fingers working his magic to bring her to the brink and send her tumbling over the edge. She titled her head back and moaned as wave after wave of intense pleasure crashed into her. Before they could drift away, she felt him enter her, powerful and deep, and he churned the fading waves back up again.

A wave of pleasure swept her up and tossed her around and she could do nothing but let it carry her off, though she grabbed onto her husband's arms, intending to take him with her.

"Not yet," Rannick said, pulling back from her to grab her legs and place them over his shoulders and gripped her bottom as he rocked her body with his powerful plunges.

Her passion swelled like a mighty wave, building in strength and anticipation of crashing along the shore only to recede with overpowering force.

She wanted to scream his name, but it came out in a soft plea, "Rannick."

He dropped down over her with a forceful thrust that sent not only his passion over the edge, but hers as well. He roared as pleasure slammed through him.

Bliss knew this time she would drown in the pleasure that hit her and crashed her hard on the shore.

Rannick felt his wife go limp beneath him and hurried off her. Her eyes were closed, and she was not moving, her body completely lifeless, and he feared she had…

He shook her. "Bliss! Bliss!"

Nay. Nay. She wanted to continue to float away on the wave of immense pleasure, but it slipped away depositing her limp and satiated on the shore.

"BLISS!"

Her eyes popped wide at her husband screaming her name.

"Good, God, woman, you frightened the hell out of me," he said, relieved to see she was all right but fearful of hugging her and robbing her of what breath had restored her.

"A wave of pleasure," she managed to say, realizing how breathless she was.

Rannick shuddered at the image of a giant wave sweeping her away from him, not able to reach her. "I will let no wave take you from me."

She smiled. "Your fault."

He went to argue when he realized she was right.

"Love the wave. Love you," she said and shuddered, recalling the overpowering climax.

He reached for the blanket to pull over her, then took her in his arms to settle comfortably. "I do love you, wife."

Bliss closed her eyes lingering in the lazy aftermath of pleasure. She did not ever think she could be this content, find this much happiness, be loved as strongly as her husband loved her. The bargain she had feared making turned out to be the best bargain of her life.

"While I would like to remain here with you, it is just after mid-day and I have responsibilities to see to," Rannick said.

"I do as well," she said on a yawn.

"Things can wait. Rest for a bit," he urged and reluctantly slipped out of bed.

Another yawn settled it for her. "Just for a bit."

Rannick dressed and smiled when he went to the bed to kiss his wife. She was already asleep. He left the room closing the door quietly behind him.

Bliss felt her husband's kiss but said nothing, feeling too tired to even say a word. Lovemaking had worn her out, though it had never done so before, but she had never felt faint before this time. And they had made love often, almost every day.

She sprung up in bed. Had she been so busy, so consumed with her husband and new home that it had slipped her mind? How could she forget something so important?

It had been two months since they had first made love and she had not bled. Her monthly bleed could be sporadic at times, a day here, three days there, but two months without seeing it at all was not normal for her. There was a good chance she was with child.

The thought brought a thrill of joy along with a dreaded fear. She would say nothing until, she was sure, and she wondered and worried what her husband would do if it proved true.

Chapter 23

"Why didn't you tell me Odran sent a warrior to us?" Rannick demanded. "How long has he been here?"

"I don't recall. I have had Lawler keeping him busy and away from you and Bliss unsure if he can be trusted," his father said annoyed. "Tell your friends to stop sending us their castoffs. Brogan sent a young woman, Damia, who is with child, here as well. Her grandfather, Harold, and sister, Lana, belonged to our clan. "Do you recall them?"

"Harold was old when I was young, and Lana worked in the keep if I remember correctly."

"She did and she was a good, obedient servant. Your mother made me let her go when she met a man from another clan when at market and wished to wed him. Harold perished in the illness that struck the clan. Damia no longer has family here and will be returned to Brogan's clan."

"Brogan sent her here for a reason and I will hear that reason before any decision is made about her," Rannick argued.

His father's fist came down on the table, he sat behind in his solar, with a sharp rap. "You do not rule this clan yet."

"Maybe I should," Rannick snapped.

His father bolted up off the chair. "Give the clan an heir and I will turn the leadership of it over to you."

Rannick wanted to let his father know that that would be a long time coming, but Bliss had made a bargain with his father and while Elysia was safely wed to Odran, there was still Annis to consider. His father could get angry enough to force a marriage on Annis and that would upset Bliss.

Instead, Rannick returned to the problem at hand.

"Odran and Brogan sent both here to me and I will find out why."

His father dismissed the issue with a snap of his hand. "Talk with them if you wish but the decision will be mine."

"Nay, Da, this decision rests with me," Rannick cautioned.

"Do I hear a threat in your tone?" his father demanded.

"Do not make it necessary." That time there was a definite threat in his tone.

His father looked ready to argue but held his tongue. "I forgot how obstinate you can be."

Rannick smiled. "I am a lot like my father."

His son's smile brought a smile to Lochlann's face. "Then the clan will be in good hands when the time comes."

"Aye, that is something you never need to worry about," Rannick assured him.

"It does my old heart good to know the Clan MacClaren will live on and I look forward to my first grandchild."

Rannick ignored another reference to an heir, moving on to another subject. "No news from any of the men we sent out to see what they could find out about this righteous group who wants to see this curse end with Odran, Brogan, and me?"

His father shook his head. "Someone riles them, convincing them that any and all problems stem from the curse."

"Has anything been heard of a speculation that the MacWilliam bairn lived and now seeks revenge?"

Anger smoldered in his father's eyes. "That is not possible. I saw the bairn and I can assure you that she was dead."

"You saw the bairn, but you did not deliver the fatal blow, an illness did," Rannick said, reminding his father of his own words.

Lochlann dropped down in the chair as if his own

weight, or perhaps the guilt, was too much for him. "I sent a message to the King that he would question no more and the matter could finally be laid to rest."

His father sounded as if he had grown tired of the hunt. If that was so, what had he truly done to see the matter ended.

"How do you truly know it was the MacWilliam bairn?" Rannick asked, needing more of an explanation that his father had previously given him.

"After a lengthy search, we found where Gunna was hiding. When we arrived there, we found an old woman. She told us that the woman we looked for left shortly after she buried a bairn. An illness had taken the barely month-old lass. The grave was searched, and the remains of a tiny lass found. The woman also described Gunna perfectly and told us that Gunna gave her coin to hold her tongue so no one would disturb the grave. We needed no coin to convince her to speak the truth."

"What happened to Gunna?" Rannick asked.

"An effort was made to find her, but it was as if she vanished, not a trace of her could be found. It was over and done and I was glad to put it to rest."

"But it wasn't put to rest, Da. The curse continues to haunt and hurt and how you expect, or even want me to have a son or daughter that would suffer the same fate is something I cannot understand." He stopped his tongue from finishing the thought in his head. *Nor do I intend to do so.*

His father's shoulders slumped along with his head. "I kept hoping that with time the curse will wane until nothing was left of it."

"Did you ever want to right the wrong done to your friend?"

His father raised his chin with effort. "I pray that you are never placed in the situation that I and your friends' fathers faced those many years ago. Brochan was a stubborn man. He would not even listen to reason when he insisted on marrying a peasant. His father and mother would have never allowed it if they had been alive. But he insisted he was in love and that nothing else mattered."

"You wed me to a peasant," Rannick reminded, the thought that he might never have met Bliss if things had been different a sharp pain to his heart.

His father sighed heavily. "I truly am sorry, son, that I could not have done better for you, but I had little choice."

"Then you should know that I would have no other woman but Bliss. I have found with her something I thought I never would with a wife—love. She is the most caring, loving soul I have ever met."

"You love, Bliss?" his father asked as if he did not quite understand.

"More than she will ever know and I would give my life to keep her safe."

"I can almost hear Brochan laugh at the irony of it," his father said, turning his head away but not before Rannick caught a glisten of tears in his da's eyes. "I recall Balloch doing the same, claiming he loved a peasant, but his father wisely put a stop to it." With a cough that almost drowned out his sniffle, he turned back around to face his son. "I hear the people are pleased with Bliss's healing skills."

"Bliss is a knowledgeable healer, Da, and she has the kindest heart. You cannot help but trust her."

"I would agree since so far she is proving true to her word, and I have no doubt she will see our bargain fulfilled."

"And if she doesn't?" Rannick asked.

"A bargain is a bargain. She fulfills it or else," his father warned. "Though I have little doubt I need to worry about that." He grinned. "The servants talk about how much time you both spend in your bedchamber. I am sure Bliss will have wonderful news for us soon." He stood. "I will have Lawler bring Bram and Damia here so you may speak to

231

both of them."

Rannick left his father's solar shortly after he did. This Bram and Damia could have news Bliss may want to hear, whether good or bad, he would keep neither from her. He didn't want to wake her if she still slept, but she would be disappointed if he didn't. He was glad to find her in the Great Hall.

"Where do you go?" he asked, seeing she wore her cloak.

"To see if anyone is at the cottage and is in need of healing," she said, going to him with a smile.

Her smile always lightened his heart, and he extended his arm as he always did to welcome her with an embrace.

"I think you should come with me. I am going to question a man and a woman. Odran sent the man and Brogan sent the woman. I thought either of them may have news about your sisters."

Bliss hugged him tight. "That is wonderful news. I cannot wait to speak with them."

Once in the solar, Rannick slipped his wife's cloak off to drop on a bench.

"I think I recall Bram," Bliss said. "If I am not mistaken, I tended him when a wound caused him to lose part of his earlobe." She scrunched her brow. "But there is more," —her eyes went wide— "now I know what it is. Lendra, one of the servants at Loudon keep, and a friend of mine, favored him, though he favored many women."

"Then you will keep your distance from him," Rannick ordered.

Bliss laughed lightly. "He showed not a bit of interest in me."

Rannick did not mind at all that his wife did not have the stunning beauty that captured every man's eye. If she did, he would forever be battling men... killing them was more likely since it would infuriate him if another man simply glanced at her.

Her plain features were just fine with him, not that he thought her plain. She had a subtle beauty that until recognized was ignored, but once discovered it was difficult not to admire it.

A knock sounded at the door and Rannick's protective instinct, though it could be jealousy that another man would find his wife attractive, had him tugging her hand for her to join him to stand behind the table before he called out, "Enter."

"Wait outside the door," Rannick ordered the two warriors who escorted Bram and Damia into the solar.

Rannick should have known his wife would not stay at his side as soon as the woman, round with child, stood before them. She went to her, and he caught Bram's glance roaming over his wife. He had good features, the kind that women would favor, and his stance was confident, and he had a good height to him.

"You should sit," Bliss said, hurrying to the young lass and taking her by the arm to help her sit in a chair near the table. "When do you expect to deliver?"

"Three months, I think, my lady," Damia said.

"We will talk once we are done here," Bliss said, sensing her husband's impatience. Besides this was not the time or place to discuss such matters with the woman. She hurried to join her husband and she almost smiled when he made sure their sides touched as if somehow it would keep her there beside him.

"We will start with you, Damia," Rannick said, sure to have more questions for Bram. "Why did Brogan send you here?"

"I asked him too. "The woman with him, Annis—"

"You saw and spoke with Annis—my sister? She is well and not alone?" Bliss asked anxiously.

Damia got teary-eyed. "Annis is the bravest woman I

have ever met. She saved me from being beaten by Lady Faline, Lord Brogan's mother. She threw herself on top of me and took the whipping with the stick to protect me and my bairn."

Bliss paled. "That would be my sister. Was she hurt badly?"

Damia rested her hand protectively over her rounded stomach. "She suffered several hard strikes before Lord Brogan arrived and stopped it."

"Annis is staying at Clan MacRae?" Bliss asked anxiously, the thought of her being in the presence of a woman whose temper could cause harm worrying her, especially with Annis not being one to hold her tongue.

Damia shook her head. "Nay, my lady. Annis, Lord Brogan, and several other people reside in the area where," —she hesitated a moment and lowered her voice to a whisper— "the witch in the hills is believed to live."

Bliss didn't bother to hide her shock. "Annis has found the witch?"

"I do not know, my lady. I have heard no such talk. All I know is that is where she and the others make their home. A craftsman joined them since they are building many dwellings and need help."

Bliss smiled, knowing how happy her sister must be since she was involved in building dwellings, or anything for that matter, an interest and love she had had since young."

"I asked to come here where my sister and grandfather reside, and Lord Brogan granted my request." Tears filled her soft-blue eyes. "I did not know my grandfather had taken ill and died or that my sister, Lana, had wed and left the clan. I do not know what to do now." She looked reluctantly to Rannick, purposely having avoided meeting his eyes before this. "Please, my lord, I beg you do not send me back to Clan MacRae. I fear I, nor the bairn, will survive. I would gladly return to Annis and Lord Brogan if you do not want me

234

here."

Bliss spoke up. "You are more than welcomed here and will not be sent back to Clan MacRae, and we can also let your sister know you are here." Realizing too late, it was not her decision to make, she looked to her husband, not surprised to see him scowling. There was a time his scowl would have frightened her, not now. She smiled and hugged his arm. "Don't you agree, husband?"

"Aye, she can stay, and her sister will be made known that she now resides here," Rannick said and called out to the guards outside the door to enter. "One of you escort Damia to the Great Hall and tell a servant to see that she is given food and drink."

Damia stood. "I am most grateful, my lord."

"Wait in the Great Hall, my wife will see you when we are done here," Rannick said.

Once the door closed, Rannick crossed his arms over his chest and settled a glare on Bram. "And why did Lord Odran send you here?"

Bliss saw that she was right. Bran was missing a chunk from one of his earlobes, though it did not distract from his good features.

"I was unwise in who I trusted and not being mindful of what I had been told and warned about," Bram admitted. "Lord Odran believes I will either learn to become a better warrior here or learn I am no warrior at all."

"I will see what we can do with you," Rannick said, "but a warning, do wrong here and I will ship you off to a foreign land and let someone else deal with you."

"I will serve you well, my lord," Bram said with a bob of his head.

"How is my sister? Is she happy with Lord Odran?" Bliss asked.

"Lady Elysia asked me not to mention that Saber is actually Lord Odran. She did not want you to worry over the news. But since you already know," —he shrugged— "one only has to see the way Lord Odran looks at your sister to know he loves her deeply and it appears Elysia feels the same about him. He keeps her well-protected. She is safe with him."

"I am glad to hear that," she said.

Her worry over Elysia was for naught. She was doing well and had a husband who would keep her safe. At least she was wed to a man she loved whether he was one of the cursed lords or not.

"You do well, Lady Bliss?" Bram asked.

"You speak to my wife only when she asks you a question. Otherwise, do not address her," Rannick ordered.

"Aye, my lord," Bram said with a nod.

Rannick saw that the order did not set well with Bram, annoyance tightening his brow. "You will train with the warriors, and you will do your chores without complaint." Once again Rannick detected annoyance in the man. Obviously, the mention of chores was not to his liking. "Also, Damia will be your responsibility. You will see her kept safe and see that she is adequately looked after... much like a dutiful husband minus the benefits of marriage."

Bram looked ready to argue as his mouth shot open.

"I would think wisely before you say anything and remember that Odran is a far more patient man than I am," Rannick warned.

Bram closed his mouth.

"Go find Lawler and see what chores he sets for you. I will have Damia wait here until you finish," Rannick ordered. He didn't look to his wife when he said, "Do you have any questions for Bram, Bliss?"

There were many things she wished to ask him about Elysia, her old home, and the people there, but she did not think her husband would be patient enough to hear it all. She would find another time to talk with Bram.

"Not at this time," she said, letting her husband know that she would speak with Bram again.

"Go!" Rannick ordered and once the door shut, he took his wife in his arms. "I will be with you any time you speak with him."

She spoke her worry. "While I do not mind you there, I believe Bram will be reluctant to fully discuss my sister with me in front of you."

"I can understand that, but—"

"I do not believe he will harm me, but I will make sure there are many around us when I speak with him," she offered.

"I am not willing to take that chance, but I will see that you speak with him while I am a short distance away." Rannick did not want to concede even that, but he could understand his wife wanting to learn all she could about what had happened to her sister since she had been gone.

"At least Elysia is wed to someone she loves. I no longer have to worry about her being stuck with a man who would treat her badly," Bliss said, relieved. "Now I have only Annis to be concerned about."

"She is with Brogan. You need not worry, he will protect her," he assured her.

"But can he protect her against a witch?" Bliss asked and shivered at the thought.

The door suddenly swung open, and Lord Lochlann entered. "Did you hear it?"

"Hear what?" Rannick asked, surprised by how pale his father appeared.

"Good Lord, Lochlann, not again," Rannick's mum cried as she rushed into the room behind her husband and into his arms.

"What's wrong?" Rannick demanded, keeping a firm grip on his wife.

"A wolf's cry loud and clear, echoing throughout the

village," his father said and shuddered.

Bliss felt every muscle in her husband grow taught and she glanced up at him. "I don't understand. Why does a wolf's cry upset everyone so much?"

Rannick looked to his father.

Lord Lochlann shuddered again. "The last time a wolf's cry echoed forcefully through the village was the day the curse was cast."

Chapter 24

Winter arrived with a flurry of snow and with the news Bliss could finally confirm without a doubt—she was with child. She had told no one and was not sure when she would, though she supposed she could not keep it long from Rannick. He would notice soon enough the faint changes in her body with how often he touched her intimately. She did not want to shy away from his touch in order to prolong telling him the news since she not only loved his touch, but also got much pleasure from it.

She wished she could share the news with her sisters and thought how Elysia must have felt the same when she had learned the news that she was with child. She had sent and received several messages from both her sisters in the last few weeks. The three had agreed they all wanted to see each other as soon as possible, but their husbands thought differently.

There was something else that disturbed Bliss. Had Annis and Brogan wed? Wagging tongues would have her believing the rumor, but Annis had yet to confirm it. She wondered if Annis kept silent on purpose. With Elysia wed to Odran and if Annis was wed to Brogan, it would mean that Bliss's sacrifice was for naught. In the end, the three had been wed to the cursed lords. But Bliss had seen for herself the way Elysia and Saber—she shook her head, not Saber, Lord Odran—felt about each other. And as for Annis, she may have fought her attraction to Brogan as he had fought his for her, but she had seen sparks of interest in both their eyes for each other. That meant she had succeeded in seeing that both her sisters got what she had wanted for them… not only to wed men of their choosing but men they actually loved.

A knock at the healing cottage door stirred her from her thoughts and she opened it, expecting Damia and smiled seeing Bram holding the young woman's arm.

"I told you to walk slowly. You almost slipped twice," Bram reprimanded the woman whose head barely reached his shoulder.

"I do not need your help," Damia said. And if your strides were not so fast, I would not have almost slipped."

"You should have told me that," Bram snapped. "Need I remind you, yet again, that I have been ordered to look after you, otherwise you would not see me."

"Something I pray for every day," Damia said as she stepped into the cottage.

"I will be waiting out here," Bram said.

"No need," Damia said and shut the door in his face and looked apologetically to Bliss. "I am sorry, my lady, but I cannot tolerate Bram at times."

Bliss thought of another couple who bickered upon meeting, memories of Annis and Brogan bringing a smile to her face.

"I could speak to Lord Rannick about it and see if he would change his mind about Bram looking after you," Bliss offered, curious how Damia would feel about that.

Damia smiled softly. "I complain about Bram, but I do not know what I would do without him. He truly does much for me. I think I complain because he complains, and I feel guilty that he has been made to look after me. Though, I do wonder why Lord Rannick assigned him the chore."

"He has not said, but I would guess he waits to learn Bram's true character," Bliss said, having realized her husband's leadership skills far surpassed his father's.

"I know many that fear Lord Rannick, but what I have seen of him since I have been here, he is a fair man."

"I believe it is more the curse they fear and blame him for all the ills the clan has suffered and for his three wives' deaths, though they were no fault of his," Bliss said. "I imagine Lord Brogan suffers a similar fate."

Damia hugged herself protectively. "Lord Brogan has not been at the keep much in the last few years. It is not a pleasant place."

The way Damia sealed her lips tightly, Bliss knew she would say no more and so she asked, "You have been feeling well?"

"Aye, much better since I arrived. Everyone has been most kind to me. I worry though," Damia said with concern. "I have been given no chore and I fear that it might mean that I am not to remain here."

"I can solve that worry right now," Bliss said, smiling. "How would you like to help me here in my healing cottage? I have settled in well here and the people have come to trust me, so I am busier than I believed I would be. I could use someone to prepare the mixtures and to tend light wounds and such. Though I propose this, do not worry and feel compelled to remain here if your sister should come for you when she receives word of your arrival here."

A smile lit Damia's pretty face. "I would welcome the chance to learn the skills of a healer, my lady. As for my sister, Lana, I would love to see her again, but this is my home and I have greatly missed it."

"Good. Then you will start tomorrow morning. I will begin to teach you the different plants and their properties, and I am pleased that you are content here and prefer to stay."

"That has much to do with you, my lady. I have seen your constant smile and pleasant nature turn many a surly face pleasant," Damia said. "And if I may say so, my lady?"

"Please speak freely, Damia," Bliss urged.

"I think many believe that if you can maintain a

241

pleasant nature wed to the cursed lord, then perhaps Lord Rannick isn't as evil as they all believe him to be."

"That brings me great joy to hear," Bliss said with a huge smile, "for it is the truth. Lord Rannick is a good man."

Bliss enjoyed her time and talk with Damia. It reminded her of talks she used to share with her sisters. The memories touched her heart, as did the knowledge that both of them were safe.

Flurries of snow were still falling when Damia left the cottage, Bliss following her out to go to the keep to fetch the fine needles her husband had shaped for her, and she had forgotten to bring with her this morning.

She smiled as she watched Bram slow his pace beside Damia, though he kept a firm hand on her arm. She wondered if their forced closeness might forge more between them. Her smile widened when she saw her husband standing outside the keep talking with Lawler. She waved and he returned it. Even at a distance, she could see the way his eyes brightened upon seeing her and it stirred her heart, not to mention sparking a bit of passion. But when didn't passion spark in her for her husband? A look, a touch, a kiss, any or all would suffice.

"My lady," Bram called out as he approached.

His strides were quick as he left Damia's side to speak with Bliss.

"My lady, Damia told me that you offered to speak with Lord Rannick about ending my chore of seeing to her care. I would prefer that you not do that. I was given a task and I intend to see it done and prove myself to Lord Rannick. Besides, Damia needs—" His eyes suddenly spread wide, and his arms shot out to wrap himself snugly around her as he tumbled them to the ground.

Bliss heard a scream and the sound of people running.

Bram pulled back after a moment and asked, "Are you all right, my lady?"

"BLISS!"

Bram scrambled to his feet, helping her up at the sound of her husband's mighty roar. Warriors hurried to form a protective circle around her and Bram, blocking her husband from view, though they parted quickly enough to let him enter before closing the protective circle once again.

"Bram saved me," she said quickly, though from what she wasn't certain.

Rannick's heart thundered in his chest as he grabbed his wife by the shoulders and fright twisted his stomach. "There is blood on your neck."

Bliss's hand went quickly to her neck and feeling no wound, looked to Bram. "You were wounded."

"A scratch to my arm, nothing more," Bram insisted.

The circle of warriors suddenly took flight, running into the woods behind the healing cottage.

Bliss shook her head. "What happened? What is going on?"

"An arrow was sent straight for you," Rannick said, anger and fear merging to worsen the twist in his gut. "If it was not for Bram stopping to talk with you and reacting swiftly…"

Bliss shivered at what he didn't say. "Bram saved my life."

"I promised Elysia I would do my best to keep you safe," Bram said, Damia standing beside him and tears pooling in her eyes.

"I will help you look after him, my lady," Damia offered.

"That would be most helpful, Damia," Bliss said before Bram could refuse the young woman's offer.

Rannick kept his arm snug around his wife and his eyes peeled on his surroundings as he got her inside the healing cottage quickly. There had been no need to instruct Lawler as to what needed to be done. He had wasted no time in sending the warriors into the woods to hunt the culprit down and to leave Rannick to see to his wife.

Bliss set to work as did Damia, following Bliss's every order, though not before Rannick took a cloth and gently wiped the smeared blood off his wife's neck while she saw to cleaning it off her hand. The fiery rage in his eyes would scorch most people, but Bliss cooled it with a soft smile and a gentle touch to his chest.

"Did you see the arrow coming?" Rannick asked Bram, reluctantly stepping away from Bliss so she could tend the wound.

"I heard it cut through the air, a skill of mine most don't know about. An arrow has a distinct sound, more so when the air is cold. It has served me well many times," Bram said. "Though, I was not sure where it would hit. That was why I wrapped myself around Lady Bliss, my lord, to shield her."

"For that I am forever in your debt, Bram," Rannick said, not truly knowing how to repay the man.

"That is not necessary, my lord. As I said, I promised Lady Elysia I would keep Lady Bliss safe if I could. I am grateful I was able to, and I am glad I was able, in some small way, to repay Lady Elysia for all she has done for me." Bram looked to Bliss. "You would be proud of your sister's healing skills and also her courage."

Bliss had enjoyed a few conversations with Bram since his unexpected arrival, but they had been brief. No doubt it had been due to Bram's unease with her husband's close proximity. It left no time to truly learn all that had gone on with her sister at Clan Loudon. And while she hoped to learn more from him, she would much rather have the chance to speak in person with her sister about it.

"I have always been proud of Elysia and now even more so from what you have said," Bliss said, glad to see Bram's wound was not severe.

It did not take long to tend the wound and while Bliss explained how Damia should care for it, on the young woman's insistence, Rannick and Bram stepped outside.

"It would take an exceptional marksman to shoot from the woods and not be seen," Bram said.

"My thoughts as well," Rannick said.

"The snow helps in tracking him."

"Another thought we share," Rannick said. "You have proven yourself to me, Bram, not only showing you would protect my wife with your life, but also by seeing to Damia without complaint while training well with my warriors. You are released from the chore of looking after her."

"If you do not mind, my lord, I would prefer to look after Damia." Bram hesitated a moment before saying, "She needs me."

"Then you will do it of your own free will, it no longer being a chore," Rannick said.

Silence fell over them both as Lawler hurried toward them.

"The culprit is dead, his throat silt," Lawler said quickly. "We found tracks and the warriors follow them now."

"Keep me apprised," Rannick ordered, though it wasn't necessary. Lawler knew what was expected of him.

Lawler nodded and hurried off and Bram, seeing Lord Lochlann approach, went inside the cottage.

"What is this I hear? Someone tried to kill Bliss?" his father asked, his face pinched with anger as he stopped in front of his son.

"Bram saved her life," Rannick said.

"Then I guess he is worth keeping."

"More than worth it, Da."

"And the culprit?" his father asked.

Rannick explained that he'd been found.

"His throat was sliced? I suppose it was payment for

245

failing his appointed task," his father said.

Rannick suggested differently. "Or it was planned from the start, a way to slow down anyone who chased after him. They would be too busy with the dead man, thinking he took his life rather than face capture, to pay attention to anything else."

"Let's hope the trackers find something," his father said. "Bliss is unharmed and feeling well?"

"Bliss is good," Rannick said, knowing his father was waiting for news. And with rumors spreading about Annis and Brogan being wed, something Rannick had not been able to confirm, he decided to make mention of it. "If the rumors that Brogan and Annis are wed turn out to be true, then the bargain you struck with Bliss is void."

His father's eyes sparked with anger. "I will have an heir to this clan, Rannick, and if Bliss cannot give you one then I will see your marriage annulled and find a wife that will produce an heir."

Rannick's hand shot out and he grabbed his father by his shirt. "I confess to you how I feel about my wife, that I love her, and yet you would dare attempt to take her from me?"

His father yanked at his son's hand, but his grip was far too strong to break his hold. "You have an obligation."

"To fuel a curse that has raged for twenty years?" Rannick argued.

"Rannick! Release your father!" his mother ordered as she came to a stop beside them. "Both of you should be ashamed of yourselves. You, Lochlann, for threatening to deprive your son of the woman he loves and you, Rannick, for laying your hand on your father, yet again."

"He deserved it," Rannick spat, releasing his father and stepping away, his anger still bubbling and ready to erupt.

"Perhaps so, since your father has no talent in weighing his words, just as you don't. You are both more alike than you realize, for your father would have done the same to his father if he had threatened to annul our marriage."

"Da loves you?" Rannick asked, surprised.

"Of course I love your mum," Lochlann snapped.

"You don't show it," Rannick accused.

"It is not your concern," Lochlann argued.

"Enough!" Lady Helice ordered. "You argue when the only concern should be about Bliss."

"I am fine, Lady Helice."

The three of them turned to see Bliss standing just outside the cottage door.

"I am unharmed and well-protected here," Bliss said and walked over to the three to slip her arm around her husband's. "Though I want you both, Lord Lochlann and Lady Helice, to know how very much I love your son and how my heart would shatter in endless pieces, never to be made whole again, if you separated us."

A pain tore at Rannick's heart at the thought. "That is never going to happen. You and I will remain together forever and beyond."

Lady Helice pressed a hand to her chest as her eyes turned teary. "I am so happy to know how much you both love each other." When her husband made no remark, she jabbed him in the side with her elbow. "Aren't you happy for them, Lochlann?"

"I will be happier when I get what I bargained for," he said with a glare at Bliss.

"These things take time, Lochlann, be patient," she said and tugged at his arm to turn and walk with her to the keep.

Rannick silently blessed his mum for seeing that the confrontation was brought to an end, but it had not truly ended. "My father will bring up this matter about an heir again. I will need to address this soon and let him know the clan will never have an heir."

Her stomach churned, knowing differently and knowing

she could not wait long as well to tell him that was not true, the clan would have an heir.

Chapter 25

Bliss woke from a sound sleep, not knowing what had interrupted her peaceful slumber. She had easily fallen asleep after making love with her husband just after they had gotten in bed. He had taken his time and while it had been enjoyable and satisfying it had lacked its usual intensity. It had been obvious to her that his mind had been elsewhere, not that she could blame him.

The search for the man who had killed the culprit had not gone well. Snow had turned heavy, and the tracks had soon been lost. That was a few days ago and nothing more had been found.

She turned on her side, her naked body having cooled from the emptiness of the bed, and she saw that her husband was standing by the hearth, his arm braced on the slim, wood mantel.

He truly was a man of fine form and strength, though it was born out of necessity. Her husband had faced more peril than most men and if he had not possessed such strength and courage, had endured despite the curse, he would not be here now with her.

That troubling thought had her hurrying out of bed and over to her husband, a chill chasing along after her. She rushed her arms around his waist and pressed as much of herself as she could against him to steal his warmth.

He brought his arm back behind him and over her to nudge her around in front of him and rest her solidly against him.

The heat from the hearth had toasted him and quickly seeped through her while the heat from the fire's flames drifted over her backside and legs, feeling heavenly.

"I thought I was quiet enough not to disturb you," he said, pressing a kiss on the top of her head as his way of apologizing for waking her.

"It was not a noise that woke me, but the emptiness of the bed," she said, resting her head on her husband's warm chest. "Share your troubling thoughts with me now that we are both awake."

He stroked her back, not able to keep his hands off her silky skin as he gladly shared the thoughts that had woken him from a restless sleep. "Some things do not make sense to me. Even if Odran, Brogan, and I die, that does not stop the curse. Our fathers still live which means so does the curse. So why kill us three and not our fathers?"

Bliss offered her own thoughts. "If I were to guess, you and the other two present a more direct threat—able to produce an abundance of heirs between all of you. Therefore, the curse would be fueled and extended for who knows how long."

"I suppose, but something still doesn't seem right about it all. Something stares us in the face, and we cannot see it and I fear the consequences if we do not at least give it thought."

"Would the problem not be more easily solved if we all, my sisters and their husbands, were able to discuss it together?" she asked, hopeful he might agree, and she would finally be reunited with her sisters.

"Most definitely," Rannick agreed but before Bliss could feel even a spark of excitement, her husband continued. "Unfortunately, it is not safe for any of us to travel right now. Odran and Brogan agree with me, especially Odran with Elysia being with child. And I do not blame him. I would worry myself senseless if that were you, and I would forbid you from going anywhere. I am relieved I do not even have to consider it."

Guilt jabbed at Bliss. She had given her word she would speak the truth to him, but she had done just that when she had told him that the mixture of plants and herbs he insisted she take was worthless in keeping her from getting with child. He had not questioned her about it since then, therefore, she had not lied to him.

"There is winter to consider as well," he said. "There is always the chance of being caught in a snowstorm. Messages will have to suffice for now. Besides, your sister will need you in the spring when it comes time for her to deliver the bairn."

If Bliss's calculations were right, she would be due sometime in the spring as well. She did not know how she would do it, but she intended to be there for Elysia when her time came.

"From Brogan's message, he and Annis have much going on with the construction of their village and the number of people who wish to reside there."

There was something in her husband's voice that made her ask, "Was there more to Brogan's message? Is Annis all right? I thought to hear from her soon but have received no message. Please tell me she is well."

"Annis is fine and is relentless in her efforts to come here to see you." His brow pinched with annoyance, and he hesitated a moment before continuing. "Brogan says that he and Annis have discovered much that I should know but not through a messenger."

"And you just decided to tell me this?" she asked, upset he had not told her.

"I only found out about it today and my first thought was that you would rush off to see Annis."

"Aye, that is what we should do. *We, not me*," she emphasized. "You should be just as eager. What if they have found the witch? That would mean there is a chance to bring the curse to an end."

251

"Or be disappointed again like so many other countless times," he confessed with a shake of his head. "I cannot tell you how often Brogan, Odran, and I faced disappointment. Or the hell I went through in foreign lands in search of someone, anyone—a demon if necessary—who could help end the misery and pain."

Bliss hurried to place a comforting hand on his chest, her heart aching for him. "I am truly sorry for what the curse has made you suffer, but you cannot give up now after all you have been through."

Rannick's hand closed around his wife's slim wrist. "It isn't that I fear what may come of it if news of the witch has been discovered. It is what I would become once again to make certain the witch tells us all we need to know."

Her brow creased with concern. "You are a good man, Rannick."

His grip on her wrist tightened. "You would not say that if you knew some of the things I have done, have been willing to do to break this curse. If it proves true that the witch has been found and she is the one who helped Lady Aila condemn us to hell, then I assure you she will rue the day she met me."

"You cannot battle a witch," she said, the thought insane and the consequences that could come of it frightening her.

"I can," —his eyes burned with fiery anger— "I already have." He pulled her against him when she went to respond, their warm naked bodies pressed tightly together. "Do not ask me to explain that. The only thing I will tell you is that when I got done, I knew I had lost not only my soul but my humanity."

"That is not true," she said as her hand went to rest on his cheek. "Your soul and humanity may have been damaged but you did not lose them. If you did, you could have never tended me with such kindness when I needed help, and you could never love me to the deepest depths of your heart the way you do." She kissed him lightly. "You will fight no witch; I will not allow it."

Anger faded from his eyes replaced by a wicked glint. "You think you can stop me, wife?"

"Aye, I can stop you," Bliss said confidently, and startled when his hands suddenly shackled her wrists.

"Tell me how you would do that," he demanded, the strength of his grip holding her firm.

She smiled softly. "I would ask you not to do it."

"And you think that would stop me?"

"Your love for me would stop you since I would remind you how very much I love you and how I could not bear to lose you, and you would know it to be true since you feel the same for me."

"My love for you is the very reason I would do whatever was necessary to make sure the witch speaks the truth," he argued. "And what if your sister did find her? How did she succeed while I failed?"

"If we went to see Annis, we would have our answers."

"You are going nowhere but to bed," he said.

Bliss stared at him for a moment, her temper sparking. "I implied we, and you referred to only me. Do not dare tell me you would go on your own to see my sister and Lord Brogan."

Rannick had no choice, he had to be truthful with her. "My father will see you kept well-protected since he believes you will give the clan an heir. A troop of warriors and my own keen skills will keep me safe. I am far more eager than you can imagine in finding out if the witch has been found."

Bliss yanked free of her husband's grip, though she was wise enough to realize it was because he had loosened his grip and allowed her to do so. Her temper flared even more when he began to don his garments.

"You intend to leave now?" she asked incredulously.

"At first light," he confirmed.

"That is why you were distracted when making love to me. You knew all this and did not tell me," she accused, upset that he kept it from her churning her stomach.

"You seemed pleased enough with our lovemaking or were you not as satisfied as you appeared to be?" he asked, a heated glare in his eyes.

She laughed, though it was not a pleasing laugh. "That is what concerns you whether you pleased me or not, not that you kept your plan from me?"

"I knew you would not be pleased with it," he said as if his excuse sufficed.

"So, if you think something will displease me, you simply will not tell me about it? Perhaps I should do the same." She reached for her shift to slip on, feeling too exposed naked, especially with her husband clothed. Her husband's hand locked around her wrist, stopping her.

"You will keep nothing from me," he ordered.

"Nay, husband," she said defiantly. "If you keep things from me, then I will do the same."

Guilt jabbed at her, since she was already keeping something from him.

Rannick yanked her close to him. "I trust you not to do to me what others have done. You promised to speak truthfully to me, and I have trusted your word. Perhaps I should have told you of my plan before now and perhaps it is no excuse to lay blame on my fear of failing to keep you safe if I took you with me, but I must see this done. I must learn what Brogan knows that he will not trust to a messenger."

"Do you not think I feel the same? Do you not think I wish to rush off and speak with my sister?" she argued. "If it is dangerous for me to go, then it is just as dangerous for you as well. What if something happened to you? Where does that leave me? I would no longer be welcomed—" She caught the lie before it spilled past her lips. She would be more than welcomed here once Lord Lochlann found out she was with child.

His hands fell away from her wrists and his arms quickly circled her. "This is your home now and always."

"It is no home unless you are here," she said and rested her head on his chest and hugged him tight. "Please, Rannick, do not go. Do not leave me."

He kissed her brow before reluctantly stepping away from her. "I will be right back."

She grabbed his hand. "Promise."

"You have my word," he said and kissed her hand before letting go.

Bliss went to the bed and sat. Tears had threatened her while speaking to her husband, so much of their conversation unnerving her. She had managed to keep them from pooling in her eyes but no more. They rose to the surface, glistening there. The guilt of not telling him that she was with child plagued her, though it could very well be his response to the news that worried her more.

Tears fell one after the other. If he truly loved her, and she believed he did, then she had nothing to fear. It was her own fears that threatened her. Fear that the unexpected news would change something between them and somehow divide them.

She could reason it was his fault for not paying heed to what she had told him and remind him that the blame was his. But she did not want blame laid on him for the child they had conceived out of love.

"Tell him and be done with it," she whispered to herself. "You owe the truth to yourself as well as him."

She brushed away her tears, not wanting him to see them.

The door opened and she sniffled the last of her tears away as quietly as she could, lifted her head, and tried to smile. Tears sprang loose once again, and she blamed the loss of control on the bairn that snuggled safely in her stomach.

Rannick's heart felt like it tore in two when he saw her tears and he rushed to scoop her up and place her on his lap after sitting on the bed.

"I am not going. I am not leaving you," he said, wiping at her tears. "I am sending two troops of warriors to escort Annis and Brogan here. I would bring Elysia here if I could, but Odran is right keeping her safe where she is since she is with child."

Words failed her, not so a response. She threw her arms around his neck and kissed him.

"I love you so much," she said a bit breathless after her vigorous kiss.

"I am a lucky man to have such a trustful wife," he said and returned her enthusiastic kiss with one of his own.

Breathless once again, she barely got out the words when the kiss ended. "I need to tell you something."

"Later," he said, turning with her in his arms to deposit her on the bed, then shedding his own garments, he dropped down to rest over her. "Right now, I need you."

He needed to say no more, for she felt the same. Her heart swelled with love for this damaged man who had managed to survive endless pain and suffering and emerge more courageous for it.

"Not as much as I need you," she whispered by his ear, then nibbled along it.

He shuddered against her, her warm breath and her teasing nibbles soared his passion. When her hand slipped down to take hold of his manhood, he tensed.

"Be careful or this will be over fast," he warned.

"Then we will start again," she said and stroked his shaft.

He grinned and the next instant she found herself with her legs in the air and over his shoulders. "We do it my way."

She gasped when he grabbed her bottom in his hands and lifted her, so that he could easily guide his shaft slowly inside her.

"I want to watch you explode with pleasure, not once but twice before I savor my own," he said and with a tight grip on her backside slammed her against him driving his shaft deep inside her.

She cried out with pleasure always welcoming the feel of him snug inside her.

All thought was lost as he took control and she gladly surrendered to her growing passion. It swirled in her and around her mounting in leaps and bounds, robbing her of any sound thought or reason. Pleasure, born of love, was all there was, and she allowed herself to sink deep into it.

"You are mine and always will be," Rannick said, reminding her, though more reassuring himself.

He withdrew until only the tip of his shift tickled her entrance and she cried out, pleading, "Rannick!"

He glared at her not with anger but with an intense love and he drove her passion to new heights.

"Mine," she said on a rushed whisper. "You are mine always."

He drove into her as he dropped down over her, and her arms went around him to hold on tight as his every thrust sent her closer to the edge of oblivion.

He cried out along with her as they tumbled together into endless pleasure, clinging tightly as they exploded, wave after wave consuming them.

Afterwards when she lay on her side, Rannick wrapped snug around her, the blanket drawn over them, he whispered in a sleepy voice, "You had something to tell me."

Bliss kept her eyes closed and kept an even breath, feigning sleep. A few minutes later her husband's even breathing sounded near her ear… he had fallen asleep.

She had to tell him of the bairn but found herself unable to. She could not wait, and she lay awake thinking of the best way to see it done.

Chapter 26

Bliss stood outside the healing cottage watching the snow falling lightly. She was excited for her sister to arrive but knew it would be a few days before she did so. She had stopped herself from telling her husband about the bairn even though the guilt ate at her. Not knowing how he would feel, she thought it best to wait until after her sister left.

She hurried forward when she spotted Damia running toward her.

"Slow down," Bliss urged when she reached the young woman and grew alarmed when she saw tears in her eyes. "Is it the bairn? Have you pain?"

Damia shook her head. "Lady Faline is here. Please, my lady, please I beg of you do not let her take me away."

"You are not going anywhere," Bliss said firmly. "This is your home and here is where you will stay."

"Damia, what's wrong? Is it the bairn?" Bram asked, hurrying toward them.

Damia turned and ran to Bram, his arms wrapping around her to hold her tight.

"Lady Faline is here," she said through choked tears.

Bram spoke with a spark of anger. "You are not going anywhere."

"I will go see to this," Bliss said. "Her visit may have nothing to do with Damia at all."

"Lady Faline always gets her way," Damia warned and huddled closer against Bram.

"Lady Faline will not take you away. I will make sure of it," Bram said confidently.

"Keep Damia out of sight, Bram," Bliss urged.

"Have no worries, my lady, I will keep her from harm," Bram assured her.

Bliss rushed toward the keep wondering if Bram realized how he felt about Damia.

"You should have told me you were coming, Faline, I would have had something prepared," Bliss heard Lady Helice say as she entered the Great Hall.

"It is not a visit, Helice. I have come to collect my servant that my son had no right taking from me and that he wrongly fostered off on you."

The woman's commanding tone had Bliss thinking that Damia was right... the woman did intend to have her way.

"Bliss, let me introduce you to Lord Brogan's mother, Lady Faline," Helice said, waving her forward anxiously.

Bliss went to Lady Helice's side and one look at Lady Faline with her hair drawn back so tightly from her face that she would not be surprised if it had stretched wrinkles away.

"Faline, this is Rannick's wife, Bliss," Helice said with a smile.

"I hope this one lasts longer than the other three," Lady Faline said, her eyes roaming over Bliss. "You are Annis's sister?"

"I am, my lady," Bliss said proudly.

"She is a brazen one trapping my son into marriage," Lady Faline said.

The news that Annis was actually wed to Brogan came as a surprise even though she had heard rumors, but she did not let it show. She did, however, correct the woman's accusation. "It would not be Annis who trapped Lord Brogan into marriage."

Faline's face contorted in anger. "You dare suggest it was my son's doing? You peasants do not know your place."

"I will not tolerate you insulting my son's wife, Faline," Helice reprimanded.

"She needs reprimanding for her outrageous remark

about my son," Faline argued.

"Have you asked your son how their marriage came about?" Helice asked.

"There is no need to. My son knows his obligation to his clan and would never marry a peasant willingly. Amuse himself with one perhaps, but not wed one," Lady Flaine said with a distasteful scrunch of her nose.

"Perhaps your son wed my sister because he loves her," Bliss said, recalling the interest Brogan had shown in Annis and the way they enjoyed bantering with each other.

"My son may dally with a peasant, but I can assure you he would never love a peasant, let alone wed one willingly," Faline said, her distaste of the subject remaining firm on her face.

Bliss forced herself to keep a pleasant tone. "Love can be unpredictable. Besides, from what I was made aware of all three lords had agreed that a search would be made among the peasants for a wife."

"Lord Balloch would never have agreed to something so absurd. He learned from his own folly of having dallied foolishly with a peasant. That horrible woman, Verbena. His father, the wise man that he was, saved him from such a dreadful mistake. He would never permit his son to make the very same one he almost did," Faline said and waved her hand dismissing the matter.

Bliss wanted to remind the annoying woman that a search had been made among the peasants since no noble would entertain an offer of marriage from the three cursed lords. But out of respect for Lady Helice, she held her tongue.

"Bring me my servant so that I may be on my way before the snow turns heavy and traps me here," Lady Faline demanded.

Bliss kept her response firm. "Damia has a home here now. She is not going anywhere."

261

"You have no authority in this matter," Lady Faline said, dismissing Bliss with the flip of her hand. "This is Lord Lochlann's decision."

"What is my decision?" Lord Lochlann asked, entering the room.

"Finally, someone with authority in this matter," Lady Faline said. "I have come to collect my servant, Lochlann. Please have her brought here so I may return home."

Bliss hurried to speak up. "Damia serves me now. She assists me with my healing."

"Nonsense," Lady Faline snapped. "Another woman can be found to help you."

"That will be Bliss's choice," Lord Lochlann commanded and turned to Bliss. "Give me a good reason why Damia would serve you better than another woman and I will allow her to stay."

Faline grinned as if tasting victory. "Do tell us, Bliss, why a peasant would need another peasant."

There was one reason Lord Lochlann would agree but was Bliss willing to expose her secret? Did she have a choice? She could not let Damia be returned to the vicious woman. Her husband was not here to hear the news, but she would have to find him and tell him before he heard it from others.

"I am teaching Damia all the different things she needs to know to deliver a bairn so that mother and child are kept safe and suffer no loss."

Lord Lochlann spoke up before Bliss could continue. "We have women here who have delivered many bairns."

Anxious with what Bliss was about to say, her stomach roiled. This was not how she hoped to deliver the news. "None have trained with me, and I want someone at least acquainted with my knowledge of safe deliveries when my times comes to deliver the Clan MacClaren heir."

Lochlann's eyes widened in shock. "Are you saying you

are with child?"

"Aye," Bliss confirmed, resting her hand on her stomach. "I am with child."

"She lies to keep me from taking the servant," Lady Faline accused.

"That is easy enough to solve," Lord Lochlann said. "I will have your word, Bliss, that you do not lie, that you are truly with child."

Bliss did not hesitate. "You have my word, my lord, "I am with child three months now."

Lochlann burst into a smile and shouted, "AN HEIR! Clan MacClaren will have an heir!" He turned his tremendous smile on Faline. "Damia stays here, Faline."

"I will not forget this, Lochlann," Faline threatened. "And why you would rejoice when a peasant carries the heir to your clan is absurd."

"Be careful, Faline, that heir just may rule over your clan one day," Lochlann warned with glee.

"Never! Never!" Faline said, wagging her finger at him and took her leave in a rush.

"You better make sure Lady Faline causes no trouble for Damia on her way out, Lochlann," Lady Helice cautioned.

"You are right," Rannick's father said, and his smile turned even larger when he looked to Bliss. "You did it. You kept your part of the bargain. You are an honorable woman, and I am proud to have you part of this family."

Bliss turned to tell Helice that she had to go find Rannick, and though her mouth fell open no words fell out as the shadowed corner released her husband to stand a short distance from her. His scowl told her all she needed to know.

Helice looked from her son to Bliss, smiling. "I am thrilled with the news, thrilled for you both." Her smile turned to a wide grin. "It looks like you were right about that mixture, Bliss." She laughed lightly. "I will leave you two to talk."

Bliss remained silent, waiting for her husband to say something.

"To our bedchamber, wife," Rannick said, pointing the way.

Bliss nodded and took the lead, her husband following in complete silence close behind her and her stomach twisting with every curve of the stone staircase.

She remained silent upon entering the room, anxious over what her husband would say.

Rannick stood braced against the door, his arms crossed over his chest, once he closed it. He stared at her, saying not a word.

Bliss sighed, the silence too much for her. "I did give you fair warning and need I remind you that you stubbornly refused to believe to me."

His response shocked her.

"I have been waiting for you to tell me of the bairn."

Her mouth fell open once again, and once again words failed her.

He pushed himself off the door and walked toward her. "I had my suspicions, but I doubted them since I watched you drink the brew day after day. It was easy to deny it to myself and certainly to my father each time he mentioned it." He stopped in front of her, his hand gently cupping one breast. "We are far too intimate with each other for me not to notice the subtle changes in your body." A tender smile crossed his face as his hand moved to gently touch at the corner of her right eye. "But it was the way you took so easily to tears that had me thinking you were right about the brew. You never shed a tear when you were in pain from your wound, and I recalled how teary-eyed my first wife got once with child. I could no longer ignore or deny what was in front of me, but I waited, said nothing, though I tried giving you a chance to tell me a few times, since I wanted to hear it from you that you were with child."

"When did you try?" she asked her shock growing.

"When I told you I would have to tell my da soon. When I mentioned Odran would not allow Elysia to travel and either would I if I knew you were with child, and when I refused to take you with me when I had planned to talk with Brogan and Annis. I thought you might mention it any of those times. I hoped you would since I wanted to hear you say it."

With tears tickling at her eyes, she said it now, "I am with child, your child, our child."

"I should be full of fear with that news and yet amazingly I feel nothing but pure joy." He cupped her face and kissed her gently, then rested his brow against hers and whispered, "I love you, Bliss, right down to my wicked soul."

She smiled and teased, "I like when you are wicked."

"Do not tempt me, wife," he warned playfully. "That is what got us into this situation."

She laughed softly. "You are happy with the news?"

"When the thought first struck me that you might be with child, I grew angry at myself and fearful for you, since the blame was mine. But in time, and with the thought having taken root, I began to favor the possibility until I hoped it was true. So, aye, the news brings me great joy."

Rannick went to kiss her again when a sudden shout and banging sounded at the door.

"Hurry! Hurry!"

They both rushed to the door and followed the servant down the stairs and outside. Rannick grabbed a cloak, hurrying it around his wife's shoulders just before they stepped outside.

Bliss halted abruptly as she caught sight of her sister Annis, a tall gray-haired man holding her back from going after Lady Faline.

"YOU LIE!" Annis screamed at Lady Faline, fighting to escape from the man that held her firm.

"How dare you accuse me of lying," Lady Faline said, anger burning in her eyes. "I know my son and he would never willing wed the likes of you and never, ever, would he love someone of such low birth. And where is he? He did not accompany you here, therefore, he cares little what happens to you." She sneered. "And you are yet to get with child. That surely must tell you he plans no future with you."

Bliss went to rush down the snow-covered stone stairs.

"Easy," Rannick said, grabbing her arm and slowing her decent as he went with her.

"That will be enough, Faline," Lord Lochlann ordered.

"I come here to fetch my servant, thinking you an honorable man, Lochlann, and would return what belongs to me. You refused and now this insane peasant nearly attacks me," Lady Faline said, shaking her head.

"Over my dead body will you take Damia." Annis said with a far more superior command than expected from a peasant.

"That can be arranged," Lady Faline said with a smile.

"Threaten my wife's sister again, Lady Faline, and I will see you suffer the fate you threaten," Rannick called out as he and Bliss approached the group.

"BLISS!" Annis cried out, tears filling her eyes as the man released her and she ran to her sister.

"I see the rumors are true about Rannick... he is more evil than human," Lady Faline said with a sneer of disgust.

Rannick walked over to Lady Faline, leaving Bliss and Annis to hug tight. "Aye, they are, and I will have no problem seeing to your demise."

"Rannick!" his mother scolded, hurrying in front of her son, though faced Faline. "My son has an excuse for his poor manners, but you Lady Faline have no such excuse for your poor behavior here today. Unless you apologize, you are no longer welcome here."

Lady Faline drew her head back as if struck. "My husband will not be happy when he hears what happened here today."

"I will make sure that Lord Balloch knows all that happened here today," Lochlann said. "Now it is time for you to depart."

Rannick turned his back on Lady Faline and went to his wife.

Annis jumped in front of her sister, her hand shooting out to jab Rannick in the chest. "You better be treating her good or you will answer to me."

Rannick stared down at her finger that continued to jab. "You know I can break that easily, don't you?"

She raised both her hands to wiggle her fingers in his face. "I've got nine more."

Bliss smiled and shook her head and said what would make all the difference to her sister. "Rannick loves me, and I love him. We are happy together."

Annis looked for confirmation, eyeing Rannick skeptically. "You truly love Bliss?"

"My word on it," he said and reached out to pull his wife into his arms.

"Well, that's a relief," Annis said. "I have been worried sick about you being wed to him, especially when your message said you were busy working in the garden. I know how you always went to the garden when you had much on your mind. And Brogan refused to let me come here and I could only take the worry for so long, so I decided to make the trip with some friends."

"Brogan does not know you're here?" Rannick asked with a slight chuckle.

"By now he probably does," Annis said. "I imagine he won't be far behind."

"I sent troops to collect the both of you," Rannick said.

"We avoided them," Annis said, pointing to the man who had kept her from going after Lady Faline.

Rannick took stock of the man. His gray hair, beard, and wrinkles noted his age, but his lean and fit body marked him as a seasoned warrior and one who had retained his strength since he had easily kept a struggling Annis at bay against Lady Faline. Seeing the group of men standing not far behind him and battle ready with their hands on the hilts of their swords and daggers, it was easy enough to surmise who they were.

"Mercenaries," Rannick said.

"Troy and friends," Annis corrected.

Annis had a far different nature from her sister Bliss and features as well. Annis's beauty startled the eyes as did her long, flaming red hair that sprung in ringlets around her head and down over her shoulders. She had the boldest green eyes he had ever seen on a woman and a brash tongue to match.

"There is much for us to discuss, Bliss," Annis said eager to speak with her sister.

Bliss could not agree more, but first... "Aye, like your marriage to Brogan."

"There is that and lots more important stuff."

"Bring your friends into the keep so they may have food and drink while we talk," Bliss offered.

Annis gave a wave to Troy and his men to follow. "I'm starving. You didn't cook the food by any chance did you?" she asked as they walked to the keep.

"I wish," Rannick said, and Annis laughed.

Chatter filled the air of the Great Hall as cloaks were shed, drinks passed around to everyone and introductions were finally just about to be made when the door crashed open.

Brogan entered, his face a fiery mask of anger as his eyes scoured the room and when they landed on Annis, he headed straight for her as he called out, "You are going to pay for this one, wife!"

Chapter 27

Bliss moved protectively in front of Annis, fearful for her safety since she had seen Brogan lose his temper when at Clan Loudon.

Annis quickly stepped around her and ran toward Brogan, smiling.

Brogan halted his steps and braced himself to catch his wife in his arms.

Annis's threw herself at her husband, her arms hooking his neck as she brought her legs up to catch at his hips, and his arm slipped under her backside to hold her steady.

"What kept you?" she asked. "I thought for sure you would catch up with me before I arrived here."

"Maybe if you hadn't set me to work on a useless chore, I would have realized it sooner," he accused, his scowl having yet to fade.

"Then you would have stopped me from coming here and I told you this could wait no longer," Annis said and gave him a quick kiss. "I missed you."

Brogan shook his head. "Do you realize the danger you put yourself in?"

"I had Troy and his mercenaries with me," Annis said as if it explained it well enough.

"That, wife, is no excuse," Brogan warned.

Annis's arms fell away from around her husband's neck and her legs from around his waist to stand in front of him. "We can discuss this later. Right now, there are more important matters that need to be addressed."

"We had agreed to wait," Brogan whispered.

"No more," she murmured and took his hand and

tugged at him to follow.

Rannick grinned as he handed Brogan a tankard of ale and kept himself from laughing when his friend downed the whole thing, then held it out to be refilled.

Unable to keep a laugh from surfacing, Rannick said, "She's a handful."

Brogan laughed himself. "In so many ways."

"And he isn't?" Annis asked with a nod at her husband. "No matter what his mum claimed or thinks, or how rude she was, my husband loves me very much." She fought the tears that threatened her and silently cursed that she was prone to tears far too often and for the most foolish things. "And while neither of us realized that our marriage came about by our own words, we are both happy that it did, and nothing or no one will change that."

Brogan shook his head, his brow creasing. "When did you see my mum?"

"I am surprised you did not cross paths with her," Rannick said. "She left not long before you arrived."

"I came the back way through the woods," Brogan said. "What was she doing here?"

One word was all Annis had to say. "Damia."

Rannick quickly assured his friend. "Damia remains with us."

Brogan smiled. "It is good to see you again, my friend, and to know I can still count on you."

"Always," Rannick said, and the two men hugged, slapping each other on the back. "It has been too long."

"Not anymore," Annis claimed confidently. "We will see each other often, since I will no longer be kept from my sister."

Rannick went to his wife to curl his arm around her waist. "You will have to travel here then, since your sister is with child."

Annis's eyes went wide. "Truly?"

Bliss smiled and nodded. "Truly."

Annis let out a squeal of delight and hurried to her sister and they hugged once again. She wiped tears away as she stepped back from Bliss. "You and Elysia will make the best mums. I only wish she was here now with us." Her eyes went wide. "How will you ever deliver Elysia's bairn when you will probably be close to delivering your own?"

"Not to worry. I will see to it," Bliss assured her and caught a look of concern on her husband's face, he just now realizing the delicate situation.

"With you both with child, it is now more important than ever to see this curse ended once and for all," Annis said. "We need to talk privately."

Lady Helice stepped forward. "I had your father's solar prepared with food and drink for you. Worry not about your friends, Annis, Lord Lochlann and I will look after them."

"Thank you, Lady Helice, that is very kind of you," Annis said.

Rannick took his wife's hand and led Brogan and Annis to the solar.

Lady Helice grabbed her husband's hand when he went to follow.

"You can see to the guests," Lochlann said. "I will hear what they have to say."

"Nay, Lochlann," Helice said softly. "It is no longer your fight. It is for your son to see to now."

"But this started with me," he insisted.

"The good Lord willing, it will end with Rannick, and he will have a good life," Helice said, and took hold of her husband's arm. "Now, what do you say we see how Annis came to be with these mercenaries."

***

Bliss sat beside her husband with her sister and Brogan

across from them at the table Lady Helice had seen set up for them in front of the hearth. There was food and drink aplenty and, after the troubling few hours, Bliss was relieved for the respite and thrilled that her sister was there to enjoy it with her. Though, she did look forward to time alone to talk with Annis.

"You are not as frightening as I thought you would be," Annis said with a nod to Rannick after a sip of wine. "Though I imagine my sister tamed you some. She is good at doing that."

"An yet she failed with you," Rannick said, with a slight rise of his goblet of wine.

Bliss and Brogan shook their heads.

Annis smiled. "Nice retort, but my sister understands about me what others do not, though Brogan was the exception. She knew taming me was not what I needed. She was wise enough and loved me enough to let me be who I am, and for that I am ever grateful." She brushed at her eyes before a tear could fall.

"The only difference between us then," Rannick said, taking his wife's hand that rested on the table, "is that your sister freed me of the heartless man I had become, to become a better man and, like you, I am forever grateful and will forever love her."

Annis looked to her sister, still smiling. "You worked a miracle."

"Did you as well?" Rannick asked. "Did you accomplish what I failed to do? Did you find the witch?"

"We found much more," Brogan said.

"But we will start with the witch because that is where it all began, "Annis said. "I believe she found me, set it in motion for me to go to her. For some reason, the time has been made right for the curse to be made right. She sent Brogan and me on a merry chase. I won't give you all the details right now, but it led us to discover that the

273

MacWilliam bairn lives and to also meet Gunna."

Bliss dropped the piece of bread in her hand and Rannick splashed his wine over the rim of the goblet, he placed it so fast on the table.

Annis continued before they could ask any questions. "Gunna posed as a woman named Luna and joined us in the village for a while. Unfortunately, she left before I realized who she truly was, though Troy knows her well. She took shelter with the mercenaries after being badly injured all those years ago and that is why she was never found."

"Gunna knows where the MacWilliam bairn is?" Bliss asked anxiously, thinking how this curse could be made to end soon and the damage and pain it could bring finally brought to an end.

"Where the MacWilliam bairn, now grown woman, is… is the problem," Brogan said. "The bairn was given to a childless couple to raise as their own so none would suspect any difference. When Gunna returned after a few months to check on the bairn, she discovered the couple had died. She had no idea where the bairn was. The only thing she knew that might have helped locate her was that two other young bairns had been placed with the MacWilliam bairn in case the ruse was discovered. And one of them had bright red springy hair."

Annis kept focused the whole time on Bliss, her heart beating wildly worried how she would take the news that they were not truly sisters.

"Are you saying that Annis is the MacWilliam bairn?" Rannick asked.

"We are saying that Annis, Elysia, or Bliss could be the MacWilliam bairn," Brogan said.

Rannick was struck silent for a moment, before stating the obvious. "That would mean the three are not sisters and that any of us three, you, Odran, or I could be wed to the MacWilliam bairn."

"Aye, that is right," Brogan confirmed.

The shock had a gasp caught somewhere inside Bliss and she was glad her husband still held tight to her hand and that he squeezed it, letting her know she was not in this alone. Never would she have suspected such startling news. It also made more real the secret her mum had divulged to her on her deathbed. But this—this unbelievable news—was difficult to comprehend let alone accept.

The silence, hanging heavily in the room, was finally broken by Annis. "This revelation changes nothing for me, Bliss. To me, we are sisters and always will be."

Bliss shook her head, seeing Annis close to tears, and she reached across the table to take hold of her hand and give it a loving squeeze. "I should have told you, but I gave Mum my word to say nothing."

Annis held tight to Bliss's hand. "You knew all this time we were not sisters?"

"I only learned it when Mum confessed it on her deathbed. She had me swear I would tell no one and I have kept my word. It was a shock to learn it, but it mattered little to me. You and Elysia are my sisters, and nothing would have changed that then nor does it now. Mum never told me of each of our true parents nor did she mention the MacWilliam bairn."

"That must have been a heavy burden to carry," Annis said.

"For Mum, but not for me," Bliss confessed. "We were and still are sisters and I was not going to let anything change that."

"I am glad you didn't, and I am grateful you kept the family together," Annis said. "But there is more you must know. It seems that though we are not sisters, we are related. We are cousins." She took a breath before delivering more surprising news. "Gunna was Aila's sister and had a daughter of her own. Fearing what might happen to the bairn

275

if discovered she was her child, she gave her daughter to the childless couple along with the MacWilliam bairn."

"And the third bairn? Who did she belong to?" Bliss asked.

"Aila and Gunna's sister—Verbena," Annis said.

"That name is familiar to me," Bliss said and quickly recalled. "Lady Faline spoke that name today. She was a peasant Lord Balloch had once loved and his father refused to allow him to wed her. Where is she now?"

"That we have not been able to find out," Brogan said. "She disappeared years ago and has never been heard from since."

"The witch had told me to find the MacWilliam lass and all would come to pass," Annis said. "I thought she meant I was to find the lass, but Brogan and I realized I was meant to find the woman who was to find the MacWilliam lass— Gunna. All has been set in motion to end the curse. We have tossed around everything we learned, thinking perhaps Bliss is the MacWilliam bairn and if you found love with Rannick the curse would be broken and eventually the MacWilliam bloodline continued."

Rannick tightened his hold on his wife's hand. "If that is so, I give you my word that I will let nothing happen to you or our bairn."

Bliss smiled softly. "I have no doubt of that." But she could not help but think of Lord Brochan who must have pledged similar words to his wife only to find the pledge impossible to keep. And fear raced through her knowing Rannick would give his life as Lord Brochan had done twenty years ago, for the woman he loved and the daughter he never got to know.

"Troy warned us against telling anyone so that we did not interfere with the curse being made right." Brogan turned his head to glare at his wife. "But someone changed her mind."

"They had enough time together to fall in love or hate each other. I had to know. We could not continue to sit back and do nothing," Annis said. "At least we know that Elysia and Odran are in love, which leaves the three of us in love, so why hasn't the curse been broken? Or does it have nothing to do with love?"

"How do you know the curse hasn't been broken?" Bliss asked.

"Attempts have been made on all our lives," Annis said.

"That may not have anything to do with the curse," Bliss said. "Someone has convinced a group of people that Brogan, Odran, and Rannick must die for the curse to end and now us wives as well since we can bear children who in their eyes will continue the curse. But hasn't life been good for us all recently? Haven't we all been happy?"

Brogan grinned. "I haven't been as happy as I have been in I cannot remember when, even though my wife can be difficult at—OW!" He rubbed his arm where Annis punched him though it was barely a tap, and he laughed. "I was missing your love taps." He kissed her quick. "Though I intend to have a word with Troy since he is supposed to be my right-hand man and he went off with you without a word to me."

"He didn't have time to alert you. He saw me leave and took off after me, his men following without question.

"You did not plan this?" Brogan asked, surprised.

"Of course, I planned it. I always make plans. You cannot succeed without plans and these plans of mine proved that. Everything went according to plan, though I did expect you to catch up with me just before arriving here so you could arrive with me," Annis explained.

Brogan shook his head and went to say something when he noticed Rannick lost in thought, staring down at his wine goblet.

"Something on your mind, Rannick?" Brogan asked.

A small grunt came from Rannick before he said, "I believe there is more to this group that hunts us. The answer to it lies with the one who leads them. But he hides his identity well." He shook his head as if clearing his thoughts. "Annis is right. A plan is needed if we are to catch the culprit."

Annis rubbed her hands together. "Time to make a plan."

***

Rannick kept his wife snug against him after a hasty bout of lovemaking. When they had retired for the night after a day full of unexpected revelations that was sure to cause difficulties ahead, he had an overpowering need to sink himself deep inside her and escape.

It was there he always felt as if they were one and, no one or anything could ever separate them. That was the escape he needed, to a place that no one could ever invade.

His hand drifted to splay over her stomach. "I should not have pounded you so hard now that you carry our bairn."

A soft yawn escaped her. "Later when I am heavily rounded, a pounding might not be wise, but you have pounded me the last three months and the bairn still does well."

"You will tell me if anything I do causes you discomfort."

"Having me followed everywhere does get uncomfortable," she said.

He poked her in the side. "That is not what I meant, wife, and you know it."

She turned to face him, his arms remaining snug around her. "I worry as you do, not just for us but my sisters and their husbands as well. I am glad we agreed that once discovered, the MacWilliam lass's identity should remain a secret between us all."

"Still, we search to make sure the curse will be brought to an end and take the chance of revealing the MacWilliam lass's identity, possibly exposing her to danger," he reminded and gave a gentle squeeze to her side. "If it turns out to be you, I will do right by you, Bliss, and see you and our bairn kept from harm."

Bliss smiled. "I have no doubt you would, but the MacWilliam lass has three courageous warriors to protect her if necessary. Whoever she turns out to be, she has nothing to worry about."

Rannick grinned. "If it turns out to be Annis, she certainly has no worries. She appears fearless."

"Blood," Bliss said. "Annis faints at the sight of too much blood."

"I have to remember that," Rannick said with a grin.

Bliss yawned and rested herself against her husband. "I am so happy Annis is here. I just wish Elysia could be here as well."

"In time, you will all be together again," he assured her.

"But it will be different," she said softly, sleep creeping up on her. "Fate has seen that none of us are who we once were."

Rannick kissed her brow and watched her drift off to sleep before he whispered, "And that is for the better."

Chapter 28

"A cottage just for healing," Annis said, glancing around. "This must make you happy."

"Much has made me happy of late," Bliss said and pointed to a bench by the table. "Sit and tell me about you and Brogan while I fix us a hot brew to chase away the chill."

Annis's face lit with delight. "I love him, though I have no idea how that came about. It surprised me as much as our marriage did."

"How is it you wed him when you were so against it?"

All delight fled from Annis's face and tears were quick to gather in her eyes. "I am so sorry, Bliss. If I had wed Brogan when I was chosen to be his wife, you would not have had to sacrifice yourself. I feel as if I betrayed you."

"Nonsense!" Bliss scolded. "If you had wed Brogan, I would have never gotten to meet Rannick, never gotten to fall in love, and never gotten to have a bairn of my own. I do not, nor will I ever regret the bargain I made to see you kept safe. I am overjoyed that you got to wed the man you loved and in your time. Now tell me how it came about."

Annis's smile returned and she chuckled. "It was our own words that did it. Remember how after you struck that bargain with Lawler, on behalf of Rannick's father, to wed Rannick and save Brogan and me from being forced to wed, that Brogan and I quickly spoke up agreeing to wed to prevent you from making such a terrible decision? That is what did it. I made the choice of my own free will as did Brogan, sealing our fate." She chuckled again. We are lucky it turned out so well. He is a good husband. He encourages me to be me. We are building the most wonderful village just as I always wanted to." The few tears that had gathered in her eyes slipped out. "I am happy, but I miss you and Elysia. I worried more about you than Elysia. She had Saber—Lord Odran—to keep her safe. You had no one. You had to face the cursed lord on your own."

Bliss reached out to give her sister's hand a comforting squeeze. "Thankfully all worked out for the best and we will soon get to see Elysia again. Though something tells me you have plans to see her sooner rather than later."

"Elysia's husband needs to know what we have discovered and the final plan we decide upon, so he can make certain she is kept safe while we dig for more answers," Annis said. "Brogan and I can take the news to her."

"I am sure Rannick will send warriors with you to see you and Brogan kept safe," Bliss said, a request she knew would not be necessary. "I can wait no longer. I am curious. Tell me about the witch."

An image of the witch came to mind as Annis spoke. "She has an abrupt and commanding manner, but then she possesses wisdom far beyond the ordinary, and I imagine it is difficult for her to tolerate fools. She speaks, yet her words are not always clear. It is as if she wants you to ponder them and decide on your own. She has a regal bearing about her and I cannot help but wonder over her origin."

"How did she come to know Gunna and Lady Aila?" Bliss asked.

Annis shook her head. "That is a question I never thought to ask."

"I wonder if Gunna will recognize the bairn she hid all those years ago," Bliss said.

"Perhaps she resembles her mum, though if that was so, surely someone would have noticed," Annis said and bounced off the bench. "Let's go ask Lady Helice about

Lady Aila. Surely, she was familiar with her."

"She will wonder why we ask," Bliss cautioned. "And if I learned one thing while here, it is that Lady Helice is much wiser than anyone realizes."

Annis sat. "At least you have a nice mother-in-law. Mine is a shrew."

"Watch your words, Annis, she is Brogan's mother," Bliss cautioned.

"You saw for yourself what an ill-tempered woman she is and if you witnessed the beating with a stick I took to protect Damia, you would have done more than swear at her." Annis grinned. "You probably would have thrown yourself over me as I did with Damia."

"You are right about that. I would never stand by and see you or Elysia hurt." Bliss turned silent for a moment. "I cannot imagine what it must have been like for Gunna to leave her sister knowing she faced death."

Tears hurried in Annis's eyes once again. "I worried every day that I was too slow in finding the witch and seeing the curse ended before it claimed your life. I still worry about it with Rannick having lost three wives."

"His wives did not die because of the curse. They were murdered," Bliss said and watched her sister's eyes spread wide. She hurried to reassure her. "Rannick keeps me safe."

"What makes you different from his other three wives?" Annis asked, shaking her head. "There is no rhythm or reason to the attacks made on our lives. Some hunt us for coins, others because they believe it is the righteous thing to do. They believe themselves warriors against evil. But who put this nonsense in their heads? Who convinced them to go after the cursed lords?"

"You have always told me a foundation is necessary when building. If you don't have something firm to hold up the structure then it will not remain firm and secure. It will eventually crumble. We need to start there—with the

282

foundation."

"And the foundation would be?" Annis asked.

"The reason this person is pitting people against our husbands. This man pays the greedy ones, but the other men fight to destroy evil. This person is after something, and he does not care who dies for him to achieve his goal."

"Power," Annis said. "It seems the more power men get, the more they want. Isn't that the true reason Lady Alia and Lord Brochan died? The King simply would not be denied gaining more power." She wrinkled her face. "But who gains power if our husbands die? Their fathers still live. It makes no sense."

"It makes sense to someone," Bliss said.

"We have to stop this madman. I need to think. We need a solid plan to—"

The door flew open, and Damia hurried in, rushing to shut the door. "I am sorry. I did not mean to disturb, but a raven chased after me and this was the closest place to escape the angry bird."

Annis stood, grabbed her cloak, and tossed Bliss's cloak to her. "Come with me."

"Stay until you feel safe, Damia," Bliss hurried to say as her sister rushed her out the door.

Annis looked around. Several more ravens had appeared diving and pecking at the guards left to watch over Bliss.

"It is the witch," Annis said, keeping her voice low. "She wants to see us."

A raven dipped down toward them, squawked and took off toward the woods behind the healing cottage.

"We follow it," Annis said.

"What if someone waits for us in the woods?" Bliss asked.

"The only one who waits for us is the witch. She commands the ravens and the wolves," Annis said and hurried Bliss along.

***

Rannick sat with his father and Brogan in the Great Hall, no one but the three men there, not even a servant. They sat at one of the tables near a corner where the shadows cloaked them.

"She is alive isn't she?" Lord Lochlann more demanded than asked. When neither his son nor Brogan responded, Lochlann's shoulders slumped. "Fergus and I both had grown tired of the endless search for the MacWilliam bairn. When a dead bairn had been presented to us, we accepted it as fact. We never bothered to correct anyone when it was assumed one of us ended the bairn's life. It was over and done, and that was all that mattered."

"The tale will continue," Rannick said. "Our only interest is to see the curse ended and along with it the pain and suffering."

He had no intention of telling his father that Bliss or one of her sisters might be the MacWilliam lass. As they all had agreed last night, that would remain their secret.

"Did you know Gunna was Lady Aila's sister?" Brogan asked.

Lochlann nodded. "Gunna showed up at the keep when Aila was about five months with child. She got on well with the servants and Aila would often laugh and tease her about being one of them. She called Gunna her most faithful, trusted servant. Gunna even referred to her as my lady or Lady Aila. I thought it strange, but afterwards I realized it was messages they exchanged in front of other people of who could be trusted and who could not. I was not among the trusted."

"What about the third sister, Verbena?" Rannick asked.

"Verbena vanished after Balloch's father threatened her.

Many believe his father had her killed so that she could never trouble his son again. Balloch was devastated, he truly loved Verbena. His father forced a marriage to Faline only a few days after Verbena vanished and threatened that he would see her sisters dead if his son searched for her," Lochlann said. "When Brochan learned of the threat to his wife, he confronted Balloch's father, cautioned battle if he dared to harm Aila. Balloch's father could be an evil man for no reason and I for one was glad fate intervened that day. Balloch's father lost his temper badly and was ready to come to blows with Brochan when he clutched his chest and dropped to the ground dead at Brochan's feet. With his father gone, Balloch pursued his search for Verbena but to no avail and then Faline announced she was with child and Balloch abandoned all efforts after that. It was troubling times for all."

"Did you know Lady Aila well?" Rannick asked.

"I knew she was a skilled healer, having helped your mother through a difficult time when she delivered you," Lochlann admitted, his eyes glazing over as if he was transported to another place and time. "Aila did not need to die. She was not a MacWilliam. I begged her to surrender the bairn so she could live. I did not see the dagger. The blood spilled so fast, her life spilling away with it. The curse continues to echo in my thoughts every day.

"She's safe. You'll never find her. And a curse on the three of you for betraying your friend. May you suffer and never know peace until you right this terrible wrong. But you, Lochlann, will suffer the worst for you were his best friend."

A shiver ran through bother Rannick and Brogan.

"How did Lady Aila come by the curse?" Brogan asked.

"A witch… is what many believed, and it could very well be how the witch in the hills was born," Lochlann said. "Though we tried, no proof could be found of a witch. After your father and I were struck by endless tragedies, I tried to think of a way to right the curse, but how did I right a wrong when not one MacWilliam lived?" He looked to his son. "That changes with your discovery. Your mother says it is now your time and I gave you my word that if you gave the clan an heir I would turn the leadership of the clan over to you. The birth of your son or daughter will be that day. Do what you will to see it is a safe day for all."

For the first time since his return home, Rannick saw in his father what he had failed to see, a tired and regretful man who wanted nothing more than peace.

A commotion at the door prevented Rannick from responding.

Lawler rushed into the room. "Hurry, ravens have gone wild attacking people."

"Ravens?" Lochlann repeated in disbelief. "We rarely see them in the village."

Brogan grabbed Rannick's arm, holding him back as Lochlann rushed to Lawler. "The witch is here!"

***

The mist rolled in fast swirling around Annis and Bliss the deeper they got into the woods, the raven leading the way.

"Do not worry, the mist always precedes her," Annis said, keeping her arm snug around Bliss's arm.

Bliss was too eager to meet the witch to worry, though she made sure to keep tight hold of Annis. Instinct, as always, had her protecting her sisters.

They stopped walking when the mist completely devoured them, and the raven could be seen no more.

"The mist will fade, and she will show herself soon," Annis whispered.

The mist did just that, began to fade until it hovered

286

from their waists down and Bliss peered through the slight haze left to see a figure draped in black standing not far from them. Her head was turned slightly to the side, a hood hiding her features.

"You are to leave the curse be. The right has been set in motion to correct the wrong and needs no help from you. It is those who seek to harm you that you most worry about and see to their demise," the witch commanded.

"Why didn't you tell me that my sisters or I may be the MacWilliam lass?" Annis demanded.

"The revelation was before your eyes, but you refused to see it," the witch snapped.

Annis let go of her sister's arm and took a hasty step forward. "I am not blind. I see things clearly. It was you who did not make it clear."

"Not make it clear?" the witch snapped. "Why did you not ever question that the three of you wed the three cursed lords? You truly believed it a coincidence?"

Annis went to argue but stopped.

"Finally, you see it—all has been set in motion with the three marriages. The rest will now follow—unless the one who intends harm succeeds. You must find the one behind it all and put an end to it before it is too late," the witch warned.

"Who is it?" Bliss asked anxiously.

"Do you not think I would tell you if I knew?" the witch snapped. "The person hides himself well, using others to achieve his goal."

"What goal?" Annis asked.

"Everlasting power," the witch said.

"There are many who want that," Annis argued.

The witch shook a finger at Annis. "I grow tired of telling you what you should realize yourself."

"Making it clear might help," Annis shot back.

"You have wisdom, woman, use it," the witch scolded.

287

"Why not just tell us—"

"She cannot," Bliss interrupted.

Annis shook her head. "Why not?"

Bliss shook her head, a stunned look in her eyes. "She fears the power of the curse because she is not the one who created it."

The witch dismissed Annis with the wave of her hand. "Go, Annis, I will speak to the wiser of the two of you."

The mist quickly swirled around Annis until she could see nor hear anything.

"Annis!" Bliss cried out, seeing the fog swallow her sister whole like some mighty beast.

"No harm will befall her," the witch assured. "You understand what others have failed to."

"Not until this moment," Bliss admitted. "Everyone assumed you provided Lady Aila with the powerful curse. But if that were true, you would have more knowledge of it. Your only choice was to wait, hide away until the time was right, and all was set in motion that would help bring the curse to an end."

"You are a wise woman, Bliss," the witch said. "And have more knowledge than you know."

The mist drifted away from the witch's legs to reveal a wolf sitting at her side.

"He appreciates your kindness," the witch said.

Bliss smiled and spoke directly to the wolf. "It is good to see you are well, my friend."

The witch's head went up as if alerted to something.

"It is imperative you find this malicious leader and put an end to his scheme, or all will be lost," the witch urged.

"BLISS!"

Bliss turned expecting to see her husband, but the mist behind her was too thick to see anything.

"Your husband is a powerful man," the witch said.

Bliss caught the annoyance in the witch's voice. "My

husband is a good man."

"BLISS!"

His shout not only sounded stronger but closer as well.

"You love the cursed lord?" the witch asked.

"I very much love my husband," Bliss said with strength and pride.

"And I love my wife," Rannick said, stepping out of the mist to take hold of Bliss's hand while he gripped a sword in his other hand. "If you harm my wife, it will be the last thing you ever do."

"You dare threaten me?" the witch snapped, and, with a slight snarl, the wolf quickly stood on all fours.

"Aye, I do," he confirmed without hesitation and with a snarl of his own.

Bliss hurried to speak up. "No one wishes anyone harm. We must work together to end the threat that can destroy everything."

"Do as I told you, Bliss," the witch ordered and pointed a finger at Rannick. "And you, cursed one, appear in my presence again without my permission and you will be the one to suffer."

"Come on my land again and summon my wife without my permission and you and I will battle," he threatened.

The witch shook her finger at Rannick. "Watch your tongue with me or I will see that you lose it."

Rannick shot back at her. "Try, and I will see that you lose your head."

The witch swirled her hand in the air, thickening the mist. "You tempt fate, cursed one, be very careful or you may lose what you hold dear."

"Bliss?" Rannick called out, her hand no longer in his.

"Rannick!" Bliss shouted, his voice in the distance and she hurried a glance at the witch. "Please do not harm him. He was only protecting me."

"He chose the wrong way to do it. Warn him to guard

289

his tongue around me or I will make him suffer for it," the witch warned. "I do not suffer foolish men lightly. They never know when their tongues do more harm than good. Go! I am done with you for now."

The mist swallowed her, taking with it the mist around Bliss and revealing her husband not far from her.

Bliss ran to him as he did to her, their arms reaching out to clasp tightly around each other.

Fear that he had lost her had Rannick's heart beating like a thunderous drum in his chest and all he wanted to do was keep his wife locked tight and safe in his arms. Unfortunately, the truth of it was that the witch could snatch her away from him at any time and that put a blood-chilling fear in Rannick.

Bliss had realized it as well and did the only thing she believed would keep her husband safe. "You will not speak with the witch again. I will see to her."

Rannick stepped back from her, though kept his hands at her waist. "That is not going to happen."

"I would listen to her if I were you," Brogan advised. "She does it for your own good."

Bliss turned to see Brogan and Annis standing a short distance from them.

"You should heed Brogan's suggestion. He knows of what he speaks," Annis cautioned.

"Except I was the one cautioning my wife to watch her tongue since it got away from her far too often with the witch," Brogan said and laughed when he felt a jab to his side. He grabbed his wife's offending finger and held it tight. "From what I've witnessed of the witch so far, I do not believe she means anyone harm. I truly think she wants this curse ended as much as we do."

"Why did she create such a powerful curse for Lady Aila in the first place?" Rannick asked.

"She didn't create the curse," Bliss said.

"Then who did?" Annis asked.

Chapter 29

Rannick stood in front of the bedchamber door he had just closed, his eyes on his wife. She stood in front of the hearth in her shift with her head bent to the flames. She had not heard him enter so deep was she in thought, but then much had gone on today.

The startling discovery that the witch did not create the curse that Aila had cast left them all wondering. Who would have such power and knowledge if not the witch?

Another witch was the only reasonable and confusing explanation, since the witch made no mention of another of her ilk. And where had Aila found this witch? Annis believed Gunna would know but it did them little good since they did not know where she was.

Rannick shook his head. This time alone with his wife was precious to him and he would not let either of their troublesome thoughts interfere with it.

He went to her, stopping behind her to rest his brow to the back of her head and slip one arm around her to splay his hand protectively over her stomach. "I will protect you both no matter what."

Her hand drifted to rest over his and she marveled at his combined strength and tenderness.

"We will protect each other no matter what," she corrected.

That she loved him with such courage amazed him and made him even more determined to make certain nothing happened to her. He had found a rare woman to love, and he was not about to lose her.

Bliss leaned back against her husband, relaxing into his

embrace. "I recalled something the healer who taught me said when I asked her how she was able to determine what troubled a person. She told me never to look far and wide, that the answers are always right in front of us, easy for us to see if we but moved the unnecessary aside. If we applied that to the present situation, we might find what we look for."

"Tonight, I look only to pleasure my wife," he said and buried his face in the side of her neck to nibble along it and send gooseflesh rushing over her.

She hunched her shoulders up as pinpricks of delight shot through her and she gasped when his hand drifted down to caress the sensitive spot that brought her even more delight.

"I have an insatiable hunger to explore your body and not only with my hands," he whispered near her ear, then bit playfully along her ear.

"I will burst with pleasure from your words alone," she said, his deft hand ensuring that.

"Good, for I intend to pleasure you multiple times tonight."

"Promise," she said on a soft moan.

His hands began to work her garments off her. "Let me show you."

When they were both naked, Bliss turned to the bed.

"Nay," he said and took her hand to lead her to the long bench in front of the hearth.

He stopped her when she went to sit after he sat. He spread his legs and, with his hands cupping her backside, drew her between them.

Bliss looked down at him, not sure of his intentions, and when his hands grabbed at her backside firmly and his mouth began to rain kisses over her stomach and drift down further, all she could do was steady herself with her hands on his shoulders.

His tongue and lips worked magic and her legs soon felt

293

too weak to hold her. She did not want to admit it, did not want the magic of his tongue to cease, but she had no choice. "My legs will not hold me much longer."

"Come down on me," he ordered with a husky need.

She glanced down when he eased her gently away from him to see his shaft engorged with passion. Desire shot through her, and she almost fell against him so eager was she to take him inside her.

"Easy," he said, guiding her with his hands still firm on her backside.

Bliss gripped the top of his shoulders to steady herself as she lowered herself down on him. She groaned with pleasure as little by little his shaft disappeared inside her, filling her with the most exquisite satisfaction.

She moved up and down on him, the feel of him gliding in and out of her causing her moans to grow. He hastened her ride, his hands forcing her to go faster, and her moans grew louder.

Bliss was swept away on a wave of intense pleasure that she feared, or hoped, would crash so hard she'd be swept away with it.

"Let go!" Rannick commanded.

She would argue, disobey him, the need to linger in such glorious pleasure so strong, but then so was his command when he issued it again.

"Let go NOW!"

Bliss let out a scream as an immense climax struck her and she was swept away in its intensity that tumbled her body and refused to let go.

"Hold tight!" Rannick ordered, his hands digging into her backside, holding her firm as he got to his feet.

In the next instant, Bliss felt her back hit the wall and her husband drive into her with such a demand that she cried out with pleasure that reignited her passion.

Rannick rested the side of his face next to his wife's as

294

once again he issued an order. "This time, join me."

"Aye," she said on bated breath and clung tightly to him.

His roar drowned out her scream as they both burst with unimaginable pleasure that lingered longer than usual, leaving them both satiated and their limbs weak.

Rannick managed to keep hold of his wife, but not for long, his powerful climax robbing him of his strength. Her heaving chest told him that she felt much the same.

Before it was too late, he took solid hold of his wife and hurried them both to the bed to fall down on it. He had enough strength left to snag her waist with his arm and move her so that her head rested on a pillow, then he spread out beside her after yanking a blanket up over them, their bodies cooling.

She cuddled against as soon as he was beside her and yawned. "That was memorable."

"We will have plenty more of those," he assured her.

She yawned again. "I look forward to every one of them."

"As do I," he said as a yawn hit him as well.

Sleep soon claimed his wife and just before it did the same to him, he prayed his wife was not the MacWilliam bairn, for if she was, he would forever worry that someone would discover the truth.

***

"How many have surrendered and offered you what they know?" Brogan asked as he and Rannick approached the pen where the imprisoned men were being kept.

"A good number of them, since only five remain," Rannick said. "It took the cold, snow, barely enough food to sustain them, and I believe seeing life, a good life, go on around them to realize their mistake."

"What did you learn from those who surrendered?" Brogan asked, gazing over the imprisoned men and seeing that it would not be long before the few stragglers surrendered.

"They have been fed some such nonsense about evil being destroyed and peace prevailing when death claimed the cursed lords. But none could tell me who led them."

"How many have you hung after they surrendered?"

"None," Rannick said, glancing over the lot of them. "I had each one escorted home to let their chieftain decide their fate."

"The evil was not as evil as they thought," Brogan said. "A wise move. They return to sing your praises of a tolerant man, which makes others question whether to believe and join whatever insane group is perpetuating this madness."

"At least it leaves them to question it, have them think, have their tongues sharing the news, their thoughts, and as you say, stop the madness. In the end, it may force whoever leads them to show himself."

"Lord Rannick!" one of the prisoners called out.

"Roland!" Sheed shouted, stumbling to his feet. "You cannot think to surrender. You lost your wife and bairn thanks to the likes of them."

The lanky, young man shook his bowed head as he stopped when he reached Sheed. "My blessed wife came to me in a dream last night and told me it was not my time. That I had a long, good life to live, and told me to stop being foolish. "I will not fail her again. I will pay heed to her word." He lifted his head. "I beg your forgiveness, Lord Rannick, and I humbly request to remain here in your clan, to make a home here. I will do whatever I must to gain your trust. I only ask for a chance to do so."

"I should trust you when you raised a sword against me?" Rannick asked.

"You have no reason to trust me. I can only hope you

296

will allow me to prove myself trustworthy since I have been far too foolish of a man since my wife and son died," Roland said.

Rannick eyed the man skeptically a moment before he spoke. "Is there anything you can tell me that would be of help to me?"

"There is not much we are told except that evil must be destroyed so that good can prevail." Roland shook his head. "But who truly knows who is good and who is evil?"

"I will give it thought, Roland, until then you will remain imprisoned," Rannick said, having had the same thought through the years and finding more evil than good... until Bliss came along.

"As you say, my lord," Roland said, lowering his head once again and walking away to sit on the cold ground in front of one of the three campfires kept burning for the prisoners.

"Sheed!" Rannick called out and the man turned an angry glare on him. "If any harm comes to Roland, the same harm will befall you."

"Sheed is the one who leads them?" Brogan asked as he and Rannick walked away, Sheed having turned his head away without responding.

"He thinks he does, but he is not intelligent enough. Someone directs him," Rannick said. "Someone directs everyone."

"No idea of who it may be?" Brogan asked.

"A name has been mentioned," —Rannick hesitated— "Jaffee."

Brogan's eyes went wide. "Bloody hell. He has been spotted in the area?"

"From what one of the captives who surrendered told me, Jaffee paid him to see that this group carried out their task. He was free to go after that. He claimed to know no more than that. When I confronted him on lies I caught him

in, it did not take him long to fall on my dagger so he would
say no more. Jaffee's name has been brought to my attention
more than once."

"Jaffee demands substantial coins for a task. It would
take a wealthy lord to pay such a price." Brogan shook his
head. "Coin is not plentiful in the Highlands. It is land that
makes a man wealthy and influential."

Both men grew quiet until Rannick finally said, "Say
what we both know."

"What is the point? It makes no sense," Brogan argued.
"Your father may own the most land in the area and coin as
well since he spent much of it to return you home." He
shook his head. "By no means does he want you dead. It
really could be any of the clans who seek to improve their
lot, which is the majority of them. I am content with the
village Annis and I are building." He laughed. "And we have
a resident witch who keeps others away."

"We have yet to discuss the obvious, Brogan," Rannick
said.

"I do not think either of us want to think that one of our
wives may be the MacWilliam bairn," he said in a whisper.
"The danger she would be in if it was discovered…" He
shook his head. "I cannot conceive it."

"But if so, do you think it could truly bring the curse to
an end?"

"I want to believe it, hope it would be true, yet fear it to
be true," Brogan said.

Rannick nodded, feeling the same. "It is a secret that
once learned must be kept at all costs."

Brogan grinned. "We'll have to get the witch to put a
spell on all those who know… to forget."

Rannick scowled. "That witch better watch her step
with my wife."

"Hold your temper with her, Rannick. She commands
the crows and wolves," Brogan warned.

"But she does not command me," Rannick snapped.

"Fair warning, my friend. She has the power to do more harm than you," Brogan cautioned.

"I know," Rannick snapped again and forced himself to hold his temper. "I have fought a witch before but seeing this witch command the ravens and especially the wolves, I realize the one I conquered had little power or she was not a witch at all, and it was not an easy victory."

"Then befriend this one before it is too late," Brogan warned.

The squawk of a raven brought them to a halt to see the large, black bird sitting on the roof of a nearby cottage. The bird looked from one man to the other, issued another squawk then took flight.

"This is not going to be an easy task," Brogan said.

"On that, my friend, we agree," Rannick said.

***

"I fear the foundation we intend to build our plan on will not be firm enough and will soon crumble," Annis said, after retiring to the solar with her husband, Bliss, and Rannick once supper was done. "This person who hunts us has proven difficult to find." She looked to Rannick. "From what you have told us, no matter how many men you and your father send out to see what can be found about the man, they return with little information. And while the men you have kept prisoners dwindle down, they have little to offer us. The person behind it all hides his involvement well." She shook her head. "And what truly disturbs me is that there have been no attempts on our lives lately? Surely with me and Brogan here, it would have been a good time to attack."

Rannick offered a possibility. "The warriors keep the village secure."

"There is something else I have noticed," Brogan said.

"Things are much different than my last visit here. I see countless smiles and hear more laughter from the clan than I can recall. I hear people talking about how hunting goes well, that food is plentiful, and that bairns are being born with no difficulty," —he gave a nod to Bliss— "because of your skills so the women say, and for the first time in a long while I have seen that no one turns their head away when Rannick passes by them."

"We see the same contentment in our thriving village," Annis said.

"Can we dare believe the curse has been broken?" Bliss said, her voice low as if fearful of suggesting such a thing.

"If not broken, perhaps at least halted," Rannick said.

"Halted for what?" Brogan asked.

They all gave thought while Rannick offered his. "For the very last thing that will break the curse for good— whatever that might be."

The thought slipped into Annis's head and from her mouth. "It must be a bairn… a MacWilliam bairn waiting to be born so that the bloodline lives again. It is the most likely thing."

Rannick looked quick at his wife. "That would mean you or your sister Elysia, one of you, is the MacWilliam descendent." He turned a hasty look on Annis. "Unless—"

"Nay, I am not with child nor am I ready to be just yet," Annis said, shaking her head. "If only the person who hunts us was aware of this information, he would stop since he would get what he wants… the curse to end. But such news cannot be shared."

"What if it could be? Not news about the MacWilliam bairn having lived and the bloodline carried on, but news that the curse has ended," Rannick suggested.

"How could that possibly be done? The curse just suddenly ending like that?" Bliss asked, though the idea did intrigue her.

"The witch did it," Rannick said with a grin. "We can start a rumor that the witch broke the curse. Word has already spread that the crows brought the witch here. All wonder why she was here. With no attempts being made on our lives and things going well, many will begin to believe it."

Brogan smiled and pointed to Rannick. "And with you not executing those men imprisoned that surrender to you, it would prove that evil lives no more in you, so the curse must have been broken."

"That would give us a firm foundation to build on," Annis said with glee. "No evil, no reason for any of us to die."

"Then the person behind this loses what he wants most… power," Brogan said.

"This could work," Annis said eagerly. "We need to start whispering where servants can hear us. How the witch claims the curse has been broken, but do we trust her word? Yet there is proof since all has been going well."

"It is worth a try," Rannick said.

"We start tomorrow," Annis instructed. "I want to see how fast it takes root and spreads before Brogan and I leave."

"We will give it two days, then take our leave," Brogan said. "Winter grows deeper, and I do not want us stuck in a snowstorm."

"Two days," Annis confirmed with a nod and a smile.

***

Annis walked with Bliss slowly down the steps of the keep, Brogan waiting below with their horses while engaged in conversation with Rannick.

"No doubt they discuss how well the ruse has been going," Annis whispered, not that anyone was close enough to hear.

"I believe it was something everyone wished to hear. Lord Lochlann and Lady Helice have appeared more at ease in the last two days. I heard Lord Lochlann tell Rannick over breakfast that it is time he takes more command of the clan."

"Brogan and I will tell Lord Odran and Elysia our plan and I will make sure to continue to spread the gossip while there." Tears began to gather in Annis's eyes as she stopped not far from the bottom of the stairs. "I cannot wait for the three of us to be together again."

"Hopefully soon," Bliss said, feeling the same.

Annis wiped at her tears. "Life is different for us now, isn't it?"

"Are you happy with your different life?" Bliss asked, the answer obvious by the way Annis and Brogan looked at each other, playfully teased each other, and the way they did not go long without reaching out to each other to hold hands or embrace.

"Surprisingly, I am," Annis said with a chuckle. "I never thought I would find a man who would love me, let alone tolerate me and my strange interest in building. I look forward to each sunrise and spending the day with him." She grinned and whispered, "The nights are pretty fantastic too."

Bliss laughed softly, thrilled that her sister had found love.

"I do hope Elysia has found the same with Lord Odran," Annis said.

"From what Bram has told me, she has, but it will be a relief when you confirm it."

"I will return after visiting Elysia and let you know how she fares," Annis said, wiping away her tears.

"I would like that," Bliss said, sniffling back her own tears. "But do not rush before you make sure all is well with her."

"On that, you have my word," Annis said.

Bliss pulled her sister into a tight hug. She was reluctant to let her go. It had been good having her here, talking with her, planning with her, seeing her happy.

Annis hugged her just as tight, just as reluctant to let Bliss go.

"Soon," Bliss whispered. "Soon the three of us will be together." Her heart hurt as she released her sister, their hands grasping in one last effort not to be separated.

"Time to go, wife," Brogan said, knowing if he did not end the sisters' good-bye they would never be on their way. He locked his hands at his wife's waist to lift her with ease and deposit her on the waiting horse, then hoisted himself up behind her.

"I can ride my own horse," Annis protested.

"Do you truly want to?" Brogan asked with a wink and a twinkle in his eyes.

Annis grinned and leaned back against him. "Nay, I am content here."

Shouts of farewell and waves filled the air as Troy and his mercenaries took the lead, Brogan and Annis behind them, and two troops of Clan MacClaren warriors trailing after them.

"They will be safe," Rannick said, standing at her side and giving her hand a firm squeeze.

"You protect them well and I am grateful. You truly are a good man, husband," Bliss said and kissed his cheek.

Rannick pulled her into a tight hug and buried his face in her hair near her ear, the light, sweet scent stirring his senses. He breathed deeply of it as if wanting always to remember it. He did not know what the future held but he did know one thing.

"We shall see if I am a good man since there is nothing I will not do to keep you and our bairn safe."

Chapter 30

Rannick reached his wife to hug her close before she could slip her garments on. She had teased him awake this morning with intimate touches and they had enjoyed a lazy bout of lovemaking. Though more than satisfied, he had the urge to feel her naked against him once more.

"I love you, Bliss," he whispered in her ear, having come up behind her to tug her back against him.

Bliss rested her hand on his arm that circled her waist and tilted her head back against his naked chest to glance up at him with a tender smile. "I am a lucky woman to have you love me."

That she thought herself lucky to be married to the cursed lord warmed his heart. "You are a brave soul for believing that, wife."

"One needs no bravery when the truth is spoken." Rannick turned her around in his arms and she hastily pressed her fingers to his lips before he could speak. "We love each other and that is all that matters." Her lips replaced her hand with a tender kiss. "I have much to do today. I can dally no more."

Rannick let her wiggle out of his embrace and got busy donning his garments. "It has been a week now and gossip goes well that the curse is dead." He chuckled. "I am beginning to believe it myself."

"People do seem more lighthearted and more engaged with one another. Illnesses have been minor and easily dispatched, and two healthy bairns were birthed easily this week." She smiled. "Best of all, no attempts have been made on our lives. I do believe our plan is working."

"Or does the truth drive the change?" Rannick asked, having spent much time considering that the curse had been halted with the possibility of the MacWilliam bloodline about to be resurrected.

Bliss went to her husband, his worry obvious with how often his hand went to rest on her stomach, a slight roundness beginning to show there. This time she placed his hand on her stomach. "He is tucked safely away, and I have no fear or worry with you nearby. I know you will always protect us." Her hand quickly went to his lips. "Do not say it. I know you would give your life for us, but it pains my heart to hear you say it."

He hugged her tight. It pained his heart as well since he would give his life for her and their bairn and that meant leaving them, and that thought caused him the most pain he had ever felt in his life.

He grabbed her wool shawl off the chest and draped it around her. "I'm starving and from the sounds your stomach is making, I'd say you feel the same."

Bliss laughed. "I am famished."

He hurried her out of their bedchamber and down to the Great Hall. Meals had become more pleasant than when Bliss had first arrived at the keep. Lady Helice often moved to sit next to Bliss since father and son talked much with each other. She got to learn a lot about the workings of the keep and the duties of a wife to the chieftain from Lady Helice, and she enjoyed the stories of when Rannick was but a young lad.

They were halfway through the meal when Lawler entered, a dusting of snow on him, with a young woman.

"Damia's sister, Lana, has arrived, Lord Lochlann," Lawler announced, stopping a short distance from the dais.

"Is it true, my lord, my sister Damia is here?" Lana asked, tossing back her hood, snow falling off it as she did.

Bliss was surprised by the contrast in the two sisters.

305

Lana had to stand a head over Damia and where her eyes were a soft blue, Lana's were more of a striking blue. They both possessed the same round face, though wrinkles marred much of Lana's face, whereas Damia had none.

"Damia is here," Lord Lochlann confirmed, "though it is Lord Rannick you speak to where your sister is concerned."

Lana bowed her head respectfully to Rannick before speaking. "I thank you for seeing to my sister, Lord Rannick."

Rannick looked past her to Lawler. "Have you sent for Damia?"

"Aye, my lord, Bram brings her," Lawler confirmed.

"Thank you again. It has been so long since I have seen her—"

"LANA!"

The joyful screech had Lana turning and running to her sister. The two hugged, tears rolling down their cheeks.

"My goodness, you are with child," Lana said after they released each other. "It appears as if I will become an aunt any day."

"A couple of weeks I believe," Damia said, wiping at her tears.

Bliss wiped at her own tears, joy filling her heart for them as it had done upon seeing Annis after too long of a separation.

"Wonderful, then there is time for you to return home with me," Lana said gleefully.

Bliss saw Bram scowl. Though he and Damia bickered, Bliss had also seen the way the two clasped hands when walking with each other. And though Bram had been freed of looking after Damia, he now spent even more time with her. It was obvious he did not like the idea of her leaving.

"Damia has a home here now," Rannick said.

Bliss was relieved her husband had spoken up, making

it clear Damia could remain here if she wished."

"She is alone, my lord. As her older sister it is my duty to look after her," Lana said.

Bram surprised everyone when he stepped forward. "I provide for her."

Lana's arm went around her sister's shoulders as if shielding her from the unknown man. "You are not family, and I will not have a man take advantage of her."

Damia quickly defended Bram. "Bram is a good man and takes no advantage of me."

"Well, he is no longer needed. You have me to look after you now and we will take our leave in a day or two," Lana said as if it were settled.

Bram shocked everyone again when he slipped Damia away from her sister to tuck her against him. "Damia and I are to wed."

Damia could not hide her shock, her eyes springing wide.

"Are we not?" Bram asked, leaving the decision to her.

Her eyes turned soft, that he gave her a choice, and she smiled. "Aye, Bram loves me and cannot live without me. Right, Bram?"

Bliss chuckled and heard her husband do the same. The woman was wise in seeing that Bram wed her for that reason, and he didn't hesitate or disappoint.

"Aye, I do love you," he said proudly.

"And I, you," Damia was quick to admit.

"Wonderful!" Lord Lochlann cried out. "Clan MacClaren keeps growing."

"Are you sure about this?" Lana asked, her many wrinkles scrunching with worry.

"I am, and I am glad you are here to meet Bram and know that I am happy. There is so much I wish to talk with you about." Damia stepped away from Bram to take her sister's hand. "Please, you will stay a few days and visit with me."

Lana smiled. "I did not come all this way to rush off. I will stay and we will talk and share smiles and laughter once again."

Damia turned, her glance going to Bliss.

Bliss raised her hand to stop her from speaking. "I have no need of your help today. Go be with your sister."

"Bram, a word," Rannick ordered when he went to follow Lawler and the two women out of the keep. He came around the dais and signaled Bram to remain where he was and walked over to him. "It is good that you spoke up and declared your feelings for Damia."

"You knew, my lord?" Bram asked, surprised.

"It was obvious to all but you and Damia. I must say I am impressed that you had the courage to speak up and in front of so many. While men charge eagerly and fearfully into battle, they are far more fearful and hesitant to claim their love for a woman. You did well."

"Fear gave me the courage, my lord. Fear of losing Damia, of never seeing her again, I could not bear the thought or the pain I felt. I have never felt this way about a woman. It caught me off guard and confused me, but when I thought of the moment I would have to bid her farewell," — Bram shook his head— "I would not be able to do it. I would not be able to let her go."

"You will make a fine husband, father, and warrior, Bram. You do the clan proud."

"Thank you, my lord, I will serve you and the clan well, and I am most grateful to Lord Odran for sending me here. If he hadn't, I would have never met Damia," Bram said and smiled.

"I will be sure to let him know that. Now go and be with your future wife. You will handfast for now and when the cleric passes through he can wed you properly."

Bram bobbed his head. "Again, many thanks, my lord."

Rannick turned and smiled, seeing his wife walking toward him. Quick strides had him by her side and his arm caught her in a snug hug. "I am grateful you had the courage to wed me."

"And I am glad your stubbornness did not stop you from admitting you loved me," she said with a soft chuckle.

"There you go thinking I am stubborn again," he said with a playful poke to her side.

She chuckled again. "I know you are stubborn, but I love you anyway."

"Pardon, my lord," Lawler said, having returned.

Rannick turned an annoyed scowl on Lawler. "What is it?"

Lawler looked to Bliss. "A young lad in quick need of the healer."

Bliss hurried out of her husband's arms. "Take me to him, Lawler."

"A cloak, Bliss!" Rannick shouted when she reached the door.

Lawler grabbed one from the many hanging on the pegs by the doors and hurried it around Bliss just before she slipped out the door.

"Your wife is quick to her task. We should do the same. There are clan matters to discuss," his father called out.

Rannick turned to see to his duties, promising himself he would search out his wife when he was done.

***

Rannick was annoyed. It wasn't until now, at supper, that he got to see his wife. It had been a busy day for them both and he had had no chance to see her. He always made sure to see her throughout the day, not only because he missed her, but he wanted to know for himself that she was safe and unharmed.

"Why do you scowl, husband?" Bliss asked, stroking the spot between his eyes that had crinkled badly.

"I have not seen you all day," he complained.

"We are together now," she offered as a way to ease his annoyance.

He leaned his head down until their brows almost touched. "It is not enough."

Bliss smiled and her whispered words faintly brushed his lips. "We have the whole, uninterrupted night in front of us, and I, for one, look forward to it."

His scowl lightened some. "We will keep supper brief."

"As you say, my lord," she said with a wicked grin.

It was less than thirty minutes later that Rannick was ready to take their leave when the door burst open, and Lawler rushed in.

"Prisoners escaped, all but Roland. He was left wounded and not by our warriors."

Rannick placed his hand on his wife's shoulder when she went to stand after he did. "You will stay here where you are safe." He turned to his father, but Lord Lochlann spoke before his son could.

"I will see her kept safe," his father assured him.

Rannick had no doubt he would since she carried the future heir of Clan MacClaren and not that his father was aware of it but also possibly a MacWilliam descendent as well.

Bliss grabbed her husband's arm as he went to rush off. "Roland may need my help."

"One of the warriors can see to his wound," Rannick said, having no intention of placing his wife in danger.

Bliss looked to Lawler. "How bad is his wound, Lawler?" The man's hesitation was enough for Bliss. "I will not sit here when someone needs my help." She interrupted her husband when he went to deny her. "Bring him here if you must, or I will find a way to go to him myself."

The stubborn set of her chin warned Rannick she would do just that. Reluctantly, he turned his head to Lawler. "Bring Roland here." Lawler hurried off, Rannick paying him no heed, his hand reaching out to grab his wife's chin. "You will wait in this room until I return, or if my father deems it unsafe. Defy me on this wife and—"

Bliss yanked her chin from his grip. "I told you, Rannick, I am a healer, and I will go where I am needed. Do not restrict me or make me defy you."

"Obey your—"

"Hush, Lochlann!" Lady Helice ordered her husband before he could finish. "This does not concern you." She tugged her grumbling husband away from the dais, giving her son and his wife privacy.

Bliss laid a tender hand on her husband's arm. "I am not a foolish woman. I will take no unnecessary chances. Besides, you have warriors follow me wherever I go. Now go and do what you must, and I shall do the same." She kissed him and whispered, "Stay safe and well," —her eyes twinkled mischievously— "though I am here if you should need to be patched up."

He could not stop from grinning. "I believe my body will need tending in certain particular areas when I return."

"I will make certain each area is properly tended," she said with a wicked grin.

Rannick snagged her around the waist and yanked her against him to plant a demanding kiss on her lips. With a quick whispered, "I love you," he left her side and headed to the door, giving a shout just before reaching it. "Pay heed, Da, my wife can be a handful."

"Worry not, son, I will see she obeys me," his da called out and Rannick's hardy laughter lingered in the Great Hall after he was gone.

"I need to fetch supplies from my healing cottage," Bliss said, running past Lord Lochlann.

311

"Wait, I will have what you need fetched for you," Lord Lochlann commanded.

"It will be quicker if I get them," she said and summoned two warriors with a flick of her hand. "Come with me."

Lord Lochlann sputtered as he tried to resume command and scowled hearing his wife laugh beside him. He shook his head and hurried after Bliss.

***

Roland was just coming to when Bliss finished tending his wound. It had not taken her long to determine that a bump to his head had knocked him unconscious, which helped him suffer less while she had tended the wound to his side.

"I am dying," Roland mumbled, cringing as the pain set in.

Bliss recalled what Rannick had told him about Roland and smiled. "Your wife says it is not your time. You have a long life to live."

Roland's eyes opened wide. "She told me that over and over in my dream." Tears glistened in his eyes. "Eliza promised me she would always look after me."

"And she has kept her promise. You will live," Bliss said with confidence. "Do not try to turn or move much. You are on a table in the Great Hall, and I do not want you falling off it. I will have you moved to the healing cottage as soon as it is deemed safe."

"The attack!" Roland gasped, then cringed when he went to move.

Bliss hurried to rest her hand on his chest. "Did you not hear me? You must remain still."

"Sheed escaped." Roland shook his head. "He had help." He rubbed his head. "I felt the blow to my head at the

same time I felt the dagger plunge into me." He shut his eyes
a moment. "Sheed was annoyed at the gossip that the curse
had been broken. He insisted it was a lie that the only way
for the curse to end was for the cursed lords to die. He
convinced the few men left that the witch used her evil to
play a trick on everyone and that the curse still existed. He
said good would prevail and free us before it was too late."

"Did he preach this belief recently?" Bliss asked.

"In the last couple of days," Roland said and shook his
head. "I thought I heard him say that the angel had arrived as
he plunged the dagger into me. Even crazier, I thought I
heard the angel respond before everything went dark."

Bliss told Roland to rest, seeing him cringe far too
much as he spoke. He needed rest to heal and as much as she
wanted to ask him more, it could wait a few hours. No news
had reached them yet of Rannick's efforts to capture the
prisoners. All remained quiet in the keep and throughout the
village as the night grew late.

Lady Helice had gone to bed, but Lord Lochlann
insisted on remaining in the Great Hall with Bliss. He now
slept with his head on his arms at a table near the hearth,
waking himself with a snoring snort on occasion.

Bliss would share what Roland had told her with Lord
Lochlann when he woke. With Sheed having gotten help
with the escape, it meant there was a traitor in the clan, and it
was most likely a woman. Sheed had referred to the angel as
she, so he must have heard a female voice. It would make
sense if one considered the deaths of Rannick's wives. A
woman would attend a birth and assist a new wife, perhaps
even attach something to a riding boot or clothing that would
disturb a horse.

She silently chastised herself for not getting to know the
servants better. It had to be someone with keep privileges
and yet she had suffered no ill effects since arriving here.
Why wait? Why not be done with another wife as quickly as

the last wife?

She had no more time to consider what it might mean, the door suddenly rushing open and Lana hurrying in.

"Please, you must come, my lady, Damia is in labor," Lana said, her face fraught with worry.

"Let me gather some things I might need," Bliss said and heard Roland groan. She went to him.

Roland struggled to lift his head.

"Rest, Roland, and worry not," she said, easing his head back down on the cloth she had fashioned into a pillow for him.

"The angel," Roland said with wide eyes. "She is here."

Bliss looked up too late. Lana was already at her side, a dagger pressed against it.

Chapter 31

"Alert anyone and I will gladly give my life to see you and your bairn dead," Lana threatened in a whisper and made sure Bliss felt the tip of her dagger at her side.

"I cannot stop warriors from following me," Bliss said, hoping the two warriors who kept watch over her would realize something was amiss.

"They will be disposed of easily enough," Lana said, her whisper turning harsher. "Now hurry and do not do anything foolish."

Roland's eyes had closed, and he appeared in a peaceful sleep. She only hoped that it was a ruse, and he could alert others. She didn't bother to gather anything, hoping the warriors might make note of it and question her intentions. Unfortunately, the two followed her out of the keep without question.

It was too late for anyone to be out, the night cold and a light snow falling. Sentinels were positioned throughout the village due to the escape but with two warriors walking behind her the sentinels paid her no heed. Possibilities ran through Bliss's head, but she dismissed most of them, fearful for the safety of the bairn she carried. Damia's eyes were wet with tears and red from endless crying when Bliss arrived at her cottage.

"I am so sorry, my lady. I do not know what happened to turn my sister so evil," Damia apologized.

Lana shook her head and glared with outrage at her sister. "Evil? You call me evil when you would rather reside here with a cursed lord than your own sister?" She shook her head. "You are misguided, and I will not leave you here to

315

rot in evil. I promised grandfather I would see you kept safe from the madness that rampages our land."

"You are the one who has gone mad. The curse is done. It has been broken," Damia argued.

Bliss was not able to stop Lana from delivering a vicious slap to Damia's face. She did, however, grab the young woman and steady her before she tumbled to the floor. The way Damia moaned and planted her hand on her stomach made Bliss realize the young woman was in labor. The frightened look in Damia's eyes told Bliss that she did not want Lana to know.

"You are a fool like the rest of them. The curse is not broken. It cannot be broken. The cursed lords must die for it to finally end, and goodness restored," Lana said and pointed the dagger she held at her sister's cloak. "Put it on. We leave now."

Bliss hurried to drape the cloak over Damia's shoulders, praying that Rannick would return in enough time to keep them from harm.

Damia let out a low moan and leaned against Bliss.

"She is in labor. Leave her here. I will go with you," Bliss bargained, knowing it would become obvious all too soon and hoping Lana would do right by her sister.

"She can drop the little bastard in the woods for all I care. No sister of mine shall bear the child of a man who belonged to the clan of one of the cursed lords," Lana said, her face twisted with a look of disgust.

Damia gasped, placing her hand over her stomach as if somehow she could protect the bairn. "Finn was a good man and husband and served his clan well."

"And yet you wed only a few months after his death," Lana accused.

"Fate sent Bram to me, and Finn would be glad for it. He would want me and our bairn protected," Damia argued. "You cannot harm my bairn. Please, Lana, do not let your hatred harm an innocent bairn."

"Time to go," Lana said, ignoring her sister's pleas.

Bliss wasn't surprised to see the two warriors who had escorted them to the cottage crumpled on the ground and hidden out of sight behind the cottage. A quick glance showed no signs of blood, and she assumed a good knock to their heads had done them both in, which meant there were others helping. She feared if there were more than just those men who had escaped, then that meant the escape had been intended to divert and that would mean that she and Damia were being led in the opposite direction of where her husband searched.

A chill of fear raced through her, and she prayed that Rannick would come to discover the ruse before it was too late.

The night wore on, the walk through the dark woods not easy as Damia's labor progressed. Bliss kept her steady on her feet while leaving as heavy footfalls as she could for Rannick to find and follow. Unfortunately, with the snow continuing to fall, she feared it might be for naught.

"You have to stop. Your sister can walk no more," Bliss said, feeling Damia collapse against her.

"It's not far now and let her drop the bairn, I care not," Lana said, reiterating her indifference and walked ahead, four men in front of her leading the way.

Fury raged through Bliss that Lana could bring such harm and heartache to her own sister. She stopped walking and eased Damia to the snow-covered ground to rest against a thick tree trunk.

"We will not take another step!" Bliss shouted.

Lana turned, her face glowing red with anger at seeing her sister sitting on the ground. She raced toward her.

Bliss hurried to steal a glance around and quickly reached out to grab a long stick on the ground, an arm's length from her, and swung it at the enraged woman when

317

she got near, catching her on the cheek, a welt swelling fast. Bliss's stomach roiled, knowing there was no way she could defend her or Damia against a dagger, but she had to try. She could not let the young woman keep walking and the bairn drop from her, and Bliss was sure she was close to delivering the newborn.

Lana's eyes sparked more with madness than with fury and Bliss braced herself for the challenge.

"Enough!" a man shouted. "You know the orders. She is not to be harmed. That privilege is for another."

"Do I get to watch when she gets what she deserves?" Lana asked.

"We will be long gone," Sheed said as he emerged from the woods alongside the narrow path. He went to Lana and glanced at the welt. "It will leave no mark. You have done good. Our reward will be great." He turned to smile at Bliss. "Your husband will find his way to you, though too late. No doubt by the time the fellow is done with you, you will have lost the bairn and probably wish you were dead."

"You are wrong," Bliss said. "Lord Rannick will find me, and it will be you who suffers for your evil deeds."

Sheed shook his head. "It is a pity you will die without knowing the truth."

"I know the truth. Lana was a good soul just like her sister until she met you and you convinced her otherwise. She worked in the keep, the perfect spot for her to be able to kill all three of Rannick's wives at your command. Since you refused to surrender as others of your group did, I can only assume that when you did not return from your mission, Lana would come for you. Or is it this man you alluded to, who will bring me great suffering, the one who aided in your escape?"

"A bit of both," Sheed said.

A loud moan had all eyes turned on Damia.

"Why did you bring her?" Sheed demanded of Lana.

318

"I did not want to leave her with those evil ones," Lana said.

"She will slow us down and be a burden. We leave her here," Sheed ordered and silenced any protest from Lana with a quick and painful grab of her jaw. "The decision is made. As soon as he arrives and we get our coins, we leave. And I will hear no more on it."

"You meant to take me and my husband captive, though the men were not aware of that, were they?" Bliss asked, anxious to learn all she could, particularly who was behind the whole scheme.

"You know nothing of what truly is going on. That fool group who believes the righteous shall prevail are being led by someone who is anything but righteous. When I discovered the truth, I used it to my advantage. Now for once, I shall be the victor."

"And who is this person who rained true evil down on all?" Bliss asked.

Damia cried out in pain, drawing all their attention.

Sheed sneered and pointed to Damia. "See to her and you," —he turned to Lana— "wait in the shadows with the horses for me. This man is not known for his kindness."

Lana nodded and did as ordered, though cast one last look toward her sister before she did.

Bliss turned to drop down in front of Damia and that was when she spotted the raven sitting on a low tree branch staring at her. Had the witch sent help?

"The bairn will not survive the cold," Damia said, tears in her eyes. "But what does it matter… we will die."

"We will not die and the bairn will survive. We will make sure of it," Bliss assured her. "I will wrap the bairn snug in my cloak and once tucked in your arm beneath your cloak there will be no worry of warmth. We will see your bairn kept safe and we will not die. I left a good trail for Rannick to follow. Now worry no more. You have a bairn eager to meet his mum."

It wasn't long after that, that thankfully, the bairn slipped out easily and with a strong cry.

"A boy," Bliss said gleefully, and Damia smiled broadly as tears of joy rolled down her cheeks.

After begging for a knife from Sheed so she could cut the cord, she wrapped the crying bairn snug in her cloak and once tucked in his mum's arms, and her cloak wrapped around them both, he quieted.

While Bliss finished settling mum and son, she whispered, "You have strength and courage, Damia. You need to sneak off into the woods and follow the raven. He waits to guide you. These men care not about you and will not waste their time looking for you." She could see Damia's reluctance to leave her. "No doubt you will meet up with Rannick, his men, and most likely Bram. Tell my husband to let the raven guide him."

"Raven?" Damia asked, confused.

"I spotted him only a few moments ago. He sits in the tree waiting. Follow where he flies. He will guide you well," Bliss encouraged.

"I will do as you say, my lady," Damia said, determined.

"Morning cannot be too far off. You need enough darkness to conceal you, so do not delay. I will go talk with Sheed and see if I can keep him distracted." Bliss squeezed Damia's hand. "Do not look back. Keep going no matter what, and when you see Rannick, tell him I love him."

"I will, my lady, you have my word," Damia promised, teary-eyed.

Bliss stood, praying that she would be able to tell her husband herself that she loved him, but she wanted him to know one last time if she never got to see him again. She went to walk to Sheed when a large man stepped out of the woods.

320

"Go now, Damia. Go and do not stop, and tell my husband that Jaffee waits for him," Bliss urged in a whisper and remained as she was so no one could see Damia leave.

Bliss had recognized Jaffee at first sight, and she knew what he wanted with her, revenge against Rannick.

"Come here, woman," Jaffee commanded, spotting her. "I have much planned for you."

***

"Something is not right, Lawler," Rannick said as they approached the village. "The men we caught were spread out wide as if they did not know where to go. They also surrendered easily as if grateful we found them, yet we found no sign of Sheed, and no one can tell us where he has gone."

"I thought the same," Lawler said and raised himself up a bit on his horse, his brow wrinkled.

Rannick looked to see what had caught his attention and saw the flames of several torches weaving throughout the village. He urged his horse into a run, his heart pounding in his chest, praying nothing had happened to Bliss. He needed only to see his father's and mother's worried faces to know his prayers had not been answered.

"Where is she?" Rannick demanded once off his horse. "You were to keep her safe."

"Damia is gone!" Bram shouted as he brought his horse to a stop at the keep steps.

"They were taken, Bliss and Damia," Lord Lochlann said.

"Who took them?" Rannick demanded.

"From what the guards who have suffered blows to the head told us—"

"Told you?" Rannick said with a growling sneer. "You did not see it for yourself? Where were you?"

321

Lady Helice stepped forward. "There will be time for blame later, Rannick. Bliss and Damia must be found."

Rannick calmed himself as best he could. "Lawler gather more men. Where are the guards who can tell me what happened, Da?"

***

"Please, Lord Rannick, let me stay at your side as we search so I may be there when Damia is found?" Bram pleaded as Rannick stood beside his horse at the edge of the woods where tracks had been found after the two guards told Rannick everything that had happened.

"Only if you can kill without thought or hesitation, Bram, for I do not intend to let the ones live who did this," Rannick said.

"You have my word on it, my lord," Bram said with a fury in his voice that confirmed he would do just that. "Why do we wait? We should leave now."

A squawk of a raven overhead had both men tilting their heads back.

"For him," Rannick said and mounted his horse.

Rannick thought he must be crazy putting his trust in a bird, but Brogan had warned him that the witch commanded the ravens and wolves, and he had had a feeling that the witch would send help. He had recalled the witch he had fought on foreign soil and her growing anger that he had been able to sense her actions. That was how he felt about the raven. He sensed the bird would appear and he'd been right.

After a while the raven slowed, and Rannick slowed his horse, a signal to his warriors behind him to do the same. That was when he heard the footfalls, a stumbling of sorts yet determined.

A cloaked figure suddenly appeared, stopping abruptly

as if in fright, then a frantic voice called out, "Bram!"

"Damia!" Bram shouted and rushed off his horse to the figure in the darkness.

Rannick heard it then, the cry of a bairn and he shut his eyes from the sharp pain that jabbed at his heart. He could not fail his wife and their bairn. He had to save her no matter the cost.

Bram's arm was firm around Damia as he walked her to his horse.

Damia rushed to speak up as soon as she was in front of Rannick. "Lady Bliss says to let the raven guide you," —she choked on her tears— "she said to tell you that she loves you. Please, my lord, please save her." She choked back more tears. "My lady also said to tell you that Jaffee waits for you."

Fright ran a chill through Rannick right down to his bones. "How many men are with Jaffee?"

"I do not know, my lord. Sheed is there along with my sister and the four men who lead the way in the woods, but I never saw Jaffee. Lady Bliss blocked me from him and the others to give me a chance to escape. She believed they cared not about me and, therefore, would not follow after me, and they didn't."

Of course, they hadn't, Bliss was right, they were not interested in Damia. Jaffee's revenge was against him, though he knew not what he had done to the man to cause such hatred.

"Take Damia and the bairn back to the keep and have my mother help them," Rannick ordered.

"I fight beside you, my lord, I will have two warriors escort her back," Bram said.

"Nay, you will go with her, and I will have no argument about it," Rannick ordered sharply. "Now go and see her and the bairn kept safe."

"I am grateful, my lord, and I am forever in your

323

service," Bram said and was soon off with Damia and the bairn.

Rannick knew he had little time before Jaffee made his wife suffer unspeakable things. He looked to see the raven circle overhead and commanded, "Take me to her."

***

"I will have my coins and be on my way before you have your fun with her," Sheed said, raising his chin, though the slight tremor in his voice betrayed his unease.

"Be gone with you," Jaffee said, licking his lips as he leered at Bliss. "You are owed nothing. You failed."

Bliss remained where she was, knowing she would be a fool to get too close to Jaffee. While his features were far from ugly, evil had somehow left its mark on him, and anyone with a sane mind would not go near him.

"I delivered her to you," Sheed protested.

Jaffee laughed, though it sounded anything but funny. "You got caught. It was that crazy woman of yours that made the capture possible."

"I did my part," Sheed protested, anger giving him unwise courage. "Give me what I am owed, or I will see the truth made known."

Jaffee laughed. "You think that matters to me. I have part of what I've hungered for and will soon have it all."

"I will have what is owed me," Sheed protested, shaking his fist at Jaffee.

"Aye, you will," Jaffee said, his laugh gone and with sudden swiftness swung his sword, slicing Sheed's hand off at the wrist.

Sheed stood staring in shock at the bloody stump and his hand on the ground at his feet.

Lana came rushing out of the woods screaming his name.

Jaffee gave a nod to one of the four men there, and the fellow grabbed Lana and walked off into the woods where her screaming abruptly stopped and the man returned, tucking his dagger back into its sheath.

Sheed paled, his mouth falling open and his eyes staring at Jaffee in desperation.

"You are a fool. You learn the truth and make demands," Jaffee said, shaking his head. "You should have held your tongue and used what you knew to your advantage once it was all done."

"I won't say anything. I swear," Sheed pleaded.

"Your word on that?" Jaffee asked with a chuckle.

Bliss could see that he was toying with Sheed and between the light falling snow, the cold, no cloak, and fear of what she would face if Rannick did not arrive on time, she began to shiver.

"Aye, I will never speak of it, never!" Sheed begged.

Jaffee handed his sword to one of his men and pulled his dagger from its sheath. "I best make sure of that. Hold out your tongue."

Sheed backed away, tears beginning to stream down his cheeks. "Nay, I beg. I will keep silent. I will say nothing."

"Aye, I am going to make sure of that," Jaffee said and turned to smile at Bliss. "Watch for you will suffer the same fate so I do not have to listen to your endless pleas."

Sheed took advantage of Jaffee's distraction and drew his dagger, running the blade across his throat before anyone could stop him.

"He was less of a coward than I thought," Jaffee said indifferent to the man's death and snapped his hand for Bliss to approach him. "Come here, I have much planned for you before your husband arrives."

"Too late. I am already here!"

Chapter 32

Bliss thought her legs would give way they trembled so badly with relief upon hearing her husband's voice. She was not surprised when he was suddenly in front of her, his back to her, shielding her from Jaffee.

"You are unharmed?" he asked without turning to look at her.

She ached for his strong arms to wrap around her tight, feel his strength and determination to keep her safe, but he was wise in keeping his focus on Jaffee. He was not the kind of man you looked away from even for a second.

"I am good," she assured him, though worry still hung heavy over her. This was far from over… a battle awaited.

"We both know we did not come alone," Rannick said, his stance confident and his hand on the hilt of his dagger ready to defend. He would let no one get to his wife—no one.

Jaffee grinned, though it did nothing to mask the anger there. "My men are being paid only if victorious. They will not fail."

"Did you meet with who pays you to see me and the two other cursed lords dead when you stopped at Clan Loudon?"

"You delay with talk in hopes your men are finished with mine in the woods and will come to your rescue." Jaffee continued to grin. "You will be sorely disappointed."

A chill ran through Bliss more from his remark than her lack of a cloak in the lightly falling snow. If warriors waited in the woods, why didn't she hear the clash of swords. Did one side more outnumber the other?

"Yet you do not answer me, which tells me you know as little as I do about who leads this insane mission," Rannick said.

Jaffee's grin turned to a snarl. "I am no fool. I learned well on who commands this senseless mission. How you have not seen the truth for yourself surprises me, but I care not about that. And I care nothing for the coins paid me. I take your life for free, and I will keep you alive so you can see how I make your woman suffer."

"That will never happen," Rannick said with such strong confidence that for a moment Jaffee looked as if he believed him. "You will die seeking vengeance and for what?"

Anger overwhelmed Jaffee's face, distorting it into a mask of evil so hideous that it had his men stepping away from him when they were already at a distance.

"You killed the woman I loved!" Jaffee cried out in torment.

Rannick shook his head, thinking of the only woman he ever killed. "Nabila, the witch I met on foreign soil, was your woman?"

"Aye," Jaffee said, pounding his chest with his fist. "She was mine. You had no right."

"She promised to help me and then after having met with her twice, she attacked me. She told me I must die and that I could never be allowed to father a child. I told her I had no intentions of doing so."

"And yet a child grows inside your wife," Jaffee accused. "Nabila could see the future. I can only assume that she saw that a child of yours must never be born and I will make sure of that.

Bliss rushed her hand to her stomach, fearful for the bairn that was just beginning to grow inside her. And fearful that her husband would do what he had repeatedly told her... give his life for her and the bairn. Not knowing what else to

327

do at the moment, she began to silently pray.

Jaffee kept talking. "Nabila warned me about a man with a scar on his face that would bring much heartache and—"

"Death," Rannick finished after Jaffee had stopped abruptly. "Too bad she failed to warn you that it would be you who gave the man the scar."

"She did warn me, but by then I did not care. I will gladly die to avenge Nabila's death and to stop you from ever having a child," Jaffee said, holding out his hand for one of his men to bring him his sword.

"If Nabila truly cared for you, why did she say nothing to me of you?"

Rage hardened Jaffee's features. "To protect me and give me a chance to avenge her and make certain that child never gets born. And I will see it done." He gripped the sword tightly in his hand.

Bliss was relieved that the darkness was fading as dawn began to make itself known, the sky faintly lighting though no sun would rise this snowy morning. And an unnatural quiet settled over the woods, the animals themselves taking shelter against what was to come. No more unseen attacks, that was until she felt the tip of a blade poked her lightly.

"My men probably have your men surrounded by now," Rannick said. "Surrender! It is over!"

"It is you who will surrender if you want your wife to live," Jaffee said with a smug grin and shouted, "LANA!"

Rannick turned to see Lana standing beside his wife with a dagger resting at her stomach.

"Lana is no Nabila, but she serves me well enough since she was far wiser than Sheed and chose the side who would be victorious."

Rannick not only saw the fright in his wife's eyes but felt her fear as well since he shared it. It amazed him to see that with her fear there was also courage, hope, trust, belief, and he wondered how she sustained them all at such a dangerous moment.

Her courage fortified his own and he turned to Jaffee and demanded, "Let her go!"

"Or what?" Jaffee laughed. "You will rain your men down upon me. They are too busy chasing after the few of my men that lead them astray." He laughed again. "But what does that matter when Lana holds a dagger to your wife? She and the child would suffer a fatal wound before you could reach her, and you could do nothing but watch her die and your child along with her."

Bliss remained still, the shock of feeling the blade to her side once again and seeing it was Lana had stilled her tongue. She feared the woman while also feeling for her. She had been manipulated by so many people that she could no longer distinguish between right and wrong. Unfortunately, that made her extremely dangerous and difficult with which to deal. But she had faith in her husband, and she hoped he had seen it in her.

"Put your sword down, rid yourself of your other weapons, and come over to me and I will see that your wife and bairn do not suffer a painful death," Jaffee bargained.

Rannick almost laughed at Jaffee's offer. He was not a man of his word. He would make Bliss suffer no matter what bargain he offered. He took a step toward his wife, saving her and their bairn more important than anything else.

"Stay where you are!" Jaffee called out.

"A final goodbye," Rannick said, hoping to get closer and saw his wife's hand that rested on her stomach inch closer to the dagger. He knew her intention and he did not hesitate. He lunged.

Lana did not hesitate either, she went to plunge the blade into Bliss's stomach and caught her arm instead. By then Rannick had Lana around the neck.

"Get her! He's mine," Jaffee screamed, and the four

329

men charged ahead.

Rannick didn't wait, he snapped Lana's neck, and released a horrific roar as he drew his sword, grabbed his dagger, and threw it at the one man. It caught him in the stomach, and he went down, blood pouring from him.

"Stay behind me!" Rannick ordered his wife as he pulled another dagger from his boot. Another man rushed to get around him at one side while another went to his other side. Rannick's sword severed the one man's arm nearly off and he flung his dagger to catch the other man in the neck just before he reached his wife. Both men fell to the ground, the one dead and the other writhing in pain.

The fourth man stopped, looked upon Rannick and his fellow comrades, and ran off into the woods.

Bliss had seen the fear that had flared in the man's eyes and understood what had made him flee. Evil had captured her husband's face as she had seen it do another time and she swore it could frighten the devil himself, but would it frighten Jaffee?

Jaffee let out an equally raging roar and Rannick was relieved to see his roar had gotten the desired results. Lawler and some of his warriors emerged from the woods.

"Protect Bliss!" Rannick shouted and with rapid speed, dropped his sword and swiped two of the daggers from the fallen men and headed straight at Jaffee on a full run, letting loose another ominous roar.

Jaffee held his sword firm and steady, prepared for the first swing, thinking Rannick foolish for fighting only with daggers. Jaffee realized too late he had misjudged Rannick's skill.

Rannick bent low and slid in the snow with ease beneath the sword Jaffee swung at him and slipped right past him though not before his dagger sliced across Jaffee's calf. Rannick was up on his feet to his full height quickly as Jaffee stumbled from his wound, giving Rannick enough time to slice his arm quick and deliver a jab to his lower back before swerving around to finish with a plunge of his dagger into Jaffee's stomach.

Jaffee stood stunned, his sword hanging from his hand, little strength left in it, as blood flowed from his wounds.

He stared at Rannick in disbelief as he wavered on his feet. "I should have paid heed to her warnings." The sword fell from his hand, and he fought to remain standing. He lost the fight and fell on his back, blood pooling his mouth. He struggled with his words. "It isn't over."

"Who? Tell me who wants me dead besides you?" Rannick urged, looking down at him.

Jaffee grinned, blood coating his teeth and spilling from his mouth along with his last words. "Family."

Rannick walked away from the dead man, his last words disturbing him. It couldn't possibly be anyone in his family. Or was it that he did not want to believe anyone in his family could do such a heinous thing?

Lawler was helping Bliss bandage her arm when he approached them. Lawler stepped out of the way to leave Rannick to finish helping.

"I will get Lady Bliss a cloak, she shivers with cold, and I let her know that Damia and the bairn are on their way home with Bram," Lawler said, then hurried off.

"Is it bad?" he asked, crouching down beside her to gently brush her hands aside to finish tying the cloth.

"I believe you stopped her before her blade could do any serious damage, but I will be able to tell more when we return home," she said and slipped her hand around the side of his neck. "I feared I would lose you when you foolishly took daggers to a sword fight, but I was amazed and relieved at how quickly you conquered the man."

He took hold of her hand and brought it to his lips to kiss her palm before moving it to rest against his chest. "Defeat was unacceptable since my heart cannot live without you."

"Good, for I plan for both of us to be around for a long time," she said with a tender smile and kissed him.

***

Rannick hugged his wife close, several blankets tucked around them since she still suffered a slight shiver. Though it was mid-afternoon, he and his wife had gotten no sleep last night. He had known there would be no stopping her once they returned to the keep from seeing that Damia and the bairn did well. They both slept with Bram keeping an eye on them when he wasn't snoozing himself on a nearby chair in Damia's cottage. Lady Helice had managed to stop the endless questions coming from Lord Lochlann, once in the Great Hall, insisting Bliss needed rest as well as Rannick. He had given her an appreciative hug before escorting his wife to their bedchamber.

He was right where he wanted to be, in bed with his wife in his arms safe, though she truly was not safe, not yet.

Bliss said what he'd been thinking, her voice heavy with fatigue. "It isn't over yet, is it?"

"I am afraid not. I had hoped Jaffee would tell me who hired him, but realized that by him keeping it from me, it left the chance he would get what he wanted... you and me dead." He kissed her brow when he felt her shudder. "Worry not, I believe we will have time to try and figure out who is behind the scheme since he will need to hire others to see his plan succeed. With Jaffee defeated that will not be easy. Others will be fearful and reluctant to take on the mission. What troubles me more is what Jaffee said about it being family." He shook his head. "It is not possible. No one in my family would do such a thing."

"Family spreads far and wide. We need to look beyond our immediate family," Bliss said and yawned. "Or perhaps

Highlander The Cursed Lord

Jaffee lied to make our search more difficult."

"A possibility," Rannick said, "Enough about him for now, tell me how Damia and her son do."

Bliss turned a wide smile on her husband. "They both do wonderful. Damia named him after his da, Finn. She was very brave being forced to deliver her son in the dark woods and with the snow falling and equally as brave to chance the escape." Her smile faded. "Her sister's betrayal pains her, and she worries you will punish her for it. I assured her you would never do such a thing."

"Damia proved herself when she escaped as you urged her to do, and she wasted not a moment in delivering your message. She has nothing to fear." He faintly touched her bandaged arm. "And your wound?"

"As I thought, not serious enough that it will not heal, though extra healing time may be required."

"Then you will be wise to follow the healer's advice," he said with a smile and a gentle kiss, relieved the wound was not as bad as he worried it might have been. His hand went to rest at her stomach. "The bairn does well?"

"He is tiny and well-protected. He does good," Bliss assured him.

"You will give birth in this bed where you and the bairn will be safe, though I will worry terribly about you."

"I will be fine, Rannick, especially with Lana not here to hurt me as she did your other wives."

Rannick shook his head. "Since you shared that news with my father and mother—"

Bliss quickly interrupted him. "I thought it would reassure him, knowing the person who had betrayed the clan was dead."

"I fear it did the opposite," he said. "He's having all the servants watched and to be honest, I am relieved he is. We have no idea who else may be among us that continues to believe the cursed lords and their wives need to die."

333

Bliss offered some hope. "That will fade as the months go by without anything horrible happening."

He wished he could feel as confident as she sounded. "You are so sure, wife?"

"I believe it," she said on a yawn. "And with things going so well, it will make it even more difficult for the person responsible for this mess to convince people that the curse still exists."

"The question is, does it?"

"Another thing I believe we will soon learn." Bliss yawned again.

"You need to sleep," he ordered and kissed her cheek.

"Later when we wake, you will make love to me."

"Is that an order, wife?" he asked with a smile.

She chuckled. "Must I make it one?"

"Never," he said and kissed her lips lightly.

She sighed. "I do not believe I can wait until tonight."

"You are too tired," he said, though wished she wasn't since her teasing demand had stirred his desire.

"A quick one," she said with a playful grin. "Then we can both sleep well."

"I can see to that," Rannick said and gently rolled his wife on her back and did as he said and, afterwards, they both slept very well.

Chapter 33

Five months later.

"I cannot believe we are all together again," Elysia said with a joyful smile.

Bliss found it hard to believe as well, looking from Elysia to Annis sitting outside with her on a blanket under a large shade tree. It was like a dream, but it wasn't a dream. It was real.

"I am so glad you convinced Odran to bring you here, to Bliss, to have the bairn," Annis said.

"It took some doing, but I had to see for myself where she lived and that her husband treated her well, even though you assured me Rannick did," Elysia said with a nod to Annis.

"True, but I assume it made a good excuse to get you here," Annis said with a laugh and her sisters joined in the laughter.

Bliss had once feared she would never see her sisters again when she had left them to fulfill the bargain she had made to see them kept safe. She never imagined how well things would turn out for the three of them.

Bliss expressed her joy with a wide smile and appreciation. "The three of us have been lucky to find such good husbands."

Annis smiled. "And who would have thought it would be with the cursed lords?"

The three chatted on and after a while silence settled amongst them.

Bliss broke the quiet, keeping her voice low. "I did not tell you what Mum told me on her deathbed because I did not think it would matter. To me we are sisters and always will be."

"Of course we are," Annis agreed.

"Sisters forever," Elysia said and hesitated a moment before continuing, "but one of us faces the possibility of—"

Bliss reached out and grabbed each of their hands, stopping Elysia from finishing. "We all face it together and as agreed we keep it a secret so our husbands will be protected as well. For if it is known, it may cause more trouble than the curse itself."

The three nodded their heads in agreement.

"Has there been any word from the witch?" Elysia asked. "I am curious as to what else she may be able to tell us."

Annis shook her head. "Nay, and I am disappointed. I thought for sure she would show herself and claim the curse broken."

"Perhaps the curse is not broken yet," Elysia said.

"But all has been going well, not just here but at your homes as well from what you both have told me," Bliss said, having enjoyed listening to how happy her sisters were in their new homes.

"I thought Gunna would return so we could find out more about Lady Aila from her," Annis said, "but Troy tells me he has heard no word from her."

"And we have only Jaffee's final word that it was family behind the scheme," Bliss said.

"But how far does Rannick's family extend with you now being his wife?" Annis asked, imagining the number of people that could be suspect.

"Are you in pain, Elysia?" Bliss asked, seeing her sister rub her rounded stomach several times while they talked.

"A bit uncomfortable that's all. I will be glad when the bairn arrives and it is done," Elysia said.

Annis chuckled. "I bet not as much as your husband. He follows you around with a worried brow that will stay permanent with how long he wears it.

Elysia and Bliss laughed.

"Rannick does the same," Annis said, pointing to Bliss, "though I can understand why with what happened to his first wife and I am so relieved that that shre—"

"Annis!" Bliss scolded before she could finish.

"I am only saying what we think. Good riddance to Lana," Annis said.

"And when are you going to get with child?" Elysia asked Annis with a teasing smile.

"I explained to Brogan that we have to time it right," Annis explained as if she was making plans to build something. "There are things in our village that must be completed as well as our cottage. And I cannot deliver the bairn in the winter since it would be too difficult for either of you to reach me, especially with having bairns of your own. So as soon as I have it all planned out, then and only then will I get with child." Annis scrunched her face annoyed, looking toward the keep. "Good Lord, what is she doing here?"

Elysia and Bliss turned to see Lady Faline and Lord Balloch approach the keep on horses, a line of their warriors spreading out behind them when they came to a stop.

Rannick was standing near talking with Brogan and Odran. Odran headed over to his wife while Brogan joined Rannick when he went to greet Brogan's parents. However, not before Rannick sent a servant inside to alert his parents of the unexpected arrival.

"I do not understand, Brogan, why you did not let me and your father know you were here," his mother admonished once off her horse. "I suffered great embarrassment hearing it from a traveling merchant."

"I planned on sending word, Mother," Brogan said, though it was not until his visit was near at an end that he intended to do so.

337

"Have you any news of an heir yet?" Lady Faline asked.

Brogan saw his father roll his eyes as he had seen him do so often throughout the years.

"That is not a question to be asked at the moment, Faline," Brogan's father reprimanded.

"When do I ask him?" Lady Faline snapped. "He barely visits with us and besides, he has a duty and if his wife cannot fulfill it—"

"Enough, Faline, this is not the place for such talk," Lord Balloch warned.

"Brogan is your reason for your visit here?" Rannick asked, an abruptness to his tone.

Lady Faline lifted her chin in annoyance. "That is how you welcome a guest?"

"We would be better prepared to welcome a guest if the guest sent prior knowledge of her visit," Lady Helice said as she hurried down the steps, her husband close behind her.

"Balloch, it is good to see you. It has been too long," Lord Lochlann said, extending his hand when he reached the man.

"It has, Lochlann, and the blame is mine for not sending notice of our visit, but my wife finally agreed it was time to apologize for her unmannerly behavior the last time she was here," Lord Balloch said. "And I also was eager to see my son, since he rarely is home anymore."

Rannick glanced back to where his wife sat and saw Odran assisting Elysia to her feet while Annis struggled to get Bliss on her feet, and he hurried to her. His hands went under her arms to easily hoist her to her feet.

Annis narrowed her eyes at him, and he waited for her to tell him she had needed no help in assisting her sister, so her words surprised him.

"What is she doing here?" Annis demanded, her focus on her mother-in-law.

"Supposedly, she is here to apologize," Rannick said,

338

his wife leaning on him a sure sign she was fatigued. It still worried him that she would be delivering Elysia's bairn since she had tired easily in the last week.

"Not likely," Annis said.

"She is a thorn in your side?" Odran asked with concern.

"More like a dagger that she twists and turns," Annis said, turning her clenched fist as if to demonstrate. "You will see it for yourself, for she is sure to berate me for not being round with child like my sisters, then she will claim I am barren and make reference to a new wife for Brogan."

"Brogan will not stand for that," Odran said in defense of his friend.

"Nay, he does not, and it is the reason he barely visits his parents, though his father has visited more with us of late," Annis said.

"Come with us, Annis," Odran ordered. "Rannick and I will protect you from her verbal arrows."

"I do not need either of you to protect me. I am not afraid of the witch." Annis shook her head. "I insult the witch saying that since she is a far better person than Lady Faline." She lifted the hem of her garments and marched off.

"Hurry!" Elysia urged. "We must keep pace and warn her to mind her tongue."

"That is Brogan's problem now, wife," Odran said, and he and Rannick laughed.

Elysia and Bliss did not. They hooked arms and hurried off as quick as their rounded stomachs would let them, their husbands shaking their heads while keeping pace behind them.

***

"You have to admit, Annis," Elysia said. "Lady Faline did give a heartfelt apology last night at supper and was even

339

quite pleasant this morning to everyone."

"She didn't mean a word of what she said," Annis said, reaching for another honey cake on the table. "I have seen her be perfectly nice one minute and a complete demon the next. I do not trust her. I never will." She waved the honey cake in the air. "I really like this healing cottage of yours, Bliss. It reminds me of the cottage the three of us shared, though it is bigger."

"I agree with Annis," Elysia said. "It feels like the way it used with us around the table talking, and it brings back many good memories." Her eyes went wide, and her hand rushed to her stomach. "That was quite a pain."

Annis jumped to her feet. "The bairn comes."

"Easy, Annis," Bliss cautioned. "Let's make sure before we alert anyone."

It took less than an hour and Annis pacing back and forth to confirm the bairn was on the way.

Bliss went to Elysia to help her to her feet. "I am going to get Elysia to the keep. You go find Odran and also get Damia and tell her Elysia's time has come. She will know what to do."

Annis nodded. "You don't want me to get Odran to help Elysia to the keep?"

Bliss smiled. "I am sure he will reach us before we make it to the keep."

Annis nodded again as she ran out the door.

Elysia stood as a pain struck and she gripped Bliss's hand.

"The pains are not far apart. You may have a quick delivery," Bliss said.

"I would very much like that," Elysia said, leaning on Bliss as they walked to the door.

They stepped outside and Bliss was surprised to see Lady Faline coming toward them and the two guards gone.

"I saw Annis running and the guards as well. Is

everything all right?" she asked. "Can I help in any way?"

"Time has come for the bairn," Bliss said, an unease creeping over her and wished this one time the guards had remained at their post, but Annis must have demanded they help find Odran.

"Good. I have been waiting for this," Lady Faline said with a smile, and her hand slipped out from the folds of her garment, a dagger firm in her grip. "You both will come with me, and I promise you that if you struggle one of you will suffer for it. Now move."

Bliss had no time to be shocked by the woman's actions. She gave a quick glance around to see if there was anyone she might be able to alert to their plight, but no one was nearby.

"Do not be foolish, Bliss," Lady Faline warned. "A quick stab to your sister's stomach and she and the bairn dies. Now start walking."

Bliss took as much of her sister's weight as she could, another pain hitting her as they entered the woods.

A few more steps had Elysia gasping. "My water has released."

Bliss's fear grew, but she did what she could to reassure her sister. "Do not worry. All will be well."

Lady Faline prodded with words. "Hurry, keep moving,"

"It was you behind it all, wasn't it?" Bliss said, wanting to keep her busy talking so she would not suspect her inquisitive glance to see what might be useful to help them escape.

Lady Faline laughed. "No one suspected a woman. Of course, I used the fanatical group that wanted the cursed lords dead to my advantage, making sure the wagging tongues spread the message far and wide. It was easy to hide my scheme among their pitiful one, convincing them a messiah would come and free them of their suffering. All was going well until you both came along and wed Odran and Rannick and ruined everything."

"How could you want your own son dead?" Bliss asked, shocked that a mother could even conceive of such a heinous thing.

Lady Faline's face twisted in disgust. "How dare you even think that. I do not want Brogan dead. I do this for him, for our clan. Brogan is the chosen one. He cannot die. I have seen him suffer wounds no one could survive, yet he did. I had no worry he would die even if wounded, though it was made clear to Jaffee that it was only Odran and Rannick plus their wives and Annis, of course, who were to die. I was very disappointed when news reached me of his death and that you and Rannick were responsible. With the group now losing momentum to see the cursed lords gone, I knew I had no choice but to see the task done myself, or all my plans would be wasted, and what better or easier way than when you and your sisters were together. When news reached our clan that not only Brogan was here but Odran and his wife as well, I knew the time had come."

Bliss realized the woman had lost all sanity and, like Lana, made her dangerous and impossible for her to see reason.

"Brogan will live on. He will rule this land and beyond when people realize he is immortal. The curse is a gift to him, and I will not have him deprived of it. Now keep walking. There is a nice cliff a short distance from here. I will cry copious tears telling the tale of how I tried to stop a madman from taking you both and watched in horror as Bliss struggled to save Elysia and you both went over the edge, the man running off in fear. Then one day, not far off, Annis will take her own life, unable to cope with her sisters' death. And all will be as it should. Now keep moving."

"We are not that far from the keep yet," Bliss whispered, pretending to hold her sister up more than needed, giving her a chance so that their whispers would not be heard. She had come to a decision after hearing how crazed Lady Faline had become. "I am going to create a diversion. You leave as soon as I do and head back to the keep. I dug my boots good into the earth as we walked. You should have no problem following the trail."

Elysia looked ready to shake her head.

"I will be fine. Rannick will come for me," Bliss whispered. "We have no time to wait with the bairn eager to be born. Cry out in pain and double over."

Elysia did as her sister told her.

Bliss wasted no time. She leaned down as if helping her sister and grabbed several rocks. "Move as fast as you can when I start throwing." Bliss sprang up and threw the first rock catching Lady Faline in the shoulder and sending her wavering on her feet. She followed fast with three more throws, then rushed the woman hoping to get hold of her dagger while Lady Faline remained stunned and disoriented.

That's when she felt a gush of water rush from between her legs.

***

"Odran!" Annis shouted and he not only came running but Brogan and Rannick did as well. "The bairn!"

Odran hurried after Annis when she turned abruptly, needing to be with his wife and know she was safe. Brogan and Rannick followed as well.

"Bliss should have her close to the keep by now," Annis said as she ran off, the three men following her.

When Elysia and Bliss were not spotted outside the keep, the small group ran inside. When the two sisters weren't found there, they all anxiously went to the healing cottage, Lord Lochlann and Lord Balloch joining them.

"Where are they?" Odran demanded, angry with worry

343

when the cottage was found empty.

"Did you talk with anyone on your way here and tell them it was Elysia's time?" Rannick asked. "And where are the guards?"

Annis cringed at her mistake. "I sent one to get Damia as Bliss wanted and the other I sent in the opposite direction from me to search for Odran. And the only person I spoke to was Brogan's mum, no one else."

"Do you know where Mum is?" Brogan asked his father.

His father shook his head. "I have not seen her since breakfast."

"We need to find her to see if she saw anything," Odran said, fear that something awful happened to his wife filling his already fearful thoughts.

"She may be with Helice. I will go see," Lord Lochlann said and hurried to the keep.

Rannick studied the ground in front of the cottage. "There are tracks leading to the woods."

"We follow them," Odran demanded and went to do just that when he spotted his wife stumbling out of the woods. "ELYSIA!" He ran to her and scooped her up as she doubled over in pain.

She buried her face in her husband's neck grateful to be in his arms, then she lifted her head and called out, "Rannick, I must speak with him."

He was at her side in an instant as was Annis and Brogan. "It was Lady Faline. She is the one behind it all. She threatened us with a dagger, and she was too close not to take her seriously. She intended to see us dead. She believes Brogan is the chosen one and will live forever." She cringed as another pain hit her. "Please go! Help Bliss. She went after Lady Faline so I could escape. Follow the trail she left for me." She buried her face in her husband's neck when another pain hit her.

"I will follow after I see Elysia settled," Odran said.

"Nay, you will stay with your wife, my friend. This is for me to see to," Rannick said.

"And for me as well, since it is my mother who has caused all the pain and suffering," Brogan said, his heart heavy with grief and disbelief.

"I go too, son," his father said. "Your mother is my responsibility."

***

Lady Faline managed to keep on her feet, still wavering a bit and brandishing the dagger wildly in front of her to keep Bliss away.

"It's over," Bliss said, keeping her distance, taking no chance that the bairn inside her would suffer harm. "Elysia has probably reached the keep by now and has informed my husband. He will follow the tracks I left and find me soon enough. You are finished."

"Then he will find you dead," Lady Faline threatened.

"Touch her and I will rip your heart out."

Bliss was shocked to see the white-haired woman who had passed by Rannick's cottage standing just a few feet away swathed in a dark cloak.

Lady Faline looked as if her eyes bulged from her head. "You?" She shook her head. "You are supposed to be dead."

"As you can see, I'm not. I was just waiting for the right time to return. That time is today. The day when the curse will finally be brought to an end. You waste your time here. Bliss is right. It is over for you."

Bliss was surprised to see a thick fog creeping along the ground and rising up swiftly. The witch was here.

"If I lose then so does she. I'll rip that bairn from her stomach," Lady Faline said, sneering and raised the dagger.

"BLISS!" Rannick roared racing into the small clearing

345

as Lady Faline lunged at his wife, the fog swiftly rising to consume the whole area. "BLISS!" he roared again and felt a hand on his arm. He grabbed it, disappointed to find it was Annis.

Bliss wanted to call out to her husband, but she feared Lady Faline might be too close, so she reluctantly held her tongue. Pain began to nag at her back letting her know labor was close at hand.

"MUM!" Brogan called out. "Stop this madness! I am not immortal, nor do I want to be. I want a quiet life with my wife and the bairns we will have. I will rule nothing but the clan when it is time for me to do so."

Lady Faline let out an angry shout to her son. "You were always a disappointment!"

"SAYS A SHREW TOO CRAZY TO SEE WHAT A HORRIBLE WOMAN SHE IS!" Annis yelled, her hands stretching out in front of her as she turned away from Rannick to find her husband. A hand suddenly grabbed her wrist, and she clenched her other hand ready to throw a punch if necessary. "Brogan!" she gasped when his face appeared through the fog, and he hugged her tight.

"ENOUGH! FALINE!" Lord Balloch cried out. "STOP THIS NOW!"

"You have always been a coward, Balloch, and I will have my revenge against everyone but particularly you by taking your daughter's life," she cried out.

Balloch shook his head and went to Rannick's side, spotting him through the fog. "She has completely lost her mind, Rannick, I have no daughter."

"I need to reach Bliss before she does," Rannick said, and a chill of fear felt as if it turned him to ice when a horrifying scream pierced the fog.

"BLISS!" Rannick shouted, fear so raw racing through him he thought it would take him to his knees.

Tears choked Annis as she clung to her husband, his

arm tight around her, but she managed to cry out, "BLISS!"

The fog began to dissipate and Rannick's heart thundered in his chest waiting for the fog to reveal what he feared... that he had lost Bliss.

All but Rannick stood in shock. He hurried to his wife, avoiding the wolf who stood over Lady Faline, her throat torn open and the wolf's mouth bloody.

Rannick grabbed his wife in a fierce hug and kissed her, resting his brow on hers when done. "I thought I had lost you. You have to stop being brave or I will lose my mind."

Bliss understood what he meant. "I had to save my sister, and never once did I fear you would not rescue me."

"If it was not for the fog..." Rannick shook his head.

"I would have fought her off until you reached me," Bliss assured him.

"There you go being brave again," he admonished.

"Nay, there I go again trusting my husband to always be there for me," she corrected.

"Always," he whispered.

They both turned when they heard Annis ask, "Are you all right, Brogan."

Rannick and Bliss looked to see Brogan and his father staring at Lady Faline from a distance, the wolf not letting them get near and Annis keeping her eyes averted with too much blood to be seen.

"Go, wolf, with my appreciation. It is done," Bliss said gently, and the wolf walked away.

Lord Balloch approached his wife's body, but Brogan stayed where he was, Annis keeping tight hold of his arm.

"I don't want to remember her that way. I have far too few good memories of her to begin with," Brogan said, turning to bury his face in his wife's mass of fiery red curls.

"We will make wonderful memories together," Annis assured him, tears trickling down her cheeks.

Balloch stood over his wife's body in silence, too

bewildered to speak.

"The witch!" Annis called out, the fog completely dissipated to reveal her presence.

"She is the witch?" Rannick asked, recognizing the woman standing there as the woman who had passed by their cottage.

"Verbena?" Balloch asked as if seeing a ghost.

"Aye, Balloch, it is me, and it is time you meet our daughter," the witch said, her glance going to Bliss.

"Good Lord, I beg you do not let the witch be my mother-in-law," Rannick whispered.

Chapter 34

"I am exhausted," Annis said, leaning against her husband.

"You were not the one who gave birth," Elysia reminded, her newborn daughter swathed in a soft blanket and tucked in the crook of her arm and Odran sitting on the bed with Elysia tucked in his arms.

"I felt like I did, it was so long and exhausting," Annis argued.

Bliss laughed. "It took less than an hour."

Rannick had worried the whole time, pacing the floor in the Great Hall along with Odran. He had seen the tiredness in his wife's eyes and her steps did not have their usual brisk pace. He also knew her thoughts were heavy over the announcement the witch had made about her being her mother and Balloch her father. She had pushed all that aside, not asking one question of either of them, her only thought was to get to the keep so she could deliver Elysia's bairn. He had been glad it hadn't taken long. Now his wife could rest, though she wouldn't until the witch revealed the truth of the past.

"The bairn has been born," Rannick said, anxious for the truth. "Tells us it all now."

The witch stepped out of the shadows in the bedchamber. "In a moment, she has arrived and will be here..."

A knock sounded at the door and Brogan opened it.

"Gunna!" Annis said in surprise when the woman limped into the room.

Gunna smiled. "I have so looked forward to this day."

She went and stood not far from the witch. "Hurry and tell them, for they have waited too long as have we."

The witch began to reveal the secrets kept these many years. "I am Verbena, Gunna and Aila's older sister... and Bliss's mother."

Bliss felt the relief in her husband as he held her close, though he whispered, "Lord help me." His relief had come from knowing she was not the MacWilliam bairn and she was glad of it herself.

"That makes you Brogan's half-sister," Annis announced with a playful poke to his side.

"I am honored," Brogan said with a charming smile to Bliss. "A warning, dear sister, our father is not as charming as I am."

"Maybe he will be now that the woman he truly loves has returned," Annis suggested with a look to Verbena.

She ignored Annis's remark and continued. "I left years ago when Balloch's father discovered I carried his son's child. His terrifying threats to see me and the bairn dead enough for me to flee in fear. Gunna and Aila urged me to go being as fearful as I was for my safety." She paused a moment before continuing. "We come from a long line of wise women and there is always one in the line born stronger than the others, capable of seeing the future, of casting powerful spells, and so much more."

"And you are the one with those powers?" Annis asked.

Verbena shook her head. "Nay. It was Aila who had such powers. She cast the powerful curse that could never be broken, only made right. She relied on Gunna and me to see her daughter protected so that when the time came the curse could be fulfilled, her daughter finally safe and the MacWilliam bloodline carried on. To see that done, Gunna and I gave our daughters along with Aila's daughter to the couple who would raise them. We feared if we were found, our daughters would be in grave danger. Gunna went into hiding while I went to increase my skills and power, but I am nowhere near as powerful as Aila had been. If I were, I would have been able to see that it was Lady Faline who was behind it all.

"When Gunna returned to check on all of you, she discovered the couple she had given our daughters to had died and the three of you had been given to another couple we knew nothing about."

"That's why you made yourself known to me to help you with your plight," Annis said.

"I saw you in a dream headed to me, which is why I gave that drunken man a message to deliver to you. You are as tenacious as your father was and as talented in building as he had been," Verbena said.

Tears began to gather in Annis's eyes as she looked to Gunna. "You're my mother."

Tears filled Gunna's eyes as well. "Aye, I am, and I am so proud of the woman you have become."

Annis went to hug Gunna and stopped, turning to look at Elysia, realizing what her revelation had revealed.

Odran wrapped his arms tighter around his wife. "That leaves Elysia the MacWilliam bairn."

Verbena and Gunna both nodded their heads.

Tears clouded Verbena's eyes as she spoke. "Your mother was an extraordinary woman and fearless in her protection of you even before you were born," Verbena said. "She and your father planned how they would save you once your mother told him that she had seen what the future held for his clan and for them and there was no changing it. Their only thought was to keep you safe, knowing they would not live to do so. It was why Gunna came to live with her so the plan could be carried out successfully and the curse would see fruition and be corrected with the birth of another MacWilliam. It was your future your mother feared most for you and the reason for the powerful curse."

351

Elysia remained silent listening, glad for her husband's strong arms around her, the news causing a shiver of fear to run through, and her heart felt heavy with a great sadness for her mother and father and that she never got to know them.

Odran felt her shiver and hugged her closer as he whispered near her ear, "You have nothing to fear. I will keep you and our daughter safe."

"Why doesn't Elysia have powers like her mum?" Annis asked. "Can't she cast a protection spell or something to keep herself safe?"

"There is only one born in each generation in our family who possesses such power. Aila was the one in ours and in yours…" Verbena looked to Bliss.

Bliss shook her head. "I possess no such power or skills."

"You commanded the wolf," Verbena reminded. "You have such power. You simply need to allow it to mature."

"Maybe she doesn't want to," Rannick snapped and sent a formidable scowl at the woman.

"Watch your tongue with me or I'll turn you into a frog," Verbena warned, her tongue sharp.

Bliss squeezed her husband's arm in a silent effort to plead with him to hold his tongue.

Gunna stepped in to help her. "Don't worry, she can't do that."

"Why? Why did I have to get you as a mother-in-law?" Rannick asked as if pleading to the heavens.

"Because the heavens smiled down on you," Verbena said with a smile that was anything but pleasant.

Elysia spoke up. "If one with powers are born with each generation, then that means one of our bairns will possess such skills."

"That's right," Gunna said.

"How would we know which one?" Annis asked.

"The child will be born with her eyes open and able to

see all from birth," Verbena said.

Elysia's eyes went to Bliss. "Was my daughter born with her eyes open?"

"Nay, and I have never seen a child born that way," Bliss said.

"Well, if your bairn isn't born with her eyes open, then it will be Annis who has such a child," Elysia said.

Annis shook her head. "Nay! Nay! Nay! Nay!"

"We will soon find out," Verbena said and looked to Bliss. "Isn't it time you tell them that you have labored since leaving the woods and your bairn will be born this day?"

Rannick stepped quickly in front of his wife. "Is this true? The bairn is ready to be born? I thought you had another month."

"The bairn has decided otherwise," Bliss said.

"I'll help deliver the bairn as I did with Elysia," Annis called out.

Bliss and Elysia laughed.

"I would like to have the honor of delivering my granddaughter," Verbena said.

Rannick turned another scowl on the woman. "Absolutely not."

"I did not ask you," Verbena snapped.

"That is enough," Bliss warned and looked to Verbena. "My husband comes first, *Mother!*" Then she turned her eyes on her husband. "Know that I wish to come to know my mother."

"I can learn to tolerate her," Rannick offered.

"If I must, I will do the same. I have been separated from you far too long," Verbena said.

Bliss sighed. "At least it is a start. Her hand went to her stomach. "Now I need to make ready for the birth of our bairn." She saw fear race up in her husband's eyes. "All will go well."

Rannick went to argue with her then recalled all the

353

times she had told him all would go well. It had not just hope, it had been that she truly knew it would be so, and his worry eased.

"Aye, wife, it will," he said and kissed her.

***

Bliss rested against her husband in bed, their daughter sound asleep tucked comfortably in the crook of her arm.

"The curse is no more, and no one hunts us any longer," Bliss said with a smile. "Life will be good from here on."

"Life is already good, Bliss. "We have pledged to keep Elysia's identity a secret even from our parents. And if it should ever become necessary, Brogan and I will be there to help Odran protect her. Though with the powerful family of wise women she comes from, Odran does not believe that will be necessary.

"That has brought great relief to Elysia," Bliss said, having spoken to her sister not long after she gave birth herself.

"Gunna sits and talks with Annis and Brogan, telling them all about Annis's father, a skilled craftsman who built many dwellings."

"Has Brogan said anything to you about his mum?"

"He tried to offer an apology to me and Odran, but we both told him it was not necessary. He could not be blamed for her madness. No doubt, it started way before the curse and perhaps worsened when she learned Balloch had fallen in love with Verbena while his father had promised Faline's family that she would wed his son only to discover his son intended to wed the peasant he loved."

"Do Verbena and Lord Balloch talk?" Bliss asked.

"You mean your father and mother?" he asked teasingly, though with a cringe when he said mother. "It will take time for the pain of the past to heal and for them to

354

talk."

"It will take time for me to come to know them both as my parents. Though I do not mind having Brogan as a half-brother," she admitted, he deals so well with Annis.

Rannick laughed. "He doesn't mind either, teasing Annis that he is more related to you than she is, of which he has received many jabs and punches that he laughs off."

She laughed at the image her husband painted. "Your mother was thrilled at the birth of her granddaughter. And I was glad to see how pleased your father was with a granddaughter. I thought he would be disappointed it wasn't a grandson."

Rannick laughed. "He told me there were plenty more bairns for me to make and one was bound to be a son." He shook his head. "I cannot believe it was your mother who changed the mixture I ordered Lawler to fetch for you."

"Lawler barely remembers meeting her," she said, recalling the man scratching his head when Verbena made mention of it.

"She put a spell on him, that's what she did," Rannick said, his brow narrowing. "Then she held her tongue, refusing to say why she did it, but I know she did it to annoy me."

Bliss chuckled and teased. "Be careful she does not turn you into a frog."

"She has no such power, but she cautions about one who may have," he said.

"A child born with her eyes open and can see all at birth... a powerful wise woman," Bliss said. "I believe that is what Nabila saw when dealing with you and what made her turn against you. She feared a woman born more skilled and powerful than herself, perhaps even the one who would be her demise."

Rannick caressed his daughter's soft cheek with his finger. "You would not believe the relief on Odran and

Brogan's faces when they learned that our daughter was born with her eyes wide open while I was struck dumbfounded by the news."

Bliss tilted her head back to kiss him, then whispered, "We are all safe now. It is over, finally done."

Rannick grinned and shook his head as he looked at his sleeping daughter, "Nay, wife, it has just begun."

Learn more about Donna, her books, and subscribe to her newsletter so you don't miss her next exciting, romantic adventure!

www.donnafletcher.com

Printed in Great Britain
by Amazon

28061244R00202